PENGUIN BOOKS

Nurses
on Call

Donna Douglas lives in York with her husband and family. When she is not busy writing, she is generally reading, watching Netflix documentaries or drinking cocktails. Sometimes all at the same time.

Also by Donna Douglas

Nurses
on Call

Donna
DOUGLAS

PENGUIN BOOKS

PENGUIN BOOKS

UK | USA | Canada | Ireland | Australia
India | New Zealand | South Africa

Penguin Books is part of the Penguin Random House group
of companies whose addresses can be found at
global.penguinrandomhouse.com

Published in Penguin Books 2024
002

Typeset in 10.4/15pt Palatino LT Pro by Jouve (UK), Milton Keynes
Printed and bound in Great Britain by Clays Ltd, Elcograf S.p.A.

The authorised representative in the EEA is Penguin Random House Ireland,
Morrison Chambers, 32 Nassau Street, Dublin D02 YH68

A CIP catalogue record for this book is available from the British Library

ISBN: 978–1–804–94371–7

www.greenpenguin.co.uk

To my sister Jane Quennell

Because we don't do things by halves

Part One

Chapter One

Maman was dying.

It seemed so wrong, when the city was bursting back to life after the long, harsh winter. The sun was shining, the trees lining the boulevards frothed with plum and cherry blossom and people sat in pavement cafés again, enjoying their café au lait and croissants as they watched the world go by.

But inside their little apartment in the shabby *arrondissement de l'Observatoire*, Romy Villeneuve was fading away. It frightened Catrine to see her looking so frail as she lay on the couch, almost too weak to move. She had always been slender, but now Catrine could feel her bones jutting as she pulled her blanket up to cover her thin shoulders.

She did her best to help lift her mother's spirits. She carefully styled her blonde hair, pretending not to notice the dry clumps that came out each time she brushed it. She applied rouge to her cheeks and her favourite Lancôme lipstick. Maman's face, though etched in pain, had lost none of its beauty. And she always liked to look her best, even though they seldom had visitors.

3

Catrine would have welcomed some cheerful company. Spending so many hours alone in the apartment gave her mother too much time to brood on the past. And that was never a good thing for her.

She often wished she could have had someone to share in the work of looking after her mother. Not that it was a burden for her, but sometimes the responsibility fell heavily on her seventeen-year-old shoulders.

But they could not afford a nurse, and her mother was adamant she would not see anyone anyway. And so it was left to Catrine to manage.

Since her mother became ill six months earlier, they had fallen into a familiar routine, just the two of them. Catrine would return from her shift at the hospital, clean the apartment and open the windows to let in the fresh air. She would make herself and her mother something to eat, and then they would sit together, and Catrine would read to her, or talk about her day. She did her best to entertain her mother with her stories of the patients at the hospital, or the other student nurses. But half the time she knew she wasn't listening.

If Maman was very tired, they would look out of the window, watching the comings and goings in the street below. One advantage of living in the cheaper, less salubrious area of the city was that there was always something lively or amusing to watch. It was better than the theatre sometimes.

But even then her mother would all too often seek out the dark and sorrowful side.

'Look at them,' she would say, pointing at a couple

walking hand in hand. 'So young and in love. And so foolish, too.'

'There's nothing foolish about being in love, Maman.'

Her mother sent her a withering look. 'Believe me, no good ever came of it, *chérie*. Look at us.' She gestured around her. 'Living in this bug-infested apartment when I could have had so much better. And all because of a man,' she said bitterly.

You mean all because of me, Catrine thought. It might have been a man who caused Romy Villeneuve's unfortunate situation, but Catrine was the reason her mother's life had been so hard, the reason she had been cast out by her own family.

She felt the weight of her mother's shame and bitterness, and sometimes it was almost too hard for her to bear.

She even felt the burden of her mother's illness, as if it were somehow her fault that she had become so sick. If Romy's life had been different, happier, perhaps she would not be embracing the idea of death so eagerly. It was almost as if she couldn't wait to leave her miserable life.

'It won't be long now,' she would sigh.

'Don't talk like that, Maman. The doctor still has hope—'

'Then the doctor is a fool. He tells me what he thinks I want to hear. But I was a nurse long enough to know the truth. I'm not going to get any better.'

But Catrine refused to give up hope. 'There must be something,' she insisted. 'Perhaps there may be some treatment we haven't tried yet . . .'

'If there is, then we probably couldn't afford it.'

'We could ask Grand-mère?'

Her mother's face tightened, and Catrine immediately knew she should not have spoken the name out loud.

'Your grandmother would never help us. And I'd never ask her.' She reached out, her thin fingers tightening around Catrine's arm. 'You must never ask her either. Promise me,' she urged. 'Promise me whatever happens you'll never go to her?'

'*Je te promets, Maman.*'

They never spoke about it again. Catrine understood why her mother was so adamant. Romy Villeneuve had asked Grand-mère for help once before.

It was a long time ago, and the memory was hazy. But there were some details Catrine would never forget. She recalled her mother dressing her up in her best clothes and taking her by taxi to a very smart *arrondissement* close to the centre of the city. She remembered the beautiful house overlooking a park, and all the steps that had led up to the imposing front door. She remembered looking up into the face of the maid who had answered the door, and the way her mother had clutched her hand so tightly as she stood on the doorstep. Catrine was too young to understand what was being said, but she remembered the quiver in her mother's voice, and the way the door had closed in their faces.

They had sat on a bench in the park and Catrine stared at the other children playing while her mother wept beside her. Catrine had never seen her cry before, and it frightened her. Almost as much as the stern face of the old woman she had glimpsed standing at an upstairs window of the house, looking down at them.

In the end her mother had pulled herself together, and they had gone to a café for a *chocolat chaud*.

'We don't need her, anyway,' Romy had muttered to herself, staring out of the window, her hands wrapped around her cup. 'We don't need anyone.'

But life had not been easy for them. Being a young, penniless unmarried mother was a constant struggle for Romy. And being an illegitimate child had not been easy for Catrine, either.

She had grown so used to the taunts from the other children at school, the whispers and pointing of the mothers at the school gates. There was never anyone to meet her because her own mother was always working, trying to keep a roof over their heads.

She was always alone in the playground because the other girls' mothers would not allow them to play with *la bâtarde*. In the classroom, the nuns would single her out and pick on her. Catrine spent a lot of her time crying, but she would never tell her mother because she did not want to burden her with even more problems. So she learned to keep herself to herself, to expect nothing from anyone.

But now her mother was dying, and Catrine would soon be completely on her own. And even though she was old enough to take care of herself, the thought still filled her with dread.

Then, one evening, she came home from her shift, bone weary as usual, to find her mother sitting up on the couch, an embroidered silk quilt draped around her shoulders. A large box sat on the low table in front of her, with an array of photographs and letters scattered around it.

Catrine recognised it at once, and her heart sank. But she tried not to show her despair.

'I hope you didn't lift that down from the top of your wardrobe by yourself?' she said.

'Who else would help me?'

'You should have waited for me to come home, I would have fetched it for you. What if you'd fallen—'

'I didn't,' her mother cut her off impatiently. 'Anyway, never mind about that. Sit down, I have something to show you.'

Catrine sat down reluctantly on the couch beside her. 'What is it?'

As if she did not already know.

'It's about your father.'

A chill ran like iced water down Catrine's spine. Her mother must be in one of her maudlin moods if she wanted to talk about him.

'What about him?' she asked.

Her mother did not reply. Instead she picked up one of the photographs and handed it to her. 'Here, look at this.'

'Maman—'

'Look at it.' Her mother thrust it into her hand.

Catrine looked down at the photograph that she had seen so often before. She immediately recognised the grand-looking building. Highwood House Hospital, on the south coast of England. Her mother had come over from France to nurse there for a few months just after the war began.

There were four young nurses in the photograph, her mother and three other young women. It must have been a windy day, judging by the way the girls had their hands clamped to their heads to keep their caps from flying away.

They were flanked by two young doctors in white coats, one short with fair curly hair, the other tall and dark.

It was the dark one who drew Catrine's eye, as it always did.

'William Tremayne,' her mother said. 'Your father. The man who ruined my life.'

Catrine stared back at the photograph. She had lost count of how many times she and her mother had been through this. Sometimes Romy was tearful, sometimes she flew into a rage. But she was always bitter.

'He was very handsome,' Catrine said quietly.

'Oh yes, he was. And charming with it. All the nurses were in love with him.' Her mouth twisted. 'What fools we were. And I was the biggest fool of them all.'

Catrine looked back at the photograph. William Tremayne was good-looking, there was no doubt of that. But he looked kind, too. Even in the faded image, she could see the warmth in his dark eyes.

'He looks nice.' The words were out before she could stop them.

'Nice?' Her mother turned on her. 'Do you think what he did to me was nice?'

'No, but—'

'He abandoned me!' Her voice cracked. 'I was all alone and pregnant and he didn't care.'

Catrine steeled herself. She had heard the story so many times she hardly needed to listen to it any more.

But she could not stop her mother going through it

9

again. It was something Romy needed to do, as if she was purging herself of the memory. She would go for weeks, sometimes months without mentioning William Tremayne's name. And then, just when Catrine was beginning to hope that she would never have to hear it again, the box would come out. Then her mother would spend hours poring over the photographs, repeating the story of how she had fallen in love with a young English doctor, how she had given herself to him because she believed he loved her too.

And how cruelly and callously he had abandoned her when she needed him most.

'Perhaps he didn't know?' Catrine said. She could see her mother slipping into the depths of depression and all she wanted was to stop her before she sank too deep. 'You didn't know you were *enceinte* yourself until you came back to France.'

'I wrote to him.'

'He might not have got the letter? You told me yourself he was just about to be posted elsewhere—'

'Of course he got the letter!' her mother cut her off. 'You think I didn't try to tell myself that? When I was all alone, wondering why he'd forsaken me, I made a thousand excuses for him, but deep down I knew the truth. He'd forgotten all about me. Or he didn't want to be encumbered with a bastard child!'

Catrine flinched at the word, even though she'd heard it whispered a thousand times.

She studied the photograph again, taking in the handsome young doctor with his unruly dark hair and tall, lanky limbs. She did not resemble him at all. She was as blonde and petite as her mother.

'I wonder where he is now?' she said.

'Probably married to some nice English girl with a family of his own. Wherever he is, he won't be struggling like us.' Romy looked around her in disgust.

'He might be dead?'

'I hope he is. He deserves to die for what he did.'

'Maman! It's a sin to speak that way.' Catrine crossed herself.

'Then I daresay I'll see him in hell soon enough,' her mother said.

She looked down at the photograph as she said it, and Catrine saw the longing in her eyes. Whatever William Tremayne might have felt, her mother had truly loved him. She would not feel so much hatred for him if she hadn't.

'Why are you telling me this now?' she asked.

'Because I want you to find him.'

Catrine looked up in shock. 'What?'

'I want you to find your father and tell him who you are.' She made it sound like the simplest thing in the world.

'But why?'

'Because I don't want you to be alone.'

Catrine looked into her mother's thin, desolate face.

'I'll be all right,' she said, even though the thought filled her with terror.

'No, chérie. You will need someone to help you when I'm gone. You need your father.'

'But you said yourself he's probably got another family by now?'

11

'All the better.' There was a gleam of malice in her mother's dull eyes. As if the idea of revenge had given her a new lease of life. 'Find him, Catrine. Show him he can't forget us.'

'I wouldn't even know where to start looking for him.'

'Even so, you must try.' Her mother pressed the photograph into her hand. 'Promise me,' she urged. 'Promise me you'll look for him when I'm gone?'

Catrine looked down at the young man with the warm smile. The stranger who was her father.

'I promise, Maman,' she said.

Chapter Two

Romy Villeneuve died three months later. No one came to mourn at her funeral, since her mother had cut off the few friends she'd had in the months since she became ill.

Catrine had wondered if perhaps her grandmother would come. But there was no sign of her, and instead she stood at the graveside alone and watched as her mother was buried in the little churchyard.

Her days passed in a blur. Her nurse training was very hard, but Catrine was grateful for it. She was kept too busy cleaning and scrubbing and studying to grieve. She worked far into the night when sleep eluded her, poring over her books, determined to do well and become every bit as good a nurse as her mother had been. But every night when she returned to their empty apartment, she was reminded of how alone she was.

She thought about her mother's dying wish. She still had the photograph of William Tremayne in her bedside drawer, and from time to time she thought about looking for him as her mother had asked, but she couldn't bring herself to do it. She had never even left Paris before, so the idea of going to England was too daunting for her. In the end she put the photograph away, because looking at it reminded her that she had broken her promise.

Living with her mother's sickness and depression was hard, but life without her was harder. Catrine was frugal, and managed to eke out her meagre student's wages and the modest savings her mother had left her, even though once she'd paid the rent and bills it left little money for food or necessities. Every night she went to bed curled up in her mother's bed, wrapped in her favourite embroidered silk quilt that still bore faint traces of her perfume. She often wanted to break down and cry, but she knew what her mother would say about that. Romy would want her to be brave and strong.

And then one evening she came home from her shift at the hospital to find the landlord had let himself into the apartment and was waiting for her.

Monsieur Durand was an oily little man, with beady dark eyes and a long, sharp nose that always put Catrine in mind of a snuffling rat. He repulsed her. He had always repulsed her mother too, but she had a way of dealing with him. Somehow Romy managed to be charming while still keeping him firmly at arm's length.

'I don't know how you can bear to be nice to him,' Catrine would often shudder.

'I do what it takes to keep a roof over our heads,' her mother had replied pragmatically. 'Anyway, he's quite harmless as long as she you make it clear you won't put up with any nonsense.'

With her mother's words in mind, Catrine squared her

14

shoulders and said, 'What are you doing here? You can't just let yourself in when you feel like it.'

'It's my apartment, Mademoiselle. I can do what I like.' He looked her up and down insinuatingly as he said it.

Catrine pretended not to notice the way his eyes followed her as she shrugged off her coat.

'I was sorry to hear about your mother.' His voice was cold and flat.

'Thank you.'

He looked around. 'How long has it been now? A month? Six weeks? You seem to be managing very well without her.'

If only you knew, Catrine thought.

'What can I do for you, Monsieur?' she asked, then immediately regretted the question when she saw the leer on his face.

'What a question. You should be careful, Catrine. You don't know what trouble you could be getting yourself into.'

She shuddered but did her best to maintain a cool demeanour as she moved past him to the small kitchen area at the other end of the room. She pretended to be making a start on her supper, but really she wanted to keep as much distance between them as she could. All the while she was conscious of him watching her with those little beady eyes of his.

'I'm putting up the rent,' he said finally.

Catrine stopped, her heart dropping. 'You can't!'

'Excuse me, Mademoiselle. But I can do anything I want.'

Once again his eyes moved up and down her body. Catrine fought for control as panic rose in her chest. She was sure this wasn't the first time Albert Durand had tried such a trick. All she had to do was stay calm and try to think how her mother would deal with the situation.

'The rent is already too high,' she stated flatly.

Monsieur Durand bristled. 'It's an up-and-coming area.'

'It's a den of thieves and ne'er-do-wells.'

'Even so, it's worth more than you're paying.' He looked around. 'Another ten francs seems fair to me.'

'Ten francs?' Catrine could not keep the dismay out of her voice. 'But I can't afford that. I'm barely managing as it is.'

'Is that so? I'm sorry to hear that, Mademoiselle.' He paused. 'I certainly don't want to see a poor young girl like you out on the streets.' His tongue flicked out, licking his thin lips. 'Perhaps we could come to some – arrangement?'

There was no mistaking the predatory gleam in his eyes. Catrine turned away, opening and closing kitchen drawers mindlessly to hide her panic and confusion.

'I – I can't afford ten francs,' she stammered. 'But I complete my first year of training in a couple of months. Perhaps when I'm paid more, I could—'

'I'm not talking about money, Catrine.'

He was approaching her now. She kept her back turned, her whole body rigid.

'I have a better idea.' His words slid out like oil, slick and persuasive. 'I'm willing to keep your rent as it is, if you're willing to be – nice to me.'

As his hand touched her shoulder Catrine swung around to face him.

'Don't you dare touch me!' she hissed.

16

She didn't even realise she had the bread knife in her hand until his gaze dropped to the blade and he took a quick step back.

'*Putain!*' he hissed, his eyes still fixed on the blade. 'You're as crazy as your mother. I should have thrown you both out years ago.'

'Get out.' Catrine advanced towards him, her hand shaking as she held out the blade before her.

'I don't know what I was thinking, letting you stay here in the first place. God knows, no one else would have anything to do with her. Dirty *salope* and her little bastard daughter!'

'Never speak about my mother like that!'

'What else do you call a woman who opens her legs for half the Allied forces? And all she ended up with was a bad reputation and a kid with no father and no name.' He looked her up and down, his eyes narrow with contempt. 'And you're no better, for all your airs and graces. You think you're in any position to turn me down? You should be on your knees thanking me for giving you the chance to keep a roof over your head.'

'I'd rather sleep in the Metro.'

'Is that so?' Monsieur Durand smiled nastily. 'Well, I hope you'll be very comfortable there, Mademoiselle.' His smile disappeared. 'You have until the end of the week to get out.'

And with that he was gone. Catrine quickly drew the bolt across the door and slumped down with her back against it. All the strength had gone out of her but her heart still beat a frenzied tattoo against her ribs.

17

She looked down at the blade she still held limply in her hand. There was no chance Monsieur Durand would let her stay in the apartment now, and she wouldn't feel safe there anyway.

So where could she go?

As if in answer to her unspoken question, she heard her mother's voice clearly in her mind.

Promise me you'll find your father.

William Tremayne's smiling face swam before her, but Catrine pushed it away furiously.

No, she thought. There must be another way.

Chapter Three

The house on the Rue Fortuny in the 17th *arrondissement* was just as Catrine had remembered it from her childhood. It was a tall, elegant building, overlooking the beautiful Parc Monceau.

The sour face of the maid who answered the door was just as Catrine remembered too, although she was at least fifteen years older, her face lined with age and her scrawny shoulders stooped.

She seemed to recognise Catrine, too. She looked briefly startled before her features settled into a scowl.

'Yes?' she said stiffly. Her accent still bore traces of a rough country twang. 'Can I help you?'

'My name is Catrine Villeneuve, and I am here to see my grandmother.'

The maid's face registered no surprise. So she did recognise her, Catrine thought.

'Madame Villeneuve is not at home.'

'When will she return?'

'I cannot say.' The maid went to close the door but Catrine put out her hand.

'Perhaps I could wait for her?'

The maid glared at Catrine's hand, pressed against the

glossy black paintwork of the door. 'That is not possible. *Au revoir*, Mademoiselle.'

Once again, she went to close the door. But Catrine remembered what had happened to her mother, the shame she had felt when the door was slammed in her face, and she was determined she would not be rebuffed in the same way. It had taken all her courage to come here, and she was not going to be put off that easily. As the door closed, she deftly sidestepped and slipped through the gap.

She found herself in a marble hall, surrounded by antiques, with a grand, sweeping staircase ahead of her.

'What are you doing?' the maid spluttered with outrage. 'You can't just barge your way in here—'

'It's all right, Sophie,' an imperious voice rang out above them.

Catrine looked up to see an elderly woman descending the stairs. She moved slowly, her spine stiff and upright. She was elegantly dressed, her silver hair expensively styled.

Catrine felt intimidated, but she reminded herself that this woman was her flesh and blood.

'*Bonjour*, Grand-mère,' she greeted her. '*Comment ça va? Je m'appelle*—'

'I know who you are!' the old woman cut her off. She nodded to the maid, who scuttled off towards the back stairs. She sent Catrine a hostile glance over her skinny shoulder and then disappeared.

Louise Villeneuve waited until she had gone, then turned back to Catrine. Her blue eyes were icy in her carefully made-up face.

'What do you want?' she said.

Catrine was taken aback. She wasn't sure what to expect from her grandmother, but her coldness still surprised her.

'I came to tell you my mother is dead.'

The old woman's face remained impassive. 'So I heard.'

Catrine wondered how she knew, but she did not ask. 'Why didn't you come to the funeral, in that case?'

'I didn't see the need, since we were not close.'

'But she was your daughter!'

'She was no daughter of mine!' Louise Villeneuve spat out the words. 'She ceased to be my flesh and blood when she gave birth to you. We hadn't seen each other for years, and that suited both of us very well.'

And yet you knew she was dead, Catrine thought. Her grandmother must have been keeping an eye on her mother, no matter what she said.

'You turned your back on her,' she said. 'She was a pregnant girl, alone and terrified, and she needed you.'

'You don't think I tried to help her?' Two bright spots of indignant colour lit up Louise Villeneuve's powdered cheeks. 'I did everything I could. I arranged a place for her to go, somewhere discreet. I spoke to the priest about adoption—'

'You wanted her to give me up,' Catrine murmured.

'Of course I did! Do you really think we could have welcomed a bastard into our midst? The Villeneuves are a good family, our name stands for something in this city. My husband was a friend of the President.' She shook her head. 'Romy could have salvaged something of her life if she'd taken my advice. But of course she was too headstrong and foolish to listen. And look what happened to her.'

She looked coldly at Catrine.

'We came to see you,' Catrine murmured. 'When I was very young.'

'Your mother thought she could get round me,' Louise Villeneuve sneered. 'Her father had just died and she had an idea that we could be a family again.' Her thin lips curled. 'Of course, I knew the real reason she'd come. She was struggling, just as I'd known she would, and she thought she could use my grief to worm her way back.' She stood upright, her spine stiffening. 'As if she could take me for a fool!'

'You turned her away.' Catrine remembered her mother's tears as they'd sat together in the park.

'I simply reminded her that she'd made her decision and there would be no going back on it.'

'But she needed you.'

'She only came to me when she was in trouble. Where was she when her father was sick and I was nursing him?' Bitterness flared in the old woman's eyes. 'I suppose that's why you're here now?' She looked Catrine up and down. 'Because you're in trouble?'

Catrine would have liked to say no, but she was desperate and she had no choice.

'The landlord of our apartment wants to put up the rent and I can't afford it,' she admitted quietly.

'So you thought you'd come here? What is it you want? Money?' Her grandmother's expression changed. 'You don't think I'd take you in?' She sounded appalled.

'I have nowhere else to go.'

'That's hardly my concern.'

Catrine was shocked. 'You're turning me away?'

'We're strangers to each other. Why should I help you?'

'But I'm your granddaughter.'

Louise Villeneuve's face was full of contempt. 'You're no family of mine. I disowned my daughter because she brought disgrace on our good name. Do you really think I would welcome her bastard into the family?' She pointed at Catrine, her bony finger laden with rings. 'You were the one who caused all this trouble in the first place. Your mother could have had a good life if it hadn't been for you. You ruined her life and everyone else's.'

Catrine gasped. 'That's not true!'

'Isn't it? My daughter could have had a husband, a beautiful home, a real family. But instead she ended up dying in squalor, and all because of you.' Madame Villeneuve stared down her nose at Catrine. 'I will give you money,' she said. 'But only on condition that you go away and never return.'

'Then I don't want your money. I don't want anything from you.'

'In that case, we have nothing more to say to each other.' Louise Villeneuve nodded towards the front door. 'I'm sure you can see yourself out. No need to trouble the servants.'

She turned her back on Catrine and headed back up the stairs.

Catrine left the house and sat in the park, just as she had years earlier. Only this time she was alone, without her mother's comforting arm around her. This time there would be no *chocolat chaud*, no promises that all would be well.

She stared at the tiny Venetian bridge that crossed the pond. It looked so pretty, surrounded by lush green shrubs

23

and flowers. But Catrine was too numb with shock to take in her glorious surroundings.

She was not surprised that her mother had never wanted to speak about her grandmother. Catrine did not think she had ever met such a cruel, heartless woman. She was amazed her mother had ever been capable of love, growing up in such a cold place.

Your mother could have had a good life if it hadn't been for you. You ruined her life and everyone else's.

Was it true? Had she really ruined her mother's life?

She remembered how they had struggled, especially when winter came and the apartment grew damp and cold. Her poor mother must have felt terribly alone, buckling under the burden of looking after a baby all by herself. Perhaps it would have been better for everyone if she *had* given her up.

She stared at the dark water of the pond. Where did she go from here? Her grandmother had been her last slim hope, and now it felt as if she was back where she started, about to be thrown out on the streets.

Promise me you'll do your best to find your father.

Once again, her mother was whispering in her ear.

It was his fault, Catrine thought bitterly. He was the one who had abandoned them.

Find him, Catrine. Show him he can't forget us.

Perhaps it was time she did just that.

Part Two

Chapter Four

London
October 1956

'Welcome to the Nightingale Hospital, my boy.'

William Tremayne placed his hand on his stepson's shoulder and guided him through the double doors that led to Fox wing, where most of the women's wards were situated.

Apart from the war years, he had spent almost his whole career at the Nightingale, since he was a young graduate like Henry. Over the course of twenty odd years, he had worked his way up from humble junior doctor to respected consultant surgeon. But he still clearly remembered his own trepidation as he had entered the hospital for the very first time.

He sensed it in Henry, too. The young man looked terrified as he stared around him. If William hadn't had his hand clamped on his shoulder he might have bolted back for the doors.

'Oh, that smell!' His wife Millie breathed it in. 'Overcooked cabbage and Lysol. It hasn't changed, even after twenty years.'

'I don't suppose it ever will,' William said.

Two porters raced towards them, pushing a patient on a trolley. The three of them pushed themselves back against the shiny beige-painted wall as it rattled past like a freight train.

Henry watched them go. 'It makes it all seem very real,' he said quietly.

'I know what you mean.' William had felt just the same the first time he had set foot on a ward. It had hit him that this wasn't just a diagram in a medical textbook, or a theory delivered in a dusty old lecture theatre. These were real people with real illnesses, and he was expected to help look after them.

'Don't worry, old man,' he reassured him. 'I'll be there to guide you. You'll be learning from the best!'

'Just don't follow his example,' Millie said.

William turned to his wife. 'And what's that supposed to mean?'

'I mean you might be a good surgeon now, but you were incorrigible as a medical student.'

'I'll second that!'

William turned to see his old friend James Bose barrelling down the corridor towards them. He was in his mid-forties, the same as William, stockily built with thinning fair curls.

'James!' Millie greeted him in delight. 'It's so lovely to see you again.'

'Likewise, my dear.' He hugged her, kissing her on both cheeks. 'You don't come up to London nearly enough.'

'I'm rather busy these days. I have the estate to run.'

'How is the old place?'

'Falling down around our ears as usual,' she grimaced.

'I have such fond memories of being stationed at Billing-hurst during the war,' he sighed.

'So do I.' William smiled at Millie. The RAF had

requisitioned Millie's family estate, and it was where they had rekindled their romance.

'Yes, well, you would say that. You ended up with the lady of the manor.'

Bose winked at Millie, then turned to look at Henry. 'And how are you, young man? Flourishing, I hope?'

'Hello, Uncle James,' Henry greeted him shyly.

'A little bird tells me you graduated from Oxford with a double first?'

'Bragging again?' Millie lifted her eyebrows at William.

'Why not? The best I managed was a shabby second.'

'That's because you didn't pay attention,' Bose said. 'Whereas I was more like young Henry here.'

He beamed at him. Henry blushed, his ears turning bright red as they always did when someone spoke to him.

'You were a swot,' William said. 'Henry isn't like that. Are you, Henry?'

'There are worse things than working hard, old boy. You should try it sometime.'

'Now, now, you two!' Millie shot them both a warning look. 'You're not setting a very good example to my son.'

William grinned at his old friend. He and Bose had been ribbing each other for as long as he could remember. They had been friends ever since college, and right through their training days. They had even served in the military together during the war.

'Talking of setting a good example,' Bose said now, lowering his voice. 'I believe the hospital committee is meeting today. No prizes for guessing what they're going to be talking about.'

'If it's the Medical Superintendent's job, then it's about time. I've been saying for months they need to get someone in place,' William said.

'You're only saying that because you want the job yourself!'

'Why not? I think I could do a good job.'

William had made no secret of the fact that he wanted the newly created post of Medical Superintendent. Not just because it was the top job, either, although the Medical Superintendent would wield a huge amount of power at the hospital – they would be in charge of the entire running of the place, overseeing the medical, nursing and administrative departments on behalf of the hospital committee. William wanted the job because he truly believed he could make a difference. He had been at the Nightingale since he was a student, he understood it better than anyone. Even if he said it himself, there was no one who came close to him in terms of expertise and experience.

'Oh, so do I, old man. You're the obvious choice. It's just a shame Sutcliffe doesn't agree.'

Frederick Sutcliffe was the chairman of the hospital committee. He was a dour man, a Methodist lay preacher with very fixed ideas about right and wrong, moral and immoral.

And for some reason, he disapproved of William Tremayne. He had been dragging his feet for weeks, apparently looking for an excuse not to give him the job.

'Well, if you'll excuse me, I have a hernia that needs my attention . . .' Bose smiled at them all. 'It was delightful to see you again, Millie.'

'You must come down to visit us at Billinghurst sometime,' she said.

'Indeed. Although I'm sure it won't be the same without the Spitfires landing on the lawn!' He nodded to Henry. 'And I look forward to seeing you on the wards, young man.'

And with that he was off, strolling down the corridor in his usual jaunty way.

'Come on,' William said when he'd gone. 'I'll show you round a ward, so you can get a feel of the place.'

He led the way to Wren, which was the Gynaecology ward and his personal domain. Most of his patients were there, although he also did general surgery when circumstances required it.

As he pushed open the doors, Millie hung back.

'Won't the ward sister mind us just walking in like this?' she whispered.

'Not me,' William grinned. 'Things have changed, my love. I'm the consultant, I can walk in whenever I please.' Although he knew even he wouldn't dare risk it on some of the other wards, where the sisters were dragons and still insisted that no one could set foot through the door without their permission.

Luckily, Jennifer Grace was the more forgiving type. She sat at her desk in the middle of the ward, a neat redhead in her thirties, with a freckled face and gentle grey eyes.

'Mr Tremayne.' She rose from her desk when she saw William. 'We weren't expecting you this afternoon?'

Her gaze moved from William to Henry and Millie. Out of the corner of his eye, William noticed his wife surreptitiously adjusting her hat and brushing down her coat.

He smiled to himself. Old habits die hard, he thought.

Even now, just the sight of a ward sister's dark blue uniform was enough to bring out the terrified student nurse in Millie.

'This is purely a social call, Miss Grace,' he said. 'I'm showing Henry here around the hospital. He'll be joining the Nightingale next month.'

'So you're following in your father's footsteps?' Jennifer Grace smiled at Henry.

'I hope so,' he said quietly.

It was all William could do not to burst with pride. Henry might not be his flesh and blood, but he had been in the boy's life since he was a toddler, and William regarded himself as his father. Henry didn't remember his real father, Sebastian, who was killed fighting for his country as a pilot in the war, but William was always careful to respect his memory.

'Not too closely, I hope,' Millie murmured, too quietly for Miss Grace to hear.

'I'm sure you'll be a great asset to the hospital,' she said.

A student nurse went by, carrying a pile of fresh linen. William caught the speculative sideways glance she sent Henry as she skimmed past them.

Henry was a very handsome young man – tall and broad-shouldered, with clear blue eyes and a mop of fair curls. But he hardly seemed aware of the effect he had on the opposite sex. He certainly did not seem aware of the young nurse's interest as he focused his attention politely on Jennifer Grace.

Perhaps his mother was right, and it was for the best that he did not take after him too closely.

Chapter Five

They said their goodbyes and left the ward, and stood for a moment in the corridor.

'Well,' Millie remarked. 'I must say Wren ward seems a much happier place than it used to be. We were there for five whole minutes and I don't think I saw a single student nurse in tears.'

'I told you, things have changed since your day.'

'I suppose so. Although I was so utterly hopeless, I'm sure I would have driven even a paragon like Miss Grace to distraction!'

'You were awful,' William agreed with a laugh.

'So were you,' Millie retaliated. 'You spent more time flirting with the student nurses than you did attending patients.'

'I'm sure Henry doesn't need to hear about that—'

'He used to come back to the hospital after a night out so he could sleep it off on the ward,' Millie went on, ignoring him. 'I remember one poor old lady in geriatrics who got up in the night to go to the bathroom, and when she came back you were curled up in her bed.'

'So I was!' William laughed. 'It gave her quite a start, as I recall.'

'It nearly finished her off. And do you remember that

33

time you decided to take a quick nap on a trolley you found in the hospital corridor?'

'And that porter mistook me for a recently deceased patient and tried to push me down to the mortuary? I don't know who was more shocked, me or him, when I suddenly sat up and demanded to know where he was taking me!'

They both laughed.

'What's so funny, you two?'

William's sister, Helen, approached them down the corridor. Millie started at the sight of her.

'You gave me such a fright!' She pressed her hand to her chest. 'As long as I live, I don't think I'll ever get used to the sight of you in that uniform.'

Helen looked down at her stiff black Matron's dress. 'It is rather daunting, isn't it?' she agreed. 'I frighten myself sometimes.'

Helen had been Matron of the Nightingale for six months now. Like William and Millie, she had begun her career in this very hospital. She and Millie had been students together, and even shared a room at the nurses' home. They had been great friends ever since.

But unlike Millie, who had given up nursing when she married her first husband, Helen had continued with her career throughout the war. Even when she married her doctor husband David and moved to the Kent countryside to be closer to William and Millie, she had worked alongside him as a district nurse at the village surgery.

And when their marriage broke up, she had returned to the Nightingale to take on the job as Matron.

It couldn't have come at a better time for her, William

reflected. Helen had never discussed her decision to end her marriage, not even with Millie. It was a mystery to both of them why she had left David when they had seemed so happy.

But returning to the Nightingale had been a lifeline for Helen. She took her nursing very seriously and had flourished in her new role as Matron. But behind her smile, William could see the lingering sadness in his sister's eyes. Her marriage break-up had affected her more than she allowed herself to acknowledge.

'I'm sorry I wasn't here when you arrived, but I've been in a meeting with the administrator. Have you enjoyed looking around the hospital, Henry?'

'Yes, thank you, Aunt Helen.'

'I suppose your mother has been telling you some terrible stories?'

'Nothing I haven't heard before.'

'They haven't put you off joining us?'

'Not at all.'

'I'm glad to hear it.' Helen smiled warmly. 'Perhaps you'd like to join me in my office for coffee before you leave?'

'Coffee? In Matron's office?' Millie looked terrified at the thought. 'I don't think I've ever been in there when I wasn't in trouble.'

'It'll make a nice change for you, then,' Helen said.

Millie looked at her son. 'I suppose we have some time before we catch our train?'

'I won't be able to join you, I'm afraid.' William looked at his watch. 'I'm due back in Harley Street at five.'

'So you won't be coming back to Billinghurst with us tonight?' Millie looked disappointed.

'I'm afraid not, darling. I'm seeing two patients and then I'll probably come back here. There's a post-op on Wren I'm rather worried about.' He glanced at Helen, who nodded. She knew the woman he was talking about. She had survived her hysterectomy, but her condition was still giving cause for concern. 'I'll probably stay at the flat tonight.'

'Oh, that's a shame.'

'Why don't you two stay in London, too? We could all go out to dinner. You too, Helen, of course.'

Millie looked tempted for a moment, then shook her head. 'It's a lovely idea, but I should get back for the children,' she said. 'And I'm meeting the estate manager first thing to discuss the tenancy on the vacant farm.'

William looked at her with pride. Not in a million years would he ever have imagined that little Millie Benedict would take to running her family's estate as well as she had. She had always been such a flighty thing when she was a nursing student, delightfully scatty and well-meaning but forever getting things wrong.

But her life had changed when she inherited Billinghurst from her father, the Earl of Rettingham. Suddenly she was left to care for the family estate, a stately home, numerous tenant farms and several thousand acres of Kent countryside.

William could never have imagined her taking it on, but the responsibility had been the making of Millie. Somehow she had not only run the estate single-handedly through the war, she had made a great success of it. Billinghurst was now flourishing under her expert guidance.

Even so, William still marvelled at the sight of his wife in wellington boots, a man's tweed cap on her blonde head, perched on top of a tractor.

William left his family to their coffee and caught the tube train back to Oxford Circus. It was half past four, and the broad shopping thoroughfare was still busy with shoppers heading home, laden with bags.

William turned down Regent Street and cut across Cavendish Square to his consulting rooms. Like many other senior doctors, he divided his time between his work at the hospital and his private practice. But unlike many of his colleagues, he had a preference for his work at the Nightingale. The introduction of the National Health Service after the war had changed everything, and William was very pleased at the way it was working. Suddenly patients who might never have been able to afford to see a doctor were coming through the doors.

Some of the other consultants had been less than impressed, but as far as William was concerned, he had become a doctor to treat everyone, rich and poor alike.

He knew his first patient was not due until five o'clock, so he was surprised when he glanced through the door to the waiting room to see a young woman seated in the corner, her face averted to gaze out of the window.

'Dr Tremayne!' Miss Jason, his receptionist, emerged from the waiting room to greet him, half closing the door behind her. She was usually such a calm, unflappable old stick, but this time she looked distinctly put out.

'What on earth is wrong?' William asked. 'And who's that in the waiting room?'

He knew it wasn't his five o'clock appointment; Mrs Hartley-Evers was one of his regulars, a woman in her late forties with recurrent fibroids.

'Well might you ask.' Miss Jason's cheeks flushed. 'She arrived half an hour ago, wanting to see you. I told her there were no appointments left this week, but she insisted on staying.' She lowered her voice. 'I was thinking about calling the police,' she confided.

'Oh no, please don't do that. She must be rather desperate if she's willing to sit there.' He looked at the young woman's averted face through the crack in the door. There was something tantalisingly familiar about her profile. 'Does she have a name?'

'I didn't ask her,' Miss Jason replied huffily. 'To be honest, I just wanted her to go away.'

'Then let's find out, shall we?' He pushed open the door to the waiting room, and called out, 'You wanted to see me, Miss—?'

She turned around to face him. She was slightly built, her delicate features framed by a short cap of blonde hair. Large brown eyes stared back at him, frank and assessing.

He would have known her anywhere.

'Villeneuve,' she said. 'My name is Catrine Villeneuve.'

Chapter Six

He knew her straight away, Catrine could tell. There was a flicker of recognition in his eyes – just fleeting, but enough for her to know.

But his face gave nothing away, his professional smile fixed in place.

His dark hair was threaded with grey and there were fine lines fanning from his brown eyes, but otherwise he looked just the same as the photograph she still carried in her pocket.

'Come through to my office, please.'

He ushered her into his surgery and closed the door behind them.

'Please, take a seat.' He indicated the chair and took a seat himself behind the polished walnut desk. 'Now, what can I do for you, Miss Villeneuve?'

Perhaps she had been wrong about him recognising her? Catrine stared back at his blandly smiling face. Her hands suddenly felt clammy with nerves. She had waited for this meeting, practised in her head what she was going to say. But now she was here, she could not seem to find her voice.

She could feel her heartbeat drumming in her ears. She'd lost count of how many days she had walked up and down

Harley Street, wondering what to do. She had sat in Cavendish Square, staring across at the glossy black front door of the private practice, trying to get up the courage to go inside.

And now here she was, and she could scarcely believe it.

'I'm sorry, Monsieur,' she blurted out finally, her words tumbling over each other in a rush. 'I'm not sick. I'm—'

'You're Romy's daughter.'

She stopped in her tracks. 'You know who I am?'

'As soon as I laid eyes on you. The resemblance is extraordinary.'

'I wasn't sure you'd remember her.'

'Of course I remember her. Tell me, how is your mother?'

'She's dead, Monsieur.'

For a moment his calm, professional mask seemed to slip. 'I'm sorry to hear that.' He stared down at his desk for a moment. 'When did it happen?'

'Two months ago. She had been ill for a while.'

He was silent for a moment, lost in sadness.

'I can still hardly believe it,' he murmured. 'She was so young . . .' Then he looked up at Catrine. 'My sincere condolences, Miss Villeneuve.'

'Thank you.'

'So what brings you here, to my office?'

'Maman said I had to find you.'

'Why?'

She looked at him. If he had any inkling of what she was going to say, then he was doing an excellent job of hiding it.

She took a deep breath. There was no going back now.

One way or another, the next words she uttered would change both their lives.

'I am your daughter, Monsieur.'

'Good God.'

The words erupted from William Tremayne's lips.

Catrine took the crumpled photograph out of her pocket, smoothed it out and put it on the desk between them. William stared down at it for a long time.

'Highwood House,' he said. 'We worked there together just after the war started.' He looked up at Catrine. 'How old are you?'

'Seventeen, Monsieur.'

He nodded, taking it in.

Catrine's gaze fell to the silver-framed photograph on his desk of William with a beautiful, smiling blonde woman and three children.

Maman was right, he had married a nice English girl and had a family of his own.

'You didn't know?' she said.

'Of course I didn't know!'

'My mother wrote to you, Monsieur.'

'When?'

'Just after she returned to France. When she found out she was pregnant.'

'I didn't get any letter from her.'

'But I don't understand. How could that be?'

'I don't know. But I swear to you, I had no idea.'

If only Maman had known, Catrine thought. Perhaps she would not have lived her whole life under the shadow of bitterness, feeling forsaken by the only man she had ever loved.

'How did you find me?' William asked.

'Through the General Medical Council register. It's a list of every doctor in the country—'

'I know what the GMC register is,' he smiled.

'The woman at the library told me about it. I did not know where to start looking for you, so I asked her for advice.'

'I see. And you say Romy – your mother – asked you to find me?'

She nodded. 'She thought you should know about me.'

But before he could say any more there was a knock on the door, followed by the receptionist's voice calling out,

'Sir, Mrs Hartley-Evers is here for her five o'clock appointment.'

'Tell her to wait, will you?' William called back.

'But it's nearly ten past.'

William muttered a curse under his breath.

'Thank you, Miss Jason.' His voice was tight with tension. 'Tell her I'll be with her in a moment.'

He turned back to Catrine. 'I'm afraid I have to see my patient,' he said. 'Miss Jason will just keep tapping on the door every thirty seconds otherwise.'

'I'll wait.'

He shook his head. 'I have someone else coming after that, then I have to return to the hospital to check on one of my patients there. I may not be finished until much later.'

Catrine looked at him. She knew an excuse when she heard one.

But at least she had fulfilled her mother's wish, although she had no idea to what purpose.

As she rose to leave, he suddenly said, 'Where can I find you?'

'I'm working at Selfridges, in the perfume department. Just across the road,' she said, then instantly felt stupid. Selfridges was the largest department store in Oxford Street, of course he would know where it was.

'And where are you staying?' he asked.

'I have lodgings in Ladbroke Grove.'

'Write down the address.' He pushed a pad of paper and a pencil towards her. As she scribbled down her address, Catrine noticed the smart headed notepaper, with his name in embossed letters across the top.

'I'll come to see you this evening,' he promised, as she handed the paper back to him.

William sat behind his desk and listened for the sound of the front door closing.

Almost immediately, Miss Jason was knocking on the door again.

'Shall I send in Mrs Hartley-Evers?' she said.

'In a moment, Miss Jason. I need to make a telephone call first.'

'But—'

'I said a moment!'

'Very well, Mr Tremayne.'

William rarely raised his voice, and he could hear the hurt surprise in his secretary's tone. She would be sulking for days, he thought. But his mind was in too much turmoil to care.

He looked down at the piece of paper in his hand. An address, in neatly looped handwriting.

His daughter's address.

He kept it in his hand as he picked up the telephone receiver and quickly dialled a number.

'Come on, come on!' he muttered under his breath as he listened to the interminable ringing tone on the other end of the line.

Finally, someone picked up.

'Bose?' William jumped in straight away, as soon as he heard his friend's voice. 'Bose, will you be at the hospital later? I really need to speak to you. Something's come up and I badly need some friendly advice . . .'

Chapter Seven

Catrine caught the tube train back to Ladbroke Grove. It was six o'clock in the evening and the Teds were already beginning to lurk in their gangs on the street corners. They looked intimidating in their long coats, with their greased quiffs and heavy, crepe-soled shoes. They didn't seem to care about anything or anyone as they insolently smoked their cigarettes and showed off to their giggling girlfriends.

A couple of them whistled and catcalled Catrine as she hurried past. She tried to feign indifference, but she was glad that the streets were still light and busy. She would never have wanted to encounter them after dark.

The area of London where she lived was run-down, to say the least. It was bounded by a railway track, the Grand Union Canal and Wormwood Scrubs prison. There was also a cemetery called Kensal Green, which sounded pretty but was anything but.

But it was cheap, which was why Catrine had chosen to live there. And being cheap, it also attracted ne'er-do-wells and foreigners and ex-convicts from the local prison – all the types who couldn't afford or weren't wanted in the smarter, more salubrious areas of the city.

Catrine rented a bedsit on the first floor of a tall, shabby Edwardian house which had once probably belonged to a respectable middle-class bank clerk or a bus inspector, but which had now been converted into dingy little flats.

A train rattled past on the metallic bridge overhead as Catrine let herself in. The aroma of curry greeted her straight away. From upstairs came the sound of music playing.

The house was occupied by a number of tenants, mostly foreigners like herself. There were people from Trinidad, Jamaica and Barbados, and an Indian family on the ground floor. There was only one English person in the house, a miserable old woman called Doris who banged on the ceiling with a broomstick and complained incessantly about everyone. She had been friendly to Catrine at first, until she learned she was French, at which point she had started snubbing her whenever their paths crossed.

Catrine's room was at the front of the house. The wallpaper was spotted with damp, but it had a high ceiling and a bay window that overlooked the bustling street market below.

The room contained a single bed, a wardrobe and chest of drawers, and two worn leather armchairs that flanked the small fireplace. There was a tiny sink in the corner which Catrine used for washing, but the main bathroom was upstairs. Like the small kitchen area on the landing, it was shared between all the residents on the first and second floors.

Her neighbours regularly argued over the four-ringed hob, but luckily Catrine did not have to cook very often. She ate what she could at the Selfridges staff canteen and then went without for the rest of the day.

This evening she had no appetite at all. Her stomach was in knots after all that had happened that afternoon.

She could scarcely believe she had met her father. It all seemed like a bizarre dream. Even though they had not said a great deal to each other, she found she could not remember a word either of them had uttered.

Except one thing.

I'll come to see you this evening.

It was more than she had expected, more than she could have hoped for. She had thought he might throw her out of his office as soon as she told him who she was.

But instead he had listened. He had seemed nice, she thought.

Well, Maman, at least I kept my promise.

She dragged one of the armchairs over to the window and sat looking out on to the street below. The market traders had long since packed up and gone, leaving behind the skeletal remains of their stalls and gutters littered with rotting fruit and vegetables.

She wasn't looking for him, she told herself. It was too early for him to come. But that didn't stop her stomach giving a jolt when she heard someone banging on the front door downstairs.

But no, it was just one of her neighbours who had lost his key again. Catrine listened to the heavy thump of his footsteps as he made his way up to the floor above hers, followed a moment later by the clamour of voices.

There was never a quiet moment in the house, but Catrine didn't mind. If she closed her eyes and listened to all the different languages and accents, she could almost imagine she was back in the *arrondissement de l'Observatoire*.

She tried not to keep looking at the time, but somehow her gaze kept straying towards the little alarm clock on her bedside table. Seven o'clock. Half past seven. Eight . . .

Surely he must come soon? She tried to work out how long it would take him to cross London from east to west. Would he travel by taxi, she wondered, or on the underground? She couldn't imagine someone as immaculately turned out as him on a dirty tube train.

She drifted off to sleep, still curled in the armchair. Once or twice she awoke with a start, thinking she heard someone knocking on the door. Out on the landing, the woman in the next room hummed to herself as she prepared her supper on the stove. A moment later Doris came thumping up the stairs in her slippers and told her that she didn't know how they carried on where she came from, but in this country no one cooked past ten o'clock at night.

Ten o'clock. Catrine blinked blearily at the alarm to make sure.

He wasn't coming. Not at this hour.

She was disappointed, but not surprised. As soon as she had walked into that smart consulting room and seen that photograph of his beautiful wife and children, she had known he would want nothing to do with her. She felt foolish for ever thinking it would be different. Hadn't her mother warned her what he was like?

Oh, Maman, she thought. *Why did you tell me to come?*

Chapter Eight

Catrine woke the following morning with a mood that matched the dull grey sky outside her window. At first she did not recall the reason for her heavy heart, but then she remembered the previous night and her wretchedness came flooding back.

She wasn't disappointed, she told herself. But she did feel lost. For the past couple of weeks, her whole focus had been on finding her father. Now she had, and he had turned his back on her, she did not know what her next move should be.

There was one thing she was certain about, however; she was never going to contact William Tremayne again.

She had already made up her mind to return to Paris when she went to work that morning. There was nothing to keep her in England now. It was better to cut her losses and go home, though she wasn't sure what kind of life would be waiting for her back in France. She had no home, no family and no future since she had given up her hospital training to come to England.

But she put all her worries aside as she joined the other girls behind the perfume counter at Selfridges.

'*Bonjour, Mademoiselle,*' Josie, one of the senior girls, greeted her with a sickly smile. She seemed all sweetness and light on the surface, but Catrine could sense the malice behind her charm.

She had been very put out since Catrine had arrived, especially after Miss Gregory the supervisor had observed how popular Catrine was with the customers. Up until that point, Josie had apparently been the top salesgirl.

'It must be your French accent,' Miss Gregory had said to Catrine in front of the other girls. 'It gives you a bit more class. The customers like that.'

Catrine had been mortified, of course. And ever since then, Josie and the rest of her gang had never missed an opportunity to belittle her. They called her stuck-up and excluded her whenever they could. They snubbed her in the staff canteen, and she was never invited on any of the outings they discussed loudly in front of her.

Not that Catrine cared. She was used to being left out. Besides, she did not have the money for nights out. Most of her wages went on paying her rent and keeping the gas meter in her room topped up. The other girls all lived at home, so they never had to worry about bills, or where their next meal was coming from.

Besides, she had nothing in common with them. All they talked about was make-up and boyfriends and the latest heartthrob in the hit parade, and Catrine didn't really know anything about any of those subjects. And even if she did, the other girls probably wouldn't want to hear what she had to say.

She fetched a duster and a tin of Mansion Polish and set to work wiping down the wooden counter before the store opened. But even that caused comment.

'Look at her,' she heard Josie whispering, as she stood in a huddle with the other girls, their arms folded. 'She's only doing it to make the rest of us look bad.'

'Sucking up to Miss Gregory, more like!' one of the other girls chimed in.

Catrine ignored them as she put all her effort into buffing up the wooden counter. She was only doing it out of habit. As a student nurse, she was used to starting each day by sweeping, scrubbing and dusting the ward. She had tried explaining this to the other girls, but they only took it the wrong way as usual and accused her of thinking herself better than them just because she'd once trained to be a nurse.

'Perhaps you should go back to your hospital, then?' Josie had sneered.

If only, Catrine thought. Selling perfume to spoilt rich women who had nothing better to do with their day but spend money hardly compared to nursing the sick back to health.

Her first customer was particularly difficult. She was one of their regulars, the middle-aged wife of a High Court judge. She was swaddled in a thick mink coat, her grey hair styled in rigid waves. Her crimson-painted mouth was pulled down in a perpetual scowl. She came in at least twice a week, and Catrine did not think she had ever seen her smile.

Now she seated herself in one of the armchairs reserved for special customers and treated Catrine like a servant, sending her scuttling here and there with an imperious wave of her hand. Soon they were surrounded by at least a dozen bottles of expensive French perfume, but nothing seemed to satisfy the woman.

'Too flowery ... too sickly ... not nearly sophisticated enough.'

'How about this one, Madame?' Catrine added another dab to the inside of her wrist, although it was hard to find a patch of skin that was not already scented. 'It was my mother's favourite.'

The women lifted her flabby arm and sniffed hard, then pulled a face.

'Oh no,' she dismissed. 'That's far too cheap. I don't want to smell like a common shop girl!'

Catrine gritted her teeth in a determined smile. She wondered if the woman had even noticed her casual insult. Probably not, she decided. She was far too self-centred to give a thought to anyone else's feelings.

On the other side of the perfume department, she was vaguely aware of Josie and another girl bickering over who was going to serve a particular customer.

No doubt it was a handsome man, she thought. They rarely showed an interest otherwise.

'Perhaps I should try the Guerlain again?' the woman interrupted her thoughts.

'Yes, of course.'

As Catrine went to fetch the bottle she had just replaced on the shelf, she ran into Miss Gregory.

'There's a man here looking for you,' she said, her voice laced with disapproval.

'For me? Are you sure?'

'He asked for you by name. I told him I do not allow my girls to receive personal visits during work hours, but he insisted it was a family emergency.'

Her mouth curled, showing that she did not believe a word of it, but Catrine was hardly listening. Her heart had leapt into her throat.

It couldn't be – could it?

'Hold this, would you?' She thrust the bottle of Guerlain into Miss Gregory's hands and hurried around to the other side of the counter. There she found a scowling Josie – and William Tremayne.

He smiled when he saw her. 'Catrine! Thank God I found you. I couldn't remember which department store you said you worked. I've just walked the length of Oxford Street. I made a terrible nuisance of myself in DH Evans!' He lowered his voice. 'I'm sorry I didn't come to see you last night. I didn't leave the hospital until nearly midnight, and I didn't think you'd appreciate my calling round so late.'

Catrine blushed, very aware that Josie was loitering nearby, listening avidly to every word.

'I – I can't really talk now,' she whispered, glancing over her shoulder.

'When, then?'

'My lunch break is at twelve.'

He thought for a moment. 'I'm supposed to be seeing a patient at half past eleven. But I can get Miss Jason to telephone and change the appointment.'

Catrine stared at him. Was he really changing his plans for her?

'You don't have to do that,' she said quietly.

'I think I do.' He sent her a level look. 'You and I have a great deal to talk about. I'll have Miss Jason book us a table for lunch. How about L'Escargot on Greek Street? It isn't too far from here. I take it you have no objection to French food?'

'No, of course not.'

He smiled. 'Splendid. I'll meet you there at noon.'

And then he was gone, sauntering out of the store without a backward glance.

Catrine watched his tall figure disappearing into the crowd of shoppers and wondered if she had imagined him.

But then she caught the look of avid curiosity on Josie's face and realised that whatever had happened, it had been very real indeed.

Chapter Nine

L'Escargot was in Greek Street, in a rather shabby area of the city called Soho, full of coffee bars and record shops and seedy basements with their curtains drawn in the middle of the day.

Catrine had lived in a similar area in Paris all her life, so she was well aware what sort of business went on behind those shuttered windows, but her mother had taught her not to judge anyone for how they made a living.

'They are only women like ourselves, struggling to pay their bills,' she would say.

The restaurant itself was small and intimate. Catrine immediately felt homesick as she breathed in the delicious aromas of garlic and butter and wine. It reminded her of the restaurant below their apartment, a cheap and cheerful place where the chef served up dishes worthy of Le Cordon Bleu.

Even as the maître d' showed her to the table, Catrine was sure William would not have made it, but there he was, waiting for her, seated at a corner table. His face broke into a smile when he saw her approaching.

'I wasn't sure you'd come,' he said, standing up to greet her.

Catrine stared at him in surprise. Was it her imagination, or did he seem nervous?

'*Pourquoi*, Monsieur? It's not every day I get the chance to eat French food again.'

His brows lifted. 'So you've just come for the food?'

'I am hungry.'

He laughed at that, and Catrine wasn't sure why. She was only being honest.

'You don't just resemble your mother in looks, I can tell,' he said. 'She always spoke her mind, as I recall.'

The waiter appeared at their table.

'Some wine, Mademoiselle?' he offered, picking up the bottle William had ordered.

'That won't be necessary—' William started to say, but Catrine cut him off.

'Yes, please,' she said. 'But I'll taste it first.'

She was aware of William's surprise as she sampled the wine, then nodded to the waiter to fill her glass. From what she could gather, girls of her age in England tended not to drink. Either that, or they got very giggly after a port and lemon.

But in France children were taught from an early age how to appreciate good wine.

They were silent for a moment as they both considered the menu.

'Would you like me to order for you?' William offered, but Catrine shook her head.

'Thank you, but I know what I want.'

Once again, she sensed William's mild surprise.

'I'm sorry if I embarrassed you earlier, turning up like that,' he said. 'I should have thought about what I was doing. But I was keen to let you know I hadn't let you down.'

The waiter arrived to take their order, which saved Catrine from replying.

William was not what she had been expecting. The fact that he'd even invited her here was a surprise to her, but she remained guarded, remembering what her mother had said about him.

Why had he wanted to meet her? Had he invited her because he wanted to get to know her, or because he wanted to let her down gently? It was impossible to tell, but as usual Catrine was braced for the worst.

'I must say, I'm rather glad I didn't see you last night.' William looked down at the snowy white linen napkin he was pleating nervously between his fingers. 'It's given me the chance to think about everything.'

Here it comes, Catrine thought, holding her breath. This was where he told her he didn't want to see her again. She wished he would wait until after they'd eaten.

'What did your mother tell you about me?' he asked.

Catrine almost smiled, thinking of her mother's bitter outbursts. *You really don't want to know*, she thought.

'She told me you met when she came to England to escape the Nazi occupation.'

'She started nursing at Highwood House Hospital, where I'd been stationed as a medic. We were expecting a huge influx of casualties when the war began, but apart from the evacuation at Dunkirk, there wasn't a lot going on for several months. In the end Romy decided she could serve her country better by going home, and I was stationed elsewhere shortly afterwards.'

'Which would explain why you didn't get her letter?' Catrine suggested.

He nodded. 'I was constantly being moved around from one military hospital to the other,' he said. 'And then I enlisted in the RAF and was sent up north for a few months. It's possible your mother's letter could have missed me, or got lost.' His eyes met hers across the table. 'I swear to you, I had no idea.'

'And what would you have done if you had known?'

He was saved from answering by the arrival of their food. The aroma of the boeuf bourguignon in front of her was delicious, but suddenly Catrine had little appetite as she waited for William Tremayne to answer.

'I – I don't know,' he answered finally. 'But I would have done the right thing by her.'

'Would you have married her?'

'If that was what she wanted.'

His lack of enthusiasm hit her like a blow. Why couldn't he lie to her, tell her that Romy Villeneuve had been the love of his life, that he would have married her and lived happily ever after? It would have cost him nothing to lie; her mother was dead, after all. She wasn't going to bind him to any promise.

But it would have made a difference to Catrine. She might have felt wanted for once, instead of a burden on everyone.

'Of course it's what she would have wanted,' she snapped.

'It would have been a better life than the one we had on our own.'

'She never married?'

Catrine stared at him. Was he truly so naïve?

'There were not many men who would take on a shamed woman and her bastard child.' She saw him wince at her bluntness, but she was too angry to care. 'Even her own family didn't want to know her once I was born.'

'I'm sorry.' William lowered his gaze towards his plate. 'I had no idea.'

'Are you married?' Catrine asked, even though she already knew the answer.

'Yes.'

'Any children?'

'Three,' he said. 'Two boys and a girl. Henry – the eldest – is Millie's son from her first marriage.'

'So you took on another man's child but ignored your own flesh and blood?'

'How could I ignore you when I had no idea you even existed?'

Catrine fell silent. All she knew was that William and his family had had a lovely life together while she and her mother had struggled.

She felt a sudden burning resentment for the smug, smiling woman in the photograph.

'Did you love her?' she asked.

William looked up at her sharply. 'What sort of question is that?'

'One you can't answer, I think. Or perhaps that is an answer in itself?'

His hand shook slightly as he picked up his wine glass. He took a long time to speak, and Catrine could see him going over the words in his mind before he uttered them.

'I thought I loved her,' he said finally. 'But you have to understand, it was a difficult time. We were very young. War had just been declared, we had no idea what was going to happen to us, whether we were going to be bombed or invaded. We didn't know if we would live to see another year, or even another week. Under those sorts of conditions, it's easy for feelings to become very intense, very quickly.'

'So you didn't love her?' Catrine said flatly.

'As I said, I thought I did. And I still remember her. As soon as I saw you sitting in my office, I could picture her so clearly . . .' His voice trailed off. 'But whether it would have endured, I don't know.' He looked up at her, his eyes dark. 'I know that isn't what you want to hear, but I'm trying to be honest with you. I'm sorry.'

'She never forgot you.' But whether it was love she felt, Catrine was not sure. Certainly by the end of her life, whatever feelings she might have had for him had crystallised into cold, bitter resentment.

The waiter came to take away their plates. He raised his eyebrows at their virtually untouched food but whisked them away without a word.

William refilled her glass.

'Tell me about yourself,' he said.

'What do you want to know?'

'What sort of work were you doing before you came to England? Or were you studying?'

'I was training to be a nurse,' she said.

'Like your mother?'

'Yes.'

'And now you're selling perfume in a department store.'

Catrine bristled at the amusement in his voice. 'It pays my rent,' she snapped. God knows, she needed the money. Coming to England had taken every franc of the modest savings her mother had left her.

William took a gulp of his wine. 'Of course,' he muttered. 'I'm sorry.'

'Are you?'

'Of course.' He put down his glass. 'Look, I can only apologise that I wasn't part of your life. But I hope I can change all that now.'

'In what way?' Catrine asked.

'I don't know.' He regarded her across the table. 'What do you want from me, Catrine?'

Now it was Catrine's turn to look away. It was a question she had not expected to have to answer. She was still reeling that he had given her the time of day.

Find him, Catrine. Show him he can't forget us.

'Where did you say you're living?' William broke the silence between them.

'Ladbroke Grove. I have a bedsit there.'

'It's not the nicest of areas, is it?'

'It's all I can afford,' Catrine said defensively.

He thought for a moment. 'I have a flat in Covent Garden that I use when I have to stay in London for work. I'm not there very often – perhaps once or twice a week at the most. You're very welcome to stay there if you like?'

Catrine stared at him warily. 'You're offering me a place to live?'

'I think it's the least I can do, under the circumstances.'

'How much is the rent?'

William laughed. 'Good lord, I wouldn't charge you anything! What do you take me for?'

Catrine hesitated. 'Why would you do that for me?'

'Because you're my daughter,' he said. 'And I'd like to get to know you, if that's what you'd like? That's why you're here, isn't it?'

Catrine considered the question. Why was she here?

Show him he can't ignore us forever.

'I'll think about it,' she said.

Chapter Ten

'You did what?'

'I know, it was foolish of me. But what else could I do?'

'Foolish? My God, man, you've invited a young woman you've barely met to move in to your flat within five minutes of meeting her. I'd say that was more than foolish. Criminally reckless, more like. Even for you.'

William looked out of the window of his office. It was a brisk autumn day, and the wind shook the bare branches of the cherry tree in the grassy quadrangle below his window. Opposite him on the other side of the quad, he could see the verandah of one of the Male Medical wards where half a dozen or so patients were enjoying the sunshine. They were supervised by a young nurse who sat hunched in a corner, surreptitiously smoking a cigarette.

He was beginning to wish he'd never gone to James Bose about his problem. But in the moment he'd panicked and needed to talk to someone. And Bose understood the situation better than anyone. He'd been at Highwood House too, he had known Romy.

Besides, his friend was only telling him what he already knew.

'I told you, didn't I? I warned you when you called not to get involved. But you have to blunder in and land yourself in this mess.' He shook his head. 'It never ceases to amaze me how you do this time and time again. As a surgeon you're constantly weighing up the consequences of your actions – you'd never act without thinking. And yet for as long as I've known you, in your personal life you've always gone with your heart and not your head.'

'I didn't know what else to do,' William said. 'For heaven's sake, the girl is all on her own in a strange country. And you should have seen the hovel she was living in . . .'

He had briefly been inside the run-down old house when he went to collect Catrine and her belongings in a taxi. The stench of stale cooking, dirt and poverty still seemed to cling to his clothes.

'From what you say it sounds as if it's what she's used to,' Bose muttered.

William felt a sting of guilt. 'Don't say that.'

He was still in a state of shock, trying to get over everything that had happened. Was it really only two days since Catrine walked into his office? It all felt quite unreal.

'You should have taken my advice and had nothing to do with her,' Bose said.

'How could I? She's my daughter.'

'You only have her word for that.'

William turned on him sharply. 'What's that supposed to mean?'

'How do you know she's not some other man's mistake?'

'You knew Romy. She wasn't like that.'

'No,' Bose agreed heavily. 'No, she wasn't. She was utterly besotted with you.'

'Don't. I feel wretched enough as it is.'

He looked back across the quadrangle. The wind had picked up. The young nurse had stubbed out her cigarette and was ushering her patients back inside.

Bose was right, he thought. Romy Villeneuve had been very much in love with him. She had put all her trust in him, given him her heart and everything else she had to give.

'I let her down,' he said.

'You mustn't punish yourself, old man. We were young, and they were difficult times. We all did foolish things.'

'But this was more than foolish, wasn't it?' William said. 'She had a child. My child. And she had to do it all alone.'

From what Catrine had told him, it hadn't been easy for her. Even her own family had turned their backs on her.

'You weren't to know how it would turn out,' Bose insisted. 'Besides, you can't change the past.'

'I know,' William said. 'But I can do something about the future.'

'Are you sure that's what you want?'

Their eyes met.

'You don't have to get involved,' Bose urged him. 'You can call a halt to it, even now.'

'But she's living in my flat.'

'Then get rid of her.'

William shook his head. 'I can't do that.'

Bose took out a cigarette and offered one to William.

'Why has she come looking for you?' he asked.

'Her mother is dead. Her grandmother wants nothing to do with her. I'm the only family she has left.'

'But you're a stranger to her.'

'I suppose I'm better than nothing.'

James Bose took a long, thoughtful drag on his cigarette. 'What's she like?' he asked.

William paused. It was not a question he could really answer.

'I barely know her,' he said. 'From what I can tell she seems rather reserved.'

'Shy, you mean?'

'Not exactly.' He shook his head. 'Far from it, in fact. She has a great deal of confidence. No, I'd say she was more – guarded,' he found the right word. 'She doesn't give much away. But then again, I've only met her a couple of times. I dropped her off at the flat with her belongings last night, and headed straight down to Billinghurst.'

'She might have cleaned you out by the time you get back,' Bose said with a grin. 'Can you imagine if you went back to the flat and found her and all your worldly goods gone?'

William looked rueful. 'It would serve me right if she did.'

'I think you could count yourself lucky if that happened.' Bose considered the tip of his cigarette thoughtfully for a moment. 'Actually, that might not be such a bad idea,' he said. 'I wonder if you should offer her money? That might be what she's come for, when all's said and done. A nice big cheque to get out of your life forever.'

'I don't want to do that,' William said.

It was odd, but he was already beginning to feel an attachment to her. Perhaps it was just guilt.

'You're taking a big risk, keeping her around,' Bose pointed out. 'What if Sutcliffe finds out? You know what a stickler he is. Finding out you'd fathered a child out of wedlock – he'd get up on his moral high horse. It would put paid to your chances of that Medical Superintendent's job, certainly.'

'That's the least of my worries,' William said. 'I'm more worried about what Millie will say than the chairman of the hospital committee.'

Bose gawked at him. 'You mean you haven't told her?'

'How can I?'

'But I thought you went home to Billinghurst last night?'

'Yes, but I can hardly drop my bags in the hall and say, "Gosh, darling, you'll never guess who turned up yesterday? My long-lost daughter from a brief love affair with a French nurse."'

'You've got to tell her something,' Bose pointed out. 'You can't keep the girl a secret forever. Unless you do decide to pay her off?' he said hopefully.

William shook his head. 'I'm not sure I could keep it from Millie even then,' he said. 'It wouldn't be fair on her.'

'So no one else knows apart from me? Not even your sister?'

'God, no! I can only imagine what Helen would make of the situation.'

He and Helen had always had a prickly relationship. Even though he was the eldest, Helen had always been the more sensible one. When they were students, she was forever saving William from all kinds of scrapes, romantic and financial.

'She's always thought I was a lost cause anyway,' he said. 'This would only prove she was right.'

'Well, I think you should tell her,' Bose advised. 'You never know, she might be able to help.'

'She'd be a nightmare about it,' William said.

'She's going to find out sooner or later. And if I know our esteemed Matron, she will be furious if she finds out you've been keeping something from her.'

He was right, William thought. But he couldn't face it. There would be all kinds of problems and difficulties that he just wasn't ready to deal with yet.

'Let's just see how it all works out,' he said to Bose. 'And then I'll tell them when the time's right.'

'Putting off the inevitable, you mean? That's so like you.' His friend sent him a shrewd look. 'Well, don't say I didn't warn you.'

Chapter Eleven

London
March 1957

As it turned out, it was six whole months before William had to face the consequences of his actions.

At first all he felt was relief that he had not been found out. But as the days turned into weeks and then months, William grew more and more guilty. He loathed keeping anything from his family, especially Millie. But the longer time went on, the harder it became to admit what he'd done.

Every day he promised himself he would tell her. But how could he? It was bad enough that he had a long-lost daughter. But to keep such a devastating secret for six months made it all much, much worse.

He should have come clean straight away, when he'd had the chance. Millie might have been more understanding then. Now, after months and months of lying, he wasn't sure even his loving wife would find it in her heart to forgive him.

And so he went on lying, making excuses whenever Henry or Helen wanted to visit. When Millie wanted to come up to London to do some Christmas shopping, he told her there was a leaking pipe in the flat and arranged for her to stay at Claridge's instead.

He felt wretched about Catrine, too. As time went on, she had begun to resent being shut up in the flat and never being allowed to meet his family.

'If you are so ashamed of me then perhaps it would be better if I were not here at all,' she had said to him.

She was very sensitive about being a source of shame, he had realised. From the little she had told him about her life in Paris, William had learned that Catrine and her mother had led a very solitary life, separated from polite society by their circumstances. Her mother had often lied and tried to pass herself off as a widow, but sooner or later their secret would always be uncovered, and they would be cast out, rejected.

The more he found out about the wretchedness of Catrine and Romy's lives, the more guilty William felt. No matter how difficult it made things for him, he could not abandon his daughter again.

Not that they had a very close bond. Catrine was still very cool and reserved with him. They did not spend a great deal of time together. If William had to stay in London for work, he would stay with Bose or at a hotel. He did not like to intrude on her space.

But the feeling wasn't always mutual. One afternoon, Catrine had unexpectedly turned up at the hospital. It was her day off from working at Selfridges, and she was bored.

'I wanted to see where you worked,' she had said.

Fortunately, William just happened to be crossing the hospital quad when he saw her strolling up the drive. He had headed her off and ushered her around the side of the building, where he'd given her a stiff warning about poking her nose in where it did not belong.

On reflection, he had reacted more harshly than he'd intended. But he'd upset Catrine and she'd fled in floods of tears. And as luck would have it, who should she run into but his sister Helen, who was crossing the courtyard at the time.

Helen had not seen them together, but she seemed to have an uncanny sixth sense where William was concerned, and somehow she had managed to connect them.

It had been a close shave. William had denied everything, of course, and Helen seemed to believe him. But he should have known that once her senses were alerted, she was like a dog with a bone.

Sure enough, late on a spring evening in March, she turned up at his flat in Covent Garden, all guns blazing. It just happened to be an evening when William had gone back to the flat to collect some belongings. Catrine had made supper, and they'd eaten together.

'Where is she?' she had demanded.

'Who?'

'You know very well who. The girl with the red scarf. The one I saw you with at the hospital.'

'I don't know what you're talking about—' he started to say, but Helen ignored him.

'So where is she?' she repeated, pushing past him. 'Hiding in the bedroom, I suppose?'

'I'm not hiding, Madame.'

Catrine stood in the bedroom doorway. His sister stared at her, lost for words. Then she turned on William.

'How could you?' she demanded. 'How could you do this to Millie and the children?'

'Please, if you'd just give me a chance to—'

'I thought you'd changed. I thought you'd grown up!'

Slowly, the truth dawned. 'You think I'm having an affair?' he murmured.

'What else would you call it?' She sent Catrine a look of disgust. 'For Christ's sake, she's young enough to be your daughter!'

'She is,' William said quietly.

'What?'

William sighed. 'Helen, I'd like to introduce you to Catrine Villeneuve – your niece.'

'My niece?'

'Catrine is my daughter.'

He looked at her with pride as he said it, but Catrine did not meet his eye. She stared boldly at Helen, her chin raised.

She was always so defensive, he'd noticed. She carried herself as if she was used to having to fight for her place in the world.

'I think I need a drink,' Helen said.

'Good idea.' He turned to Catrine. 'Would you do the honours?'

They all moved to the living room, where Catrine poured them each a brandy from the crystal decanter. She poured one for herself, too. William noticed his sister's disapproval as she watched her take a sip.

Not that Catrine seemed to care. William could not help

admiring her composure as she seated herself on the couch between them, her legs curled underneath her. She seemed utterly unfazed by Helen's arrival, while William could feel his nerves rising.

His sister always had that effect on him.

'How long has this been going on?' Helen asked.

'Six months.'

'Six months?' Helen repeated incredulously. 'You've kept it a secret all this time?'

'I needed time to think.'

'Think about what?'

'I just wanted to get used to the idea, I suppose.'

William could feel himself squirming under his sister's questioning. Helen was four years younger than him, but she had a way of making him feel like a schoolboy. He could only imagine how much the student nurses must have dreaded being summoned to her office.

'And what about your mother?' Helen turned her attention sharply to Catrine.

'She is dead, Madame.' Catrine's voice was flat, devoid of emotion.

'Romy was a nurse,' William put in. 'She and I met when she was stationed briefly in England just after the French occupation.'

Helen ignored him. 'Did you always know who your father was?' she asked Catrine.

Catrine nodded. 'Maman told me all about him.'

She glanced at William as she said it, and he saw the accusation in her eyes.

He wondered what Romy had told her about him. He didn't blame her for being bitter. She had deserved better from him.

'But you knew nothing about her?' Helen asked him.

'No,' William said quietly. 'No, I didn't. Apparently Catrine's mother wrote me a letter . . .' He trailed off.

'But you didn't receive it?'

He shook his head.

Helen turned to Catrine. 'What made you come to England to look for my brother?' she asked, in that clear, precise voice that William imagined struck terror into student nurses.

It certainly struck terror into him.

'Maman wanted me to find him.'

'And now you've found him,' Helen said. 'So what are you going to do?'

'I – I don't understand—'

'How long are you planning to stay?'

'I don't know.'

'Surely you must have thought about your future?'

'I . . .' It was the first time William had seen Catrine falter, and he immediately jumped to her rescue.

'This is her home for as long as she wants to stay here,' he said.

Catrine looked at him, and for a moment he caught the faintest hint of warmth in her brown eyes.

'And what does your wife have to say about this?' Helen said sharply. 'She does know about this, I take it?' She looked from one to the other. 'Oh, William! Please tell me you've told her?'

74

'I didn't know what to say at first,' William admitted sheepishly. 'And then, as time went on, it's just become more difficult—'

'So you decided to say nothing at all?' Helen finished for him. 'How typical of you, always trying to take the easy way out.' She turned to Catrine. 'I'd like to speak to my brother in private, if you don't mind.'

Catrine's expression hardened. 'If you're going to talk about me, then I should be here,' she said firmly.

William looked from one to the other. Neither of them moved. They were like two cats in an alley, their spines arched, each waiting for the other to yield. And he was caught squarely in the middle.

'Give us a moment, Catrine. Please?'

She glared at him mutinously. Then she got up and stalked out without a word.

No sooner had she left than Helen turned on him.

'What on earth are you thinking?' she demanded. 'I wish you'd told me sooner.'

'So you could talk some sense into me?' William said bitterly.

'Someone should! For heaven's sake, William. Why did you ask her to move in with you?'

'You sound like Bose,' he muttered.

'You've told James Bose about this?' Helen looked horrified.

'I had to talk to someone.'

'And it didn't occur to you to speak to your own wife?'

He fell silent.

'What do you think she'll say?' he ventured at last.

'God knows. If she's got any sense she'll leave you.'

His head shot up. 'Don't say that! She wouldn't – would she?'

'No,' Helen conceded. 'No, she probably wouldn't. But she should. You deserve it.'

'I had no choice. I was only trying to do what was right.'

'Right for whom?' Helen paused. 'How do you even know she's your daughter?'

'She has a photograph—'

'I'm sure there are lots of young nurses who still carry a photograph of you. That doesn't mean anything.'

'She's my daughter,' William insisted. 'I know she is.' She might look like her mother, but she had his brown eyes. He could see the resemblance every time he looked at her.

'So when will you tell Millie?' Helen asked.

'Soon.'

'When? Tomorrow? This week?'

'I'm not sure.' Helen had a horrible way of cornering him so that he felt like a fish wriggling on the end of a hook.

'You'd better tell her soon, Will, or I'll tell her myself. I mean it. She deserves to know.' She looked at him consideringly. 'Unlike you, Millie's no fool. And if I've had my suspicions then I'm sure she has, too.'

'I know.' He buried his face in his hands. 'I'll tell her, I promise.'

Helen faced him, her expression serious. 'I hope this doesn't end badly for you,' she said.

'I'm sure she'll understand—'

'I'm not talking about Millie. I know you want to do the right thing, Will. But I wish you'd thought about all this more carefully. That girl—' she glanced past him towards the bedroom, biting her lip.

'What about her?'

'I'm worried, Will. If this gets out it could ruin your reputation. Not to mention the shame it will bring to the family.'

'Aren't you being rather melodramatic?'

'I don't think so.' She shook her head. 'Just promise me you won't be an idiot?'

'Bit late for that, don't you think?'

He smiled weakly, but Helen did not smile back.

Chapter Twelve

Helen's words stayed with William after she had left.

He poured himself another brandy and sat on the couch, brooding about what she had said.

Deep down, he was worried that his sister was right. He had acted impulsively, without any thought for the consequences.

But what else could he do? He felt so badly for Catrine, he knew he had to make it up to her for what she had been through.

He was still brooding on it when Catrine appeared in the doorway.

'It's all right, she's gone. It's safe to—' His gaze dropped to the battered suitcase she was holding. 'What's this?'

'I'm leaving.'

'Why?'

'I should never have come. I know I'm not wanted here.'

'That's not true. I want you here.'

'I heard you telling your sister you had no choice.'

He flushed guiltily. 'That isn't what I meant. You're part of my family. Of course I want you here.'

'Then why haven't you told anyone about me?'

'I'm sorry,' he said. 'As I said to Helen, I was just waiting for the right time—'

'Your sister doesn't think I belong here.'

'I promise you, Helen isn't usually that fierce,' he said. 'She's actually very kind when you get to know her.'

'I don't think she wants to get to know me.'

For a moment her aloof mask slipped and he caught a glimpse of the forlorn, frightened young woman beneath.

'I'm sorry,' he said. 'But you must understand, Helen is very – protective of me. Even though I'm the eldest, she's always been the sensible one. She was forever getting me out of scrapes when we were young.'

'Scrapes?'

'Trouble, I suppose you'd say.'

'And is that what I am? Trouble?'

His sister's words of foreboding flashed into his mind.

If this gets out it could ruin your reputation. Not to mention the shame it will bring to the family.

'Not at all.' He shook his head. 'This has all been a shock to her, that's all. She'll be fine once she's had time to get used to the idea.'

'And what about your wife?'

William took another gulp of his drink. He could feel Catrine watching him carefully. It felt as if she was testing him somehow.

'Perhaps it would be better if I left?' she said. 'Then you wouldn't have to tell anyone. You could carry on with your life as if I didn't exist.'

'Do you really think I could just forget you? You're part of my life now, Catrine.'

She stared down at the floor, so it was impossible to read the expression on her face.

'Helen was right about one thing, though,' he said.

She looked up at him sharply. 'What's that?'

'You need to think about your future. You can't go on selling perfume in Selfridges forever.'

She bristled defensively. 'It's a job.'

'I know, but you could do better. Have you thought about taking up your nursing studies again?'

'Here? In London?'

'Why not? I'm sure you'd have no difficulty finding somewhere to train.'

'I'll think about it.' Her face was aloof and impassive as always, but the gleam in her brown eyes told him she was interested.

'Good.' He set down his glass. 'Now, I think I'll go to bed. It's been rather a long evening, all things considered.'

As he rose from his seat, Catrine said, 'What do you think your wife will say?'

William paused as once again his sister's words came unbidden into his head.

If this gets out it could ruin your reputation. Not to mention the shame it will bring to the family.

He smiled weakly. 'We'll find out soon enough, won't we?'

Catrine sat at the window and looked out.

The flat, as William called the apartment, was in a smart mansion block on Long Acre, in a place called Covent Garden. It was a few streets away from a bustling fruit and vegetable market, and early in the morning Catrine would wake up at the crack of dawn to the sound of vans and lorries arriving, the shouts of the wholesalers opening up their stalls and the rattle of the porters' trolleys over the cobbles.

She loved to sit at the window and watch them at work. Her English was already very good, but listening to them shouting to each other had taught her a great deal of vocabulary she had never learned from her mother. Not all of it suitable for a young lady, as William told her when she had tried it on him.

At night, when the market was closed, the theatres would open and the area would be transformed. This was what Catrine saw now as she looked out of the window. Below her, the streets were thronged with smartly dressed people heading home from the Royal Opera House and the Theatre Royal on Drury Lane.

Sometimes the two worlds would collide, and she would see gaggles of actors emerging from the smoky late-night bars just as the market porters were arriving to start their day.

This was what she saw as she sat at the window in the early hours, although for once she was too restless to take an interest. The evening had left her shaken and unable to sleep.

She could not stop thinking about what had happened. Had William really meant it when he'd said she was part of his life? He had seemed sincere, but she couldn't allow herself to believe it was true.

She kept reminding herself what Maman had told her, that William was not a good man, that he was not someone to be trusted. He was the reason her mother had been so unhappy for so many years.

And yet he had been so welcoming to Catrine since she had first arrived. He had allowed her to stay at his flat, and he'd made a real effort to get to know her.

Not that she had made it easy for him. She still kept him at arm's length, telling herself that it was all too easy, too good to be true. Sooner or later he would let her down, abandon her the way he had abandoned her mother.

He would certainly forsake her if his sister had anything to do with it. Helen McKay's haughty disdain had reminded Catrine of her grandmother. And like Grand-mère, she had made it very clear that she wanted nothing to do with her long-lost relative.

Your reputation could be ruined. Not to mention the shame it will bring to the family.

Bitterness hardened her heart. Was that all anyone thought of her? She had tried so hard to make herself worthwhile, to prove herself. But all she would ever be was a shameful secret, to be hidden away and never spoken about.

Well, she wasn't going to allow herself to be hidden away again. William Tremayne and his family were going to know all about her, one way or another.

Chapter Thirteen

'Do what?'

Elsie Parsons sat back in her chair and planted her hands on her eight-months pregnant belly.

'You want me to do what?' she repeated, glaring across the table. From behind her, beyond the makeshift curtain screen, came the sounds of clinking cups and saucers, babies crying and the murmurs of mothers-to-be as they waited for their antenatal appointment in the draughty church hall.

'I – um . . .' Dora could almost feel the young midwife trembling beside her. 'I just wondered if you wouldn't prefer to have your baby at the hospital?' the girl ventured finally.

'And why would I want to do that?' Mrs Parsons' eyes narrowed.

The midwife, whose name was Lucy Cornish, shot a nervous look at Dora. 'It might be a good idea, given your age—'

'My age?' Mrs Parsons bristled.

Miss Cornish checked her notes. She was a fresh-faced young woman of twenty-three, and this was her first pre-natal clinic in Bethnal Green.

It wasn't going very well so far. Her plummy voice and air of condescension wasn't going down at all well with the expectant mothers of the East End.

Poor girl, Dora thought. She was doing her best to appear confident, but she was coming across as a bit of a know-all.

'You are nearly forty,' she was telling Elsie Parsons now. 'Delivering a baby at your age might be considered a risk.'

'Cobblers!' Elsie Parsons scoffed. 'My mum had our Alan when she was forty-two.'

Dora hid her smile behind her hand. Elsie Parsons was a mother of five. She probably knew a lot more about the grim realities of childbirth than Miss Cornish did.

A confused blush rose in the young midwife's cheeks. 'There's also the question of your accommodation,' she went on, consulting her notes.

'My what?'

Don't, Dora prayed silently. *Don't say it.* She could already see the light of battle in Elsie Parson's eyes.

'Your home, Mrs Parsons,' the young woman continued, oblivious. 'It's hardly an ideal place to give birth, given the conditions you and your family live in.'

Elsie Parsons shifted her bulk to lean across the table, and for a moment Dora feared she might be about to grab the hapless midwife by her throat.

'Are you suggesting my house ain't clean?' she hissed.

'No, no! Not at all.' Lucy Cornish rushed to reassure her, but the damage had already been done. 'But surely you'd rather give birth in a nice hospital, with pain relief and doctors on hand? And you could rest in the hospital for a week afterwards. That would be nice, wouldn't it?'

'Oh yes, that would be lovely,' Elsie Parsons agreed. 'But

what am I supposed to do with my five other kids while I'm putting my feet up in the hospital? My old man works nights and when he is at home he's either fast asleep or useless. And I've got to keep an eye on my old mum, too. And she's got the whelk stall to run, so don't tell me she can lend a hand with the kids.'

'Yes, but ...' Lucy Cornish looked helplessly at Dora, who shrugged back.

'Listen, love,' Elsie went on in a more conciliatory tone. 'I had all this before with the last midwife when she tried to get me to have our Colin in hospital. And I'll tell you what I told her. I've given birth to all my children at home, and they've all been born fine and healthy. I've got no need of all that messing about.'

The toddler in the pram beside her starting to whinge, and she lumbered to her feet.

'Now, if there's nothing else, I'd best go and get the tea on before the rest of them get home from school,' she said.

'That's all for now,' Dora said, as she watched her shrugging on her coat. 'Make sure you pick up your vitamins on the way out, won't you? And we'll see you next week.'

'I'll be here, love. Unless this little one decides to make an appearance!' Elsie patted her bump with a grin.

She left, and Lucy Cornish stared after her resentfully.

'Honestly, some people just don't want to be helped, do they?' she muttered. 'I can't imagine why she'd want to give birth in that hovel!'

Dora stared at her. 'I know Elsie Parsons,' she said. 'Her home might be small and overcrowded, but it's spotless.'

'There are eight of them crammed into three rooms! Can you imagine?' The midwife looked appalled at the thought.

I don't have to imagine, Dora thought. Her own mother had brought up five children in a cramped little terrace on Griffin Street, very similar to the one the Parsons family lived in now. And her grandmother had lived with them, too.

She clearly remembered her mother giving birth to little Alfie in the bedroom upstairs, while Dora cooked tea for her siblings in the kitchen. Then, when the midwife had gone, she'd made her mother a cup of tea and they'd all crowded round the bed to meet the newest arrival.

Miss Cornish had a long way to go to understand such a way of life. She had come to the East End fresh from her training, armed with a smart new uniform and all kinds of modern theories about childbirth and antenatal care. She hoped the girl would be willing to learn.

'You've got to know who you're dealing with,' she told her. 'It's no use handing out the same advice to everyone.'

She pulled aside the curtain and looked out at the rows of women waiting to be seen. Some were chatting, others reading magazines. A woman in the corner was busily knitting a pair of pale blue bootees.

'Every one of these women is different,' she said. 'They're all pregnant, but they've all got their own stories, and you need to help them all in their own way. Take that one, for instance.' Dora pointed to a young woman who sat flicking through a copy of *Woman's Own*, but hardly looking at the

86

pages. 'She's clearly a first-time mum, so she'll need lots of reassurance and support. She'll welcome any advice you can give her. But that one . . .' She pointed to a harassed-looking woman with a baby in her arms, who was trying to stop a fight between the two young children at her feet. 'She's been through it all before. She doesn't need telling what to expect. But she still needs your help, although I daresay she'll be too proud to ask for it.'

'How do you know that?'

'Look at her.' The woman wore a shabby coat that had seen better days, but the children were dressed immaculately. 'There's no point telling her to make sure she gets enough fresh fruit and vegetables. If there's money for such luxuries, she'll make sure her children are well fed before she sees to her own welfare.' Dora studied the woman's wan face. Around her left eye she could see the faint traces of a fading bruise. No doubt she'd borne the brunt of her old man's temper.

Dora bunched her own hand into a fist at her side. She'd known enough cruelty at the hands of her vicious stepfather to understand the life of fear the poor woman probably endured.

Dora had learned to fight back, but she understood others were not so lucky. Especially if they had three children to feed, and another on the way. A pay packet was a pay packet at the end of the day, even if it did come with a beating.

'How will I know how to help if she doesn't ask?' Miss Cornish interrupted her thoughts.

'You'll know,' Dora said. 'Just listen to her. She'll let you know when she's ready.'

She looked back over her shoulder at the young midwife. Lucy Cornish looked quite overwhelmed. No doubt she thought she would just be dispensing vitamins and weighing newborns, not listening to emotional problems and dealing with domestic disputes.

'You'll get used to it,' Dora assured her cheerfully. 'You'll find it's a fulfilling part of the job, once you get to know people.'

'I'm not sure they'll want to get to know me.' Lucy gazed gloomily out at the rows of expectant mothers. 'They don't seem to like me much.'

'Oh, they're bound to be a bit wary at first. But they'll take to you soon enough.'

'And what about her?' Lucy nodded towards the corner of the hall. 'What's her story, do you think?'

Dora followed her gaze to where an unhappy-looking woman sat slightly apart from the others. An older woman sat beside her, her hands folded in her lap, mouth clamped in a stern grimace.

Dora recognised her, and felt a tug of sadness.

'Brenda Cashman,' she said.

'You know her?'

'Oh yes, I know her. She used to go to school with my younger sister, Bea.'

'Let me guess,' Lucy considered the woman for a moment. 'She looks too old to be a first-time mother. Mid-thirties at least, I'd say. But she looks nervous, doesn't she? And she's brought someone with her for moral support.'

'I don't know about support,' Dora said ruefully.

'What do you mean?'

'You'll find out,' Dora said.

Brenda Cashman was smiling as she stepped behind the curtain for her appointment ten minutes later, the old woman following close behind.

'Perhaps you'd like to wait for your daughter outside?' Lucy suggested, but the woman cut her off.

'Daughter-in-law,' she said abruptly. 'And no, I don't want to wait outside. I want to know what's going on.'

Her mouth firmed, as if that was the end of the matter. Dora looked at Brenda, who shrugged helplessly.

'She can stay if she wants,' she said. 'I don't mind.'

Brenda was a gentle, softly spoken woman, tall and slender with pale skin, light brown hair and a sweet smile. Her mother-in-law, by contrast, was dumpy and pugnacious-looking, with a tight perm dyed an alarming shade of auburn. She planted herself in the only available seat, her battered handbag on her lap, so that Lucy had to scurry off and fetch another chair for the expectant mother.

'It's nice to see you, Brenda,' Dora greeted her warmly. 'How far along are you?'

'Nearly four months,' Brenda beamed.

'That's wonderful news. I expect you'll feel baby move in a few weeks.'

'I can't wait!' Her eyes lit up, like an excited child.

'God willing,' her mother-in-law grumbled. 'Although she got this far last time, and look what happened.'

Brenda's smile faded. 'You don't need to remind me, Ma,' she mumbled.

'You've been pregnant before, Mrs Cashman?' Lucy Cornish consulted the notes in front of her.

'Seven times,' her mother-in-law answered, before Brenda had the chance to reply. 'And every time she's managed to lose it.' She glared at Brenda as if she had done it on purpose. 'Seven miscarriages in five years,' she muttered. 'That ain't right, is it?'

Dora and the young midwife looked at each other.

'Let's examine you, shall we?' Lucy Cornish suggested brightly. 'Get undressed and hop up on the bed.' She glanced at the older woman. 'Are you sure you don't want to wait outside, er . . .'

'Enid Cashman,' the old woman finished for her. 'And no, I'm staying right here, if you don't mind.'

It was a statement, not a question. The way she was planted in the chair, wild horses would probably not have moved her.

Dora watched as Lucy carried out her examination. She might have some high-minded ideas, but there was no questioning her abilities as a midwife. She was brisk and efficient as she went about palpating Brenda's tummy, checking the measurement of the fundus.

'The doctor reckons there's nothing wrong with her, but I ain't so sure,' Mrs Cashman said. 'I can't understand it. By the time I'd been married three years I had three healthy kids. I popped them out easy as anything. The midwife said it was like shelling peas,' she said proudly.

Dora glanced at Brenda. 'Not everyone's as lucky as you,' she said. 'It takes a while for some people.'

'Yes, well, I wish she'd hurry up.' Enid Cashman glared

at her daughter-in-law. 'She ain't getting any younger, and neither am I. And my Joe deserves to be a father.'

'I'm doing my best, Ma,' Brenda muttered through gritted teeth.

'How far along did you say you were?' Lucy Cornish asked.

'Nearly four months. Why?'

'You have a fundal height of three fingers above the symphysis pubis. That's rather small for sixteen weeks.'

'What does that mean?' Brenda Cashman sat up on the bed, her face full of distress. 'Is there something wrong with the baby?'

'I knew it!' Her mother-in-law looked grim. 'I said you should be showing by now, didn't I? My Jeannie's barely four months gone, and she's already out here.'

She held her hand out to indicate a swollen belly. Dora remembered Mrs Cashman's daughter Jeannie coming in for her first antenatal appointment a couple of weeks earlier. Dora suspected she'd been eating for two since before the baby was conceived.

'Calm down,' Dora stepped in quickly, seeing Brenda's face crumple. 'There's nothing to worry about, honestly. You won't do yourself any good by getting anxious.'

'Did you hear that?' Enid Cashman turned on her daughter-in-law. 'You're probably causing all these miscarriages with your fretting.'

And you're not helping with your constant nagging, Dora thought.

'It's nothing to worry about, honestly,' she reassured Brenda, who was trembling like a leaf, her eyes full of tears.

'These measurements are never that accurate, you can't take them as gospel.'

Lucy Cornish opened her mouth to speak, but Dora sent her a quick, silencing look.

'As long as you're feeling well and getting plenty of rest and good food, that's all that matters.' Dora patted Brenda's hand.

'Oh, she's doing that,' Mrs Cashman interrupted. 'My Joe treats her like a bloody queen.' She glared jealously at her daughter-in-law.

'Why don't you come in again next week, and we'll examine you again,' Dora said. Then, lowering her voice, she added, 'And perhaps you could leave your mum-in-law at home next time?'

'I'll try.' Brenda Cashman gave her a watery smile.

'I wonder why she keeps trying?' Lucy Cornish said, when the pair of them had gone. Brenda seemed in better spirits, although her horrible troll of a mother-in-law was still muttering under her breath as they left. Dora could only imagine what she was saying to her poor daughter-in-law. 'I mean, you'd think after seven miscarriages she'd want to give up, wouldn't you?'

'I don't think she dares,' Dora said. 'You saw how Enid Cashman was with her. She's obsessed with the idea of her son carrying on the family name. Besides, I think Brenda really wants to be a mum. She lost both her parents and her sister in the war, so she had no one until she met Joe. She's desperate to have a family of her own.'

'Not as desperate as her wretched mother-in-law!' Lucy remarked.

'I know,' Dora smiled. 'And it's not as if she ain't already got more grandchildren than she can count. Her two daughters are both sickeningly fertile.'

'Poor Brenda, that can't be easy for her either, seeing her sisters-in-law having babies around her.'

Dora looked at her approvingly. It was nice to see Lucy Cornish was already showing some understanding and compassion for her patients.

'No, it isn't,' she agreed. 'And it certainly doesn't help that Jeannie is pregnant again. I'm sure Enid Cashman never stops comparing them.'

'Poor woman,' Lucy sighed. 'I hope she manages to come in by herself next time.'

'Me too,' Dora said. Although from what she'd seen of Enid Cashman, she didn't think it was very likely.

Chapter Fourteen

Holmes was one of the Male Surgical wards at the Nightingale Hospital. In Matron Helen McKay's days as a student it had been a general surgical ward, but since the expansion of the hospital it now specialised in gastro-intestinal patients – or 'tums and bums', as the younger nurses nicknamed it.

When Helen was training, the girls had all dreaded a stint on Holmes, mainly because of the fearsome reputation of the ward sister, Mary Lund. And twenty years later, things had not changed. Miss Lund might have retired, but her place had been taken by Ruth Redmond, a woman with an even sharper tongue and more exacting standards than her predecessor, if that was humanly possible.

Even Helen was slightly intimidated by Miss Redmond. They were roughly the same age, both in their early forties, and the ward sister barely came up to Helen's shoulder in height. She was a small, bespectacled woman with pointed features and wavy brown hair. But she scarcely ever smiled, and behind those glasses her grey eyes glinted like cold steel.

As Helen conducted her regular morning ward inspection, she could sense Ruth Redmond's keen glance flicking around behind her, looking for faults. Helen even found herself nervously brushing invisible specks off her own black dress.

Everything was perfect, of course. The dark wooden

parquet floor was carefully polished, the glass in the tall windows sparkled, and all the beds had perfectly mitred corners and smooth counterpanes.

Helen knew Miss Redmond would have already been around each of them in turn, measuring the turn-down of each top sheet with her forearm to make sure they were all uniform.

And even if Miss Redmond missed something, which was highly unlikely, then the ward maid would certainly have picked it up. Annie Chadwick had been the maid on Holmes ever since the war, and took her responsibilities very seriously indeed.

Helen could see her now out of the corner of her eye, just beyond the door at the end of the ward that led to the kitchens. She was lurking in the shadows, a mop in one hand, bucket in the other, eyeing them suspiciously. She and Ruth Redmond had an uneasy relationship, to put it mildly. On the surface it was all politeness, but underneath tensions simmered.

There might have been a power struggle going on between ward sister and maid, but at least they were united in their passion for a clean and orderly ward. There was almost no need for Helen to carry out her inspection, although she made a show of running her finger along the bedrails and checking each water jug had been properly topped up, just because she knew it would be expected of her.

'I trust everything is in order, Matron?' Ruth Redmond said tightly.

'Of course, Miss Redmond. I would expect nothing less.'

But it wasn't just the cleanliness of the ward she was

95

there to inspect. Helen also liked to keep an eye on the patients and nurses, too.

She had a particular interest in the two student nurses who had been assigned to Holmes ward for this rotation.

First there was Nurse Riley. Young Winifred Riley was the daughter of Dora, one of Helen's oldest friends. She and Dora had both trained with Helen's now sister-in-law Millie.

They could not have come from more different backgrounds – Millie was the daughter of an aristocrat, while Dora was brought up in the back streets of Bethnal Green – but the three of them had formed a friendship that had lasted more than twenty years. Together they had endured a war, widowhood and all kinds of other family dramas, big and small.

There had been a time when Helen and Dora had drifted apart, but Winnie's arrival as a student at the Nightingale had brought them all together again.

To look at them, no one would ever guess that Winnie was Dora's daughter. She did not have her mother's red hair or freckles. She was tall like her father, with his black curls and intense blue eyes. But she definitely had her mother's indomitable spirit and caring nature.

And then there was Nurse Trent, a ravishing redhead who still managed to look like a pin-up girl even in her shapeless, blue-striped dress and starched apron. Her face looked as if it had been freshly scrubbed, and Helen wondered if Miss Redmond had sent her to the bathroom to wash off any vestiges of make-up.

At least she had given up her scarlet lips and painted nails, although she still tried to sneak on to the ward with a touch of rouge and mascara on her lashes if she thought she could get away with it.

Even so, Helen was pleased with the girl's progress. Vivien Trent was a very different girl from the young tearaway who had roared through the hospital gates on the back of her boyfriend's motorbike that first day of training. Underneath those tight sweaters, high heels and backcombed hair, she was very intelligent and a natural nurse. But it had taken a long time for her to buckle down and realise it.

She had even tried to quit her training, but thankfully she had changed her mind about leaving. The new National Health Service needed many more girls like Nurse Trent.

But now she and Nurse Riley were exchanging wary looks as they stood behind Miss Redmond. Helen noticed how they kept glancing back over their shoulders towards the far corner of the ward.

'Is there something wrong, Nurses?' she asked.

Ruth Redmond looked at them both sharply. Winnie Riley blushed as she replied,

'The patient in number ten is waiting for a bedpan, Matron.'

'Then he'll just have to go on waiting!' Miss Redmond cut in before Helen could speak. 'The bedpan round was half an hour ago.'

Helen frowned. 'But if the patient needs attention—'

'He's already had far too much attention!' Two high spots of colour lit up Miss Redmond's cheeks. 'It will do him no harm at all to learn we're not all here at his beck and call,' she added in a low voice.

Helen glanced towards the far end of the ward, where

the patient in bed ten lay quiet and uncomplaining. He was clearly from the Commonwealth, his skin dark against his striped pyjamas.

She turned to Winnie. 'Fetch him a bedpan, Nurse Riley.'

'Yes, Matron.' Winnie sent her a quick, grateful look then hurried away to attend to the patient. Miss Redmond tightened her lips but said nothing.

'And what do you want?' She took her suppressed fury out on the unfortunate young medical student who had just entered the ward. It was Helen's nephew, Henry.

'I – I . . .' He stopped in his tracks, clutching his notes to his chest like a shield. 'Mr Fletcher sent me to check on the laparotomy he did yesterday,' he stuttered.

'Yes, well, you'll have to come back later. Well, don't just stand there!' Miss Redmond flapped her hands at him, ushering him back towards the double doors. 'Surely you can see Matron is doing her rounds?'

'I – er . . .' He shot Helen a quick look of dismay.

'It's all right, Sister. I think I've seen everything I need to see.' Helen turned to the student. 'Go and check on your patient, Dr Tremayne,' she said with the slightest of winks.

'Thank you.' He blushed deeply to the roots of his fair hair and then hurried away, still clutching his notes to his chest.

Once again, Miss Redmond was tight-lipped. 'I remember the days when we ran the wards,' she said. 'Now it seems as if people are allowed to come and go as they please. Not to mention ordering us about.' She sent a malevolent glance in the direction of bed ten, now concealed behind pulled curtains.

Helen left the ward but waited in the corridor for a few minutes. She knew that one of the staff nurses would have been on the telephone as soon as she had left, warning the next ward she was on her way. She could just imagine Miss Farrell on Male Orthopaedic twitching at the double doors, waiting for her arrival.

A moment later the doors to Holmes ward opened and Henry appeared, his head down, studying his notes. He was so focused on his work he didn't notice Helen until he'd cannoned straight into her.

'Oh, I'm terribly sorry – Aunt Helen!' Henry's face relaxed when he saw her.

'How was your patient?' she asked him.

'Still alive, thank goodness.' He glanced towards the doors leading back to the ward. 'Miss Redmond is rather terrifying, isn't she?'

'Ward sisters go out of their way to frighten medical students,' Helen assured him. 'It's to make sure they don't get too big for their boots.'

'Not much chance of that,' Henry said ruefully.

It was all Helen could do not to put her arms around him. She had to remind herself that he was a man now, and not the little boy she had once known.

They might not be related by blood, but young Henry felt every bit as much Helen's family as her brother William's own children, Charlotte and Timothy. Perhaps it was because he was Millie's son. Whatever the reason, she felt so proud of him, and she was sure William must have felt the same. It was a great compliment that his stepson had chosen to follow him into the medical profession.

'How are you getting on?' she asked.

'I still find dealing with real patients a bit daunting,' he admitted. 'There's so much to learn, and I don't want to get anything wrong. My mistake could mean life or death to someone.'

'It's good that you feel that way,' Helen said. It made a change from the usual types who donned a white coat and immediately thought they knew everything.

But it worried her that after six months at the hospital Henry was still plagued by such nerves. Helen had often wished the junior doctors took their duties more seriously, but she was worried Henry might have gone too far the other way. There was a risk he would end up paralysed by fear.

He was nothing like his stepfather in that respect. William might be a very gifted and well-respected consultant now, but as a young man no one would have called him dedicated. He was more interested in flirting with the nurses and running up a tab in the students' union bar.

'By next year this will all be second nature to you,' she said soothingly. 'Just ask your father.'

'Chance would be a fine thing,' Henry muttered.

'What do you mean?'

'I hardly see him.' He lowered his voice. 'He's too busy with *her.*'

'Catrine?'

He nodded, scowling at the name.

William had kept his promise to tell the family. Millie, as Helen suspected, had been very understanding about it, and immediately insisted that Catrine should be welcomed into the family at once.

But Henry clearly saw things differently.

'I hear she's going down to Billinghurst at the weekend to meet everyone?' Helen said.

'So I'm told. Are you coming?'

Helen nodded. 'Your mother has asked me to be there. I think she wants some moral support.'

'Don't we all?'

Helen looked at him consideringly. 'What do you make of it all?'

'Does it matter what I think? All I know is I never see Father any more. We were supposed to be having dinner last night, but he cancelled at the last minute because *she* had a migraine.'

His resentment was written all over his face.

'I suppose he's trying to make it up to her for all those years he wasn't in her life,' she said.

'He could hardly help that, could he? Anyway, now it feels as if we've all been pushed out to make room for her.'

Helen stared at him. Henry was such a quiet, affable young man, it was rare to see him so disgruntled.

'I'm sure things will settle down in time,' she said.

'I hope you're right.' His eyes met hers. 'You've met her, haven't you? What did you make of her?'

Helen considered the question. Various words came into her mind. Cool, aloof, defensive. 'She struck me as being very confident,' she said at last.

'Nothing like me, then,' Henry said dolefully. 'I can't wait to meet her.'

Chapter Fifteen

April 1957

On the twenty-fifth of April, Elsie Parsons gave birth to a bouncing baby boy.

Dora went to visit her on the Monday morning, a couple of days after the birth. As District Nurse for the area, it wasn't really her job to check on new mothers, but she had to pay a routine call on Elsie's mother, who suffered from chronic arthritis.

She found Elsie in the kitchen of the Parsons' terraced house on Russia Lane. She was standing at the sink, up to her elbows in soapy water. Washing festooned the tiny kitchen, draped on wooden clothes horses and gently steaming on the airer above Elsie's head. By the back door, yet more laundry was steeping in a zinc bucket of Reckitt's Blue.

Little Colin was on the rug in front of the fire, playing with a toy train. He had been unceremoniously dumped from the battered pram to make way for the new arrival, who slept peacefully in the corner.

Elsie's thirteen-year-old daughter Doreen was also there. She had dragged the mangle in from the back yard and was slowly cranking the handle as she fed a pillowcase through the rollers.

Dora didn't question why she was not at school. It was the East End way for children, especially girls, to stay at home and help their mothers when they were needed.

'Should you be up and about?' Dora asked, as she slipped off her coat and hung it over the back of a chair.

'Who else is going to keep this house going?' Elsie replied over her shoulder as she scrubbed at a shirt collar with a chunk of red carbolic soap. 'I can't keep Doreen off school forever, and Mum's got the whelk stand to worry about. Someone's got to take care of everything.'

'Your mum's out? In this weather?' Dora looked out of the window towards the back yard. It was a dull grey morning, and rain streamed down the glass.

'You try stopping her!' Elsie said grimly.

'Like mother, like daughter.'

'I suppose so.' Elsie sent her a sheepish smile. 'Sorry you've had a wasted journey. But the kettle's there, if you want to stick it on?' She nodded towards the stove.

'I can't stop too long,' Dora replied regretfully. 'But while I'm here, I might as well say hello to the new arrival.' She looked towards the pram. 'May I?'

Elsie nodded. 'Have a cuddle, if you want. He's due his feed soon, anyway.'

Dora picked the infant out of his pram, carefully supporting his downy head. He stirred, opened his eyes and gave her a dark, unfocused look before closing them again and going back to sleep. Dora breathed in the milky smell of him, and was immediately transported back to the moment she held her own babies for the first time.

'He's beautiful,' she said. 'And so contented.'

'Oh, he has his moments, I can tell you that!' Elsie shook her head. 'Another bloody boy, can you imagine? That makes five of the little buggers. We'll have enough for a football team before long.' She smiled at her daughter. 'Still, we're more than a match for them. Eh, Dor?'

'I'll say.' Doreen picked up a sheet from the pile of soaking washing and started to feed it through the mangle, straining to turn the handle.

'He's a dear little thing.'

'Not so little! Eight pounds ten ounces when he was born.' Elsie dried her hands on a towel and took the baby from Dora, ready for his feed. 'Proper little bruiser, he is. Didn't half hurt when I gave birth to him.'

'You should have gone to hospital,' Dora said. 'You could have had gas and air.'

'Not a chance!' Elsie unbuttoned her blouse and set the baby to her breast. 'And I must say I was very relieved when the old midwife turned up and not Miss Cornish. I wasn't looking forward to having that little madam standing over me, telling me to do this and that. As if I don't know what I'm doing by now!'

Dora tried not to smile. Elsie Parsons was not the only expectant mother who preferred Miss Evans, the senior midwife. She was sure Lucy Cornish would find her feet soon, but the women of the East End had seen too many changes over recent years to appreciate any more.

Doreen was struggling with the mangled sheet, so Dora went to help her. They each took an end and started to fold.

'What have you decided to call him?' she asked.

'Johnnie. After Johnnie Ray.'

104

Dora looked at Doreen. 'Was that your idea?'

The girl grinned. 'I wanted to call him Elvis, but Mum wouldn't hear of it!'

'Can you imagine? Bloody Elvis Parsons.' Elsie shook her head.

'Oh, I don't know. It might have suited him.'

'He's got the quiff already.' Elsie teased at the baby's shock of dark hair, making it stand on end.

'Perhaps you could call the next one Chuck, after Chuck Berry?' Dora suggested.

'Next one? Not likely!' Elsie shook her head. 'My days of having babies are over, I reckon. Don't get me wrong, I love my kids, but I can't be doing with it at my age.' She looked down at the baby in her arms. 'No, I reckon little Johnnie here will be the last.'

Just then the back door opened and Elsie's mother shuffled in, carrying two brown paper bags.

'Bloody hell, it's perishing out there – oh, hello,' she said when she saw Dora. 'What are you doing here?'

'I came to see you,' Dora reminded her.

'Oh, so you did. Sorry, love, it completely slipped my mind.' She dumped the bags on the table and started to take off her coat. 'Our Elsie's got you working, I see?' She nodded towards the sheet Dora was folding.

'I don't mind helping out. How are you, anyway?'

'Oh, I'm all right. Soldiering on, you know how it is.'

'Arthritis playing you up again?'

'Not a bit.'

But Dora noticed how she winced painfully as she tried to shrug off her coat. Freda Baines was a tough East End woman who wouldn't complain if her leg fell off. Even if it did, she would probably be out the next morning, running her whelk and winkle stall in Columbia Road market.

She'd been running that stall for as long as Dora could remember. At night, when the market closed, she would pick the whole lot up and push it around the streets, selling outside the pubs of Bethnal Green.

'Sorry you had a wasted journey, love,' Freda said as she sank on to one of the kitchen chairs.

'Not at all. It gave me a chance to see the baby.'

'Lovely, ain't he?' Freda smiled at the infant in her daughter's arms. 'And no trouble at all.'

'All right for you to say,' Elsie grimaced. 'What are you doing back so early, anyway?'

'There was no one about on the market, so I decided to close up the stall. Ended up bringing most of it home.' She nodded towards the bags on the table. 'You might as well take some home with you, Dora.'

'Oh, no, I couldn't.'

'Go on. We won't eat them all, and they'll only go to waste otherwise. And I know how much you like them!' She gave her a toothless grin.

'Well, in that case I won't say no.' Dora reached for one of the brown paper bags. Her mother would be delighted, she thought. It would be a real treat for her.

But as she opened the bag she caught the sour fishy smell, and suddenly bile rose in her throat. She gagged, tears springing to her eyes.

'What's wrong?' Freda, her daughter and granddaughter all stared at her in concern as she thrust the bag away from her.

'I don't know. It was the smell – it just made me feel sick.'

'They were fresh off the boat this morning,' Freda said defensively.

'Here, you ain't pregnant, are you?' Elsie Parsons grinned mischievously. 'I went right off whelks when I fell with little Johnnie. Couldn't even have them in the house.'

Dora shook her head. 'It's too late for that. I've started going through the change.'

'I thought that too, when I had my youngest,' Freda said. 'When I stopped getting my monthlies I was convinced it was my age. Until our Alan popped out and surprised us all. It was a right shock, I can tell you!'

'Well, I don't think that's going to happen to me.' Dora eyed the bag of whelks gingerly. 'But I'd best leave those behind, just in case. The smell's really turning my stomach for some reason, and I don't want to start being sick in the middle of my rounds.'

Dora tried to put it out of her mind as she headed off to see her next patient, but she couldn't seem to shake off the troubling thought.

Her monthlies had been erratic for a while, but she couldn't remember the last time she'd had one. Was it two or three months? She had no idea. Like the constant weariness that seemed to assail her, she had just put it down to the inevitable changes in her body as she got older. She was forty-three years old, after all.

But what if Freda was right? What if she was pregnant?

Chapter Sixteen

May 1957

Catrine was supposed to be travelling down to Billinghurst with William on the following Friday, but on the morning they were due to leave, he told her that he would have to stay in London to perform an emergency operation.

'But it doesn't mean we have to change our plans,' he had said. 'You can still catch the train down to Kent and I'll join you later.'

'Go alone?' Catrine was horrified. 'But I can't!'

'My dear, you managed to travel from France to a strange country by yourself, I'm sure this won't be difficult for you. Besides, you won't be alone,' he'd added. 'Henry will be catching the same train. You can keep each other company.'

Catrine stared at him, appalled. Did he really not understand how awkward it would be? She was already nervous at the idea of meeting his family, but the thought of having to spend two hours on a train in the company of a stepbrother she had never met filled her with absolute horror.

Her feelings must have shown on her face because William looked amused and said, 'Don't look so worried, I'm not sending you into a den of lions. My family can't wait to meet you, I'm sure they'll make you welcome. Millie will send a driver to meet you both at the station, and I'll be there as soon as I can.'

In spite of his reassurances, Catrine was still wary as she made her way to Victoria station to catch the train down to Billinghurst.

Whatever William said, she was not expecting his family to like her. Even if they were not outwardly hostile like Helen, they were bound to resent her coming into their lives. How could they not?

But Catrine was prepared for them. She was not going to cower in the shadows in shame any more. She had a right to exist, to be seen and heard, just as much as anyone else.

The mid-afternoon train was nearly empty, and Catrine was pleased to have the carriage all to herself. And as the station clock ticked nearer to the hour and Henry still did not arrive, her relief grew. She had not been looking forward to being stuck on a train with him.

Although she felt as if she already knew him. There were photographs of him all over the flat, and William was forever boasting of his accomplishments, telling her how studious and hard-working Henry was, and how proud he was that he had chosen to study medicine at the Nightingale.

The platform guard's whistle blew shrilly, followed by a huff of steam from the engine. Catrine sighed with relief and took out her book. She could relax for a couple of hours at least.

But as the train began to slowly pull out of the station,

suddenly the door to her carriage flew open and a young man threw himself in, amid a messy flurry of bags, coat, hat and flailing limbs.

Catrine lifted her gaze from her book to look at him. So this was Henry Tremayne. He looked just like in his photographs: tall and broad-shouldered with fair hair, blue eyes and angular cheekbones. His suit was well-worn and slightly old-fashioned, certainly nothing like the drainpipe jeans and drape coats Catrine was used to seeing on the street corners of London.

She watched as he made an unnecessary commotion of taking off his dripping raincoat and shoving it and his cumbersome bag into the luggage rack overhead. Then he sat down opposite her and tossed his hat on to the seat next to him.

She waited for him to introduce himself but instead he took out a textbook and started to read.

Finally she could stand it no more.

'You're Henry?' she said.

'That's right.'

'I'm Catrine.'

'I know.'

No smile, no 'pleased to meet you'. Catrine retreated back to her book, thoroughly offended.

She was even more offended a few minutes later when he pulled a packet of Woodbines out of his pocket and lit one up.

Catrine cleared her throat. 'Excuse me?'

'Oh, sorry. Do you want one?' he offered her the packet.

'I don't smoke. And I'd rather you didn't, either.'

He frowned. 'But it's allowed.'

'I know, but I don't like it.'

'Then perhaps you should sit somewhere else?'

'Perhaps *you* should sit somewhere else?'

'I'm quite happy here, thanks.'

'I was here first.'

He took a long drag on his cigarette, then settled back and blew the smoke out in a long, deliberate plume towards the ceiling.

'I'm not going anywhere,' he said.

'Neither am I.'

They glared at each other for a moment. Then Catrine got to her feet and reached up to open the window.

'What are you doing?' Henry asked.

'Opening the window – what does it look like?'

'But you'll let the rain in.'

She ignored him as she struggled with the catch. It was so stiff it hurt her hands, but Henry did not offer to help. He settled back in his seat and watched her.

'Suit yourself,' he shrugged. 'It's you that's getting wet.'

He was right. Catrine had the seat closest to the window, and as the train moved she found herself spattered by a fine spray of rain. It hit her face with icy darts, but her pride would not allow her to close the window or move because she was acutely aware of Henry watching her with amusement from the opposite corner of the carriage.

Instead she sat, turning the soggy pages of her book and surreptitiously wiping her damp cheeks with her sleeve whenever she thought he wasn't looking.

And so they sat in silence for two hours, both absorbed in

their books. Or at least, Henry seemed to be absorbed. Catrine was too annoyed to concentrate on her novel.

She was stunned at Henry's rudeness. She had been looking forward to treating him with cool disdain, but he had completely taken the wind out of her sails.

It was a relief when they finally reached the tiny rail halt of Billinghurst. William had warned her it was hardly a station, more just a short stretch of platform in the middle of nowhere, with a small bridge across the rails and a gate that led to the road.

'No one ever gets off there,' he had told her.

As the train slowed down, Henry stood up and started dragging his belongings out of the luggage rack.

'Can I help you?' he offered, as Catrine reached for her own bag.

'No, thank you,' she refused stiffly. It was a bit late for him to decide to be gallant.

'As you wish.'

He glanced down at the book she had left on her seat, his eyebrows lifting. Catrine had set herself the challenge of reading only in English to improve her vocabulary, but she was in need of some comfort so she had brought one of her favourite children's stories, *The Little Prince*, in her own language.

She quickly snatched up the book and stuffed it into her bag.

A damp drizzle was falling when they got off the train. Catrine stepped down and headed purposefully towards the bridge, leaving Henry on the platform, struggling with his raincoat.

William had told her that the driver would be waiting for them on the other side of the bridge, but there was no sign of anyone.

'If you're looking for the car then you're out of luck,' Henry said, as he caught up with her. 'I daresay Ma has forgotten to send the driver again.'

Catrine stared at him, appalled. 'But how could she? She knew we were coming.'

'Oh, she's always doing it. I'm sure she has other things to think about besides your visit.'

Catrine stared up and down the empty, rain-washed lane. It was hard not to feel insulted that she had been so easily forgotten.

Or perhaps she had not been forgotten? Perhaps it was a deliberate slight, meant to put her in her place.

'Where are you going?' she said, as Henry hitched his bag over his shoulder and started off up the lane.

'Walking home. What does it look like?' He glanced over his shoulder at her. 'You can come with me, if you want?' He did not sound very enthusiastic about the idea.

'I think I'll stay here and wait.'

'Suit yourself.'

He trudged away from her, up the lane. Catrine paused for a moment, the drizzle dampening her hair and face. Then she picked up her own bag and followed him.

Chapter Seventeen

It wasn't in Henry Tremayne's nature to be boorish or inconsiderate. He had been brought up by his parents to be polite and respectful, especially to ladies.

And most of the time he was too painfully shy to open his mouth to a stranger, let alone be rude to them.

But there was something about Catrine Villeneuve that irked him so much he even forgot to be nervous.

He had not been looking forward to meeting her. Even before their paths crossed, he was already tired of hearing her name. Every time he telephoned home, his mother would talk about Catrine and how excited she was to meet her.

And as for his stepfather ... William certainly never seemed to have any time for Henry any more now Catrine was there.

Henry had been looking forward to spending time with his father once he started studying at the Nightingale. He was even supposed to be staying at the flat in Covent Garden, but now his place had been taken by Catrine.

He was already inclined not to like her, even before they met. And their first meeting had not been promising.

Henry knew he had not helped matters. His nerves always made him brusque, and he had felt so foolish because he'd nearly missed the train. He could almost feel her looking down her nose at him as he'd clambered on board, and that had set him on edge.

Perhaps he should have tried to make conversation with her but he was too shy, and besides, he had a lot of studying to catch up on. The other student doctors in his digs had decided to have a party the previous evening, and there had been drinking and noisy carousing far into the night.

Henry had not been able to sleep through it all, which did not help his mood. Then, after he'd finally dropped off in the early hours, he was so tired he had overslept, which was why he had nearly missed the train.

Anyway, Catrine hadn't tried to talk to him either, apart from rudely insisting he put out his cigarette. Even then, Henry might have done as she'd asked if she hadn't been so demanding about it. She acted as if everyone should jump whenever she snapped her fingers.

Henry smiled to himself, remembering the look on her face when the car was not there to meet her. He was secretly glad his mother had forgotten yet again to send Bennett to pick them up, even if it did mean a long walk in the rain.

'How much further is it?' Her voice was a whine of complaint.

'Only a couple of miles. Although there's a shortcut we could take?'

'Then why are we not taking it?' she snapped, turning up her collar against the drizzling rain.

'If that's what you want?'

He went a few yards further up the road, then stopped.

'It's just this way,' he said.

Catrine stared at the battered old stile. 'What's this?'

'The shortcut. It'll only take five minutes this way.'

She paused, looking down at her shoes, and for a moment he thought she'd balk. But then she slung her bag over the stile and scrambled after it.

Henry automatically went to offer his hand to help her, but Catrine ignored it.

He averted his eyes, trying not to notice how her skirt rode up over her knees. She was hardly dressed for a country walk. And her bag had landed in a muddy puddle, he noticed with grim satisfaction.

It must have been raining for several days, because the fields were deeply rutted with thick black mud. Even Henry struggled with it.

He felt slightly bad for Catrine, who was picking her way gingerly several yards behind him.

'Are you sure you don't want me to carry your bag?' he asked.

'I can manage.' No sooner had the words left her lips than she missed her footing and sank up to her ankles in mud. Henry reached out to catch her as she overbalanced but she shook him off irritably.

'I said I don't need your help!' she snapped.

'Suit yourself.'

The mud gave a sucking sound as she pulled her foot out. Once again, Henry felt a pang of guilt for bringing her this way.

They crossed another field and clambered over another stile.

'I thought you said it was a five-minute walk?' Catrine grumbled.

'It is – usually. I can't help it if you're slow, can I?' Henry snapped back. 'Anyway, once we get to the top of the hill you'll be able to see the house.'

He always liked taking the shortcut, because it afforded the best view of Billinghurst. The ground rose to a small crest, and once they reached the top they would be able to see the house nestling in the shallow valley below them, surrounded by a patchwork of fields.

He stopped at the top and waited for her to catch up.

'Here we are,' he said, pointing ahead of them. 'Billinghurst Manor.'

Even in the drizzling rain, the house looked magnificent. From a distance it appeared more like a castle from Arthurian legend, with its crenellated roof, mullioned windows and thick walls of golden stone.

'It's been in my mother's family for five hundred years,' Henry said with pride.

He looked sideways at Catrine, waiting for her reaction. But her face was impassive as she stared down at the house.

'Shall we go?' she said. 'I want to get changed out of these wet clothes.'

She led the way down the hill without waiting for an answer. Henry stared after her, deflated.

He'd so wanted her to be impressed, but she'd completely taken the wind out of his sails.

They approached the house through the side lane, bypassing the main gates. Henry had already realised that Catrine would not be remotely moved by the grandeur of the long, gravelled drive, the rose gardens or the ornamental fountains. She seemed determined not to notice anything as she stared grimly ahead of her, dragging her mud-spattered bag. She looked thoroughly bedraggled, her shoes and stockings caked in mud and her beret sodden with rain.

As they skirted the side of the house, his mother came rushing out from the kitchen garden to greet them. She was looking harassed as usual, dressed in muddy gumboots with his grandfather's old mackintosh thrown over her flowery dress. Her blonde curls were windblown and her cheeks pink.

'You're here! Oh my God, I'm so sorry, I completely lost track of the time. Can you forgive me? I've just sent Bennett down to the station. No doubt he'll be very cross about his wasted journey.'

She held out her arms. Henry automatically moved forward to hug her, but his mother had already swept Catrine into a suffocating embrace.

'Darling girl, what must you think of us? Your father will be completely furious with me for abandoning you.' She released Catrine and held her at arm's length. 'It's wonderful to meet you at last. I can't tell you how much I've been looking forward to it.'

'*Merci*, Madame. Thank you for inviting me to your home.' Catrine's reply was stiff and formal. It wouldn't have hurt her to smile, Henry thought sourly.

'Oh, it's your home too, now. At least, I hope you'll think of it that way.' His mother looked her up and down. 'But look at the state of you! Henry, what on earth have you done to the poor girl?'

'We took the shortcut,' Henry said.

'Why on earth did you do that? You would have been far

better coming round by the road. It's scarcely further than the shortcut, and far less muddy.'

Henry could not meet Catrine's eye, but he could tell she was utterly furious. She clearly couldn't take a joke.

'Let's get you inside so you can get changed out of those wet clothes,' his mother went on. 'Honestly, I can't imagine what my son was thinking, dragging you across those muddy fields.'

'*Merci*, Madame.' Catrine flashed him an accusing look. She understood exactly what he'd been thinking, he could see it written on her face.

As his mother led the way round to the front of the house, there was a sudden flurry of barking and shouting and Lottie and Tim came running towards them, followed by their three dogs.

Henry braced himself, ready for the usual greeting, but Shadow the black Labrador and Mint the Border collie headed straight for Catrine, nearly knocking her off her feet. Even Biddy, the family's elderly Labrador, plodded stiffly past Henry towards her.

'You must excuse them, they're so badly behaved.' Millie grabbed Shadow's collar and dragged him away. 'We've tried to train them, but they don't listen to a word we say.'

'Are you talking about the dogs, or the children?' Henry asked, winking at his brother and sister. But neither of them noticed him. They were too busy staring at the new arrival.

'Both!' Millie sighed. 'But at least the children don't bite if they get over-excited.'

She turned to the boy and the girl, who were staring at Catrine with wide eyes. 'Lottie and Tim, come and meet

119

Catrine. Honestly, they've been so excited to meet you all day, and now look at them. They've gone shy.'

'I'm not shy.' Lottie, who was eight years old and the elder of the two, looked Catrine up and down. 'You're as old as Henry,' she said with evident disappointment.

'Lottie!' His mother laughed. 'I do apologise for my daughter, she tends to speak her mind. When I told her she was going to meet her sister, I think she expected a play-mate, someone of her own age. Didn't you, darling?' She ruffled the girl's blonde hair.

'Catrine will have to play with Henry instead,' Tim piped up.

'I don't think so,' Henry muttered under his breath.

'Let's all go inside and get dry, shall we?' his mother said brightly.

She took Catrine's arm and led the way up the broad stone steps into the house. The children and dogs crowded around them, eager to get close to the new visitor, leaving Henry to trail behind.

Chapter Eighteen

William had not told her he lived in a palace.

'A country house,' he'd called it. But this was more like a grand chateau. It was certainly a million miles from the squalid little apartment in the *arrondissement de l'Observatoire*.

Inside the house was as impressive as the outside. The double doors opened into a vast hall, with a sweeping staircase, antique furniture and an array of gilt-framed portraits adorning the walls.

Catrine gawped. She had thought her grandmother's house was magnificent, but Billinghurst made it look like a hovel.

But Millie Tremayne did not seem impressed with her surroundings. In fact, she kept apologising for them.

'I'm sorry it's all so shabby and run-down,' she said. 'We do our best to maintain it, but it's a losing battle most of the time.'

'It's beautiful,' Catrine said.

'Do you think so?' Millie looked pleased. 'You should have seen it when my father and grandmother were alive. It was glorious then. But it never really recovered from the RAF taking it over during the war.' She gazed around her with a sigh. 'All the pictures and antiques had to be put away in storage, but they still caused a lot of damage to the furniture and the fittings. You can still see the marks on the wall in the dining room where the officers hung their dartboard, and where the young pilots scribbled their names on the William Morris wallpaper. But we haven't had the heart to cover them up,' she sighed. 'So many of those poor boys didn't come home, and it's the last memory we have of them.'

She smiled at Catrine. 'I'm sorry, I'm talking rather a lot, aren't I? You must forgive me, I tend to chatter when I'm nervous. It drives everyone mad! Come with me, I'll show you up to your room.'

Catrine was puzzled as she followed Millie up the sweeping staircase. What on earth did she have to be nervous about? This was her home, she belonged here. Catrine was the outsider. If anyone should be feeling anxious, it was her.

William's wife was hardly what she had been expecting. She had pictured a cool, aristocratic beauty, with her grandmother's *hauteur*. Millie was certainly beautiful, with her heart-shaped face, blonde curls and sparkling blue eyes, but there were no airs and graces about her. Catrine might have mistaken her for one of the staff if she hadn't known better.

Millie showed her to her room. It was beautiful, with richly coloured rugs on the polished wooden floor, and a mullioned window that looked out over the front of the house. The room was dominated by a huge four-poster bed draped with brocade.

'The moths have been at the curtains, I'm afraid. And it's a bit chilly, too.' Millie gazed at the empty fireplace. 'I'll get Polly, my maid, to light it for you before you go to bed. But Mrs Winn, the housekeeper, is very strict with us, and doesn't like us to waste coal once spring comes, no matter how cold it is outside!' She gave Catrine an apologetic smile.

'I'm sure I shall be very comfortable.'

'Oh, well, I don't know about that!'

They stood in awkward silence for a moment, neither of them quite knowing what to say next.

'Would you like Polly to help you unpack?' Millie asked finally.

'No, thank you. I can do it myself.'

Millie looked at her admiringly. 'Gosh, your English is so good, it puts us all to shame. My governess did try to teach me French when I was a child, but my grandmother didn't approve. She thought everyone should speak English.' She pulled a face. 'Well, I'll leave you to it. Dinner is at seven o'clock.'

'Thank you, Madame.'

'Please, call me Millie. Madame makes me sound far too grand.' She went to the door, then turned back. 'We are glad to have you here, you know,' she said. 'I can't imagine what your father was thinking, keeping you from us for all this time. But at least you're here now.'

Another quick smile and then she slipped from the room, leaving Catrine alone at last. Finally she allowed herself to let out the breath she felt as if she had been holding ever since she arrived.

She crossed to the window and looked out. In front of the house, beautifully manicured lawns flanked the long drive. They were dotted with rose bushes, and a pair of ornamental ponds, one on either side.

It truly was like a palace.

Catrine felt a tiny dig of resentment under her ribs, remembering the shabby apartment she and her mother had shared, with its damp and its bugs and the lecherous, grasping landlord. And all the while, William and his family were living here, within these gilded walls, with their portraits and their four-poster beds. They had never wanted for anything in their lives.

Yet Millie had been so friendly and welcoming, far more than Catrine had imagined she would be. But then, she could afford to be generous and open-hearted. She hadn't been embittered by the kind of humiliation and rejection that Romy had faced. She'd never had to live her life as an outcast.

And she'd had William at her side to love and support her, which was more than Catrine and her mother had ever had.

Catrine quickly unpacked her bag and changed into fresh clothes. She was sitting at the dressing table brushing her hair when she realised she was being watched.

She caught a movement in the mirror's reflection and looked round sharply to see little Charlotte standing in the doorway.

She looked very like her mother with her fine blonde hair and wide blue eyes, but there was a boldness about her as she stared at Catrine.

'What do you want?' Catrine asked, turning back to her reflection.

'Are you really my sister?'

'I'm your half-sister.'

124

'What does that mean?'

'It means we have the same father but not the same mother.'

Charlotte tilted her head thoughtfully. 'You mean like Henry has the same mother as us but not the same father?'

'That's right.'

'But he's still our brother. That's what we call him.'

Catrine had no answer for her, so she picked up a pin and started to fix her hair in place.

'Where is your mother?' Charlotte piped up again. 'Is she dead, like Henry's father?'

'Yes.'

'Henry's father was killed in the war. Did your mother die in the war too?'

'No.'

'Where do you come from?'

'France.'

'Where is that?'

'Across the sea, a long way from here.'

'Can you ride a horse?' Charlotte abruptly changed the subject.

'I don't know. I've never tried.'

Charlotte stared at her incredulously. Then she said, 'I could teach you, if you like? But you can't ride my pony, Sienna. You'd be far too big for her. Can you play chess?' she changed the subject again.

'Yes. I used to play all the time with my mother.'

'We'll have a game later. But I'm warning you, I'm very good.'

And modest with it, Catrine thought. 'I'm sure you are.'

'Honestly, I bet you won't be able to beat me. No one can. Except Henry and Uncle David.'

'Uncle David?'

'He was Aunt Helen's husband, but they're getting divorced,' she replied, matter-of-factly. 'He's a doctor, like Daddy.'

'Ah.' William had told her that Helen's marriage had ended. Was that why she was so sour?

Charlotte twisted a pale strand of hair around her finger. 'Are you going to come and live with us at Billinghurst?' she asked.

Catrine put down her hairbrush and turned in her seat to face her. 'You ask a lot of questions, don't you?'

'It's the only way I learn things.'

Catrine turned away, trying not to smile. Charlotte was very precocious, but she couldn't help being amused by her.

'I hope you do come to live here,' Charlotte went on. 'I've always wanted a sister. It's better than having two brothers, don't you think?'

'I wouldn't know,' Catrine said. 'I don't have any brothers or sisters.'

'Yes, you do, silly. You've got us.'

Catrine stared at her in the reflection of the mirror. But before she could reply, Millie's voice came drifting from the landing.

'Lottie? Where are you?'

'I'm talking to Catrine.'

A moment later Millie appeared in the doorway, looking distracted.

'I thought I told you not to bother our guest?' She sent

Catrine an apologetic look. 'I'm so sorry. I hope she hasn't been making a nuisance of herself?'

'Not at all.'

'Really? There's a first time for everything, I suppose.' Millie turned to her daughter. 'Come on, let's leave Catrine alone. I'm sure she could do with a rest from us all before dinner.'

She ushered the child away, leaving Catrine on her own.

She found she was smiling as she turned back to the mirror. But then she caught herself, and her smile faded.

She couldn't allow herself to be beguiled by the family's charm. It was all a façade, an illusion. She did not belong, and they didn't really want her there, either. Even Millie, with all her smiling warmth, must resent her deep down.

How could she not? After all, Catrine had come and disrupted her perfect family life. She wouldn't be human if she didn't feel some bitterness about it.

And Catrine was sure that bitterness would surface eventually. Sooner or later she would be rejected, and she had to prepare for it.

Chapter Nineteen

Helen arrived in Billinghurst late in the afternoon, and took the shortcut across the fields to the manor house.

The path was churned with mud, which coated her rain boots and spattered her skirt and stockings, but she would rather have waded waist deep through a quagmire than take the main road through the village.

She could not face running into any of her former neighbours. The break-up of her marriage had caused a great deal of gossip in the village, and Helen was not ready to answer anyone's questions, no matter how well-meaning.

Nor was she ready to see Lowgill House again. She had spent so many happy years living in the cottage and helping David with his GP practice. She feared all the memories that might come rushing back if she saw the house again.

She arrived at the house and went straight around to the back to divest herself of her wet clothes. She was in the boot room pulling off her mud-caked wellingtons when Millie appeared in the doorway.

'Where's Will?' she asked. 'Is he not with you?'

Helen frowned. 'I thought he was coming down this morning with Catrine and Henry?'

'So did I, but there was a last-minute change of plans.

Here, let me help.' Millie reached down and pulled Helen's boot off. 'It's rather vexing, really. I wish he'd been here when she arrived. It might have made things a lot easier.'

'So Catrine came by herself?'

'She travelled down with Henry on the train. Although I gather from the rather frosty silence between them that they haven't exactly hit it off,' Millie said ruefully.

'William should never have sent her by herself,' Helen said.

'I'm sure he couldn't help it,' Millie said. 'If he's needed for an emergency operation then there isn't much he can do about it, is there?'

'All the same, he shouldn't have left it to you to deal with her. It's not fair on either of you.'

It was so typical of her brother to do exactly what suited him without a thought for the consequences.

Helen shrugged off her coat and hung it up to dry. 'Where is Catrine now?'

'In her room. She's been shut away all afternoon.' Millie looked anxious. 'I've tried to coax her out but she insists she's resting. I'm just worried she's decided she hates us all!'

'Nonsense, how could she possibly hate you?'

'I don't know. But she seems rather – chilly. She barely said a word or cracked a smile when I met her.'

'I think that's just the way she is,' Helen said. She had certainly struck her as being very guarded and aloof.

'Perhaps she's just shy?' Millie suggested. 'It's probably utterly terrifying for the poor girl to be here, among strangers. Oh, I do wish Will would hurry up and get here. He's

129

the only one who really knows her.' She looked at Helen, hope sparking in her eyes. 'Although you met her once, didn't you? Perhaps if you went up and saw her—'

Helen shook her head. 'No, thank you. We didn't exactly hit it off either.'

Thinking about it now, she realised she had been a little harsh to the young girl when they'd first met – but she had been in a state of shock and scarcely thinking straight.

Millie bit her lip. 'Oh dear, this is not going nearly as well as I'd hoped. I so wanted Catrine to feel welcome.'

'I'm sure she'll come out of her shell at dinner,' Helen comforted her.

'Speaking of dinner,' Millie said. 'I meant to talk to you about that.' She looked decidedly uncomfortable. 'We have an extra guest coming tonight. I hope you don't mind?'

She didn't have to say his name. It was written all over her face. Helen's heart sank.

'Oh, Millie, you haven't invited David?'

'He invited himself,' Millie insisted. 'He telephoned a couple of days ago and said he wanted to talk to you about something.'

Helen stiffened. 'If it's to do with the divorce then he should speak to my solicitor.'

'I don't know what it's about,' Millie said. But her face told a different story.

'What is it, Millie?' Helen asked. 'What's going on?'

'It's better if you speak to David,' Millie murmured, her cheeks flushing. 'It's between you two.'

'But you know about it?'

'Let's go into the drawing room, shall we?' Millie deftly changed the subject. 'I'll ring for some tea. You never know, my husband might finally decide to join us.'

'Or Mademoiselle Villeneuve?' Helen suggested.

'Oh gosh, I doubt it,' Millie laughed. 'Anyway, I hope Will gets here soon. He'll know what to say to her because I certainly don't.'

'I still think it was very unfair of him to dump her on you,' Helen said. 'It's a horribly uncomfortable situation. I mean, how are you supposed to—'

She broke off as Millie clutched her arm, stopping her in her tracks. Helen followed her gaze to see Catrine standing at the foot of the stairs.

For a moment they all stared at each other. Millie recovered herself first.

'Catrine,' she said, her smile quickly back in place. 'Here you are at last. Would you like some tea? Helen and I were just going to have some, if you'd like to join us?'

'No, thank you.'

'Are you sure? Perhaps you'd like to come and sit with us? We could have a chat—'

'No, Madame. I would hate to make you feel – *uncomfortable*.' She looked directly at Helen as she said it. Then she turned on her heel and headed back upstairs.

'Oh dear,' Helen said.

Millie looked distraught.

'Do you think she heard what we said?' she whispered.

No sooner had she said it than a distant bedroom door slammed, making the chandelier shiver above their heads.

'I would assume so,' Helen said dryly.

'Oh dear, now we've offended her.' Millie looked anxious. 'Should I go up and speak to her, do you think?'

Helen shook her head. 'If I were you, I'd leave well alone. Least said, soonest mended and all that.'

Chapter Twenty

Dusk was gathering when William finally arrived.

Catrine stood at the bedroom window, hidden behind the heavy brocade curtain, and watched as the family spilled out of the house to greet him. Children and dogs tumbled down the steps, and Catrine saw William squat down and open his arms to greet them.

Henry and Millie came out too, and William warmly embraced them both in turn while the two younger children clung to him, wrapping their arms around his legs.

They all seemed so happy and carefree, it gave Catrine a painful tug in her chest to think how different their lives must have been from her own.

And here she was, on her own, watching from a distance.

It reminded her of all the times she had stood in the shadows in the school playground, unable to join in with the other children's games.

'We can't be your friend because you don't have a father,' they'd said to her when she'd tried to approach them.

'Jeanne Moreau doesn't have a father and you still play with her.'

'That's different. Jeanne's papa was killed in the war. No one knows where your papa is.'

'I don't care,' Catrine had declared. 'I don't want to play your stupid games anyway.'

And so she had hidden her hurt feelings behind a wall of haughty indifference. And she was doing the same now, pretending she did not care that she didn't belong.

William must have asked Millie where she was, because his wife pointed up to the window. William looked up as Catrine quickly ducked behind the curtain, out of view.

The next moment, William had forgotten her as he linked arms with his wife and headed up the steps to the house. She saw the adoring way Millie looked up at him, her face radiant with happiness.

Had her own mother looked at him that way? she wondered.

She had just returned to reading her book when there was a knock on her door.

'Catrine?' William's voice called out softly. 'Catrine, are you all right?'

Catrine stiffened, holding her breath.

'Catrine?' William knocked again. There was a squeak as the brass doorknob turned and Catrine was glad she'd turned the key to lock it.

'I told you, didn't I?' she heard Millie whisper. 'She's been shut away all afternoon. I didn't know what to do.'

'Perhaps she's resting?' William said. 'Let's give her some time. We'll see her at dinner.'

Their footsteps receded back along the landing, and Catrine went back to her book. But the words jumped in front of her eyes and she could no longer concentrate.

She could not avoid them forever. As seven o'clock approached, Catrine knew she would have to join the rest of the family for dinner.

She dressed carefully. She had brought one good dress with her from France, a pretty pale blue silk that had once belonged to her mother. She was not going to have them all looking down their noses at her, thinking she was some kind of poor relation. She would prove she was every bit as good as the rest of them.

As she approached, she could hear laughter coming from the drawing room. She hesitated on the threshold and peeped in through the crack in the half-open door.

Henry and his stepfather were laughing together about something. Henry looked more animated than when Catrine had seen him earlier. It was as if he came to life in his father's presence.

William was the first to spot her. He was still dressed in the clothes he had been wearing when he arrived. The hems of his trousers were spattered in mud.

'Good lord.' He looked her up and down as she stood framed in the doorway. The others all turned in her direction.

'Gosh, don't you look pretty?' Millie said. She was wearing a moth-eaten jersey over her flowery dress.

'*Pardon*,' Catrine murmured. 'I thought we would be dressing for dinner . . .' She looked around and caught Helen's eye. She was sitting in the corner, nursing a sherry. She was wearing an old tweed skirt and a thick twinset.

'Not for fifty years,' Henry muttered into his glass. He

was smirking, Catrine noticed. Enjoying every minute of her discomfort, no doubt.

What had she done to offend him so much?

'It's all my fault,' Millie said quickly. 'I'm sorry, Catrine, I should have explained. We would love to dress for dinner, but the dining room gets so chilly in the evenings. I think we'd all freeze.'

Catrine looked around at the others, hot colour flooding her face. 'I'll go and change—'

'No, please don't. You look far too beautiful. Here, take this.' Millie snatched an embroidered shawl from the back of the sofa and handed it to her. 'Just to put around your shoulders if you get cold.'

'No, thank you,' Catrine refused stiffly.

'Are you sure? It is rather chilly—'

'I said no!' Catrine snapped.

Millie flinched, and Henry and his aunt glanced at each other. William said nothing but his dark look spoke volumes.

'It's past seven,' he said curtly, his eyes not leaving Catrine. 'Perhaps we should go into dinner.'

'But David isn't here yet,' Millie pointed out.

'Then we'll start without him.' William's voice was clipped with irritation.

'No need,' said a voice from the doorway. 'Here I am.'

'Sorry I'm late,' he said. 'I had to go and see a patient.'

David McKay's arrival seemed to lift some of the awkward tension from the room, although Catrine noticed that Helen had suddenly become very stiff in the presence of her estranged husband. They greeted each other formally, like

136

strangers. Unlike William and the rest of the family, who hugged him like an old friend.

At least it took some of the attention off her. William was even smiling as he introduced them.

'Catrine, I'd like you to meet David McKay, my brother-in-law and one of my greatest friends. David, this is my daughter Catrine.'

He must be a great friend if William had let him in on her secret, Catrine thought as she shook his hand.

'*Bonsoir, Mademoiselle Villeneuve. J'espère que vous passez un bon séjour en Angleterre?*'

'Show-off,' Helen muttered.

'*Vous parlez bien français, Monsieur,*' Catrine replied, with a quick sideways look at her aunt. Helen was not looking at him, but her lips curved faintly, almost as if she could not help herself smiling.

Catrine wondered why their marriage had ended. David McKay did not look like the type to do anyone a great wrong. He resembled an amiable professor, with his greying hair and old tweed jacket with leather patches on the elbows. His deep brown eyes twinkled behind his spectacles when he smiled.

'Shall we go in to dinner?' Millie suggested. 'Mrs Winn will be in a terrible tizz otherwise, and I don't want to upset her.'

Millie was right, the dining room was frigidly cold. The tyrannical housekeeper who apparently ruled the roost had lit a fire in the grate, but it was too small to be of any use in the long room. The heat barely reached the far end of the long, polished dining table where Catrine sat.

She really wished she had accepted Millie's offer of the shawl. Why did she have to be so defensive all the time?

Mrs Winn might be a tyrant when it came to the household purse strings, but she certainly knew how to cook. Dinner was a delicious chicken chasseur, served with creamy mashed potatoes and buttered green beans.

'I asked Mrs Winn to prepare something French, in your honour,' Millie explained. 'I was rather terrified about what she might come up with, since she isn't exactly well-travelled. I hope it's all right?'

'It's delicious, Madame. Thank you,' Catrine replied.

Millie flushed pink with pleasure, and Catrine was touched that she had gone to so much trouble for her. But at the same time she couldn't forget the way she and Helen had sniggered like schoolgirls about her.

William was talking about the reason he was late. Apparently he'd had to wait for a new anaesthetist because he suspected the one on duty had been drinking.

'I'm going to have to speak to Sutcliffe about him,' he was saying. 'I hate to do it because the old man's been there for donkey's years. But I can't have him in the operating theatre if he's going to endanger the patients.'

'He was an old sot when I was there,' David agreed.

'Were you at the Nightingale Hospital?' Catrine asked him.

'Yes, I was in charge of the Casualty department. That was where I met Helen.'

He looked across the table at her and Helen dropped her gaze awkwardly.

'It was a very long time ago,' she mumbled.

'I remember it as if it were yesterday,' David replied.

Catrine looked from one to the other. So Helen must have left him, she thought. She wondered why.

Whatever the reason, David was obviously still in love with her. He couldn't seem to stop looking at his wife – but her gaze darted everywhere in the room except towards him.

David started talking to Catrine, asking her questions about her life in France. She answered him politely, but soon their conversation fizzled out and they both ended up being drawn to what was going on at the other end of the table.

All the focus seemed to be on Henry and his studies.

'Mr Witter speaks very highly of your work,' William was saying. 'He says you have all the makings of a promising young doctor.'

'A chip off the old block,' David McKay smiled.

Henry blushed, but he looked very pleased with himself, Catrine noticed.

'We'll see about that,' William said. 'You and the rest of your student intake will be coming under my wing soon. Then we'll see what you're made of!'

'Don't frighten the boy,' Millie chided him.

'What about your lodgings?' David asked. 'Do the students still get up to all sorts of high jinks like they did in my day?'

Henry nodded. 'Yes, they do.'

'They're probably even worse than we were,' William said.

'And do you join in, or are you one of those swotty types who lock themselves in their room to study?'

Henry opened his mouth to speak, but William got in before him.

'What do you think?' he said. 'This is my son we're talking about, David. I daresay no young nurse is safe. Eh, Henry?' He reached across and ruffled his fair hair. 'Anyone you've got your eye on?'

'Not particularly,' Henry said.

'Prefer to play the field, eh? That's my boy,' William said proudly.

'William! Don't encourage him,' Millie said. But she was smiling when she said it.

Catrine felt a sting of jealousy as she looked at them. This was supposed to be about her and her introduction to the family. And instead it was all about Henry and his wonderful achievements.

David must have noticed her sullen look because he said,

'I'm sorry, Catrine. All this shop talk must be very boring for you?'

'Oh no, Monsieur, I understand all about hospital life,' she said. 'I was training to be a nurse before I came to England.'

'Really?' David was interested. 'So you're following in your father's footsteps too?'

'No, I'm following in my mother's,' Catrine corrected him firmly. 'She was a nurse.'

'Of course.' He had the grace to look embarrassed. Then he added, 'Have you thought about finishing your studies in England?'

'Well—'

'What a good idea,' Millie said enthusiastically.

'I hope you're not suggesting she should train at the Nightingale?' Helen put in quickly.

Catrine looked at her aunt. Out of the corner of her eye, she saw Henry smirking down at his plate.

'Yes,' she said. 'Yes, that is exactly what I would like to do.'

Chapter Twenty-One

William was beginning to wish he'd stayed at the hospital. Even the complex hysterectomy procedure he'd spent most of the day performing suddenly seemed simple compared to the minefield he now found himself in at the dinner table.

'Out of the question,' Helen said flatly.

'Why?' Catrine asked.

'I would have thought that was obvious.' His sister was tight-lipped.

No one else spoke. William's heart went out to Catrine. She suddenly seemed very young and forlorn, sitting on her own at the end of the table in her pretty blue silk dress.

'I don't think we should dismiss the idea out of hand,' he said.

Helen snapped round to look at him. 'Have you taken leave of your senses?' she demanded. 'You know what this will mean for you, don't you?'

'What?' Catrine looked from one to the other. 'What will it mean?'

'It means your father would kiss goodbye to any chance of that Medical Superintendent's position, for a start,' Helen said, her gaze still fixed on William. 'You'd be lucky if you kept your job, once Frederick Sutcliffe got wind of it.'

'Frederick Sutcliffe?' Catrine looked blank. 'Who is he?'

'The chairman of the hospital committee,' William explained. 'He's a very – moral man.'

'He already dislikes you,' Helen pointed out bluntly. 'I'm sure he'd jump on any excuse to get rid of you. If he were to discover that you'd fathered an illegitimate child—'

'So you're ashamed of me?' Catrine turned to William.

'No,' Millie said. 'No, of course not. Are you, William?'

'No,' he said quietly.

'Besides, it was eighteen years ago,' David pointed out. 'You were young and foolish then. And you had no idea you even had a child.'

William stared down at his plate as the conversation swirled around him.

'Nevertheless, it would still be held against him,' Helen insisted. She turned to William. 'You deserve this job, William. You've worked too hard to throw it all away.'

He was silent for a moment. He knew Helen was right. He desperately wanted the Medical Superintendent's job.

But could he really put his career before his family? Catrine deserved better than that.

'Perhaps we could find a way?' he said. 'Maybe if we kept your identity a secret?'

'So you are ashamed of me?' Catrine turned on him angrily. 'You are proud that Henry is studying at your hospital, but I would be an embarrassment to you!'

'No! It's not that at all—' William started to explain, but Catrine had already fled the dining room. The poor girl looked close to tears as she hurried away.

Dinner was a subdued affair after that. As soon as it was over, David also took his leave.

143

'I'm sure you have a lot to talk about,' he said. 'I'll be in the library with a brandy if you need me.'

William watched his friend go. He would dearly have liked to join him, but he knew he had to stay and deal with what was to come.

'She's terribly upset, poor girl,' Millie said reproachfully.

'I know,' William sighed.

'She's probably sulking,' Helen said.

'Helen!'

'It's true. She's put out because she didn't get her own way.' She turned to William accusingly. 'She's had you twisted round her little finger for the past six months, and now you've finally said no to her and she doesn't like it.'

'That's rather harsh, don't you think?' he said.

He could not forget Catrine's face as she had left. It was not the look of a petulant child throwing a tantrum; she had been genuinely hurt.

'She's got a point,' he said. 'She is family, after all. Why should she be left out?'

'You're not seriously thinking about it?' He looked up to see Helen staring at him. 'You are, aren't you?'

'No,' he said, then added, 'but Catrine has to do something. She's too bright to go on selling perfumes for the rest of her life.'

'Fine,' Helen said. 'I can think of a dozen hospitals in London who would probably be glad to have her. I could even write her a reference if necessary.'

'But her family is at the Nightingale,' Millie said.

'Which is precisely why she shouldn't be there,' Helen pointed out.

'Aunt Helen is right,' Henry muttered. 'She'd only end up causing trouble for all of us.'

William and Millie looked at each other, and he could tell they were both thinking the same thing. It wasn't like Henry to say a bad word against anyone.

'But Helen could keep an eye on her,' Millie said.

'I most certainly could not!' Helen replied with asperity. 'I have enough to do without playing nursemaid to your daughter,' she told William.

William fell silent. He was caught in the middle, and it wasn't a comfortable place to be.

He could completely understand what Helen was saying and he agreed with her. She was only trying to protect him, after all.

But he also sympathised with Catrine. She was his daughter and it was only right she should be with her family. She had been left out in the cold for too long.

'I meant what I said earlier,' he said. 'What if we could keep it a secret?'

Helen stared at him. 'I can't believe you're even considering it. Do you seriously believe it wouldn't come out?'

'Why should it? I certainly wouldn't say anything, and neither would you.'

'Aren't you forgetting someone?' Helen said.

'I'm sure Catrine would be very discreet if it meant she could study at the Nightingale.'

'Discreet!' His sister laughed. 'If you think that then you're even more naïve than I thought.' She shook her head. 'It's obvious to me the girl is out to make trouble for you, William. Why do you not see that?'

'You really don't like her, do you?' William said.

'I don't trust her,' Helen replied. 'I'm only looking out for you. Someone has to be sensible. I can see right through her, even if you two can't.'

'Me too,' Henry murmured.

'I just feel I owe her this chance,' William said quietly.

'You're making it sound as if you've done her a terrible wrong.'

'Perhaps I have.'

'How? You didn't even know about her until six months ago!'

William paused. 'She and her mother have had a terrible life,' he said at last. 'I can't make it up to Romy, but perhaps I can make amends to Catrine for what she's been through.'

'Even if it means giving up your career?' Helen said. 'Because that's what you'd be doing if this came out.'

William glanced at Millie. He could see by the look in her warm blue eyes that she agreed with every word he said.

'Would you give her a chance if I was willing to take the risk?' he asked Helen.

She sighed. 'I suppose so,' she agreed grudgingly. 'But I still think you're a fool. You mark my words, William. That girl will bring you nothing but trouble!'

Chapter Twenty-Two

Helen went into the garden to calm down after her conversation with William and Millie. It had stopped raining at last, and the air was fresh and cold.

She perched on one of the low walls around the ornamental fountain. The damp cold of the stone seeped through her skirt, but she barely noticed as she shakily rifled in her bag for her cigarettes. Clamping one between her lips, she searched again for her lighter, then realised she had lent it to Henry earlier.

She was just about to put the cigarette back when there was a soft click behind her and a voice said,

'Allow me.'

Helen swung round and felt a slight jolt at the sight of David's face, illuminated in the flicker of the lighter's flame.

Forcing herself to stay calm, she leaned in and lit her cigarette.

'I thought you were in the library?'

'I needed some fresh air. May I?' he gestured to the wall beside her. Helen shifted her shoulders in a careless shrug, even though her heart was beating unsteadily against her ribs.

'How did it go with William?' he asked.

'My brother is a fool.'

'It went well, then?' He looked amused. 'I thought not. You only smoke when you're under stress.'

Helen looked down at her cigarette. She was about to argue then she realised he was right.

'Do you want to talk about it?' he asked.

'My smoking?'

'Your brother.'

'Definitely not.' She shook her head. There was a lot she wanted to say, but she was too angry to trust herself.

They sat in silence for a while. Then Helen said,

'What did you want to talk to me about?'

He frowned. 'What?'

'Millie said you had something you wanted to discuss with me.'

'Oh, that.'

'If it's about the divorce—'

'It isn't.'

They were still sitting uncomfortably close. She was suddenly aware of the heat from his body, the clean, soapy smell of his skin.

'Well?'

David was silent for a long time, and Helen could see him mentally composing what he was going to say.

'One of the consultant physicians at the Nightingale has fallen ill,' he began.

'Dr Prendergast,' Helen nodded. 'I understand he's been prescribed a couple of months' bed rest.'

'Someone needs to fill in temporarily, and Frederick Sutcliffe asked if I'd be interested.'

Helen looked sideways at him. 'How does Frederick Sutcliffe know about you?'

Even in the darkness she could see him blushing. 'William and a couple of others may have put in a good word,' he admitted finally.

'I knew it!'

Helen took another puff on her cigarette. Her brother seemed determined to make her life difficult, one way or another.

'And I take it you said yes?' she said.

'Would you rather I'd said no?'

Helen paused. She wasn't sure she had the answer to that question.

It shouldn't matter to her what he did. They were separated, he was free to do whatever he pleased.

And yet it still bothered her. The Nightingale was her place, her sanctuary. It was the place where she could start to put her life back together after the break-up of her marriage. How could she rebuild her life without David when he was still a part of it?

'And there are no other physicians in London who could do it?' she said.

'I'm sure there are, but they asked me. And I must say, I jumped at the chance to go back to the Nightingale. I rather miss working on the wards.'

'What about the surgery here?'

'I'm getting a locum to fill in.'

He was watching Helen expectantly, waiting for her reaction. She forced herself to stay calm, even though she felt as if she was falling apart inside.

'When do you start?' she asked.

'Next month.'

'So soon?'

'Old Prendergast can't put off his bed rest.' He paused. 'It'll only be for a couple of months. You're all right about it, aren't you?'

'Does it really matter what I think?'

'Of course it matters. I won't do it if you really hate the idea.'

She looked at him. He meant it, she realised. But at the same time she knew she could not take this away from him.

'As long as it doesn't affect the divorce,' she said.

He frowned. 'In what way?'

'We're supposed to live apart for two years, remember?'

'So we are.' His jaw tightened. 'Well, I'll just have to make sure I keep my distance from you, won't I? I'm sure we can both remain professional if we set our minds to it. Aren't you?'

Even in the gathering gloom, she could see the glint of challenge in his eyes. He was testing her, she was sure of it.

'I'm sure that won't be any problem at all,' she said primly.

Chapter Twenty-Three

Winnie and Viv were reaching the end of their allocation on Holmes, the Male Surgical ward, and they couldn't have been more relieved about it.

'Only another two weeks,' Viv said as she and Winnie scrubbed down the dressing trolleys with methylated spirit. 'I dunno about you, but I reckon I've seen enough backsides to last me a lifetime!'

Holmes mainly dealt with gastro-intestinal procedures, such as laparotomies and proctoscopies, as well as appendectomies and ulcer surgery. It was hardly the most glamorous nursing work in the world.

And because it was Winnie and Viv's first time on the ward after passing their Preliminary Training, they were given the worst and most lowly jobs. Their daily work included helping the ward maid with the cleaning and dusting, dealing with bedpans and helping to change the patients' dressings. This involved boiling and sterilising all the equipment, preparing the clean dressings and assisting the sterile nurse by removing and disposing of the patients' soiled dressings.

This particular job earned them the title of 'dirty nurses', much to the amusement of the medical students and junior doctors.

Unfortunately, two of them happened to be on their way to the ward at the same time as Winnie and Viv.

'Look out, here come the dirty nurses!' one of them nudged his companion. 'Do you girls live up to your names?' he grinned.

'No, but you certainly live up to yours,' Viv retorted. Which made Winnie laugh, because this particular doctor was called Andrew Fule.

'I think you'll find it's pronounced "Few-l",' he said.

'I speak as I find, Dr Fool.' Viv pushed her trolley faster towards the ward doors. Unabashed, the young doctor followed her.

'You can't ignore me forever,' he said.

'I'm doing a good job so far,' Viv replied. She strutted on ahead of him with her nose in the air. The young man hurried to catch up with her, nearly pushing Winnie out of the way.

'Watch it!' she said, as her trolley veered to one side, tipping its contents.

'Here, let me help.' The other student rushed to her aid.

'Thank you.' Winnie smiled gratefully at him. 'It's nice to see someone has some manners.' She glared at Dr Fule's turned back.

Henry Tremayne blushed to the roots of his fair hair. Poor boy, he was so shy he couldn't even look at a nurse without turning beetroot.

They reached the doors to the ward, but as Viv went to go through them Dr Fule put out his arm, barring her way.

'Do you mind?' she snapped.

Andrew Fule smirked. 'I'm not letting you pass until you agree to go to the pictures with me.'

'For heaven's sake, Fule, leave her alone!' Dr Tremayne sounded impatient. 'We're here to examine a patient, not bother the nurses.'

'Speak for yourself,' Dr Fule grinned. He turned back to Viv. 'So what do you say? When are we going out together?'

'I'm not sure. I'll ask your girlfriend when you're free, shall I?'

That wiped the smile from his face. 'I haven't got a girl-friend,' he mumbled. 'Nothing serious, anyway.'

Tell that to Camilla, Winnie thought. It was common knowledge around the nursing home that Andrew Fule was dating Camilla Simpson, a girl from their set. Lord knows, she never shut up about it. The way she talked about him, anyone would think they were picking out rings.

Everyone else might have been able to see that she was just another conquest for him, but Andrew was Camilla's first boyfriend and, as far as she was concerned, he was the love of her life.

They'd all tried to warn her off, of course, but Camilla was utterly besotted and wouldn't hear a word against him.

'I know what he used to be like,' she would say. 'But he's different now he's with me.'

Andrew Fule certainly didn't seem like a changed man as he loitered in the doorway now, desperately trying to chat up Viv Trent.

He might have kept her there forever if the door hadn't suddenly swung open, hitting him in the back of the head.

'Where are my dirty nurses?' The ward sister, Miss Redmond, glared at Winnie and Viv. 'Oh, there you are. When you're quite ready, Staff Nurse Jessop is waiting for you to begin the dressings round.'

'Yes, Sister. Sorry, Sister.'

Her hostile gaze fell on Henry and Andrew. 'And what are you two doing here? Apart from distracting my probationers?'

Dr Tremayne turned puce and even Dr Fule's unshakeable confidence seemed to have suddenly deserted him.

'We – we've come to look at a patient, Sister,' he stammered at last.

'Well, you won't be able to see him from here, will you? Go on,' she ushered them towards the doors. 'Do what you're supposed to be doing and then go. And if I see you hanging around my nurses again I shall be having words with your superior. Is that understood?'

'Yes, Sister,' Henry Tremayne mumbled.

'Poor Henry,' Winnie sighed, as the two doctors hurried on to the ward with their heads hung. 'It wasn't his fault, was it? He's so nice.'

'At least he keeps his hands to himself, unlike the rest of them,' Viv said grimly.

Winnie glanced sideways at her. 'He likes you.'

Viv said nothing as she pushed her trolley through the door to where one of the staff nurses was waiting to begin the dressings round.

She must be used to it, Winnie thought. She couldn't think of a single junior doctor who didn't have their eye on

Viv Trent. Not to mention quite a few of the seniors and housemen, too.

It was hardly surprising. She was a real glamour girl, with her pretty, freckled face, luxurious auburn hair and shapely curves that even her striped uniform could not hide.

And now she was single again. She had finally broken up with her tearaway boyfriend Roy after several weeks of indecision.

Winnie was glad her friend was free of him at last. Roy had been a bad influence on her. He resented the fact that Viv was bright and ambitious and wanted to make something of her life, and he did his best to get in the way of her studies. It had taken her a while to realise that he didn't have her best interests at heart.

She had driven Winnie to distraction in the early days of their training, with her insouciant attitude and constant rule-breaking. But now she had really buckled down to her studies and they had become firm friends. They had a lot in common, with them both being cockney girls from the East End. Although in many ways they couldn't be more different. Winnie was hard-working and studious, while Viv still liked to push the boundaries a bit, with her bright red lips and mascara on her lashes.

'Wakey, wakey, Nurse Riley!'

She looked round to see Staff Nurse Jessop smiling at her. Angela Jessop was one of the nicer senior nurses, a plump, smiling contrast to the snarling ward sister.

'Shall we get on?' she said, nodding towards the dressings trolley.

'Yes, of course. Sorry.' Winnie followed her dutifully to the first bed and pulled the curtains round for privacy. As she opened the sterile gloves for Nurse Jessop to put on, she could hear Miss Redmond berating another probationer, an Irish girl called Phil.

'Why hasn't this water jug been refilled? And why has this sheet come untucked at the corner?'

'I'm sorry, Sister, I—'

'I don't want to hear excuses, girl! See to it immediately.'

Phil's footsteps skittered off, moving as quickly as she could without breaking into a run.

'Honestly, I wish Matron wouldn't keep taking all these Irish girls,' Winnie heard Miss Redmond saying. 'They're so dirty and slovenly, and you can hardly teach them anything.'

Winnie caught Angela Jessop's eye as she removed the soiled dressing with forceps and dropped it into the bowl at the bottom of the trolley. The staff nurse's expression gave nothing away, but Winnie could tell she was thinking the same thing as her.

Miss Redmond was well-known in the hospital for her lack of tolerance towards foreigners of any kind. Whether patients or nurses, she disliked them all and did her best to make their lives a misery.

It wasn't the first time she'd picked on poor Phil. For the whole three months of their ward allocation, she had singled out the hapless student nurse for harsh criticism. She had once even managed to blame Phil for an untidy linen cupboard that had happened while she was having a day off.

They discussed it on the way back to the nurses' home

after their shift. Phil was still downhearted after her latest telling-off.

'I do my best, but I just can't seem to please her,' she sighed.

'It ain't your fault she's a mean old bag,' Viv replied with feeling.

'She's really got it in for me.' Phil looked doleful. 'And it's not just her, either. Some of the patients are just as bad. They act like I'm not good enough to bring them a sodding bedpan just because I'm Irish!' She shook her head. 'Sometimes I just feel like going home.'

'Don't do that,' Winnie pleaded. 'It's only for a couple of weeks and then we'll all be moved to new wards.'

'I can't wait,' Phil said grimly.

For the first three months of their probation, the students had all been housed in the old nurses' home, a slightly shabby Gothic house with bits missing from the war. Once they'd passed their Prelims, they'd been moved around the corner to a smart, modern two-storey block with its own kitchen and radiators, and pipes that didn't creak and shudder every time anyone turned on a tap.

A pair of glass double doors led to the airy hallway painted shiny beige, with a payphone on the wall and a large noticeboard filled with flyers and timetables and rotas and reminders about laundry day.

No sooner had they walked in than Camilla Simpson appeared in the doorway that led to the nurses' lounge.

'Have you heard the news?' she said eagerly.

'What news?' Winnie's gaze flew immediately to the noticeboard.

'There's a new girl.'

'How do you know?'

'I had to come back to my room to collect a clean apron at lunch time and I saw the Home Sister showing her around. She's on our floor, in the room next to you, Riley.'

Winnie and Viv looked at each other. They were neighbours, but there was an empty room on Winnie's other side. It had been left vacant after Susan Barlow, one of the nurses from their set, had decided nursing was not for her and enrolled in secretarial college instead.

'Where did she come from, I wonder?' Viv said, as they climbed the stairs to the first floor.

'That's what I want to know,' Camilla said eagerly. She was slim, with long, shiny brown hair and sharp features. Her nose was slightly pointed, which was quite appropriate since she was always trying to poke it into other people's business.

Camilla was the bossy one, the know-it-all of the set. She put herself in the centre of everything, always organising outings and activities for the rest of the group. Winnie suspected she did it because she was afraid of being left out.

'Perhaps she's joining our set now Barlow's gone?' Phil suggested.

'Oh, I don't think so,' Camilla said quickly. 'That wouldn't be allowed, would it?'

'There's only one way to find out, ain't there?' Winnie went up to the girl's door and knocked.

'What are you doing?' Camilla stared at her, horrified.

'Introducing myself to our new neighbour, what does it look like?'

The others all hung back, watching avidly. It took several

moments before the door opened and a young woman stood there.

She was slightly built and barely came up to lanky Winnie's shoulders. A cap of short blonde hair framed her delicate, elfin face. She stared at Winnie with enormous brown eyes fringed with dark lashes.

'Yes?' Her voice was husky, with a distinct foreign accent.

'Hello, I'm Winnie Riley. From the room next door.'

The girl said nothing. She didn't even smile. She just went on staring at Winnie with that unnervingly steady gaze.

'You just arrived today?' Winnie ventured. The girl nodded. 'What's your name?'

The girl hesitated for a moment. 'Catrine Villeneuve,' she said at last.

'You're French?'

'Yes.'

Another pause. Winnie glanced back at the other girls, who were all nodding encouragingly, urging her on.

'We were wondering,' she said, 'would you like to come down to the lounge with us? We could have a chat, get to know you properly—'

'No,' the girl said flatly. 'No, I don't think I would like that.'

And with that she promptly closed the door in Winnie's face before she could say another word. It was all so sudden, Winnie went on staring at the door for a few seconds before she even realised what had happened.

Everyone was silent for a moment. Then she heard Viv Trent laughing.

'Well,' she said. 'I reckon that's you told, ain't it?'

Chapter Twenty-Four

Catrine turned the latch and pressed her ear to the door to listen. Outside on the landing, the girls were talking about her in low voices. Then she heard someone laugh and the others joined in.

For a moment she was tempted to open the door and speak to them. That girl Winnie had seemed nice, and Catrine was feeling very alone since she'd arrived at the nurses' home.

But no sooner had the thought come into her mind than she heard the sound of doors closing as the girls returned to their rooms.

It was too late. She'd made a first impression on them, and they wouldn't be bothering her again.

She set about her unpacking. Her room was much nicer than the one she'd had at the Sacré-Coeur. That had been as old and bare as a monastic cell, but this was light and airy, with primrose-yellow walls and a window that overlooked the main hospital building.

She took her time unpacking, even though she did not have many belongings – just a few clothes and the textbooks she had bought for her course. She had a single photograph of herself with her mother. She still had the photograph of William Tremayne, but she kept that tucked away in the lining of her suitcase.

There could be no connection between them, nothing to give any hint that she was his daughter. As far as he was concerned, she did not exist.

She still felt utterly humiliated every time she thought about that night at Billinghurst. The way they had all joined forces against her. The looks on their faces, as if they could not possibly contemplate allowing her to join their ranks.

Even when William had come to her later and told her she could train at the Nightingale, she had refused to be mollified. Especially when he told her that she was not allowed to breathe a word about her relationship to him or to Helen.

'You do understand, don't you?' he'd pleaded.

Of course she understood. She had been hearing the same message all her life.

She was too shameful, a secret to be hidden away in a corner and never spoken about.

She felt the same humiliation the following morning, when she reported to Helen McKay's office.

She had expected to be assigned to a ward, but instead the matron had announced that she would have to undergo three months of Preliminary Training School.

'No,' she said. 'No, that will not do.'

Helen blinked at her. 'I beg your pardon?'

'You cannot send me back to Preliminary Training. I have already been through training at my old hospital, in Paris. I was working on the wards for nearly a year before I came to England.'

'That may be so,' Helen said tautly. 'But how do we know

161

whether the training you've received is up to our standard?' She shook her head. 'You will have to undergo PTS again.'

This had nothing to do with standards, Catrine thought. Helen was trying to goad her. She could see the gleam in her aunt's eye as she faced her across the desk.

She shook her head. 'I will not do it,' she declared. 'I will start on the ward, like everyone else.'

Angry colour rose in Helen McKay's face. 'You will do as you're told! The very fact that you're in my office questioning my authority tells me a great deal about your suitability for training at this hospital.'

'I passed the entrance examination, yes?'

'Yes,' Helen admitted reluctantly.

'*Bien*. Then I must be suitable.'

'There's a great deal more to being a good nurse than having an adequate standard of English and arithmetic, Miss Villeneuve.'

'I know that, Matron, since I've worked on medical and surgical wards. I also have experience of orthopaedics and fever nursing.'

They stared at each other, eyes locked. Helen thought she could intimidate her, in her stiff black Matron's dress and starched bonnet. But Catrine was not a frightened little student. She had been through too much to be scared by a bully like Helen McKay.

Even so, she was still the matron, and Catrine knew she had to treat her with respect. If she didn't, Helen would not hesitate to get rid of her.

'Please, Matron,' she said, trying to sound subdued. 'All I want is a chance to prove myself.'

Helen hesitated, and Catrine could see the battle going on behind her eyes.

'Very well,' she said at last. 'You will report to Miss James in the Preliminary Training School – for an initial assessment,' she went on quickly, as Catrine opened her mouth to argue. 'If she believes your basic skills are up to our standard, then I will consider putting you on a ward. Is that acceptable to you?' she asked, her voice laced with sarcasm.

Catrine nodded. 'Thank you, Madame,' she said.

She couldn't hide her smile as she left the office. She suspected it would be the first of many battles between them, but at least she had won this round.

Helen sank back in her chair with a sense of relief. She had always known William's daughter would be difficult, but she hadn't expected to encounter trouble from her before she had even set foot on a ward.

It was bad enough that she had her father wrapped around her little finger. But if she thought she could do the same to Helen, then she was in for a nasty surprise.

She had barely recovered from Catrine's visit when her secretary buzzed through on the intercom to announce that Dr McKay was in the outer office and wished to speak to her.

Helen sighed. Today was proving to be a trial and she had not even started her morning rounds yet.

She managed to fix a professional mask in place by the time he walked into her office.

'Are you sure now's a good time?' he said.

'Of course.'

'Really?' He tilted his head. 'You seem rather tense.'

'What makes you say that?'

'I can tell. Also, I noticed Mademoiselle Villeneuve leaving as I came in.'

'Ah.'

'I take it you've been locking horns?'

'You could say that.'

'I hope you showed her who's boss?'

Helen flicked a glance at the door. She was rather afraid that Catrine had got the better of her this time.

'What do you want to talk to me about?' she asked.

'Chlorothiazide.'

'Chlorothiazide?'

'It's a new drug for treating—'

'A diuretic,' Helen finished for him. 'Used for treating excess fluid in congestive heart failure and hypertension.'

His brows rose. 'You've heard of it?'

'I read *The Lancet*. It was approved for clinical use earlier this year.'

'I was going to introduce it to treat some of the patients with long-term heart conditions. I believe it could improve their quality of life a great deal.'

'I think that would be a very good idea.'

'I'm glad you approve.'

She pulled her gaze from his and looked down at the ink-stained blotter in front of her. 'The nurses will need training.'

'That's what I wanted to talk to you about.'

They discussed the drug and its application on the ward.

Then Helen said, 'I'll speak to the medical ward sisters about it. Perhaps we could have a meeting in a few days?'

'Whenever you're ready.'

She opened her desk diary and suggested a date.

'That suits me.' David rose to his feet. 'I'll leave you to organise it with the ward sisters, shall I?'

'I'll speak to them this afternoon.'

'Thank you.'

As he went to leave, he turned and said, 'You look very smart, by the way. The Matron's get-up suits you.'

'Thank you.'

Helen looked away so he wouldn't see her smile.

Chapter Twenty-Five

'His daughter?'

Dora froze where she stood in the back yard, her hands raised in the middle of pegging out her husband's shirt. She stared at Helen, who stood in the doorway.

'You won't tell anyone, will you?' her friend said anxiously.

'What do you take me for?' Dora shook her head and went back to her washing. 'My lips are sealed, you should know that.'

Helen smiled with relief. 'That's why I told you. I had to talk to someone. And Millie said she didn't mind if you knew.'

'So no one else knows?'

'Only the family. And David,' she added.

Dora reached down to the laundry basket of wet clothes at her feet and pulled out her son Danny's vest.

'Well, I never,' she said. 'I always knew your William was a bit of a rascal in his younger days, but I never imagined anything like this.'

'Neither did I,' Helen said gloomily.

'And he had no idea?'

Helen shook her head. 'He never heard from this woman again after she left England. Catrine says her mother wrote him a letter, but it must have got lost somewhere on the way from France.'

'That doesn't surprise me.' She knew how long her own husband's letters had taken to arrive during the war. And then there had been those few months when they'd stopped coming completely and she'd feared the worst.

As she raised her arms to pin another vest to the line, her jumper rode up, revealing the slight swell of her belly under her skirt. Dora quickly pulled it down, sure that Helen must have noticed. But her friend was so wrapped up in her own problems, she was oblivious to anyone else.

'How did William take it?' she asked.

'He was as shocked as the rest of us – at first. But now he seems to have welcomed her with open arms.' There was a hint of bitterness in her voice.

'What about Millie? It must have been a shock for her, too.'

'Oh, you know Millie. She takes everything in her stride. She feels terribly for the girl. All she wants to do is take her under her wing and look after her.'

'That sounds like Millie,' Dora smiled. 'But I suppose the girl could probably do with a mother after losing her own. She must be feeling very lost, poor mite.'

'Oh, there's nothing poor about her. Believe me, she's remarkably self-possessed. Cold, even.'

Dora frowned at her friend. It wasn't like Helen to be so critical. Under that cool, unflappable exterior she was very warm and compassionate, but for some reason she had really hardened her heart against Catrine Villeneuve.

She thought about what her daughter had told her about the new girl in their nursing block.

167

'Our Winnie says she keeps herself to herself and doesn't want anything to do with the rest of them. But perhaps she's shy and still finding her feet?'

'I don't know about that,' Helen replied. 'She seems to have everyone dancing to her tune. Even Miss James the Sister Tutor has fallen for her charm.'

'You've never made her go through PTS? I thought you said she had experience?'

'I had to make sure she was good enough.' Helen looked slightly defensive.

'And was she?'

'Miss James had nothing but praise for her,' Helen said dryly. 'She said she'd seldom seen such an able student.'

'Well, that's good news, ain't it?' Dora reached down for another piece of washing from the basket. 'I'd snap her up and put her straight on the ward if I were you.'

'Oh, I shall. Don't worry about that.'

Dora looked at her friend's enigmatic expression. 'Why do I think you're up to something?'

'I'm going to send her to Holmes ward.'

'Tums and bums? That's the ward my Winnie's on. She reckons the sister's a right old—' Realisation dawned. 'That's why you're sending her there, ain't it?'

A slow smile crossed Helen's face. 'I shall enjoy seeing what Miss Redmond makes of her. Mincemeat, I should think!'

Dora frowned. It really wasn't like Helen to be so malicious. She usually cared a great deal for her nurses' welfare.

'Blimey, you really have got it in for her,' she said.

She put a hand to her lower back, which was starting to

ache. It was a sharp reminder of why she had invited Helen round. She desperately needed someone to talk to herself.

She pegged up the last of the wet clothes and then said, 'Right, that's done. Let's go inside and have a proper natter, shall we? I've got a bit of news of my own to tell you.'

Helen glanced at her watch. 'Sorry, love, I have to go. I have a meeting with the medical ward at eleven.'

Dora stared at her. 'You can't stay for a cup of tea at least?'

'I'm afraid not.' Dora's disappointment must have shown on her face because Helen looked at her watch again and said, 'Look, I'm sure I can spare another five minutes. What's this news you want to tell me?' She smiled brightly.

Dora smoothed down her skirt with her hand, feeling the slight rise of her belly underneath. Whatever she had to say would take a lot longer than five minutes.

'It will keep till next time,' she said.

'Are you sure?' Helen looked worried. 'I hate to rush off when you've been so patient, listening to me going on about my problems . . .'

'It's all right, honestly. You get to your meeting.'

'I'll come round for that cup of tea as soon as I can, I promise.'

Dora said goodbye to her friend and then carried the empty laundry basket back into the kitchen and set it down on the table.

Her mother Rose was on her hands and knees in front of the fireplace, polishing the grate.

'You shouldn't be doing that,' Dora said over her shoulder.

'I ain't useless, Dor.'

'You ain't well, either.'

'Nonsense, I'm as fit as a fiddle.' But Dora noticed how long it took her mother to scramble to her feet. 'I'll put the kettle on, shall I?'

'You sit down, Mum. I'll do it.'

She watched her mother out of the corner of her eye as she sank into the armchair beside the fireplace. Rose Doyle had recovered remarkably from her stroke the previous year, but she was still frail and unsteady on her feet.

'Your friend gone, has she?' Rose asked as she watched Dora filling the kettle.

Dora nodded. 'She had to get back to the hospital for a meeting.'

'That's a shame. I heard you chatting – it sounds like she had a lot to get off her chest.'

'Yes, she did.'

'It's a pity you didn't get to tell her your news.'

Dora froze, the kettle still in her hand. 'What news?'

Her mother smiled knowingly. 'Oh, come on, Dor! I'm your mother. You might be able to pull the wool over every-one else's eyes but you can't fool me.' She nodded to her daughter's belly. 'You're expecting again, ain't you?'

Dora stared at her. 'How did you know?'

It was a daft question. Rose had given birth to five chil-dren of her own, so she knew what to look for better than anyone.

'I can tell. You've got that look about you. Besides, you've been sick as a dog every morning and you're never ill. How far along are you?'

'I'm not sure.' Dora pressed her hand to the swell in her skirt. 'I was thinking I might not even be—'

'Come off it, love. You're supposed to be a nurse, ain't you? You know as well as I do you've got a bun in the oven. And ignoring it won't make it go away.'

'You're right,' Dora sighed. Although that was exactly what she had been doing these past few weeks.

'Have you told Nick yet?' her mother asked. Dora shook her head. 'Don't you think he should know?'

'I ain't had the heart to tell him. I didn't know what he'll say.'

'Well, there ain't much he can say, is there? And if I'm not mistaken, you're going to start showing soon. Then you won't have to tell anyone.' Rose smiled wryly. 'I'm right in thinking it weren't planned?'

Dora buried her face in her hands, finally giving way to all the emotions she had kept so tightly inside her. 'Oh Mum, what am I going to do? Danny's nearly eleven now. I thought I was done with all that baby business. I'm too old to go through it again.'

'Don't look like you've got much choice in the matter, does it?' Her mother sighed. 'Why don't you put that kettle on? Then we can have a proper chat . . .'

Chapter Twenty-Six

On the morning she joined Holmes ward, Catrine followed the stream of girls heading from the nurses' home to the main hospital building.

The tall girl, Winnie, and her redheaded friend Viv dragged their feet behind the others, she noticed. The Irish girl, Phil, was even further behind, in conversation with her friend Bernadette.

No one spoke to her, or waited for her to catch them up. After a few days of Catrine refusing their invitations and cutting conversations short, they had given up trying with her.

It was better this way, she told herself. She would do better without the distraction of friendships.

Besides, they never lasted, in her experience. Sooner or later she knew she would find herself on the outside again. Better not to allow herself to get close to anyone, then she'd have nothing to lose.

They arrived on the ward just as the weary-looking night nurses were waking up the patients with their tea.

'You're a sight for sore eyes,' one of girls greeted them, stifling a yawn with the back of her hand.

'Bad night?' Winnie asked.

'We had a ruptured appendix brought in. Luckily Mr

Bose was on, and the patient seems to be doing well. And the suspected ulcer in bed four needs a gastric fluid sample before he eats or drinks anything. Hopefully one of the medical students will tip themselves out of bed, otherwise one of you will have to do it.'

'I can do it,' Catrine said. 'I've used a nasogastric tube before.'

She saw Winnie raise her eyebrows at Viv and immediately wished she hadn't said anything.

'Have you, indeed?' The night nurse raised an eyebrow. 'As I said, hopefully the med student will be along soon. Anyway, I've just given my report to the Night Sister. She'll tell you what's what. I'm off to bed.'

Once they had spoken to Miss Campbell the Night Sister, they were dispatched off to their various duties before the ward sister arrived to start the day.

Catrine and Phil were sent to the kitchen to help the ward maid with breakfast.

'It's this way,' Phil said, pointing towards the double doors at the far end of the ward. 'Just follow the sound of singing and you'll find Annie.'

Annie, the ward maid, a scrawny little woman in her fifties, was dressed in an enormous green apron. She stood at the stove in the ward kitchen, humming tunelessly under her breath as she stirred a large pot of steaming porridge.

'Oh, hello,' she glanced over her shoulder at Catrine in the doorway. 'You're new, ain't you, love?' she greeted her in a cheery cockney accent.

Catrine nodded.

'She's French,' Phil said.

'French, eh? You're a long way from home, ain't you? I've never been further than Clacton myself.' She grinned, showing a sparse arrangement of teeth. 'Be a love and go round and take the breakfast orders, will you?' She nodded towards the door. 'Tell 'em it's porridge or boiled eggs this morning.'

'It's porridge or boiled eggs every morning,' Phil said.

'Porridge is my speciality.'

Catrine peered at the unappetising-looking grey sludge the maid was stirring in the pot. As if she'd read her thoughts, Phil murmured, 'If that's her speciality then I dread to think what the boiled eggs are like, eh?'

Catrine smiled at her reluctantly.

She went and took the orders while Phil stayed in the kitchen with Annie, spreading margarine on slices of bread. When Catrine offered to swap jobs with her, she shook her head and said,

'Sister prefers me to stay in here. She doesn't like me taking orders or serving meals.'

'Why not?' Catrine asked. Phil and the ward maid looked at each other.

'It's on account of her being Irish,' Annie said. 'Sister don't care for foreigners.'

'I wonder what she will think of me?' Catrine said.

Annie sent her a shrewd look.

'That remains to be seen, don't it?' she said.

Miss Redmond finally made her appearance as they were clearing away the breakfast dishes. Catrine and Phil quickly dried their hands and changed their aprons and went to join Winnie and Viv and the staff nurse for her inspection.

The ward sister's keen eyes sought out Catrine immediately.

'Ah, the new girl,' Miss Redmond sniffed. She was in her fifties, short and squat with piercing dark eyes and a jowly face that quivered when she spoke. 'What's your name?'

'Villeneuve, Sister.'

Miss Redmond's eyes narrowed. 'What sort of name is that?'

'It's French, Sister.'

'Oh, I'm never going to remember a foreign name. I shall call you Nurse Frenchie.'

Catrine opened her mouth to protest, but Winnie's silent shake of the head stopped her.

'You should know I don't trust the French,' Miss Redmond went on. 'They have no backbone. And they're not clean, either.' She glared at Catrine. 'Show me your hands.'

Catrine held them out to her. Miss Redmond leaned in and inspected them closely.

'Not good enough,' she declared. 'You'll need to wash them before I'll allow you on the ward. Well, don't just stand there – go on!'

Catrine stomped off to the bathroom, silently furious. How dare she speak to her like that? She had known ward sisters to be strict in Paris, but none of them had been as rude as Miss Redmond.

'Take no notice,' Annie whispered, sidling up behind her. 'I told you, didn't I? She's always nasty to the foreign nurses. Gives them the worst jobs, she does. You should see how she treats poor Phil.'

After the breakfast dishes were washed up and the beds

were made, it was time for the dressings round. Miss Redmond sent Catrine off with Viv to prepare the trolleys, one for each side of the ward.

'Hello, hello. Who do we have here?'

Catrine looked over her shoulder to see two young men in spotless white coats standing in the doorway. One of them was well-built, with hazel eyes and sandy curls.

The other was Henry.

He and Catrine looked at each other. It was hard to tell which of them was more appalled.

'What time do you call this?' Viv said. 'If you've come to do that gastric fluid sample then you're too late. The Night Sister had to do it, and she wasn't best pleased.'

'I overslept,' the sandy-haired young man shrugged, his attention still on Catrine. 'I'm Andrew,' he introduced himself. 'And this is my friend Henry. Say hello, Henry,' he encouraged him.

Henry was silent.

'You'll have to excuse him,' Andrew laughed. 'He tends to be struck dumb in the presence of a beautiful woman. Especially Nurse Trent here.'

'Shut up, Fule,' Henry mumbled. He was puce in the face now, his colour deepening every second.

Catrine was surprised. And she'd thought he was such a ladies' man, from the way he talked to his father!

'Mind you, he's so shy he even gets embarrassed by the female corpses in anatomy lessons. Isn't that right, Tremayne?' He turned back to Catrine. 'And what's your name?' he asked.

'None of your business,' Viv Trent snapped, before Catrine could reply. The young doctor grinned.

176

'Oh dear, Nurse Trent. Are you jealous because you're not getting all the attention for once? Never mind, at least you've still got Tremayne's undying adoration.'

'When you've quite finished, we're supposed to be checking a post-op drain,' Henry hissed. 'Mr Bose will be here in a minute.'

'Don't be such a frightful old bore, Henry!' the young man laughed. He blew Catrine a kiss and then strolled off, Henry at his heels. Henry did not even spare a glance in her direction.

'Stay away from that one,' Viv Trent advised. 'Or you'll have Camilla Simpson to reckon with.'

Catrine thought about the nosy girl with the sharp features and shiny brown hair who never stopped asking questions.

'She is his girlfriend?' she asked, curious in spite of herself.

'So she reckons. Although she's more serious about it than he is.' Viv shook her head. 'I dunno why she bothers with him, I really don't.'

The two doctors were still on the ward when Catrine returned with the dressings trolley ten minutes later.

She pushed the trolley to the first bed and was just pulling the curtains around when Miss Redmond's voice rang out from the other end of the ward.

'What do you think you're doing, Frenchie?'

Everyone fell silent. Catrine stuck her head around the curtain to see the ward sister advancing towards her.

'You asked me to do the dressings round, Sister.'

'Not on your own!' Miss Redmond's beady eyes gleamed. 'You're only a dirty nurse, Frenchie.'

Catrine looked around her in confusion. Everyone had stopped what they were doing to watch her.

What did she mean? Was it another disparaging reference to her being French? She looked down at her hands, which she had just finished scrubbing again. The skin around her cuticles was nearly raw.

'Good gracious, girl. Do you not know what a dirty nurse is?' Miss Redmond sent her a withering look. 'Your job is to take off the soiled dressings. One of the staff nurses has to put on the clean one.'

Catrine looked across the ward to where Viv stood. She had been joined by Staff Nurse Jessop, who was clearly in charge.

'Oh, but I've done it before,' Catrine said. 'I did all the dressings on the surgical ward at my last hospital—'

As soon as the words left her lips she knew it was the wrong thing to say. An ominous silence fell, and Miss Redmond's jowls quivered threateningly.

'Did you now?' The ward sister's thin lips curled. 'I don't care how things were done at your last hospital, or how woefully low their standards were. This is my ward and I decide who does what and when, not the other way round. Is that understood?'

'Yes, Sister.'

'I can't believe my ears! Imagine, a probationer trying to take charge and tell me how to run my ward.' Miss Redmond glared at Catrine. 'Because of your impudence, you can go and clean the bathrooms. And I mean scrub them, not the way you'd do them at your French hospital.' She pointed towards the double doors. 'And I shall be checking on you to make sure you've done it to my satisfaction!'

Catrine turned on her heel and walked away in the direction the ward sister was pointing. She kept her head up and her eyes fixed straight ahead of her as she walked the length of the ward.

As she reached the double doors, Henry Tremayne stepped forward and held them open for her.

'After you,' he murmured.

'Thank you.' She could not bear to look at him. She could only imagine the mocking smile on his face.

Chapter Twenty-Seven

By the time Henry returned to Holmes ward later that afternoon, Catrine was back on the ward.

His gaze found her immediately. She was pushing a drip stand down to a bed at the far end, where Staff Nurse Jessop was waiting for her.

'Well, well,' James Bose said. 'So that's her, is it? The famous Catrine?'

Henry instinctively looked around to check no one had heard. Even when he spoke quietly, Mr Bose's booming voice seemed to carry down the length of the ward.

The consultant laughed. 'It's all right, my boy. I'm not going to incriminate anyone!' He leaned in conspiratorially. 'I've always been good at keeping your father's secrets,' he whispered.

Henry nodded. Of course he could trust his Uncle James. He and his father were the closest of friends.

He had enjoyed his time under James Bose's tutelage. Mr Bose was very chummy with the students, unlike most of the other consultants. But even though Henry had known him all his life, he was still terrified of making a mistake in his presence.

'She looks rather full of herself, doesn't she?' Bose went on. 'A very confident young woman, I think.'

'Yes. Yes, she is.'

Henry remembered the look of utter determination on Catrine's face as she'd walked up the length of the ward earlier on. Miss Redmond had just given her a dressing-down in front of everyone but she did not look in the least bit humiliated.

Henry wasn't sure he could have kept so much composure in the circumstances. He would probably have tripped over his own shoelaces as he left.

Catrine Villeneuve must have ice running through her veins, he thought. She was far too sure of herself for anyone to ever put her in her place.

'Anyway, enough about her,' James Bose interrupted his thoughts. 'Let's have a look at Mr Perkins's lungs, shall we?'

He had been summoned by Miss Redmond to look at a patient who was having trouble with his breathing following a laparotomy, and he had asked Henry to accompany him.

Henry knew it caused resentment among the other students that he was often chosen for special treatment by the consultants.

'Must be nice to have friends in high places,' they would grumble.

If only they knew, Henry thought. He dreaded being singled out, because he always seemed to make a fool of himself.

He was determined not to let his nerves get the better of him as he stood at the bedside of poor Sidney Perkins, who was propped up in bed and looking very unwell indeed. His breathing was shallow and laboured, and his lips were tinged with blue.

Miss Redmond had joined them. She stood on the opposite side of the bed, listening in respectful silence as the consultant held forth.

'Lung complications are more common in abdominal cases than any other type of surgery,' James Bose was saying. 'Why do you think that might be?'

'Er . . .' Henry stared at Mr Perkins, as if the man's pale face would give him the answer he needed. 'Pain at the site of the wound restricting free respiration?'

'And?'

Henry stared across the bed at Miss Redmond's impassive face, his brain a blank. Then, suddenly, it came to him.

'Limited movement of the incised abdominal wall?' he suggested.

To his immense relief, James Bose nodded. 'And how would you treat Mr Perkins's condition?'

Henry felt the heat rising from his underneath his collar. He knew this. He had studied it over and over again. But the information always eluded him when he needed it most.

He closed his eyes and tried to picture what was written in his medical textbook.

Treatment for bronchial conditions . . .

'Application of poultices to the chest wall,' he began to recite. 'Medical diathermy, expectorant mixtures, steam tents, antitoxic sera—'

'Look at him,' Bose interrupted him impatiently. 'The man is slowly but surely turning blue. What does that tell you?'

'Anoxaemia, sir.'

'Precisely. We need to get some more oxygen into him. But how much, would you say?'

Henry did the quick mental calculation. 'Six to ten litres per minute, alternated with carbon dioxide in oxygen to initiate deeper respiratory movements,' he said.

'Very good. Now fortunately, like all good nurses, Miss Redmond has already anticipated the need for oxygen and has everything prepared.' James Bose nodded to the ward sister, who in turn gestured down the ward.

A moment later a couple of student nurses appeared, one pushing the trolley laden with various rubber tubes and a Woulfe's bottle, while the other dragged an oxygen cylinder on a stand.

Henry was dismayed to see it was Catrine and Viv Trent who had been given the task of setting up the equipment.

He automatically stepped back to give them room to carry out their work, but James Bose said,

'No, Doctor Tremayne. I'd like to see you administer the oxygen, if you please.'

Henry looked panic stricken. 'Me?'

The consultant's smile didn't waver. 'It's a procedure nurses can do very efficiently, but you should be able to do it yourself, should the need arise.'

Henry glanced around at the ring of expectant faces. Miss Redmond, Viv Trent and Catrine. He could feel his skin burning so hot, he thought he might melt into a puddle of embarrassment.

Calm down, Henry. You can do this.

He looked at the oxygen cylinder and the items on the trolley. He turned on the oxygen, checked its flow against the water in the Woulfe's bottle then adjusted it.

So far, so good. Now all he had to do was put in the nasal catheter.

He hoped no one would notice how much his hands were shaking as he greased the tip of the catheter. As he turned back to the patient, he caught sight of Viv Trent. He saw her encouraging smile, as if she was silently urging him on.

Catching her eye made him panic. Without thinking, he pushed the rubber tubing in.

'Backwards, not upwards.'

Henry looked up sharply. It was Catrine who had uttered the words, her attention focused on the man in the bed.

'I know what I'm doing,' he snapped.

He inserted the tube, then deflected it downwards. But he was so annoyed at Catrine's intervention that he went too far and too fast. The next moment the patient was coughing and retching.

'You've gone too far,' Bose said. 'Three inches into the nasopharynx, no further than the base of the uvula.'

Before he knew what was happening, Catrine had elbowed him out of the way and was pulling the tube out.

'What do you think you're doing, Nurse?' Miss Redmond snapped.

'Saving this patient from choking.'

Henry stood back lamely as she took charge. He felt utterly humiliated.

'Leave it,' the ward sister said. 'You should not interfere when the doctor is working.'

'But—'

'I said leave it, Nurse!'

Catrine hesitated for a moment, then let the tubing drop

from her hands. Miss Redmond pulled herself upright, her mouth pursed with disapproval.

'This is the second time today I've had to speak to you about your behaviour,' she said. 'If there is a third time then it will be your last.'

Catrine pressed her lips together, as if it took all her effort not to speak. Henry could sense the resentment coming off her as he quickly inserted the catheter, properly this time.

'Thank God for that,' James Bose breathed a sigh of relief as they watched the nurses walking away. 'I was afraid you were going to make a mess of it again.'

So was I, Henry thought miserably. It was nothing short of a miracle that he'd managed to carry out the procedure.

'I must say, I'm glad Sister put Nurse Villeneuve in her place. Talk about overstepping the mark!' Bose shook his head.

'The patient was choking,' Henry said quietly.

'There was no harm done. Don't look so glum, old chap. Everyone makes mistakes.' Mr Bose slapped him on the shoulder. 'Your concentration slipped for a minute, that's all. Too many late nights, I expect.' He grinned conspiratorially. 'I know what you young students are like, burning the candle at both ends. Your father and I were just the same. Although he was far worse than me,' he added. 'Just try and stay away from too many late-night parties, that's my advice.'

Henry smiled weakly. 'I'll try,' he said.

He returned to his lodgings later to find Andrew Fule preparing for another night out.

He stood at the mirror in the bedroom he and Henry shared, teasing his hair with Brylcreem. His clothes were strewn all over their room, as usual, and he had doused himself in so much Aqua Velva it made Henry's eyes sting.

'You're going out, I take it?' Henry said.

'Indeed I am.'

That was a relief, Henry thought. At least he would be able to study undisturbed.

Andrew was silent for a few moments as he studied his reflection. Henry opened his book at the chapter on post-operative complications and began to read.

'What do you think about Frenchie?' Andrew asked.

'Who?' Henry asked absently, not looking up.

'Frenchie. Nurse Villeneuve? She's quite a looker, isn't she? And you know what they say about French girls, don't you?'

'I don't, and I don't care to, either,' Henry said through gritted teeth.

He was still smarting over the way she had humiliated him earlier. Every time he closed his eyes, he could see the pitying look on Viv Trent's face as Catrine snatched the tube out of his hand.

'I'm not sure who I prefer, her or Viv Trent.' Andrew leaned closer, artfully smoothing a greasy curl on his forehead. 'Frenchie's got that petite Audrey Hepburn charm, while Trent's pure Marilyn Monroe.'

'And there was me, thinking you only had eyes for Nurse Simpson?' Henry muttered.

Andrew's grin widened. 'Nothing wrong with playing the field, old man. How can I possibly limit myself to one girl when this place is full of pretty faces? It's like living in a sweet shop and only eating humbugs for the rest of your life. You should try it some time.'

'Eating humbugs?'

'Playing the field, you idiot.' He slapped Henry on the shoulder. 'Right, I'm off. Don't wait up for me, will you?'

No sooner had he uttered the words than the sound of music and laughter drifted up from downstairs.

Henry put down his book. 'What's going on now?'

'Oh, didn't you know? Some of the other chaps are having a get-together,' Andrew replied carelessly. 'I'm surprised they didn't mention it.'

'No,' Henry said, glaring towards the door. 'They didn't.'

'I suppose they assumed you wouldn't want to join them. You never usually join in with anything.'

Just try and stay away from too many late-night parties, that's my advice.

James Bose's words came back to taunt him.

'No,' he said. 'I wouldn't.'

Chapter Twenty-Eight

In Helen's experience, most senior doctors tended to think of themselves as superior beings, far above anyone else. Perhaps it was because everyone treated them like gods.

Their arrival on a ward would be greeted with a great fanfare, even greater than when Matron did her rounds. They would make their way around, followed by an awestruck gaggle of medical students and nurses. Even the most outspoken ward sister would be rendered respectfully silent, offering no opinions unless she was asked.

Most of the senior doctors wouldn't even look at the patients, let alone talk to them. They would stare at their notes, bark some orders to the ward sister and then move on.

Helen had only known two doctors who did not behave like that. One was her brother William.

The other was her husband.

From the first moment she had met him while working together in the Casualty department, Helen could see David McKay was different. She had never known a doctor show such tenderness to his patients. He looked them in the eyes when he spoke to them, held their hands when they were distressed, and talked to them as if they were human beings and not just a collection of troubling symptoms.

He was talking to Barbara Howard now, perched on her bed despite the disapproving glare of Miss Gould the ward sister, explaining exactly how her new medication was working.

And working it clearly was. After taking chlorothiazide for a few days, Mrs Howard was showing a great improvement in her condition.

She was no stranger to the ward, Helen reflected. The thirty-eight-year-old mother of four had suffered from mitral stenosis after a bout of rheumatic fever when she was a girl.

'And you're sure there's nothing else you need to tell me? No headaches or blurred vision?' Mrs Howard shook her head. 'What about rashes or itchy skin?'

'Not at all, Doctor. I'm as right as rain.'

'That's good news,' David said. 'You're certainly looking well, I must say. It seems as if the pills are working.'

'Oh, I'll say they are, Doctor.' Barbara Howard beamed. 'You've given me a new lease of life, I reckon.'

'Well, I wouldn't be swimming the English Channel just yet, my love.' David looked rueful. 'We can't guarantee to keep you out of hospital forever, but hopefully your visits should be fewer and further between. Not that we don't like seeing you,' he added with a wink.

'She's right, you know,' Miss Gould said as they moved away from the bed. 'You have given her a new lease of life. I must have seen the poor woman at least half a dozen times, and she's never looked so well. She's got a lot to thank you for, Doctor.'

A faint blush rose in David's face.

'It's the treatment she should thank, not me,' he said.

Just then, a student nurse sidled up to tell Miss Gould there was a telephone call for her. The ward sister excused herself and hurried to take it, leaving Helen and David alone together.

'You shouldn't be so modest,' Helen said. 'Mrs Howard might never have had that medication if you hadn't introduced it.'

'I'm sure someone else would have thought of it sooner or later,' David shrugged. 'I'm just glad it worked so well for her.' He glanced towards Barbara Howard's bed. 'Hopefully the poor woman will be able to spend more time with her family, and less lying in a hospital bed.'

He looked every bit as pleased and relieved as the patient, Helen thought. That was so typical of David.

After more than a week of him being at the Nightingale, she had grown used to seeing him on her daily ward rounds. David had kept his promise to remain professional at all times, and so after a while Helen had begun to let her guard down in his presence.

She did not want to admit it, but she had even started to look forward to running into him on her rounds. His cheerful warmth always seemed to bring out the best in people. Even Helen had caught herself smiling once or twice.

And then he made a comment that changed everything.

'Just like old times, isn't it?'

Helen stared at him. 'What?'

'You and me working together. It reminds me of those days in Casualty, when we first met.' He was smiling when he said it, completely oblivious of the effect his words were having on her. 'Do you remember—'

'I thought we agreed to keep things professional between us?' Helen cut him off sharply.

'I was only saying—'

'Please don't.' She didn't want to be reminded of those days, when their love was new, and she was happy and full of hope for the future.

Before time tarnished everything.

'It's all in the past,' she said. 'If we're to continue working together we need to concentrate on the future.'

'Of course. I'm sorry.' He looked crestfallen. 'I didn't mean—'

But Helen was already hurrying away, putting as much distance between them as she could.

David McKay could have kicked himself as he watched his wife walk away.

Why had he said it? He'd known it was the wrong thing to say as soon as he'd seen the look of dismay dawning on Helen's face. And after he'd worked so hard to gain her trust, too.

But things had been going so well between them and he'd been so elated over Barbara Howard's treatment, for a moment he had forgotten himself. He had overstepped the mark and taken them right back to square one.

Perhaps he shouldn't have come back to the Nightingale after all. He was enjoying his work at the hospital, but Helen was still clearly uncomfortable with him being there, and he didn't want that. This was her place, her refuge, and he had blundered into it.

He was foolish to think it could have been different. When William had first suggested David step in and temporarily take over from Dr Prendergast, he had jumped at the chance. He told himself that he had missed the wards, but really, if he was honest, he had been hoping that it might give him the chance to rekindle his relationship with Helen.

After all, the Nightingale had been where their love story started.

Not that it had been love at first sight. David had not been impressed by Helen when she first took charge of the Casualty department. She was too young in his opinion, and had only been given the job because her mother was on the Board of Trustees. But gradually she had impressed him with her cool competence and the fact that she did not take nonsense from anyone – especially him.

She might have won him over, but he'd had an uphill battle to make her feel the same. She was a young widow, having just lost her first husband after a tragically short marriage. She was not ready for love again. It had taken her a long time to allow herself to fall for him. And even then it had taken them nearly losing each other during the war for them both to realise how they truly felt.

But it had been worth the wait. They had married and settled in Billinghurst, and they had been idyllically happy.

Or so David had believed. But apparently Helen did not feel the same.

He had been knocked for six when she suddenly told him she wanted to end their marriage. Even after she took the job as Matron of the Nightingale, he could not quite believe that it was happening. Helen was his life, his whole world. It seemed unthinkable to him that she would ever leave.

But in the weeks that had followed, he'd had more time to reflect. And even though her leaving had come as a dreadful shock, in a way he was not really surprised.

He had sensed her pulling away from him, even though he tried not to admit it. Even though outwardly she seemed as contented as she had always been, underneath her smile, he had sensed her sorrow in their marriage.

And he thought he understood why, too.

They had both looked forward to starting a family after their marriage. Whenever they talked about their future there was always a handful of children included in it. They'd even chosen Lowgill House to set up the GP practice because it was so perfect for a growing family.

But it hadn't happened. As the months and then years went by and the children did not come, they had gone through disappointment and heartache together. Yet while David had come to terms with their situation, he realised now that his wife had not.

Of course he had been aware of her sorrow, even though she tried to hide it from him. But he hadn't talked about it, preferring to give her time to grieve for her lost dreams in her own time. He thought that when she was ready she would come back to him. It might not have been the life they had planned, but they would still be together and happy.

Instead, Helen had decided to go on without him.

Did she blame him? he wondered. Was that why she had

left him? He'd never dared to ask her. The end of their marriage had been so swift and sudden, he'd had no time to consider why it had happened until weeks later.

And now it was too late.

'Doctor McKay?'

He turned to see the ward sister, Miss Gould, looking at him.

'Would you mind taking a look at the peptic ulcer in bed six, sir? I know you prescribed antacids, but Mr Hargreaves thinks it should be taken out.'

'Let's have a look, shall we?'

David glanced back over his shoulder at where Helen had gone.

She was right, he thought. It was all in the past.

Chapter Twenty-Nine

On Sunday night, the notice went up on the board in the hallway of the nurses' home, listing the various wards to which students would be sent for the next three months.

Winnie and Viv were jubilant as they were being sent to Wren, the Gynae ward.

'Mind you, I wouldn't mind where I went, as long as it's a long way away from Miss Redmond!' Winnie said.

'We'll never have to hear her calling us dirty nurses again!' Viv laughed.

Catrine envied them. She had been on the ward just over a week and she had already had more than enough.

She searched the list for her name, although she knew it would not be there. She had another three months to endure before she would be moved to a new ward.

Helen McKay was testing her, she was sure of it. And even though every day was a struggle for her, she was determined not to give Helen the satisfaction of seeing her give up.

'Are you going to Wren?' Camilla Simpson sidled up to them. 'So am I. Won't that be fun?'

Catrine noticed the look Winnie and Viv gave each other. She had noticed Camilla Simpson wasn't very popular among the rest of the set, mainly because she was always trying to tell the others what to do. She always seemed to know best, and she was constantly poking her nose into everyone else's business.

'Andrew is joining Mr Tremayne's staff for the next few weeks, so I'll be able to see him every day,' Camilla went on happily.

Once again, Winnie and Viv exchanged a meaningful look. But Catrine was not interested in Camilla Simpson's love life. She was more relieved that she would not have to cross paths with Henry Tremayne any more, since he was in the same cohort of students as Andrew and would also be moving to work with William.

They had been avoiding each other studiously since the incident a week earlier. Catrine was still smarting over the fact that she had been scolded for trying to correct his mistake.

He had been clumsy and inept, but she was the one who ended up being punished for it. It hardly seemed fair.

It sickened her to see him with the other students, following Mr Bose on his rounds. From what she could tell, Henry seemed to get a much easier time of it than the other young men. James Bose was forever singling him out and praising him to the skies.

She wasn't the only one who noticed it; she had heard Andrew Fule complaining to another student that Henry Tremayne was a favourite, and that none of the rest of them ever got the chance to shine.

'I wonder who's going to be taking our places on Holmes?' Winnie said, looking back at the list.

'Peggy, Alice – and Louise Charles,' Camilla said promptly.

They all looked at each other.

'Poor Lou,' Viv said. 'Miss Redmond's going to lead her a dog's life, ain't she?'

'Not necessarily,' Camilla said. 'I'm sure if she works hard, Miss Redmond won't have any chance to complain.'

'Don't you believe it,' Winnie replied. 'If she can't find a reason to pick on her, then she'll probably invent one. You know how much she hates the foreign girls.'

Catrine left them talking and went back to her room. As she reached the first-floor landing, she heard Camilla whispering,

'Did you see that? She didn't say a word to us.'

'Leave her be,' Winnie said. 'She's just a bit quiet, that's all.'

'But she never joins in with anything. You never see her in the lounge or the kitchen. She just stays in her room the whole time.'

'Nothing wrong with keeping yourself to yourself,' Viv joined in. 'You should try it sometime, Camilla.'

Catrine smiled at that.

'Well, I think she's stand-offish,' Camilla declared. 'I asked if she wanted to join my whist tournament yesterday, and she flat out refused. Why do you think that was?'

'Because she ain't an old maid in her sixties?' Viv suggested.

Catrine's smile widened. Winnie and Viv had made the past few days working on Holmes ward almost bearable. They were always giggling and cracking jokes together. And even though Catrine never joined in, they still made her smile.

*

Miss Redmond looked over the new nurses, and immediately ordered Catrine and Lou to go to the bathrooms and get on with the cleaning.

This came as no surprise to Catrine. She was always sent to clean the bathroom, or the kitchen, or to organise the linen cupboard. Any lowly job on the ward was always given to her.

She was usually on her own, so it was quite nice to have company for once. Lou Charles was a pleasant, cheerful girl who seemed happy to chat while Catrine listened.

She told her how she had come to England with her parents a few years earlier. Her father had got a good job on the railways, while her mother cleaned offices in the early morning and evening, and looked after Lou's three brothers in between.

Lou said she had jumped at the chance to train as a nurse in England, because the same training in Jamaica was expensive and her family could never have afforded it.

'I'm grateful, but I do miss home sometimes,' she said wistfully.

'This is your home now, surely?' Catrine said.

'Yes, I suppose it is.' But she did not look convinced.

Catrine perked up when Lou told her about the family's lodgings in Ladbroke Grove.

'I lived there too, when I first came to England,' she said. It seemed like a long time ago now.

'Then I don't need to tell you what it's like,' Lou said. They looked at each other for a moment and then they both laughed.

'What's all this? You're not here for your own entertainment, you know.' Miss Redmond appeared in the doorway almost immediately. 'Haven't you finished this bathroom yet? Perhaps if you spent a little less time laughing and joking and more time working, you might get it done quicker.'

'It's finished now, Sister,' Catrine said.

'Is it? Let me see.'

Catrine and Lou stood stock-still as the ward sister prowled around the bathroom, peering at the taps and plug-holes and running her finger along the shelves. They hardly dared to look at each other.

'You think this work is adequate?' Miss Redmond said at last. 'The chrome is still filthy. Do it again, and this time I want to be able to see my face in it.'

'If I had a face like hers, I don't think I'd want to see it in anything!' Lou muttered, as the ward sister stalked out of the room.

As the morning went by, Catrine noticed how Miss Redmond gave Lou all the dirtiest jobs. While the rest of them were allowed to help with the dressings and to do TPRs, Lou was put to work scrubbing bedpans. If anything was spilt, Lou was summoned to clean it up. But at lunch time, when the trolleys of hot food arrived from the kitchens, there was no sign of her.

'Best if you stay out of the way, Charles,' Miss Redmond told her bluntly. 'The patients don't like girls like you touching their food.'

It came as a shock to Catrine, and she looked around to

see if anyone else had reacted. Peggy and Alice were staring at their shoes, pretending they had not heard. Staff Nurse Jessop blushed, although neither she nor Staff Nurse Philips said anything.

Catrine stared at Lou. She looked embarrassed, her eyes downcast. But she did not seem at all surprised about it.

As soon as she could, Catrine went to find her in the kitchen, to make sure she was all right.

'I suppose so,' she said, although she looked as if she'd been crying. 'I'm used to it, really. Mum says we've got to get a thick skin now we're living here.'

'But it was so rude and unfair. You shouldn't have to put up with it.'

'It happens all the time. If it wasn't Miss Redmond, it would be someone else.' Lou smiled wanly. 'I should probably thank her. I've seen the looks some of the patients have been giving me. It was only a matter of time before one of them told me to go back where I came from.'

Catrine knew what she meant. She had heard some of the horrible comments the men whispered amongst themselves. Poor Lou, she didn't know how she put up with it.

That afternoon, Catrine was given the job of sitting with a post-operative patient. She helped Staff Nurse Jessop put him in the dorsal recumbent position with his head low and turned to the side, as the staff nurse instructed. She then covered him in a blanket and fetched several hot water bottles, which she tucked in at his feet and all around him.

And then she sat and waited.

It was some time before the anaesthetic wore off and the patient finally started to rouse from his deep slumber. He stirred, and shifted his head slightly. His eyes flickered open, saw Catrine sitting at his bedside – and then he promptly vomited.

It all happened too quickly for her to grab the bowl. All her attention was on pressing his lower jaw forward and tilting his head to stop him choking.

By the time Miss Redmond appeared through the curtains surrounding the bed, Catrine was in a very sorry state, with vomit dripping down the front of her apron and pooling in her lap.

'What on earth—?' The ward sister took in the scene. 'Oh, for heaven's sake! Why didn't you fetch the bowl?'

'I didn't have time, Sister.'

'You should have had it ready.' She pulled open the curtain and called out up the ward, 'Nurse Charles, fetch the mop.'

'I can do it.' Catrine reached behind her to unfasten her sodden apron, but Miss Redmond stopped her.

'You've done enough. Nurse Charles!' Her voice rose.

'Yes, Sister?' Lou appeared in the gap in the curtains.

'Fetch a mop and clean this up.'

'I'm the one who caused the mess,' Catrine said. 'I should be the one to clean it.'

Miss Redmond turned slowly to face her, her eyes like chips of black ice.

'Are you questioning me, Nurse Frenchie?' She spoke slowly, her voice ominous.

Catrine looked at Lou. She looked wide-eyed with panic.

'Yes,' she said.

'What did you say?' Miss Redmond stared at her, as if she could not quite believe what she was hearing.

Catrine looked back at Lou, saw her shaking her head. But it was too late to take the words back now.

'You always give Nurse Charles the worst jobs,' she said. 'You never give her anything important or useful to do. All she ever does is clean toilets and scrub bedpans and clean up after everyone. I don't think it's fair.'

'You don't think it's fair?' Miss Redmond repeated slowly. Her face was stiff with shock.

'She's training just like the rest of us. How can she be expected to improve if you treat her like a maid?'

A long silence followed her words. Catrine felt the atmosphere grow heavier, pressing down on her. Outside the curtains, a deathly hush had fallen over the whole ward.

Miss Redmond stared at her, speechless. And then her thin lips curved in a nasty, insinuating little smile.

'What a speech,' she said. 'Let's see what Matron makes of it, shall we?'

Chapter Thirty

'I knew you wouldn't be able to stay out of trouble for long.'

Helen was almost glad her intuition about Catrine had been proved correct. After talking to Dora, she had started to wonder if perhaps she was being unfair towards the girl.

But then Miss Redmond had telephoned, so enraged about what Catrine had done she could barely sputter out the words.

Not that Catrine seemed in the least bit repentant as she faced Helen across her desk, a truculent look on her face.

'Well?' Helen said. 'What have you got to say for yourself?'

'It is Miss Redmond who should be here, not me,' Catrine said. 'She is the one who is wrong.'

'She says you questioned her authority in front of the other nurses and the patients.'

'Why shouldn't I? She was being unfair to Nurse Charles.'

'In what way?'

'She treats her badly, just because she is foreign. She won't even let her serve food to the patients, because her hands are black.'

Helen stiffened. 'I'm sure that can't be the only reason.'

'It is. She says all the nurses from the Commonwealth are dirty and slovenly, and they should go back to their own country. She says they are taking work from decent British girls.' She parroted the words.

'But the girls from the Commonwealth *are* British.'

'You should tell that to her, not me.'

Helen looked at Catrine. If she was honest, she'd had her doubts about Miss Redmond. She had heard tales, and even seen for herself the way she treated anyone she deemed 'foreign'.

But it was a question of discipline. She could not take a student's side against a ward sister. It was simply not done.

'Nevertheless, you should not have spoken to her like that,' she said. 'If you had any concerns you should have come to me.'

Catrine's lip curled. 'Oh yes, I'm sure you would have been *très compatissante*,' she said.

'What's that supposed to mean?'

'I think you are not interested in anything I have to say because you have already made up your mind about me.'

'I—' Helen opened her mouth to deny it but the words would not come. 'I had a feeling you were a troublemaker,' she said at last. 'And it seems you have proved me right. Miss Redmond tells me this is not the first time you have been insolent towards her.'

'I do not understand this word. But if insolent means I do not put up with bullies, then I think I am.'

Helen stared at her. Catrine had her arms folded across her chest, her expression one of absolute defiance.

'I don't think you quite understand how serious this situation is,' Helen said. 'Miss Redmond has made it very clear she does not want you back on Holmes ward—'

'Good,' Catrine said. 'I do not want to go back.'

'Nor can I imagine any other ward sister would want you, once word of this gets out.'

That seemed to sink in. Catrine's belligerent expression faltered slightly.

'What are you saying?' she said.

'I'm saying I don't think there is a place for you at this hospital.'

Catrine stared at her. For a moment Helen thought she saw tears glittering in the girl's brown eyes, but she blinked them back determinedly.

'I'm sorry,' Helen said quietly. 'I promised my brother I would give you a chance, and that's what I've done. But unfortunately—'

'No.' Catrine found her voice again. 'You did not give me a chance. You never wanted me here. And you have been looking for a reason to get rid of me since I started.'

For a moment, Helen was lost for words. Then she said,

'I'll admit I was against the idea. I had a feeling you would bring trouble. But as for looking for a reason to get rid of you—'

'So you want me to leave?' Catrine said.

'I can't see any other course of action, can you?'

Catrine stared at her in silence, and for a moment Helen thought she might argue. Then she turned on her heel and headed for the door.

'Catrine?' Helen called after her.

The girl turned slowly to face her. 'Yes?'

'Don't forget, it's your own behaviour that's brought about your downfall. It was nothing to do with me.'

Catrine smiled a slow, derisive smile. 'If that is what you want to think,' she said.

Catrine left, and Helen sank back in her seat and let out the breath she had been holding.

She was not sure why, but Catrine Villeneuve had a way of getting under her skin.

You did not give me a chance. You never wanted me here. And you have been looking for a reason to get rid of me since I started.

Her words gave Helen a guilty pang, because part of her knew the girl was right. She had been against Catrine coming to the Nightingale. And every day since she had arrived, Helen had been waiting for a telephone call from Miss Redmond.

Frankly, she was surprised it had taken this long.

But had she really wanted it to happen? That was a question she did not know how to answer.

The knock on the door jolted her out of her reverie.

'Come in,' she said, gathering herself.

Angela Jessop entered. Jessop was one of the two staff nurses on Holmes, a plump, smiling young woman who was usually full of bounce and confidence. But today she seemed nervous.

'May I speak to you, Matron?' she asked.

Helen glanced at the clock. It was past three. 'I usually only see nurses first thing in the morning, unless it's an emergency—'

'It is, Matron.'

Helen regarded her in surprise.

'In that case, I suppose I'd better hear what you have to say.'

Staff Nurse Jessop took a deep breath. 'It's about Nurse Villeneuve.'

Helen suppressed a sigh. 'Go on.'

'What she did was wrong,' Angela Jessop said. 'She should never have spoken to a ward sister like that.'

'I'm glad to hear you say so, Nurse.'

'But she was right in what she said,' Jessop went on, her words tumbling out in a rush. 'Miss Redmond is always very unfair to the foreign nurses. Staff Nurse Philips and I have noticed it for ages. But neither of us had the courage to speak up before.'

'Until Nurse Villeneuve decided to stir up trouble.'

'She wasn't trying to stir up trouble, Matron.' Angela Jessop looked earnest. 'Honestly, she's put up with a lot herself and never said a word. Sister has been very unkind to her, too, and she's never complained. She only spoke up when Miss Redmond started picking on someone else.'

Helen was surprised. She would have thought Catrine would be the first to whine if she was ill-treated.

'I know I'm speaking out of turn, but I had to say something.' Nurse Jessop lowered her gaze. 'I know Villeneuve should be punished, but she is such a good nurse. She's very diligent in her duties, and she never complains, whatever Miss Redmond asks her to do.'

'You think she's capable?' Helen asked.

'Very capable, Matron. She's an asset to the hospital. It would be a shame if she ended up being dismissed over this.'

Helen studied her carefully. A sheen of perspiration stood out on the young woman's smooth brow. It must have taken a great deal for her to approach Helen the way she had.

'I see. Thank you, Jessop. I will consider what you've told me.'

'Thank you, Matron.'

Helen went on staring at the door long after it had closed behind Nurse Jessop.

Catrine Villeneuve, an asset to the hospital? She would never have imagined it.

One way or another, it put her in a very difficult position.

'Suspended for the rest of the week? Is that all?' Camilla Simpson could barely keep the disgust out of her voice. 'If you ask me, you got away lightly.'

'We all thought you'd be dismissed,' Winnie agreed.

'So did I,' Catrine said. Even now, she couldn't quite believe she wasn't packing her bags. Helen had said there was no place for her, only to change her mind later.

Even better, she was being moved straight away from Holmes ward. As the matron had tersely informed her, Miss Redmond did not want to see her again. Which suited Catrine very well indeed.

She had been the talk of the nurses' home ever since word got around about what she had done. Catrine had been dragged from her room in the nurses' home down to the lounge to tell her story.

'I wonder what old Redmond said when she found out you weren't getting the boot,' Viv chuckled. 'I daresay she would have been apoplectic.'

'She probably wanted your head on a spike outside the ward,' Winnie said. 'To stop anyone else getting the same idea.'

'I wish I could have been there to see her face when you had a go at her!' Viv said.

'It was a sight to see,' Lou told them. 'I thought she was going to explode.' She looked at Catrine. 'Thank you for sticking up for me,' she said quietly.

Catrine gave an embarrassed shrug. 'It was nothing.'

'Nothing?' Winnie said. 'You stand up to one of the biggest bullies at the Nightingale and you call it nothing?'

'Even I wouldn't have dared do it,' Viv agreed. 'And you know me, I love a good scrap!'

'Well, I think it was a silly thing to do,' Camilla declared. 'You could easily have been kicked out. Besides, you can't go round arguing with the ward sisters whenever you feel like it. It upsets the whole system of discipline.'

'You make it sound like the army!' Winnie said, as the other nurses roared with laughter.

'It is, in a way.' Camilla looked serious. 'The hospital runs on a strict hierarchy, just like a military regiment. Those at the bottom have to respect the ranks above them and learn to carry out their orders, otherwise the whole thing falls apart.'

'Yes, sir!' Viv gave her a mocking salute. 'Whatever you say, sir!'

'It depends who's giving the orders, don't it?' Winnie chimed in. 'If someone's using their power to be cruel or bully the person below them, then I reckon it's right to put a stop to it.'

'Catrine put a stop to Redmond, all right!' Phil laughed. 'I reckon she'll think twice before she picks on another black girl. Or an Irish one, come to that!'

Catrine looked around the circle that surrounded her. They were all laughing, enjoying the moment immensely. All except Camilla, who still looked sullen.

They were treating her as if she was some kind of hero for what she did. But Catrine hadn't meant to cause so much trouble, for herself or anyone else. All she'd done was speak up for what she felt was right. She'd acted without thinking, and in doing so she had nearly handed Helen McKay the very excuse she needed to get rid of her.

And yet she hadn't. Catrine was still mystified as to why.

'I'm going back to my room,' she said quietly.

'Can't you stay a bit longer?' Lou asked. 'Frances and I are making some West Indian food for everyone tonight. It would be nice if you could join us? As a thank you,' she added shyly.

Catrine was about to refuse, but then she changed her mind. What would be the harm in joining them, just this once, she reasoned. They were all so happy, it seemed wrong to spoil the good mood.

And besides, it was just one night of celebration. She wasn't deluding herself that it meant they were friends or anything.

'I'd like that,' she said.

'Well, I won't be able to join you,' Camilla announced. 'I have a date. With Andrew.'

She looked around, as if she expected them to be impressed. They all stared back at her blankly.

'We'll see you later, then,' Winnie said. 'Have fun, won't you?'

Camilla could hear the other nurses chattering and laughing together in the kitchen as she put on her make-up ready for her date.

She almost wished she had not promised to go to the pictures with Andrew tonight. She would have liked to stay in with the other girls, just so she could keep tabs on what was going on. She loathed missing out on anything.

Part of her was annoyed that they were even having this dinner together when she couldn't be there to share it. Not that she enjoyed Lou and Frances's West Indian food, any more than she liked the curries Maya was always cooking up. They were far too spicy for her, and they always left the kitchen reeking for days afterwards. And even though she would never have admitted it to the other girls, she secretly thought Miss Redmond had a point about the Commonwealth girls. They were different. Her father and mother always said so, and she agreed with them.

But she tolerated Lou and Frances and Maya because they were in her set, and they were supposed to stick together.

So it wasn't fair that Catrine Villeneuve seemed to be part of their group now. She hadn't enrolled with them, or trained with them. She wasn't even particularly friendly to them. So why should she be included?

But that was Villeneuve all over, she thought. She always seemed to get special treatment. First she'd been allowed on the wards without going through the Preliminary Training

School. And now, when she should by rights have been packing her bags, instead she was downstairs, being feted by the other girls as if she was some sort of hero, like Robin Hood.

Camilla had no idea why Catrine was treated so differently, but she knew there must be a reason. And she meant to find out.

Chapter Thirty-One

Dora stood sideways and looked at her reflection in the full-length bedroom mirror.

She did not even have to run her hand over her nightdress to see the swell in her belly now. She was surprised none of the midwives at the clinic had noticed it yet.

More to the point, she wondered how Nick hadn't noticed – although she had been very furtive about getting changed and ready for bed every evening. She also pushed him away when he tried to put his arms around her in bed. He had said nothing about it, but he was clearly surprised because she usually welcomed his advances.

Tonight she didn't have to hide herself away because she was alone in the house. Nick had taken himself off to the pub a few hours earlier. It had almost been a relief to see him go because he was in such a foul temper.

But bad mood or not, Dora knew she had to tell him about the baby when he came home. She could not put it off any longer.

She had made up her mind to tell him about the baby earlier, when he came home from work. She had been thinking about it all day, going through it over and over again, practising what she could say.

She had even cooked him his favourite shepherd's pie for tea, hoping it might put him in a good mood.

'I dunno why you're worrying so much,' her mother had said as she watched Dora mashing potatoes. 'I'm sure Nick will be delighted when you tell him.'

'I wish I had your confidence, Mum.' Dora didn't even know how she felt about it yet, let alone her husband.

'You know how much Nick loves his kids. And yours are growing up so fast, two have flown the nest already. I reckon he'll love the idea of being a dad again.'

'Will he?' Dora tried to think positively, like her mother, but doubts still crept in.

Neither of them were spring chickens any more. Would they have the energy for a new baby? And much as he loved his children, Nick had often said how glad he would be when they were all off their hands and it was just the two of them again.

'What's going on, Dor?' her mother said gently. 'I thought you liked being a mum?'

'I do. But I'm forty-two years old, for goodness' sake. I could be a grandmother by now.'

If truth be told, she was embarrassed. She had seen older women like herself, slinking into the antenatal clinic, sitting among all the young mothers. She had seen the way the other mothers looked at them, how the midwives smirked behind their backs.

'And how am I going to tell Winnie and Walter?' she said. 'They'll be mortified, I'm sure.' She shook her head. 'I just don't know what everyone will think.'

'Since when did you ever worry about what people think?'

Dora smiled reluctantly. 'I s'pose you're right.'

Her mother reached over and patted her hand. 'Anyway, the way you're starting to show you won't have to tell anyone soon. So you'd best get a move on, my girl!'

The shepherd's pie was in the oven and Dora had arranged for their youngest son Danny to have tea at her sister Josie's house, so the house would be quiet for once.

Or so she'd thought. But just as Dora was in the middle of laying the table the back door flew open and her youngest sister Bea tumbled in, herding her two young daughters into the kitchen.

'What's all this?' Dora asked.

'Do you mind having them?' Bea was already pulling off their coats. 'I've been called in to work and there's no one else to mind them.'

Dora looked at her two nieces, then at her mother.

'Can't someone else look after them? Only it ain't really convenient,' she said.

'I just told you, I couldn't find anyone else. Anyway, it'll only be for a few hours.' She planted a kiss on each of the little girls' heads. 'Be good for your Auntie Dora, won't you?'

And then she was gone, as quickly as she had arrived.

'Bea, wait!' Dora called out, but all she could hear was the slam of the back gate and the sound of her sister's high heels clattering along the back alley as she hurried away.

She looked back at the little girls' beseeching faces.

'I take it you ain't had any tea?' she said. They shook their heads.

'Mum didn't have time,' the eldest, Shirley, spoke up.

Dora sighed. 'I s'pose you'd better wash your hands. I'll be dishing up soon.'

'If Bea's going to work then I'm Gracie Fields,' her mother declared in a low voice as the girls stood at the sink, jostling to wash their hands under the tap.

'I know,' Dora agreed. 'She really thinks we're daft enough to be taken in by her.'

'Did you see how she was done up to the nines? She'll be meeting a man, I'll bet.'

'I hope he's better than the last one.'

'Mum's going out with Uncle Bob the tallyman,' little Joyce piped up from over by the sink, earning herself a sharp nudge from her sister.

'She told us we weren't to say anything,' she hissed.

Dora's mother rolled her eyes heavenwards but said nothing.

The children were squabbling over the soap when Nick came in. One look at his unsmiling countenance and Dora had realised he was not in a good mood.

'I see the smell of food has brought all the waifs and strays to the table again?' he said grimly.

Dora glanced at the children. 'You don't mind, do you?'

'Don't look like I've got much choice, does it?' He'd sat down and pulled off his boots, caked with mud from another day on the building site. 'I s'pose their mother's out on the town again?'

'She says she's working.'

216

'And you believe that?'

'What do you think?'

Dora looked at her husband. Nick usually came home tired but in good spirits. But tonight he seemed grumpy and unsmiling.

She had waited for him to come over and put his arms around her the way he usually did, but he did not move.

'Are you all right?' she asked.

'Why shouldn't I be?'

'I dunno. You just seem to have the hump, that's all.'

'Perhaps I was looking forward to a bit of peace and quiet in my own home.' He glared at the two little girls.

Dora glanced at her mother, who shrugged helplessly back. She knew Nick could be a moody devil when it suited him, but he'd mellowed in his old age and now he usually loved nothing more than being surrounded by family.

He had eaten his tea in surly silence. Then, afterwards, he had announced he was going down to the pub for a pint.

'Do you have to go?' Dora asked, as she watched him shrugging on his coat. 'I need to have a quiet word with you.'

Just at that moment Joyce and Shirley came shrieking past, playing a game of tig.

'Not much chance of that in this house,' Nick muttered. 'I can hardly hear myself think.'

He did not kiss her before he left, which was unusual. Dora knew he had something on his mind, but she couldn't imagine what it might be.

Had he guessed the truth about her pregnancy? She thought she'd kept it hidden from him, but he wasn't daft.

*

Nick didn't come home until after closing time, by which time Dora was already in bed.

She could tell straight away that his night in the pub had not improved his mood, but she tried to make light of it.

'I was going to send out a search party,' she said. 'I thought you said you were only going for one?'

'There didn't seem much point in coming home early, since the place was a mad house.' He sat down heavily on the bed and started to unbutton his shirt. 'I take it Bea remembered she'd abandoned her kids here?'

Dora nodded. 'I didn't think you minded them coming round?'

'I'd prefer a bit of peace and quiet now and again. We're too old for kids running around.'

Dora's heart sank. 'We've still got Danny,' she reminded him. 'He's only eleven.'

'Yes, but he's growing up fast.' Nick shrugged off his shirt. 'I met Billy Parsons in the pub.'

'Elsie's husband? How are she and the baby doing?'

'Better than him, I should think. Christ, you should have seen him. Turns out he's there every night till closing time, just to get away from all the crying. He says the house looks like a laundry, with dripping nappies hanging up every-where.' He shook his head. 'Talk about drowning his sorrows!'

'I saw him and Elsie pushing the pram round Victoria Park the other day,' Dora said. 'He seemed happy enough to me.'

'Probably just putting on a brave face,' Nick said.

Dora watched her husband undress. Even in his forties

and after nearly twenty years of marriage, the sight of his hard muscled body still had the power to stir her.

Which is what got you into this mess in the first place, she reminded herself.

She had to tell him. Whatever he might think of it, she had to say something.

'Nick, I—'

'I'm sorry,' he cut her off.

Dora stared at him. 'What?'

'I was in a foul mood when I came home earlier, and I took it out on you. I shouldn't have done that. It wasn't your fault.' He lowered his gaze. 'I've got something to tell you,' he said quietly.

Dora's stomach clenched. 'What is it?'

'I've been laid off.' He lifted his blue gaze to meet hers. 'The corporation have said they don't need us after the end of the week.'

'Oh.' Dora understood his disappointment. After ten years, the council had finally got around to replacing the old prefabs that had been put up after the war. Nick had been taken on to help the corporation builder, and it had meant several months of lucrative work for him and his gang.

'You always knew it was going to end one day,' she said.

'Yes, but I thought it would carry on until the end of the year at least.' He looked worried.

'You're a good builder,' Dora said. 'You'll get more work soon enough.'

'I hope so. But in the meantime the next few months are going to be a bit of a struggle.' He reached for her hand. 'I'm sorry, Dor.'

'Don't be.' She squeezed his fingers. 'Like I say, something will come up soon.'

'And in the meantime, we might have to stop taking on your sister's kids so often,' Nick said. 'We'll only just about manage ourselves, without having extra mouths to feed.'

Dora fell silent as Nick pulled her into his arms for a hug. She couldn't tell him, not now.

'Right,' he said when he'd finally released her. 'What was it you were going to say to me?'

'It can wait.'

'Are you sure?'

'It ain't the right time.'

But even as she said it, a small, insistent voice inside her head whispered that it couldn't wait. There would never be a right time, and he had to know sooner or later.

She took a deep breath. 'Actually—' she began. But no sooner had she spoken than there was a knock on the door downstairs.

'At nearly midnight? Someone's having a laugh,' Nick grumbled, pulling on his shirt.

'Who is it, I wonder?'

'If it's your bloody sister coming round again looking for more favours, I'll swing for her!'

Dora sat up in bed, listening to the sound of her husband's footsteps stomping down the stairs. Her heart was beating a frantic tattoo against her ribs. She always feared a knock on the door late at night because it invariably meant bad news.

She instantly thought of her son Walter, away on National

Service in Egypt. Or perhaps Winnie had had an accident at the hospital?

She couldn't bear it any longer. Jumping out of bed, she pulled on her dressing gown and ran down the stairs after her husband.

She fully expected to find a policeman on the doorstep, so it came as a shock to see Joe, the husband of Brenda Cashman, one of the expectant mothers at the clinic. The woman who had already lost seven babies and was praying with everything she had that her eighth pregnancy would be a miracle.

'I – I'm sorry,' he stuttered. 'I didn't know who else to call . . .'

One look at his distraught white face, and Dora was already pulling on her coat over her nightdress.

'I'll fetch my bag,' she said.

Chapter Thirty-Two

There was a new patient on Wren ward when Helen did her rounds the following morning.

'Mrs Cashman,' Jennifer Grace said. 'Came in late last night with a threatened miscarriage.' She nodded towards the curtains pulled around the bed. 'I thought I'd let her sleep this morning. She had quite a night of it, poor love.'

'How many weeks is she?'

'Twenty-two, according to her notes. Apparently this is the furthest she's ever got with a pregnancy.'

'She's had previous miscarriages?'

'Seven, according to her husband.' The ward sister looked sympathetic. 'No wonder they were both in such a state when she started to haemorrhage.'

'Was it bad?'

'Bad enough.' Miss Grace's sombre expression told Helen all she needed to know.

Helen glanced back towards the curtains. 'What has she been told?'

'Just that we need to keep her in to rest for the next week or so. Dr McKay has prescribed morphia to calm her down.'

'Dr McKay?' Helen snapped back to look at the ward sister. 'Has he seen her?'

Miss Grace nodded. 'He was on night duty when she was admitted. Dr Swithin will be coming in this morning to take over her care, but I don't think there's much he can do. Only time will tell now,' she said. But her doleful look told a different story.

'I'll just look in on her before I go.'

Helen tiptoed over and lifted the curtain to peep inside. Brenda Cashman seemed to be asleep, her brown hair fanned out on the pillow around her. Her face was as pale as the white linen on which she lay.

Helen was just about to let the curtain drop when Mrs Cashman's eyes flickered open.

'I'm not asleep,' she said.

'Then you should be.' Helen slipped inside the curtain to stand at the side of her bed. 'The doctor says you need rest.'

'I'm trying. But every time I fall asleep I keep having the most horrible dreams. And then I wake up and realise it wasn't a dream after all.' Her grey eyes filled with tears. 'I'm going to lose my baby, ain't I?' she said quietly.

Only time will tell. Helen remembered the ward sister's grave expression as she had said those words.

'You mustn't talk like that.' Helen sat down on the chair beside her. 'We're going to do everything we can for you.'

'It's just like the last time. And the time before that.' Brenda Cashman turned her face away from Helen. 'I really thought this time it would be different. I just felt it. I thought this time we might have a chance . . .' A fat tear rolled down her cheek. 'It's all I've ever wanted,' she whispered. 'To be a proper family. Joe and me and our baby.' She turned back to look at Helen, her face suddenly urgent. 'I can't lose this baby,' she said. 'I can't. This is my last chance. If I lose it, I'll lose everything.'

'You're not going to lose your baby.'

She hadn't realised what she'd said until she saw the hope dawning in Brenda Cashman's eyes. 'Do you mean it?'

'We'll do everything we can.'

'Promise me.' Her fingers tightened around Helen's hand. 'Promise me my baby will be all right.'

Helen saw her own pain and desperation mirrored in Brenda Cashman's face. She had never suffered the agony of losing a baby, but she still understood the woman's yearning, her sadness.

Only time will tell.

'I promise,' she said.

Just at that moment the curtain rattled back and David McKay stood there.

'Oh, hello,' he greeted Helen. 'Am I interrupting something? I've come to check on Mrs Cashman, but I can come back later—'

'No, please go ahead. I was just leaving.' Helen released the woman's hand and rose to her feet. 'I thought Dr Swithin was looking after her?' she said in a low voice.

'He is. But since Mrs Cashman and I got to know each other so well last night, I wanted to see how she was.' He grinned at the woman in the bed, his dark eyes twinkling behind his spectacles.

'I'm feeling much better, thank you, Doctor.'

'You're certainly looking a lot brighter than the last time I saw you.' David picked up her notes and scanned them briefly before turning back to her. 'No pain? No more haemorrhaging?'

Mrs Cashman shook her head. 'I think it's going to be all right this time. Matron reckons so, too. Don't you, miss?' She beamed at Helen as she said it.

'Is that right?' David McKay sent Helen a penetrating look. 'Well, I'm not as all-knowing as Matron, but as your doctor I'd advise you to take care of yourself and rest as much as possible for the next few days.'

'I'll stay in bed for the next five months if it means my baby is safe,' Brenda smiled.

'Indeed.' David's eyes met Helen's again.

'Dr McKay is right, you should try to sleep if you can,' Helen said quietly.

'I'll do my best.' Mrs Cashman settled down beneath the covers, smiling like a contented child. The troubled look that had shadowed her face when Helen first saw her seemed to have disappeared.

Helen knew David would follow her. She had almost reached the doors when she heard his voice behind her.

'Might I have a word, Matron?'

She pushed her way through the doors into the corridor outside. If this conversation took the direction she thought it would, she did not want the nurses on the ward to hear it.

'What was all that about?' he asked. 'You do know she's going to lose the baby, don't you?'

Helen winced. 'You can't be sure of that.'

'I saw her, Helen. She was haemorrhaging badly. If the foetus has not separated already, it will in the next few days.'

'It might not—'

'It will, Helen. And you giving her false hope is not going to stop that.'

'Then why didn't you tell her the truth?' Helen squared up to him until they were eye to eye. 'Why didn't you say to her there and then that there was no point in her trying to rest, because she was going to miscarry anyway?'

Now it was David's turn to wince.

'You couldn't, could you? Because you knew it would break her heart.'

A pair of nurses sent them an interested sidelong glance as they scuttled past.

'Her heart is going to be broken anyway, whether it's now or next week,' he said. 'Filling her with false hope is not going to change that.'

'But surely any hope is better than none if it helps her to bear the next few days?' Helen reasoned. 'She needs something to cling on to, a reason to go on.'

'And she's going to feel ten times worse when those hopes are dashed.'

'Everyone needs hope to cling on to. Once that's gone, there's nothing left.'

'Is that what happened to us? Did you run out of hope?'

Helen stared at him, shocked by the sudden turn in the conversation. Seeing the yearning in his dark eyes filled her with panic.

'This is not about us,' she snapped.

'Perhaps it should be?' He gave her a searching look. 'Is it something we should talk about, Helen?'

Her heart was beating fast against her ribs. She felt trapped, panicky.

She couldn't talk about it. It would mean going somewhere she did not want to go, probing secrets about herself she could not face.

'I have nothing to say,' she said.

Chapter Thirty-Three

June 1957

Brenda Cashman was knitting. The furious click of her needles could be heard up and down the ward as she worked row after row, her fingers moving feverishly.

'It's a matinee jacket,' she told Catrine proudly when she brought her a cup of tea that morning. 'I've finished the back and both the fronts, and now I've just got to do the sleeves. Look,' she held up her work to show her.

'It's beautiful.' Catrine admired the intricate lacy stitching.

'Oh, I don't know about that. I ain't much of a knitter,' Brenda blushed with pleasure at the compliment. 'But I thought I'd have a go. You've got to do something to pass the time, ain't you? You'd drive yourself silly otherwise, all this sitting around.' She looked around the ward. 'Not that I ain't grateful to you for looking after me,' she added hastily. 'But it ain't what I'm used to, believe me.'

She wasn't the only one, Catrine thought. In the week since she'd been transferred from Holmes to Wren ward, Catrine had discovered that East End women never stopped working. They were used to being constantly active, cleaning, shopping, doing laundry or looking after their kids.

'Stopping in bed,' as they called it, was akin to idleness, and something they never did. The nurses had a terrible job trying to get them to rest.

They certainly weren't used to being waited on. Catrine had grown accustomed to their endless apologies whenever she brought them their meals or topped up their water jugs.

'I'm really sorry to trouble you, ducks,' they would say. 'You must think I'm a right nuisance.'

Miss Grace the ward sister was forever scolding the women for sneaking out of bed and trying to help. Only that morning, two of them had tried to help move the beds into the middle of the ward while the ward maid polished the floor.

At least Brenda Cashman had more sense than to start shifting furniture. She was happy to do anything to keep her baby safe. Although after a few days of bed rest, Catrine could sense even she was growing restless.

Not just restless, either. Miss Grace had warned them to try to keep her spirits up. With nothing else to occupy her, it was all too easy for her to brood.

Now, as she looked wistfully down at her knitting. Catrine could see Mrs Cashman's mind starting to wander.

'Here, drink your tea.' She pushed the cup towards her. Then, leaning in, she whispered, 'I can see if there's a biscuit in the kitchen, if you promise not to tell anyone?'

That brought a smile back to her face. 'Thanks, love. But don't go to any trouble on my account. You girls do enough for us already.'

'It's what they're here for, my dear.'

Catrine turned to see Helen McKay standing behind her, tall and formidable in her stiff black dress.

She steeled herself, expecting a scolding for chatting to a patient for too long. But Helen barely seemed to notice her as she smiled at Mrs Cashman.

'How are you feeling this morning?'

'Very well, thank you.'

'Would you mind if I came and sat with you for a bit?'

'Not at all. I'd be glad of the company.'

Helen McKay pulled out the chair at the woman's bedside.

'I'll have a cup of tea, if you please, Nurse,' she said to Catrine as she sat down.

'Yes, Matron.'

Camilla Simpson was helping with the tea trolley – although she had not shown much interest in the task until she saw Helen McKay sitting by Mrs Cashman's bed.

'Is that for Matron? I'll take her tea over to her.' She snatched the cup and saucer from Catrine's hand.

'If you like.' Unlike Camilla, she had no desire to try to impress Matron. It was a pointless task, anyway. Helen McKay had long since made up her mind about her.

Even so, Catrine had been careful not to give her any more reason to complain. Since being sent to Wren ward she had worked hard and done her best to stay out of trouble.

It was not that difficult for her. Unlike the dreaded Miss Redmond, Wren's ward sister Jennifer Grace was kind and compassionate, to her students as well as the patients. She took time to show them how things should be done, and Catrine had learned a great deal from her.

She was younger than Catrine had expected, too. All the ward sisters at the Sacré-Coeur had been at least a hundred years old, so she was surprised to find Miss Grace was in her thirties, a petite redhead with a ready smile and eyes that brimmed with warmth and laughter.

Camilla Simpson returned.

'Matron comes to sit with Mrs Cashman every morning,' she remarked. 'Why do you think she does that?'

'I don't know,' Catrine said. 'Perhaps she's worried about her?'

'I expect she's wondering when she's going to lose that baby.'

'Don't say that!'

'Why not? Everyone knows it's going to happen. Everyone but her.' She looked over to where Mrs Cashman was chatting happily to Matron. 'Someone should tell her not to waste her time with that knitting of hers. Then perhaps we wouldn't have to put up with those wretched needles clicking all the time.'

Catrine looked back at Mrs Cashman. 'I think while she is knitting she can tell herself there is still hope,' she said.

Camilla frowned. 'Well, that's just nonsense.'

Catrine shook her head as she pushed the trolley down the length of the ward. Camilla Simpson might be a very capable, practical nurse, but she lacked any kind of empathy or imagination when it came to understanding the patients.

When they reached bed three, they found the curtains pulled around the bed.

'Miss Grace said not to disturb her,' Camilla said. 'She only arrived last night.'

Catrine nodded in agreement. 'She's probably resting.'

'Hiding, more like. You know what she's in for, don't you?' She sent Catrine a knowing look. 'Another backstreet abortion.' She shook her head. 'The night nurse said she's in a terrible mess. Everything's turned septic.'

'Poor woman.'

'She's only got herself to blame,' Camilla said. 'She should never have done it. Who in their right mind would get help from someone like that?'

'Perhaps she had no choice,' Catrine said.

In the few days she had been on Wren, she had learned a great deal about the women and the kind of lives they led. She understood the desperation that led to them taking matters into their own hands, often with terrible consequences.

'She should have thought about that before she got herself pregnant, shouldn't she?' Camilla said.

'She didn't get herself pregnant,' Catrine pointed out quietly. 'How do we know the father didn't abandon her?'

'More fool her for not saving herself for marriage, then. Women who have babies out of wedlock are no better than they ought to be.'

'You know nothing about it!' Catrine snapped. 'How dare you judge someone when you don't know their story?'

She hadn't realised she'd raised her voice until she saw Winnie and Viv staring at her from the other end of the ward. Even Miss Grace, sitting at her desk in the middle of the ward, lifted her head briefly to frown at them.

Catrine immediately glanced to see if Helen McKay had noticed, but the matron was still intent on her conversation with Brenda Cashman.

'I was only passing comment,' Camilla said huffily.

'Well, don't,' Catrine said. 'Don't you remember what Miss Grace said when we first started?'

The ward sister had taken all the students aside on their first morning and explained that they had all kinds of women there, many of them going through great personal difficulties and facing situations that could change their lives.

'As well as good nursing care, you're going to need a great deal of tact, discretion and sensitivity,' she had told them.

As the days had gone by, Catrine had started to understand what she meant. Alongside the septic and self-induced abortions, there were also women like Brenda Cashman, who wanted nothing more than to have a baby and couldn't manage it.

It was hardly surprising things got a little tense at times, and it was important the nurses were careful and discreet.

Unfortunately, Camilla Simpson was neither.

Catrine looked across at Winnie and Viv. She wished she had been paired up with one of them instead.

It surprised her that she seemed to be part of their circle now. After that night in the kitchen when Lou and Frances had cooked them a meal, she had slipped into a friendship with the other girls. She had even been to the pictures with Peggy and Alice.

Catrine was still cautious. Especially after what Camilla had just said about the poor woman in bed three. She knew the other girls probably looked down their noses on unmarried mothers too, and she was afraid they would reject her if they knew her past, so she was always careful not to give too much away about herself. But spending time with them was far nicer than being alone in her room with her books every night.

They finished the tea round and were washing up in the kitchen when Miss Grace came to find them.

'We've got a prolapse coming in shortly, and we'll need a bed for her,' she said. 'Make up bed twelve, will you? Mr Tremayne will see her when he comes to do his rounds.'

Camilla instantly took charge, ordering Catrine to fetch the linen from the cupboard. Catrine noticed how she liked to act as if she was somehow senior, just because she'd been at the Nightingale for longer. But Catrine had given up arguing with her about it.

They got to work, watched by the woman in the next bed.

'Who's this for, then?' she asked, setting down her copy of *Woman's Own*.

Catrine opened her mouth to give a vague reply, but Camilla got in before her.

'A prolapse, apparently.'

'Ooh, that sounds nasty.' The woman pulled a face. 'My sister had one of those. Still, I s'pose it could have been worse.' The woman nodded knowingly towards the other end of the ward. 'How's that one getting on? The one who arrived last night?'

'The septic abortion?' Camilla shook her head. 'Not much hope.'

'Shame.'

Catrine stared at Camilla. What had happened to discretion at all times? she wondered.

'We're not really supposed to talk about it,' she said.

'Oh, I won't tell a soul,' the woman assured her.

I wasn't talking to you, Catrine thought, glaring at her partner. Camilla had an expression on her face as if butter wouldn't melt.

'I daresay Mr Tremayne will be coming in to look at her, once she arrives?' the woman went on. 'I always look forward to seeing him. He's so nice, ain't he? And handsome, too. Do you know, he puts me in mind of Gregory Peck.'

Catrine smiled to herself, glowing with quiet pride.

That's my father you're talking about, she wanted to say. Sometimes, when she heard the nurses talking about him, the words almost burst out of her.

But then she remembered her promise. She had to remain a stranger to her family so as not to embarrass them.

'I wonder if your Andrew will be coming with him?' the woman said to Camilla.

'I hope so,' she said.

'Has he popped the question yet?'

Camilla shook her head. 'Not yet. But I don't think it will be long before he does.'

'Love's young dream, eh?' the woman beamed. 'Have you got a boyfriend, love?' she asked Catrine.

'I . . .'

'No, she hasn't,' Camilla put in quickly.

'Oh well, never mind. There's plenty of time, ain't there?' She reached over and patted Catrine's hand. 'You never know, you might find yourself someone just like young Andrew.'

Catrine glanced across the bed at Camilla's smirking face.

I hope not, she thought.

As they walked away, she said quietly, 'I don't think you should be so familiar with the patients.'

Camilla turned on her. 'Sister's always telling us to be friendly.'

'Being friendly is one thing, but they are not your friends. You should not be talking about your boyfriends or gossiping about the other patients.'

'I do not gossip!' Camilla's face flamed. 'And I won't be told what to do by you, either. Who do you think you are, anyway? You're not one of us. You don't even belong here!'

Catrine watched her flounce off, her chin lifted in defiance.

Who do you think you are? You're not one of us. You don't even belong here.

She could not have imagined how much her words hurt.

Chapter Thirty-Four

'Mrs Cashman seems in good spirits this morning,' Helen remarked when she spoke to Jennifer Grace later.

'Yes, she's doing very well.'

'What does Dr Swithin say about her?'

Miss Grace looked sombre. 'He's afraid it may still be inevitable that she loses the baby.'

'But she hasn't had any more bleeding? No pain?'

'No, Matron.'

'Then there's hope for her yet. As long as she stays rested and doesn't allow herself to get agitated.'

'Yes, Matron.' But the ward sister did not look very optimistic, Helen noticed.

She shifted her gaze to the far end of the ward. 'I notice you're having another bed made up,' she observed. 'Who is it for?'

'Mrs Finch. She's being admitted with a severe prolapse. Mr Tremayne is due to operate on Wednesday.'

Helen watched Catrine and the other student making up the bed.

'What do you think of Villeneuve?' she asked.

'I'm very pleased with her. She's turning out to be an excellent student.'

Helen turned to her in surprise. 'You've had no trouble with her?'

'On the contrary, she's very diligent. I never have to tell her anything twice. In fact, she quite often understands what's needed before I ask it of her. A natural nurse, I'd say.'

'Really?' Helen looked back at Catrine. She hadn't expected quite such fulsome praise.

'Perhaps what happened between her and Miss Redmond was just a clash of personalities?' Miss Grace said.

Helen turned to look at her. 'How effectively a nurse works on the ward should not depend on whether or not she gets on with the sister in charge,' she reminded her.

'No, Matron. But I don't think Nurse Villeneuve is the only one who's ever found Ruth Redmond difficult. Quite frankly, it would take a saint to put up with her!'

'That may well be, Miss Grace. But it wouldn't do to let the students know that.'

'Of course not, Matron.' A blush rose in the ward sister's cheeks.

'Now,' Helen said, looking around the ward. 'Is there anything else I need to know before I go?'

'We had a new admission late last night. A septic abortion. We're keeping her comfortable and Dr McKay is treating the infection, but he – oh, here he is now,' she looked past Helen's shoulder towards the door. 'He can tell you more about it himself.'

Helen watched David McKay striding down the ward.

'We were just talking about you, Doctor,' Jennifer Grace greeted him with a smile.

'Something good, I hope?' He looked from the ward sister to Helen and back again.

'We were just discussing the new patient.'

'Ah, yes. Miss Griggs.' Once again, Helen was struck by the way he always used a patient's name. Most doctors just referred to them by their symptoms. 'How is she doing?'

'She survived the night, which is something,' Miss Grace replied.

'It's more than I imagined. I'd better take a look at her.'

Just at that moment a porter arrived, pushing a woman in a wheelchair.

'This must be Mrs Finch,' Jennifer Grace said. 'I'll have to go and meet her and make sure she's comfortable.' She turned to David. 'Are you all right to check on Miss Griggs by yourself, Doctor, or shall I fetch one of the nurses?'

'I'll be fine on my own. Unless Matron wants to come with me?'

Helen looked from one to the other. 'Of course,' she said lightly.

One look at Maud Griggs, and Helen could tell she was in a bad way. She was restless, sweating and feverish. When Helen checked her pulse, it skittered under her fingers.

She checked her notes and noticed she'd been vomiting frequently but her urine output was extremely low.

David was calm and detached as he carried out his examination, and even managed to raise a smile from her. But Helen could see the quiet despair in his dark eyes.

He knew as well as Helen did that once septicaemia had taken its grip on her, it would not let go.

Helen filled the water glass from the jug and held it to

239

Maud Griggs's lips, encouraging her to take a drink even though she was reluctant to do so.

'You have to get plenty of fluids, my dear,' she said. 'Flush all the poisons out of your bloodstream and get those kidneys working, eh?'

'She's quite right, you know,' David said. 'The sooner we get all this nasty stuff out of you, the sooner you'll start to feel better.'

It wasn't until Helen had pulled the curtains back around the bed and they were halfway down the ward that he said, 'If I could get my hands on whoever did that to her, I'd string them up. Bloody backstreet abortionists! They're nothing more than heartless butchers.'

'It might have been anyone,' Helen said. 'An aunt or a friend or a neighbour. They might have thought they were helping her.'

'Whoever it was, I'd like to see them suffer half of what she's going through.'

'Will she die, do you think?' Helen asked.

'I don't know.' David looked bleak. 'We're pumping sulfanilamides into her, so we'll just have to see what happens.'

'Where there's life, there's hope.'

'Now you and I both know that's not true,' David said ruefully. 'Speaking of which, I see Mrs Cashman is still here?'

She was surprised he remembered her, since he'd only dealt with her briefly when she was admitted. 'Yes,' she said. 'And she's doing very well.'

'Miss Grace tells me you visit her every day?'

'I try to see all the patients every day,' she reminded him.

'But you don't sit at everyone's bedside for half an hour, do you?' He looked at her consideringly. 'What is it about her? Why is she so special to you?'

Helen was instantly defensive. 'I had no idea Miss Grace reported to you about my movements,' she said.

'She's concerned about you, as am I.' He touched her arm. 'Be careful, Helen,' he warned. 'No good can come of you getting too involved.'

Helen stared down at his hand, resting on her arm. Then, slowly and deliberately, she detached herself from his grasp.

'I'm sure I don't know what you mean,' she snapped, and walked away.

Chapter Thirty-Five

Just before lunch, William Tremayne arrived on Wren ward, followed by a gaggle of eager-looking medical students.

Catrine had got used to seeing her father on his daily round. Unlike most consultants, who swept past the junior nurses without a second look, William took his time to greet them all politely as they formed a guard of honour at the door beside Miss Grace.

She liked to think the smile he gave her was slightly warmer than the others, but it might have been wishful thinking on her part. Other than a brief 'Good morning', he did not acknowledge her at all.

But at least he looked at her, which was more than could be said for his son. Henry strode past Catrine every day with his nose in the air and his gaze fixed forward, as if it was beneath him to even look at her.

This morning he lagged at the back of the group of students. He looked as if he hadn't slept. His white coat was rumpled and his eyes were bleary.

'Dr Tremayne looks like he's had a night on the town,' Winnie observed, as they followed Miss Grace down the ward.

She was probably right, Catrine thought, remembering the way he'd bragged to his father at Billinghurst. She certainly had no sympathy for Henry Tremayne.

It was unfortunate that his cohort of students had been assigned to William Tremayne just when she had left Holmes ward. It seemed as if Henry was destined to follow her, dogging her steps wherever she went.

Luckily they managed to ignore each other most of the time. Catrine was determined their paths should not cross. She certainly wasn't going to try to help him again.

Miss Grace guided William to the patient he had come to see. She had only been on the ward for barely an hour, but Mrs Finch had already made herself quite at home. Her bedside table was cluttered with magazines, fruit and bars of chocolate, and her bedclothes were rumpled and strewn with sweet wrappers and odd bits of sewing.

Catrine wondered if Miss Grace was blowing a gasket behind her benevolent smile.

She looked back at Henry. He really did look rather unwell, she thought. There was a sheen of perspiration on his pallid brow.

'Now, as well as her prolapsed uterus, Mrs Finch here has been suffering from stress incontinence,' William quoted from her notes. 'Would anyone like to suggest what might be causing this?'

'Cystocele?' a thin young man with dark hair spoke up.

'Correct, Dr Oliver. And what is that, exactly?' He looked around expectantly.

'The anterior wall of the vagina is stretched and forms a sac, which causes the bladder to herniate,' the young man answered again. William gave him a strained smile.

'My goodness, Dr Oliver, you are keen to impress this morning.' A ripple of appreciative laughter went through the students. 'Now would someone – someone else, that is,' he said, as Dr Oliver opened his mouth again, 'like to tell me what the treatment for this might be?'

He looked around for a moment, and Catrine could see the raw panic on Henry's face, and then the relief as William's gaze finally settled on the student beside him.

'Dr Davis?'

'Anterior colporrhaphy, followed by posterior colpoperineorrhaphy?' the young man replied promptly.

'Exactly. Thank you, Dr Davis. Now, if Mrs Finch wouldn't mind, perhaps one of you would like to examine her to see what I'm talking about?' Once again his eyes skimmed the gaggle of students. This time they settled on Henry. 'Dr Tremayne?'

Catrine could see the smirks on the faces of the other students as Henry stepped forward. He was gulping so hard, his Adam's apple was bobbing frantically.

Then Miss Grace drew the curtains round the bed so Catrine couldn't see any more. But when they were drawn back five minutes later she could tell by William's frown and the downcast look on Henry's face that the examination had not gone well.

'Well, I think poor Mrs Finch has had more than enough of us, so we'll move on, shall we?' William said briskly.

'I wonder what happened there?' Viv whispered.

'I dunno, but no one looks happy about it,' Winnie hissed back.

'I'll talk to Andrew later and find out,' Camilla said, a determined look on her face.

Shortly after William Tremayne had left the ward, it was time for lunch. Catrine helped serve the patients' meals and then went to light the urn for their tea.

As she approached the kitchen she heard the others talking. She pushed the door open to see Camilla holding forth to Winnie and Viv.

'Oh, it's only you.' Camilla relaxed when she saw her. 'I thought you were Miss Grace.'

'What's going on?' Catrine asked, looking from one to the other.

'Camilla was just telling us what happened with Mrs Finch,' Winnie explained.

'And what did happen?' Catrine looked at Camilla, but she was tight-lipped. Whatever secrets she had, she didn't seem to want to share them with her.

'He made a complete mess of the examination, apparently,' Viv said. 'Poor Henry.'

'And poor Mrs Finch, by the sound of it,' Winnie said.

'He made an absolute chump of himself,' Camilla said, unable to stop herself. 'Andrew said his hands were shaking so much he could hardly put on his gloves, let alone examine her. In the end Mr Tremayne lost patience with him and took over. He wasn't best pleased about it.'

'I'm sure he wasn't,' Winnie said. 'Fancy his son showing him up in front of everyone.'

Catrine turned away to arrange the teacups on the tray. It was all she could do to stop herself smiling.

Not such a chip off the old block now, she thought.

'It must be difficult for Henry, too,' Viv said sympathetically. 'Imagine your dad being one of the best surgeons in the hospital. I expect it's a lot to live up to.'

'Andrew says that's the problem,' Camilla said. 'Henry Tremayne is very clever, but he's a bundle of nerves because he's so terrified of letting his father down. Although of course, Mr Tremayne isn't really his father,' she added.

'What do you mean?' Viv asked.

'He's his stepfather,' Catrine said without thinking.

The others fell silent behind her. She looked over her shoulder to see them all staring at her.

'How did you know that?' Camilla asked.

'I – I don't remember,' Catrine turned back to arranging the teacups. 'Someone must have mentioned it.'

'I didn't think anyone else knew.' Camilla sounded accusing.

'I knew,' Winnie said. 'My mum trained here with Henry's mother. She married William Tremayne when Henry was a baby.'

Catrine glanced back at her, silently grateful. For a moment she'd thought she had given herself away.

'Anyway, Andrew says Henry's desperate to prove himself worthy of the great Tremayne name,' Camilla went on. 'Although he doesn't seem to be doing a very good job of it so far,' she smirked.

'Poor boy,' Viv said.

'Oh, I wouldn't feel sorry for him,' Camilla said.

Catrine was thoughtful as she stared at the hissing urn, waiting for the water to come to the boil.

She wasn't sure whether to feel sympathy for Henry or not. She had always assumed that life would be so easy for him, but now she saw that wasn't the way at all.

But then, Henry probably didn't help matters.

'Perhaps he wouldn't be so hopeless if he worked a bit harder,' she said.

'What do you mean?' Viv asked.

'He's always living it up with the other medical students, isn't he?' She looked back over her shoulder at Winnie. 'You said yourself he looked as if he'd had a night on the town.'

Winnie laughed. 'I was joking!'

Catrine looked at her blankly. 'You don't think he was at a party all night?'

'More like in the library all night.' Camilla sent her a pitying look. 'Andrew says he's always studying. He's never set foot in the Students' Union bar, and if there's a party at their lodgings he's usually shut away with his books.'

'That's because he's so shy,' Viv said.

Winnie sent her a sideways look. 'You do like him, don't you?'

'Give over! I told you, he ain't my type,' Viv replied. But she was blushing when she said it.

'Are you going to let that urn boil dry?' Camilla snapped at Catrine. But Catrine was no longer listening to any of them.

Chapter Thirty-Six

At two o'clock, the first of the afternoon visitors arrived on the ward. Miss Grace had the afternoon off, so it was left to Staff Nurse Potter to ring the hand bell that signalled the start of visiting time.

Each patient was allowed two visitors per day, and strictly no children were allowed, much to the daily disappointment of the mothers on the ward.

Very few husbands and boyfriends visited during the afternoon, since they tended to be working and came in the evening instead. Several had their mothers or friends coming to see them, and there was usually a clamour to get out on the verandah, where they were allowed to smoke a cigarette.

Viv Trent always volunteered to go out there with them, and Catrine suspected she took the opportunity to have a sneaky smoke too. She certainly always came back smelling of minty chewing gum.

But Viv didn't dare risk it this time as Matron decided to pay her second visit of the day, just minutes after Staff Nurse Potter had rung the bell.

The young nurses exchanged looks of consternation.

'Not again!' Winnie hissed. 'She can't keep away, can she?'

'She's probably come to keep an eye on us, since Sister's not here.' Viv looked annoyed. 'Bang goes my ciggie break!'

Whatever the reason, Helen McKay looked as if she was there to stay as she took her place at the sister's desk in the middle of the ward. Catrine tried to ignore her and go about her tasks, but she was aware of Helen watching her as she moved about the ward.

Just waiting for me to make a mistake, she thought. But she was determined not to give Helen the satisfaction as she stood at the doors, helping to direct the visitors to the right beds.

Brenda Cashman had a visitor, too. Catrine had noticed the woman immediately among the others filing in through the doors just after the bell rang. She was small and dumpy, with rusty-looking dyed hair and beady eyes. And while the other visitors had smiles on their faces, her pinched mouth was set in a tight line.

She was empty-handed, too, unlike the others, who carried bags filled with fruit and chocolates and magazines for their loved ones.

'It's all right, I know where I'm going,' she snapped, pushing past Catrine as she tried to help her.

Catrine watched as she made her way purposefully down the ward to where Mrs Cashman was sitting up in bed, still knitting. She noticed the flash of dismay that crossed Brenda's face when she saw the woman approaching.

'All right?' the woman greeted her coldly.

'Hello, Ma.' Poor Brenda sounded defeated.

'Joe said it was best if I didn't come and see you, but I

can't hold my peace any longer. You and me need to have a heart-to-heart, girl.'

At that moment, Nurse Potter called Catrine away to help Maud Griggs, who had been vomiting and needed cleaning up.

When she emerged a few minutes later, the curtains were pulled around Brenda Cashman's bed.

That was odd, Catrine thought. Brenda usually liked to see everything that was going on around her.

Had something happened? Her heart thumped in her chest. But no one seemed to be rushing to help. There were no doctors on the ward, and Matron was still sitting at Sister's desk, going through some paperwork. Although Catrine noticed that she, too, kept looking towards the closed curtains.

Catrine hovered on the other side of the curtains, listening. Through the crack she could see Brenda sitting up in bed, her head bowed like a child's, as the older woman leaned in towards her, talking quietly.

'Of course, you know what will happen if you lose it, don't you?' she was saying.

'I ain't going to lose it.'

'Why do you think they're keeping you in here?'

'The doctor says I've got to rest—'

'Oh, don't be soft! Everyone knows this baby's going to go the same way as the rest of them. And then where will you be, eh? Of course, you can't expect my Joe to stay with you if you lose another one,' she went on. 'It wouldn't be right.'

'What – what do you mean?' Brenda's voice trembled. 'Joe wouldn't leave me. He says it doesn't matter—'

'Oh, I know what he says. But I'm his mother, I know what he's really thinking.' She leaned in closer. 'Family is everything to him. You know how much he's always wanted children.'

'I want them too.'

'I know, but you can't have them. And if you really love my son you'll leave him, set him free to find someone who can give him what he needs—'

'Excuse me.' Before Catrine knew what she was doing, she'd whipped the curtains open.

The old woman turned round to glare at her. 'What do you want?'

Catrine ignored her, looking at Brenda. 'I'm sorry to disturb your visit, Mrs Cashman, but I'm afraid it's time you rested.'

Brenda stared at Catrine for a moment, and she could see the tears shimmering in the woman's eyes.

'What are you talking about?' the older woman interrupted, her beady eyes narrowing. 'It's visiting time.'

'Yes, but Mrs Cashman needs as much rest as possible. I'm sorry, but I'm going to have to ask you to leave.'

'I am a bit tired, Ma,' Brenda Cashman said.

'But I haven't said everything I came to say—'

No, but you've already said more than enough, Catrine thought, glancing at Brenda.

'What seems to be the trouble?'

Suddenly there was Helen McKay, standing behind them.

'She says I've got to leave.' The old woman pointed an accusing finger at Catrine. 'But visiting time ain't over for another hour.'

There was a brief silence, and Catrine instantly knew she was in trouble again. She steeled herself, but then,

'Nurse Villeneuve is quite right. Mrs Cashman needs as much rest as possible.'

Catrine stared at Helen, scarcely able to believe her ears.

'Well, I've never heard the like!' The old woman huffed irritably, but Helen McKay stood her ground.

'If you wouldn't mind?' Helen was already pulling back the curtains. She was smiling, but there was a hint of steel in her dark eyes.

Finally, the old woman gave up and got to her feet. 'All right, I'm going. But I'll be back, Brenda,' she said.

'And I'll know better than to let you in next time.'

Catrine hadn't realised she'd muttered the words aloud until she caught the knowing look Helen McKay was giving her.

'I couldn't have put it better myself, Nurse,' she said.

Chapter Thirty-Seven

Catrine was late.

William sat at their usual table at L'Escargot, his eyes fixed on the door, waiting for her to arrive.

No matter how many times she kept him waiting, it always made him nervous. He couldn't help thinking each time that this would be the day she didn't come, that she would decide she'd had enough.

He wouldn't blame her. After everything he'd put her through, he deserved to be rejected. She owed him nothing. And yet, as he nursed his untouched glass of wine, he found himself willing her to walk through the door.

When did he become so attached to her? he wondered. Less than a year ago they had been strangers. But slowly over time his fondness for her had grown, until now he could not imagine his life without her in it.

And then he looked up and there she was, threading her way between the tables towards him. William felt a surge of quiet pride. He smiled and waved at her, but she didn't smile back. She never did.

She was always very cool. He wondered if she was still angry with him over the way she had been treated – he wouldn't have blamed her. It must have been wretched for her to be forced to stay in the shadows, unacknowledged and nameless.

She deserved better, he thought. Catrine and her mother had always deserved better.

It was just one of the many reasons he had to feel guilty.

'Hello, my dear.' He stood up and pulled out her chair for her, then leaned in to kiss her. Catrine proffered her cheek coolly, then sat down opposite him.

'I ordered some wine for us. I hope that's all right?' he said.

'Fine.'

She seemed even more distant this evening, William noticed with a flutter of panic.

'*Comment ça va?*' he asked.

'*Je vais bien, merci.*' Her attention was on the menu the waiter had just handed her, even though she always ordered the same food. Snails, followed by a *salade Niçoise*. She would pick at it slowly, savouring it like a true Frenchwoman.

'Millie is looking forward to you coming down to Billing-hurst for her birthday this weekend. And the children are beside themselves, as you can imagine.'

Catrine smiled politely. But before she could reply, the waiter arrived to take their order.

William watched her across the table. There was definitely something amiss, he decided.

'You are all right about coming down?' he said, when the waiter had gone. 'I know it was rather daunting for you last time—'

'Yes, I am happy to come. It was very kind of you to invite me.'

'Of course you're invited. You're one of the family.'

Catrine did not reply, but the chill in her dark eyes spoke volumes.

She had stopped talking about the situation at the Nightingale, but William knew it was still there, a barrier between them.

But what could he do about it? He was helpless, she had to understand that.

'You seem to have settled down very well on Wren ward?' He tried again to make conversation.

'Yes. I like it very much.'

'What do you think of Miss Grace?'

'She is very – *sympathique*.'

'Not like Miss Redmond?'

Her face fell. 'Not at all.'

'Helen tells me you're doing very well. She's rather impressed with you, in fact.'

That made her look up sharply. 'Is she? She told you that?'

William smiled, seeing the eagerness in her eyes. So much for being cool, he thought. That guarded exterior was all a front. Underneath it, she was as desperate for love and approval as anyone else.

Seeing it made him feel even more guilty.

He nodded. 'I believe you've won her over.'

Catrine shrugged, her implacable mask back in place. But William could tell she was delighted.

Their food arrived and he made a few more attempts at conversation, but he could tell Catrine was preoccupied by something. She picked at her food even more slowly than usual, turning it over with her fork but eating nothing.

255

In the end, he could stand it no longer.

'What's wrong?' he asked. 'You have something on your mind, I can tell.'

Catrine had always been direct – sometimes painfully so. But this time her gaze dropped back to her aimlessly twirling fork.

'I am not sure I should say,' she said.

'If it's troubling you then you should tell me.' He leaned closer. 'Go on. What is it? Has something happened? Are you in trouble?'

'Not me.' She lifted her gaze to meet his at last. 'Your son.'

'Henry?' All sorts of thoughts rushed through his mind at once. 'He's in trouble? How do you know?' He could not imagine him confiding in Catrine. From what he could gather, the pair did not even speak.

Unless she'd found out from someone else. An awful thought occurred to him.

'Oh God, is it a girl?' he said. 'Has he . . . ?'

Catrine shook her head. 'It is not a girl,' she replied. 'It is you.'

'Me?'

'He is afraid of you.'

William laughed. 'What are you talking about? Henry isn't afraid of me. Why should he be?'

'Not you, perhaps. But your . . .' she paused, and he could see her searching for the right word. 'Your reputation,' she said finally.

'My what?' William frowned, baffled. 'You're going to have to explain yourself, my dear. You're not making sense.'

'He is worried about letting you down. You must have noticed how nervous he is when he is around you on the ward?'

William suddenly remembered Mrs Finch, the poor woman with the prolapse on Wren ward. He had asked Henry to carry out the examination on her, thinking it would be an easy task for someone as bright as him.

And yet he had not been able to manage it. William could still picture him, pale and trembling, rivulets of sweat running down his temples as he fumbled his way through the exam. He could see the embarrassment on the faces of the other students as they watched him, some looking away, others hiding their smiles behind their hands.

William had been mortified, and so disappointed and angry with his son that he could not bring himself to speak to him afterwards. He had left the ward without saying a word to Henry.

Now, thinking about what Catrine had said, he realised how cruel that must have seemed to the poor boy. He must have been crushed.

'But I don't understand it,' he said. 'I've never put pressure on him. I've never expected anything of him.'

'You might not think so,' Catrine said. 'But he is constantly hearing what a brilliant surgeon you are, and how everyone expects him to follow in your footsteps. He is desperate to live up to your name and be the man you want him to be. How do you say? A chip off the old block,' she said mockingly. 'But I do not even think you know your son.'

'What do you mean? Of course I know him.'

'Do you know that he lies to you? He does not go to parties, and I think he is too shy to even speak to a girl. But he will never tell you that.'

William stared at her across the table. This was all a revelation to him, and yet it made sense.

He suddenly felt a huge sense of sorrow for his son.

'All he wants is to make you proud,' Catrine said.

'But I am proud of him,' William insisted. 'How could I not be? He's a fine young man and I love him with all my heart.'

'Then I think perhaps you should tell him that, not me,' Catrine said.

Chapter Thirty-Eight

Henry had hoped that he would not have to come face to face with Mrs Finch again after his last unfortunate meeting with her.

But the day after her prolapse operation, he was given the task of checking her sutures.

Mrs Finch looked dismayed as Henry approached her bedside.

'Hello, Mrs Finch,' he greeted her. 'How are you feeling?'

'Like I've been kicked up the jacksy by an elephant,' she replied frankly.

'Oh. Right, I see.' Henry checked her notes. 'Is the pain relief helping at all?'

'I'll say it is. Until they wear off, and then it's bleedin' agony. If you'll pardon my French.'

'I – um – I'd like to take a look at you, if you don't mind?'

She eyed him warily and for a moment he thought she was going to refuse. He wouldn't have blamed her, either. But then she sighed and said,

'Go on, then. I don't suppose you can do any more damage, can you?'

Henry pulled the curtain around the bed, flinching as the metal rings screeched along the pole. God, he couldn't even do that properly.

His trepidation must have shown on his face because Mrs Finch smiled and said,

'Don't look so worried, love. I don't blame you for being nervous last time, what with your boss breathing down your neck like that.'

'Actually, I'm his father.'

Henry swung round, shocked to see his father had just stepped through the curtains behind him. Miss Grace was with him.

'Well, I never.' Mrs Finch looked from one to the other. 'I can't see a family resemblance, I must say.'

'That's because he takes after his mother.' William winked at Henry, who immediately felt himself blushing.

'I'm sorry,' he said. 'I thought I was supposed to be doing the post-op check. But if you'd rather do it—'

'Oh no, you can do it,' William waved away the note Henry was trying to hand him. 'I'll just observe.'

Henry caught Mrs Finch's look of sympathy as he removed the pad and set about his examination.

The next few minutes passed in a blur. A hundred thoughts raced through Henry's head at once as he tried to remember to check the sutures were holding in place and make sure there was no sign of infection. He asked questions about bowel movements and bladder emptying frequency, but he was in such a blind panic he scarcely listened to the answers.

Fortunately Miss Grace was there to help make sense of it all. Her quiet, smiling demeanour helped to calm Henry's raging nerves, to the point where he even found the presence of mind to order eight-hourly catheterisation.

But he was still berating himself as he left Mrs Finch's bedside a few minutes later.

'I forgot to discuss pain relief with Miss Grace,' he said.

'She already has it in hand,' his father said calmly.

'And the ends of those sutures looked as if they might cause irritation—'

'We can check them again tomorrow.' He laid a reassuring hand on Henry's shoulder. 'Calm down, son. You did very well.'

'Thank you.' But Henry was still annoyed with himself. Was there more he could have done? Had he put the patient sufficiently at her ease? He couldn't imagine he had, since he was a bundle of raging nerves himself.

He left the ward, and his father followed him.

'Before you go, there's a question I wanted to ask you,' he said.

'Oh yes? What's that?'

He expected his father was going to ask him about his mother's birthday that coming weekend. But William surprised him by saying,

'Why did you choose to go into medicine?'

'Oh dear,' Henry said. 'Was my bedside manner that bad?'

He laughed nervously, but his father's expression was deadly serious.

Henry considered it for a moment. 'I wanted to follow in your footsteps,' he said at last. 'You've always talked about how much you loved being a doctor and saving lives, and I wanted to do the same.' He frowned at his father. 'I thought it was what you wanted me to do. Wasn't it?'

'Of course I was delighted,' his father said. 'But you know I would have been proud of you whatever you did.'

'You sound as if you think I've chosen the wrong career!' Once again, Henry gave a nervous laugh. His father was so rarely serious, it was beginning to make him uneasy.

'I just want to make sure you're happy, that's all.'

'What's all this about?' Henry frowned.

'I've been talking to Catrine. She's worried about you.'

Henry stopped in his tracks. 'Worried?'

'She thinks you're trying so hard to impress me and live up to the family name, it's making you a nervous wreck.'

A tide of mortification washed over him.

'I don't know why Catrine should be such an expert on how I feel, since we've barely spoken,' he snapped.

'It isn't only her. I've noticed it too.' His father turned to him. 'I just wanted you to know that I'm proud that you've decided to go into medicine, but I don't expect you to emulate me or my career. You might decide surgery is not for you, and you'd rather become a physician, or a GP. As long as you don't go into orthopaedics,' he said. 'I think I'd have to disown you in that case!'

Now it was his turn to laugh while Henry stared at him, utterly shocked.

'Anyway, it's probably not a good idea to try to emulate me,' his father went on. 'I was hardly a perfect student in my younger days. I must say, I'm rather pleased to hear you'd rather swot up in the library than get drunk in the bar.'

Blood rushed to Henry's head, making him dizzy. 'What are you talking about? Did Catrine tell you that, too?'

'She said it was common knowledge that you're shy. But

there's nothing wrong with that,' his father assured him. 'We can't all be the life and soul of the party, can we?'

Henry was so mortified he couldn't even listen as his father told him again how proud he was. All he could think of was that he wanted to get away, to separate himself from his humiliation and give vent to his suppressed rage.

Rage that was directed at one person.

Finally his father walked away, leaving Henry standing alone in the corridor. He stood for a moment, and then kicked out in a blind fury. He hadn't even realised what he was doing until he saw the dusty imprint of his shoe on the shiny green wall.

'You should be careful,' a voice behind him said. 'Some of these walls still have cracks in them from the war. A kick like that could have the whole place down.'

He swung around to see James Bose standing at the other end of the corridor.

'I'm sorry,' he mumbled.

'It's quite all right, my boy. We've all had moments like that, I'm sure.' He walked towards him. 'May I ask what's caused it, if that's not too personal a question?'

Henry thrust his hands into the pockets of his white coat, his shoulders hunched. 'It's Catrine,' he mumbled.

'Ah, of course. I thought your sister might be the reason.'

'She's no sister of mine!'

'That bad, eh?' James Bose tilted his head consideringly. 'Why don't you come to my office? Whatever your problem is, you look as if you could do with getting it off your chest.'

*

Henry refused the whisky James Bose offered him – 'for medicinal purposes, obviously' – because he wasn't used to strong drink. But James poured himself a glass and settled comfortably behind his desk.

'Tell me everything,' he said.

'She's been telling tales to my father,' Henry muttered. 'She told him I'm not coping with my studies, that I'm shy and nervous and a social outcast.'

'She's hardly wrong about that, is she?'

'That I'm a social outcast?'

'No, you young fool. But you have been struggling lately, if I'm not wrong?' James regarded him kindly. 'I think you have the makings of a good doctor, if only you could get over your blasted nerves!'

'Not as good as my father,' Henry said gloomily. 'Sometimes I feel as if I'm an embarrassment to him.'

'Nonsense,' James Bose insisted. 'Your father is extremely proud of you.'

'Not as proud as he is of Catrine. She's perfect.' He struggled to keep the bitterness out of his voice. 'She's the one who should be following in his footsteps, not me. He'd never be embarrassed about her.'

'I know that's not true,' James Bose insisted. 'Why would he refuse to acknowledge her for so long otherwise?'

'I suppose it's only natural,' Henry went on, ignoring him. 'She is his flesh and blood, after all. I'm only his son by marriage. He's bound to feel closer to her. And she's so confident and accomplished, too. She knows exactly what she's doing, while I'm just hopeless . . .'

'Now, you listen to me,' James said briskly. 'I happen to

know your father loves you very much. He's regarded you as his son from the moment he married your mother. And as for Catrine, I think he's acting out of guilt.'

'Guilt?'

'Because he wasn't in her life when she was younger.'

'How could he have been, when he didn't even know she existed?'

James Bose hesitated. 'Well, quite,' he said at last. 'But I think he feels bad that he couldn't have helped her more.'

Henry stared across the desk at him. James Bose looked down into his glass, as if he could not quite bring himself to meet his eye.

Suddenly a casual remark from the older man came back to him. Henry hadn't noticed it earlier, but now the words were loud and clear in his mind.

'What did you mean earlier when you said my father had refused to acknowledge her for so long?' he asked.

'I don't recall saying that—'

'You did. I remember your exact words.'

'Well, he hasn't acknowledged her, has he? And it was a very long time before he even told his own family about her.'

James Bose was blustering, Henry thought. Now why would he do that?

And then another remark came back to him, one from a distant conversation on the day Catrine joined the Nightingale.

I've always been good at keeping your father's secrets.

'Uncle James, is there something you're not telling me?' he asked.

'I can't imagine what you mean,' he mumbled. He set

down his glass. 'Now, if you don't mind, I have patients to attend to—'

He started to his feet, but Henry blocked his way.

'I want to know,' he said.

'Know what, dear boy?'

James Bose met his gaze for the first time. His expression was disingenuous, but Henry could see the flicker of panic in his eyes.

'Whatever it is you and my father are not telling me,' he said.

Chapter Thirty-Nine

Frederick Sutcliffe sat behind the desk of his office.

Like the man himself, the room was sparse, almost monastic. The bookshelf behind him was filled with meticulously ordered files of notes and ledgers. The polished desk in front of him was bare, apart from a pristine blotter and the worn leatherbound Bible that Sutcliffe carried with him at all times.

It sat between them now, prominently displayed. William felt as if it was judging him, rather like Sutcliffe himself.

Frederick was a lean man in his late fifties, sparse grey hairs plastered over his balding scalp which gleamed under the harsh overhead light. His face was so fleshless, William could almost see the sharp structure of his skull protruding through his skin.

'I've received a complaint,' he said. His voice had a whiny note to it that grated on William's nerves.

'Oh yes?'

'A Mr Carr. He says his wife was due to have an operation last week, but it was cancelled at the last minute to make way for another patient.'

'Let me think . . .' William paused for a moment. 'Ah, yes. Mrs Carr. She needed some fibroids removed, as I recall.

And yes, I believe I had to postpone her operation until the following day due to a more urgent case coming in. It's standard procedure when there is an emergency admission,' he reminded Sutcliffe.

'That's not the point.' Frederick Sutcliffe consulted the letter in his hands, although William had no doubt that he had already memorised every word. 'It's the nature of this emergency admission that concerns Mr Carr and myself.' He took a deep breath, and William knew what was coming next. 'I understand the woman in question had –' he paused, as if he could not quite bring himself to say the words, '– a self-induced abortion,' he muttered through rigid lips.

'What of it?' William said.

Frederick Sutcliffe stared at him, blinking very fast. He had pale, watery eyes that reminded William of a rodent. 'Do you really think a person like this should take precedence over a woman of good moral character?'

William pressed down his irritation. 'I think that if a patient is haemorrhaging freely and about to die from a septic, lacerated uterus, she should certainly take precedence over one who is sitting up in bed chatting and reading *Woman's Weekly*,' he said. 'Or are you saying I should judge my patients on their moral character before I agree to operate? Perhaps I should get the anaesthetist to question them on their favourite Bible passages before he puts them under?'

'There is no need for sarcasm, Mr Tremayne.' Frederick Sutcliffe was tight-lipped. 'As chairman of the hospital committee, it is my job to uphold the moral values of the Nightingale. I question whether people like this should even be treated here.'

268

'It's a hospital, for Christ's sake, not a finishing school!' William's gaze fell on the Bible lying on the desk between them. 'Correct me if I'm wrong, but didn't even Jesus wash the feet of fallen women?'

'Please do not quote Bible scripture to me, Mr Tremayne,' Frederick Sutcliffe said tautly. 'Now, I trust you will consider my comments and act accordingly in future?'

I'll act how I damn well see fit, William thought.

'Of course,' he said.

As he got up to leave, he said, 'She died, by the way.'

'Who?'

'Maud Griggs. The backstreet abortion?' he reminded him. 'Mrs Carr, meanwhile, is recovering nicely and due to be discharged in a week or two. So having to wait a day to get her fibroids removed doesn't seem to have done her any harm at all.' He nodded to the letter in Sutcliffe's hands. 'Perhaps you'd like to tell that to her husband?'

Frederick Sutcliffe stared at the door for some minutes after it had closed. He prided himself on being an even-tempered man, but William Tremayne always seemed to leave him fuming.

Everyone else on the hospital committee seemed completely enamoured of him. They all thought he was the natural choice for Medical Superintendent. He was an excellent surgeon, they said, who had spent most of his career at the Nightingale. He was dedicated to his work and his patients. All the clinical staff adored him, and even his fellow surgeons – not the easiest of people, in Frederick Sutcliffe's experience – admired him.

But there was something about him that got under Frederick Sutcliffe's skin. It was the arrogance of the man. The way he'd stood in front of him just now, not in the least bit cowed, and tried to lecture him on the Bible. Him, a Methodist lay preacher! He doubted if William Tremayne had seen the inside of a church in years.

He had no doubt that if William Tremayne were to become Medical Superintendent there would be many more such clashes. Which was why he was dragging his feet over giving him the job. The hospital needed a Medical Superintendent who shared Frederick Sutcliffe's moral values.

But with every passing day, the committee was urging him to make a decision. And with William Tremayne the obvious choice, it seemed as if he would be forced to accept him.

Unless God saw fit to answer his prayers and delivered him a miracle.

Frederick Sutcliffe reached out, pressed his palm against the worn leather cover of his Bible, and closed his eyes.

Chapter Forty

On the following Friday, William drove Catrine down to Billinghurst for his wife's birthday weekend.

She was glad of his support after the last time she had visited. She had felt very alone then, surrounded by strangers.

She had been worried that Henry might be travelling down with them, but William had turned up to collect her alone.

'He's getting the train later. He said he had some studying to do in the library,' he said as they set off. 'But between you and me, I think he might be avoiding me.'

'Why?'

'I spoke to him about what you told me.'

'And?'

He didn't take it very well.' William looked rueful. 'He was so mortified it made me realise you were probably right.'

'Did you tell him it was me who'd talked to you?'

'Yes. Why?' He sent her a sidelong look. 'Don't you think I should have?'

Catrine shrugged. 'It does not matter. It is just another reason for him to hate me, I think.'

'Oh, I'm sure he doesn't hate you.'

I'm sure he does, Catrine thought. It was written all over his face every time he looked at her.

'I'm grateful to you, anyway,' William said. Then he added, 'How did you know what was going on? You barely speak to Henry. I'm his father and yet I couldn't see anything was wrong.'

Catrine was silent for a moment, gazing out at the streets of London as they rolled steadily past the window.

'I think I have learned how to understand people,' she said at last. 'I can read their faces, the look in their eyes. It sometimes tells a different story to what they are saying.'

'Did your mother teach you that?'

'Yes,' she said. 'But not in the way you think.'

She paused, wondering whether to say any more.

'Maman loved me with all her heart,' she said. 'But she could be – difficult. Her life was not easy, and sometimes . . .'

'Sometimes she took it out on you?' William finished for her.

Catrine lowered her gaze to her hands. It felt disloyal, confessing the secret she had kept for so long.

'She did not mean it,' she said quietly. 'She was so often angry and disappointed, I think. And sometimes she would be so sad that I was worried she might – do something,' she said quietly. 'I had to find a way to read her feelings, to keep us both safe.'

'My God,' William said. 'You shouldn't have had to deal with that burden. You were just a child.'

'There was no one else,' Catrine shrugged.

'I'm sorry,' he said gruffly. 'I should have been there.'

'How could you be? You didn't know I existed.'

William was silent as he concentrated on the busy London traffic. But she could see a tense muscle working in his jaw.

She didn't have to read his thoughts to know he felt guilty. It was written all over his face.

'It was not so bad all the time,' she said. 'We were happy often. Maman loved me, and she took care of me. She could have given me up as Grand-mère wished, but she kept me.'

It was important that he understood that. She did not want him to think her mother didn't love her. But she wanted him to understand the kind of life they'd had.

She had never told anyone before. She was starting to trust him, she realised.

The straggling suburbs of London gave way to a patchwork of green and gold fields and lush hedgerows.

Catrine noticed that the landscape was dotted here and there with curious-looking circular buildings, each with a tall pointed roof. She had seen them from the train window the first time she'd travelled down to Billinghurst. William told her they were called oast houses, and that they were used for drying hops to make beer.

After a while, the road narrowed to a maze of country lanes. Finally they passed a painted wooden sign at the side of the road that announced they were entering the village of Billinghurst.

Catrine hadn't had the chance to see the village before, and she was charmed by the thatched cottages, duck pond and village green. It was just like a picture on a chocolate box.

'You see that Georgian house, overlooking the green?' William pointed to an elegant building with a pale blue front door. 'That's Lowgill House, the doctor's surgery. Helen used to lived there with David.'

Catrine turned around in her seat to look at the building as it disappeared behind them. It was a beautiful house. She could not imagine what would make Helen McKay give up her life in such an idyllic place.

'Why did she leave Dr McKay?' she asked the question that had been troubling her ever since she'd met the couple.

'God knows,' William sighed. 'As far as anyone could see, they were very happy together.'

'She must have said something to you, surely?'

He shook his head. 'I've asked her, obviously. But all she'll say is that she did what was for the best. Although I don't think David sees it that way,' he said. 'He's still heartbroken, poor chap.'

Catrine wondered if she should tell him about the rumour that was circulating on the ward, that David McKay had started taking an interest in Miss Grace. They certainly seemed very friendly, from what she could see.

But she wasn't sure if William would take kindly to gossip about his sister.

'Is he coming this weekend?' she asked.

William laughed. 'Oh no. I don't think I'd dare invite him after the way Helen reacted last time.'

'But they seem to be on good terms?' Catrine said. 'Whenever I see them together on the ward they're always quite civil with each other.'

'Yes, they are. But I wouldn't expect either of them to allow their personal life to affect their work. They're both far too dedicated for that.'

'So you don't think they'll get back together?'

He shook his head. 'Nothing would make me happier, but I know Helen. Once she's made up her mind, she rarely changes it.' William sent her a sidelong look. 'Except for you,' he said. 'You seem to be the exception that proves the rule.'

'In what way?'

'I told you, she's very impressed with you. She says you're a very able nurse, and a hard worker.'

Catrine smiled to herself as she looked around at the scenery. Wonders would never cease, she thought.

They left the village and followed another winding country lane until they reached the tall wrought-iron gates of Billinghurst Manor. They passed through them and started up the quarter-mile of long, straight gravel drive, flanked on either side by ornamental gardens.

As they approached the house, Catrine spotted Millie outside on the front lawn. She was wearing old corduroy trousers and an embroidered cotton blouse. Her blonde hair was covered by a silk Hermès scarf tied under her chin.

She waved and followed the car back up to the front of the house. As soon as Catrine got out of the car Millie rushed forward and enveloped her in a hug.

'It's so lovely to see you again,' she smiled warmly. 'You're the first to arrive. I've had your room prepared for you, if you want to go straight up?'

'My room?'

'The same one you had last time. It looks over the garden and you seemed to like it last time.' Millie faltered. 'Why? Did you hate it? I can easily move you to another room if you'd prefer?'

'No. No, I'm happy with that room, thank you.'

Catrine turned away quickly so Millie could not see her blushing face.

Your room.

It was such a casual, throwaway comment, and yet it felt like the world to her.

As William was taking the bags out of the car, Lottie burst out of the house and came running down the steps towards them. She was dressed in breeches and boots, her fair hair pulled back in plaits that bounced down her back.

'I'm going riding,' she announced. 'Do you want to come? You can meet my pony, Sienna.'

Millie turned to her daughter. 'Now what have I told you? Give your sister a chance to breathe, she's only just arrived.' She looked ruefully at Catrine. 'I'm afraid she won't give up until you go. She's talked about nothing else all day.'

Catrine stared at Lottie's bright, eager face.

Your sister.

She was going to correct her, to point out that she was her half-sister, but for once she did not have the heart to do it.

'I don't mind,' she said. 'I'll go upstairs and change.'

'That's very good of you, my dear.' Millie turned once again to Lottie. 'Did you hear that? Catrine is going to indulge you. Not that you deserve it, you little pest.'

'Hurry up, won't you?' Lottie said to Catrine, ignoring her mother.

Her room was just as she remembered it. Catrine found herself smiling as she unpacked. Much to her surprise, she realised she was actually looking forward to the weekend ahead of her.

At the bottom of her suitcase was the gift she had bought for Millie. She hadn't known know what to get her, so in the end she had chosen a bottle of Guerlain's Shalimar.

There was a knock on the door. Catrine quickly stuffed the perfume back into her suitcase and covered it up with her clothes.

'Come in,' she said.

Millie entered, her arms full of clothes.

'Since you're going to the stables, I thought you might like to borrow some of my old riding breeches?' she said. 'They should fit you, and I don't want you to get your nice clothes dirty.'

'Thank you.'

Millie set them down on the bed. Catrine waited for her to go, but she paused.

'I was afraid we'd scared you off last time,' she said. 'But I'm very happy you came back.'

Catrine looked into her eyes, so warm and blue and full of love.

'So am I,' she said. And she was surprised to realise she meant it.

Chapter Forty-One

There was no one to greet Henry when he arrived at Billing-hurst in the late afternoon.

'Hello? Anyone home?' He wandered from one empty room to the other, hearing only his echoing voice and the sound of his footsteps until,

'I'm in the library,' Aunt Helen called out.

Henry went to find her. She was standing at the window, looking out.

'Where is everyone?' she asked.

'Outside.' She turned back to look out. 'I think your sister is trying to teach Catrine how to ride.'

Henry joined her at the window. His mother, stepfather and Lottie were in the cobbled yard to the side of the house. Catrine, wearing a pair of his mother's riding breeches, was attempting to mount a horse while the others looked on.

Henry recognised the horse as Dilly, a docile little bay and one of her mother's favourites. He'd ridden her himself when he was a small boy.

And it was just as well she was a mild-mannered old thing, because Catrine was making an awful job of scrambling on to her back, even with the help of the groom. The rest of the family was helpless with laughter.

'Looks as if she's really made herself at home, doesn't it?'

Helen spoke aloud the words that Henry had been thinking.

He looked sharply at her. She was smiling when she said it, as if she was genuinely pleased.

'You make it sound as if that's a good thing?' he said.

'Isn't it?'

Henry fell silent, staring out of the window. Catrine was still trying in vain to mount the horse. And the more she failed to swing her leg over Dilly's fat flanks, the more red-faced with frustration she became.

It would have been quite amusing to watch, if Henry hadn't been seething with resentment.

He was still utterly furious that she had gone to his father behind his back, spreading lies about him. Wasn't it enough that she had all his father's attention, without her trying to humiliate him?

'I thought you didn't like her,' he said to his aunt.

'I must admit, my opinion has changed since she came to the Nightingale. She's really settled in. She works hard, and she's a natural when it comes to nursing. And she's not embarrassing your father, which is what really concerned me.'

Unlike me, Henry thought. He seemed to embarrass his father every day.

Out in the yard, a spontaneous burst of applause broke out as Catrine finally managed to hoist herself up into the saddle. He watched William leading her around the yard, saw the proud way he smiled up at her.

The whole family adored her. She had even managed to win over his aunt. Now Henry had lost his only ally, he was entirely on his own.

Not only that, Catrine's star seemed to be rising, while his was sinking fast.

At that moment his mother looked up and saw him. She waved, gesturing for him to open the window.

'Darling! How long have you been home?'

'I arrived about twenty minutes ago.'

'Why didn't you come and join us?'

'You were having so much fun, I didn't like to disturb you.' He looked acidly at Catrine as he said it.

'Come out,' Lottie said. 'You can help us teach Catrine to ride.'

He looked at his sister. Lottie would usually have been clamouring for his attention, but now she hardly bothered to look at him.

Then his eyes met Catrine's, and for a moment he thought he saw a flash of pity.

'I think I have had enough,' she said.

'But you've just got the hang of it!' Lottie protested.

'It is enough riding for one day.'

Catrine tried to dismount, but her foot got stuck in the stirrup and she overbalanced, falling on to her backside on the cobbles.

Pride comes before a fall, Henry thought, stifling a laugh.

And he knew something that would make Catrine Ville-neuve take a hell of a tumble . . .

Chapter Forty-Two

Catrine wondered if she was the only one who had noticed Henry's dark mood.

Everyone else seemed oblivious to it, but she had noticed the sour look he had given her as he slammed the window shut.

It was hardly her fault that his family were taking an interest in her, she thought. She'd done nothing to demand their attention. She didn't even want to go riding. She had been assured that her horse was a 'delightful little thing', but she still seemed huge and intimidating to Catrine, and lurching around in the saddle had made her feel slightly sick.

When the riding lesson was over, Catrine returned to her room to change then headed straight for the library. She'd meant to spend the time until dinner hiding away with a good book, but when she entered the library she found Lottie playing chess with Henry. William was sitting in the armchair, reading the newspaper.

She was just about to creep away when Lottie spotted her and called out,

'Catrine! Come and play with us.'

'Oh, no, I don't want to disturb you—'

'Don't go,' Lottie implored.

Catrine looked at Henry's turned back. It was as if she wasn't even there.

'Perhaps I will watch you for a while,' Catrine said.

'No, you must play,' Lottie insisted. 'I'm bored with playing against Henry. He's always beating me.'

'You'll only improve if you play against someone better than you,' Henry muttered.

'I know,' Lottie said to Catrine. 'Why don't *you* play against Henry?'

'No!'

'I really don't think that's a good idea—'

They both spoke at the same time.

'Oh, please!' Lottie begged. 'It will be fun. And then I can play against the winner.'

Once again, Catrine looked at Henry's hunched shoulders.

'Go on,' William looked over the top of his newspaper at them. 'It will be interesting.'

'What do you think?' Catrine said to Henry.

Henry did not reply as he snatched up the pieces and rearranged them on the board. Catrine pulled up a chair to sit opposite him.

'Black or white?' he muttered, without looking up at her.

'You choose.'

'You're the *guest*.' He emphasised the word.

'Black,' she said. She could tell straight away from his glowering expression that she'd made the wrong choice.

'Henry always plays black,' Lottie put in.

282

'Then he should have chosen when he had the chance,' William said from behind his newspaper.

'It doesn't matter,' Henry mumbled.

Catrine caught his sulky expression as they faced each other across the board. He was acting like a petulant child, she thought.

She studied the pieces in front of her. Lottie sat between them, her chin resting in her hands, watching avidly. The only sounds in the room were her soft breathing and the ponderous ticking of the long case clock.

Out of the corner of her eye she noticed that William had lowered his newspaper and was also watching them.

She made the first move with one of her centre pawns. Henry promptly advanced one of his own pawns to meet it.

Almost immediately, Catrine slid her bishop out to level with her pawn. Henry met it with his knight.

Catrine frowned. What was he doing? He was supposed to be good at chess. Had he not heard of the scholar's mate? It was one of the most basic gambits in the game.

She looked at him across the board. His face was impassive, but he was gnawing at his thumbnail.

She picked up her queen and moved it. Henry immediately moved his other knight to block her way, and then—

Catrine saw the look of dawning realisation on his face. It was a stupid move. In his panic, he'd exposed the puny pawn that protected his king.

Lottie spotted it too. She started jumping up and down with excitement.

'Looks like she's got you there, old chap,' William grinned.

Catrine looked across at Henry. He looked stricken. It was the same look she'd seen the other day, when he was doing his rounds with William.

Her hand hovered over the queen, ready for checkmate. Then she reached for her bishop instead.

Lottie let out a squeal of outrage. 'Why didn't you move your queen? You could have beaten him!'

'Could I?' Catrine feigned surprise. 'Oh, I didn't notice.'

Henry refused to meet her eye as he moved his next piece, but Catrine could see the colour creeping up from his shirt collar.

They played out the rest of the game and Henry beat her easily. Catrine was just relieved it was all over. All she wanted to do was escape back to her room.

'I take it you did that on purpose?' William said when they were alone.

Catrine was about to deny it when she caught his eye.

'The game was more important to him than it was to me,' she said.

William returned to his newspaper. 'He won't thank you for it, you know,' he said. 'Henry is no fool. And he has his pride.'

He was right, of course.

Catrine was in her room getting ready for dinner when there was a knock on the door and Henry burst in.

'Do you mind?' Catrine turned on him. 'I might have been getting dressed—'

'What do you think you're playing at?' Henry interrupted her.

Catrine turned away from him, back to her reflection in the dressing table mirror. 'I don't know what you mean,' she said, fiddling with her earring.

'Oh, come on! Even Lottie could see you were letting me win that chess game. Did you want to make me look a fool, is that it?'

'Why would I let you win if I wanted you to look foolish?' Catrine reasoned. But Henry was too angry to listen.

'That's why you went behind my back to my father,' he said. 'You're trying to make yourself look good by making me look bad.'

'I was only trying to help,' she said.

'No, you weren't. You're trying to push me out so you can have my father all to yourself.'

'Now you're being ridiculous.'

Catrine watched his reflection with amusement. He reminded her of a caged bear in a zoo, pacing up and down the room.

'Stop being so dramatic,' she said. 'It was only a chess game.'

Henry stopped dead, glaring at her reflection. His face was dark with anger. 'You shouldn't be here,' he hissed. 'No one wants you here. You don't belong in this family.'

He could not have delivered a more devastating insult if he'd tried. His words felt like a punch, knocking the wind out of her.

You don't belong here.

She had grown up hearing those words, feeling like an outsider. But not any more.

'You're wrong,' she said. 'This is my family too. I have as much right to be here as you do.'

'Then how come—' he broke off.

'What?'

'Nothing,' he said sulkily.

She put down the earring she had been fiddling with and rose to her feet. 'What were you going to say?' she demanded.

He faced her across the room. 'Why don't you ask my father?' he said.

'Don't you mean *my* father?'

She would never have said it. She didn't even mean it. But she was so shaken from what Henry had said that she wanted to lash out, to hurt him as much as he'd hurt her.

But her words seemed to unlock something inside Henry. He smiled slowly, his handsome features twisting in spite.

'Of course,' he said, his voice soft. 'Your father. You think you're so special, don't you? William Tremayne's long-lost daughter. The child he never knew he had.'

There was something about the way he said it that made the hairs prickle on the back of her neck. Suddenly she wanted him to stop, to hold back the words he was about to release.

'Henry—'

'Except he did.'

The world seemed to stop for a moment. The ticking of the clock and the distant hum of voices from downstairs ceased abruptly, leaving only a tense, silent void.

Even the air seemed to disappear; suddenly, Catrine found herself fighting to breathe.

'What do you mean?' Her words came out as a whisper.

'I spoke to James Bose. He's been friends with my father for years, right from when they were at college. He knows all his secrets.'

He looked straight at her, his mouth twisted in a knowing, malicious smile.

'My father received that letter from your mother,' he said.

Chapter Forty-Three

'You're lying,' she said.

'I don't care if you believe me or not, but it's the truth.'

She shook her head. 'He told me he'd moved on, been stationed elsewhere. The letter got lost—'

'He was still at Highwood House,' Henry said. 'James Bose says he remembers him receiving it. He says he panicked and threw it on the fire.'

On the fire.

Catrine pictured her mother sitting down to write that letter. She imagined how alone and scared she must have felt, how she must have agonised over every word. It would have been the most important letter she had ever written; her future, her very survival depended on it. She would have poured all her fears into it, imploring William not to abandon her, to save her from her lonely fate.

And he had tossed it on the fire as if it were nothing.

All her old hatred and resentment rose up inside her. And to think she'd started to like him, to feel part of his family. Just like her mother, she had let her guard down, put her trust in him, and he'd betrayed her.

Never again.

*

Catrine sat down on the bed after Henry had gone, her mind spinning. She didn't know what to think, what to do.

Even now, she could feel herself making excuses for William, wanting desperately to believe that it wasn't true.

Henry might be lying. He was jealous of her, he'd made that plain enough. Perhaps he was trying to hurt her, to drive a wedge between her and her father?

But even as her mind scrabbled to believe it, she knew it wasn't the truth.

She looked around the room. Her room, Millie had called it. But now the walls seemed to be closing in on her.

She didn't want to believe it because she'd grown fond of this place, and the family who lived there. She had started to think she might have finally found somewhere to belong, among people who cared about her.

And now, in the space of a few minutes, all that had gone and she was alone again.

The dinner bell rang, shattering the peace. Catrine jerked at the sound of it.

Her first instinct was to ignore it, to shrink away and hide and never come out. The last thing she wanted to do was sit down among all those people, to look at their blandly smiling faces and pretend that all was well. She couldn't do it, she wouldn't be physically able.

But she couldn't hide away, either. And why should she? She had no reason to feel ashamed. She had not lied or betrayed anyone.

She forced herself to go downstairs, moving stiffly, like an automaton. Her blazing anger had seeped away, leaving her numb.

Just one more dinner, she told herself. *Sit there, smile, say nothing and then you can escape.*

But her nerve nearly failed her when she saw them all gathered around the table, waiting for her. Millie, Helen, Henry – and William. Catrine could not bring herself to meet his eye as she took her place at the far end of the table.

'Are you all right, my dear?' Millie asked her. 'You look rather pale.'

Catrine did not lift her gaze to look at her. 'Just a headache,' she murmured.

'Oh, I'm sorry to hear that. Can I fetch you an aspirin?'

'No, thank you.'

The meal was served. Catrine's stomach roiled as it was put in front of her. Even the smell of it made her feel sick.

She picked up her knife and fork, but no matter how hard she tried she could not force down a single bite.

It was too much to hope that Millie wouldn't notice.

'Now you're not eating,' she said. 'Goodness, I do hope you're not sickening for something?'

'Perhaps it's a migraine?' Helen said. 'You should lie down with a cold compress after dinner.'

'Now Henry doesn't seem to be eating, either,' Millie said worriedly.

Catrine glanced up briefly. Henry sat at the other end of the table, staring down at his plate, looking pale and tense.

'It must be catching,' William said.

'Don't say that,' Millie begged. 'It would be such a miserable birthday if we were all in our beds.'

'We can't have that, can we?' William smiled fondly at his wife. The sight of them made Catrine feel even more sick.

He looked as if he didn't have a care in the world. And why should he? He had everything he wanted in life.

The dinner limped on. The servants removed Catrine's untouched plate and replaced it with another course.

The conversation swirled around her, but she scarcely listened. Fortunately no one seemed to want to involve her in it.

She risked another glance at Henry. He was picking at his food with little enthusiasm, a fixed smile on his face. Strangely, she couldn't even feel angry with him. All her feelings were focused on the man who had betrayed her.

'What about a game of charades after dinner?' William suggested.

'Good idea,' Millie said. 'Have you ever played charades, Catrine?'

Catrine stared at her father. 'Oh yes, I know all about charades.'

'I don't think Catrine is well enough for silly parlour games,' Helen said. 'Nor Henry, come to that.'

Catrine caught Henry's eye. He looked utterly stricken.

Millie looked from one to the other. 'You two have been awfully quiet. Is there something going on?' She sighed. 'Oh dear, you haven't had words, I hope?'

Catrine rose to her feet. 'Excuse me, Madame. I would like to go to my room.'

'Of course, but—'

She did not wait to hear the rest. As she reached the stairs, she heard Millie say,

'I knew she was upset about something. What on earth have you been saying to her, Henry?'

Catrine was throwing her clothes haphazardly back into her suitcase when there was a knock on the door.

'Catrine?' She stiffened at the sound of William's voice. He was the last person she wanted to see, but at the same time her rage would not allow her to ignore him.

'Come in.'

'I just wanted to make sure you were ' His gaze fell to the suitcase on the bed. 'What's going on?'

'I'm leaving.'

'Why?'

She ignored him, turning away to fold up her nightdress. She couldn't even bring herself to look at him.

'The last train left hours ago.'

'Then I'll walk. I need to get away. I can't stay here.'

'What's brought this on?'

As she turned back to stuff her nightdress into her bag, William reached out and grasped her wrist. 'Catrine, tell me!'

She stared down at his fingers, circling her wrist. 'Did you know about me?'

'What?'

'Before I came to look for you. Did you know about me?'

The colour drained from his face. He released his grip and sat down on the bed.

'How did you find out?' he said heavily.

At least he didn't try to deny it. Catrine wasn't sure she could have stood another lie.

'Your good friend James Bose told Henry. And he took great delight in telling me.'

'Bose had no right to say anything.'

'No, but you should have. Or did you think I'd never

find out?' She could feel her anger rising, and fought to keep control.

William lifted his gaze to look at her. He looked defeated.

'I'm sorry,' he said. 'You're right, I should have told you. And believe me, I wanted to. You don't know how many times I've—'

'So why didn't you?'

'I didn't want to lose you.'

His words took her by surprise. Catrine stared at him in silence.

'When you first appeared, I – I couldn't face up to what I'd done,' William went on. 'I felt so guilty, realising what you and your mother had gone through. I suppose up until then I'd managed to convince myself that what I'd done didn't matter, that Romy had found someone else, got married. I told myself you had a happy life and a loving family—'

'Like yours, you mean?' Catrine said bitterly.

'Yes, I suppose so.' William's shoulders slumped. 'I felt so guilty about what you'd gone through, and at first all I wanted to do was make it up to you. But then, as time went by and I got to know you, I realised I couldn't tell you the truth. I was scared that if you found out you wouldn't be able to forgive me. And I couldn't bear the thought of losing you.'

Catrine stared at him. Was he lying again? It was so hard to know. Now her trust in him had been shattered, she could not believe anything that came out of his mouth.

'How am I supposed to forgive you?' she said. 'You abandoned my mother, left us alone—'

'I know. There was no excuse for what I did. Except that I was young and selfish.' He lifted his gaze to meet hers. 'I thought it was over between us. When Romy sent me that letter, I panicked. I didn't know what to do.'

'And so you threw it on the fire?'

'Yes,' he admitted heavily. 'I talked to James, and he said I should ignore it. We were moving on, being stationed elsewhere. The war was going on all over Europe, and none of us knew what was going to happen. I let myself be persuaded that I shouldn't allow one mistake to ruin my life—'

'It ruined my mother's life,' Catrine said quietly.

'I had no idea of what she was going through.'

'She was an unmarried mother! What did you think would happen to her?'

'I didn't know!'

'And you didn't care, either. You didn't care if we lived or died, as long as you were free to have the life you wanted.' She looked around the room. 'I don't blame you,' she said. 'I'm sure my mother would have liked this life, if she'd had the chance.'

'You're right,' he said. 'I deserve everything you say to me. I let you and your mother down. But you coming back to find me has given me the chance to make amends, to give you the life you should have had.' He looked at her imploringly. 'Won't you give me that second chance?'

Catrine stared at him coldly.

'My mother did not get a second chance. Why should you?'

She snatched up her suitcase from the bed.

'Wait,' William said. 'At least stay until the morning. You've got nowhere else to go.'

'I don't care,' Catrine said. 'I won't stay here another night. I don't belong here. This is your family, not mine.'

Chapter Forty-Four

Helen was standing in the hall when Catrine dragged her case downstairs. One look at her face told Catrine that she knew what was going on.

'You're leaving,' she said.

'Yes.' Catrine lifted her chin defiantly. 'And you're not going to stop me.'

'I'm not going to try.' Helen's gaze dropped to her suitcase. 'But where will you go at this time of night?'

'I don't know and I don't care.'

'Well, that sounds very practical, I must say.' Helen paused for a moment, then said, 'Wait there a moment.'

She disappeared into the drawing room. Catrine edged towards the front door nervously, ready to run if one of the family appeared. She did not have the strength to face any of them.

A moment later, Helen reappeared. She was wearing her coat and carrying a set of car keys.

'Come with me,' she said, breezing past Catrine to the front door.

'Where are we going?' Catrine asked as they headed out into the cool night.

'I'm taking you somewhere you can stay for the night.'

She led the way around the side of the house to where Millie's sporty red car was parked.

'She said I could borrow it,' Helen said, jingling the keys. 'I'm afraid it's not exactly practical for a chilly night, but luckily we're not going far. Well, don't just stand there – get in,' she said. She sounded so brisk, Catrine felt compelled to follow her instruction.

They drove to the village and parked close by the green. 'Here we are.'

Even in the darkness, Catrine recognised the elegant Georgian cottage with its shiny brass plate by the front door.

Lowgill House Surgery.

'There's a locum, but he doesn't stay here at weekends,' Helen said as she unlocked the front door.

Inside the house was just as she'd imagined. It was elegant and tasteful but homely. The duck-egg blue walls were hung with paintings, and the dresser was filled with beautiful hand-painted china. Everything looked as if it had been lovingly and carefully chosen. But Catrine noticed that Helen kept her eyes down as she went around the house turning on the lamps, almost as if she couldn't bear to look around her.

'I'll look in the kitchen and find you something to eat,' Helen said. Catrine shook her head.

'I'm not hungry.'

'In that case, I'll make a bed up for you—' She started towards the stairs, but Catrine said,

'I can do it myself if you tell me where to find the linen.'

Helen looked as if she was about to refuse. Then she smiled and said, 'I suppose you do know how to make a bed, don't you? The linen cupboard is at the top of the stairs, at the far end of the landing. It's right next to the bedroom you'll be using.'

The room couldn't have been more different from the wood-panelled splendour of the bedroom at Billinghurst. But it was cosy and comfortable, and it was a long way from William Tremayne and his family, which was what Catrine most wanted at that moment.

She had just finished making up the bed when Helen came up the stairs. She immediately stood to one side, her hands behind her back, as if awaiting inspection.

Helen smiled. 'It's all right, Nurse Villeneuve, you're not on duty now.' She handed her a hot water bottle. 'Here, I've brought you this. It will take the chill off the sheets. I've also found some medicinal brandy, if you'd like me to fetch one for you? It's very good for shock.'

'Thank you,' Catrine said. She needed something to fortify her. Her rage had ebbed slightly, leaving her feeling numb and exhausted.

She quickly changed into her nightclothes and was in bed by the time Helen returned with the brandy.

'Here,' she handed it to her. 'Now, is there anything else you need before I go?'

'No, thank you. Except for this—' She held out the bottle of perfume she had taken out of her suitcase.

'What's this?' Helen asked.

'It is a birthday present for Millie. Will you give it to her for me? Tell her I am sorry I didn't get the chance to wrap it.'

Helen looked down at the bottle in her hands and Catrine could have sworn she was blinking back tears.

'Are you sure you don't want to give it to her yourself?' she said quietly.

Catrine shook her head. 'No,' she said quickly. 'I can't go back there.'

'I understand.' Helen paused for a moment. 'I know why you had to leave,' she said quietly. 'Henry told us what happened.' She looked at Catrine. 'All I can say is I'm sorry. I've spent my life making excuses for my brother's behaviour, but I can't this time. What he did was shabby and appalling, and I don't blame you for being angry.'

'So you didn't know?'

'Of course I didn't! If I had, I would have made William face up to his responsibilities. Which is probably why he didn't tell me,' she added quietly.

At least she wasn't lying, Catrine thought. Her face was taut, and she looked every bit as upset and disappointed as Catrine.

'What will you do now?' Helen asked.

'I don't know. But I know I can't stay. Not now.' She paused. 'I think I'll have to go home.'

'Back to France, you mean?'

'Yes.' But even as she said it, sadness overcame her. She hadn't realised how attached she had become to the Nightingale until she was faced with the prospect of leaving it.

'Perhaps you should take a few days to think about it?' Helen suggested. 'I'll speak to Miss Grace and tell her you're on leave until further notice.'

'No,' Catrine said. 'I would like to work if I can. The ward is very busy, and I know Sister needs me. And if I am not there, the other girls will ask questions . . .'

Helen nodded understandingly. 'Then why don't I put you on nights?' she suggested. 'That way you won't have to see anyone if you don't want to.'

Catrine nodded gratefully. She couldn't face the thought of seeing William again. Not yet.

Maybe not ever.

'Now get some sleep,' Helen said.

Catrine settled down, pulling the bedclothes up around her. Helen immediately stepped forward to tuck her in, like a child. She was surprisingly tender, and Catrine caught a glimpse of what a good nurse she must have been.

'I'll come and see you in the morning, and give you a lift to the station,' she said. 'If that's what you still want?'

'I'm not going to change my mind,' Catrine said firmly.

'Let's not make any rash decisions until you've had time to think about it.' Helen gave the covers a final tweak, then turned to go.

When she reached the door she turned back.

'If it means anything, I'm sure William is truly sorry for what he did,' she said. 'I know you've come to mean a great deal to him. And to all of us.'

She left, and Catrine listened to the sound of her footsteps descending the stairs, then the front door closing softly behind her. Only then did she allow herself to give in to the tears that had been threatening to burst out of her. Her head ached with the effort of holding in her emotions.

Her body was tired, but her mind fizzed with thoughts and ideas.

She couldn't stop thinking about what William had done.

It didn't matter how remorseful he was. He had abandoned her mother, and he had lied to her.

She was angry with him, but even more angry with herself for allowing herself to believe him. He had held out the promise of a new life and a family of her own, and she had been so desperate she had let down her guard and reached out for it, only to be let down again.

She should have listened to her mother. Romy had told her that he was a liar, the man who ruined her life.

He should pay, Catrine thought. He'd taken away her mother's happiness, so she should take away his.

Don't make any rash decisions until you've had time to think about it.

Helen's words came into her mind, but Catrine pushed them aside. It might be wise advice, but she was too angry to listen to wisdom.

The only one who was going to regret her decision was William Tremayne.

Chapter Forty-Five

'You mean to tell me you knew about her all this time, and you didn't say anything to anyone?'

William had seldom seen his wife so outraged. Millie was such a sweet-natured soul, she tended to see the best in everyone.

But from the way she faced William now, there was no doubting her utter contempt and disgust.

And he deserved it. There was nothing his wife could say that could make him feel any more wretched than he already was.

'You lied to me, too,' Millie said. 'You should have told me.'

'I know,' he said heavily. 'Believe me, there are a lot of things I wish I'd done differently now.'

He looked at Henry, who sat silently in the corner. 'You should have talked to me before you went to Catrine,' he said.

'She deserved to know,' Henry muttered. But from the way he hung his head, he realised he'd played a big part in what had gone wrong.

William couldn't be angry with him, because he knew deep down what Henry said was right. Catrine did deserve to know the truth. Henry had only done what William had been too cowardly to do for the past eighteen years.

'That poor girl,' Millie said. 'As if she hasn't been through enough already, losing her mother. And now this.' She shook her head in sorrow. 'And she was so happy, wasn't she? Just a few hours ago, I was thinking how well she'd settled in. She'd just started to trust us . . .'

The front door opened and they all looked around sharply.

'That must be Helen coming back,' Millie said. 'Do you think she'll have Catrine with her?'

William hardly dared to hope. But that didn't stop his heart sinking when his sister walked into the drawing room alone.

'How is she?' Millie asked.

'Very upset, as you can imagine. I've taken her to Lowgill House for the night.'

'But she'll be on her own! I should go to her.' Millie started to her feet, but Helen shook her head.

'Best leave her for now,' she said. 'I don't think she wants to see anyone just yet.'

She glared at William when she said it.

'What did she say?' he asked.

'No more than she's said to you, I'm sure.' Then she added, 'But she did say she was going to go back to France.'

'No!' Millie looked distraught. 'She can't go.' She turned to William. 'You've got to do something,' she pleaded.

'What can I do?'

'I don't know, but you need to make her stay. She's part of our family now.'

He turned away, blinking back the tears that suddenly sprang to his eyes.

Millie was right, she was part of their family. And he'd driven her away.

'I don't think there's anything he can do,' Helen said. 'Since he's the reason she's leaving.'

'And I'm sure you're heartbroken she's going,' William turned on her, guilt and sadness making him snap.

'What's that supposed to mean?'

'You never wanted her here in the first place. You certainly never wanted me to acknowledge her.'

'You kept her a secret from your own family for six months!'

'Yes, but you're the one insisting that I keep her a secret at the hospital. How do you think that makes her feel, having her own father walking past her as if she's a stranger?'

'Why not tell the world, then, if you're that upset about it? I'm not stopping you,' Helen shot back. 'Oh, I forgot. You want that Medical Superintendent's job, don't you?' Her face flamed with anger. 'You agreed it was a good idea at the time, so don't try to pretend differently now!'

'Stop it, both of you!' Henry begged.

'Henry's right,' Millie said. 'Squabbling isn't going to help anything.'

William stared into his sister's eyes. Without thinking, they'd found themselves toe to toe, shouting into each other's faces in a way they hadn't done since they were children.

'You're right,' Helen said quietly. 'I think we've all let her down in one way or another.'

'But can we make it up to her?' Millie said. 'Is there some way of showing her how much she means to us?'

Helen shook her head. 'I think it's too late for that,' she

303

said. 'From what I could see, Catrine Villeneuve is finished with this family. And I'm afraid I can't say I blame her.'

'I'm so sorry, William. I never intended this to happen. I wish I'd never said anything to Henry.'

James Bose was full of apologies when William telephoned him. It was late in the evening and his friend had answered the phone bleary with sleep. But William could not wait until the morning to confront him over what he had done.

'No,' William said. 'You shouldn't.'

'I didn't mean to tell him, honestly. But he'd already worked it out. You know I would never have willingly broken your confidence.'

He sounded so wretched, William felt the heat of his anger ebbing away. James had always been one of his most trusted friends. He had kept his secret for so many years, and William knew deep down that his friend would never have deliberately betrayed him.

Besides, Henry had already told him that he'd forced Bose into his confession.

'I know,' he sighed.

The truth was, William was the only one to blame. He was the one who had decided to turn his back on Romy and his unborn child all those years earlier. The burden was his and his alone.

It was time he faced up to the truth of who he really was.

'I don't know what to do,' he said. 'Catrine is going back to France. I can't lose her.'

'Perhaps it's for the best?' James suggested gently. 'You've taken a huge risk having her here for this long. Frankly, it's a miracle you haven't been caught out. If Frederick Sutcliffe was to find out—'

'Damn Frederick Sutcliffe!' William cut him off. 'I've got bigger things to think about.'

'Bigger than the Medical Superintendent's job?' Bose said. 'I hardly think so, Will. You've wanted that position for years. It means everything to you.'

'Catrine means everything to me.'

He hadn't realised it until he said the words out loud.

'From what you've told me, it sounds as if you've already burned your bridges with her,' James replied bluntly.

'Don't say that.' There had to be a way of winning Catrine back, to show her he'd changed, that he'd learned from the mistakes of his past. To show her that he wanted her in his life more than anything . . .

A plan slowly began to form in his mind.

'If you want my advice, you should just let her go,' James continued. 'Honestly, it will be best for everyone. You've got to know each other, she's satisfied her curiosity about you. Now she can go home and you can both go back to your lives. Believe me, it's the only sensible thing to do.'

He was right, William thought. But . . .

'Since when have I ever been sensible?' he said.

He heard his friend sigh on the other end of the line.

'I do hope you're not intent on doing something rash?' he said. 'Listen to me, William. You've already made enough mistakes in your life, don't you think?'

'Yes,' William said. 'Yes, I have.'

Which was exactly why he did not intend to make another one.

Chapter Forty-Six

'Have you heard? Catrine's moving to nights.'

'Never! Since when?'

'Tomorrow, according to the Home Sister. She's upstairs now, packing her bag to move to the Night Nurses' Block.'

'That's a bit rum, ain't it?'

'That's what I thought. No one moves to nights out of the blue like that. Not without a good reason, anyway.'

'I wonder what's happened.'

Camilla slumped in her armchair in the students' common room and listened to the other nurses talking. She had plenty to say on the subject, but for once she was too annoyed to join in.

She had been hoping to talk to the girls about her own problems. Her boyfriend Andrew had cancelled their date the previous night, and that morning she'd caught him flirting with a pro behind the Casualty block.

He'd insisted it was all innocent, and of course she believed him. She knew only too well that lots of the other students had their eye on Andrew, and she didn't blame him for being tempted. He was a red-blooded man, after all. But it had still upset her, and she really wanted to discuss it with the other girls.

But it seemed all they wanted to talk about was Catrine.

'I saw her in the dining room at lunchtime,' Maya was saying. 'She looked so sad. And she hardly touched her food.'

'I noticed her, too,' Phil agreed.

Camilla glared at the Irish girl. She was sitting right in front of them, and no one seemed to have noticed how upset she was. It wasn't fair. Catrine wasn't even in their set, and yet they were all so concerned about her.

'Something must have happened to her while she was away this weekend,' Winnie said. 'I wonder if we should go and speak to her?'

Viv Trent shook her head. 'I don't think that would be a good idea,' she said. 'You know what she's like. She prefers to keep herself to herself.'

'You're right,' Winnie agreed. 'But I hate to think of her upset. What do you think caused it?'

'Something happened while she was away, if you ask me,' Bernie said. 'Where did she go, does anyone know?'

They all shook their heads.

'She wouldn't say,' Viv said. 'And as far as I know, she doesn't have any friends or family here.'

'Perhaps it's a secret boyfriend?' Phil suggested.

'Speaking of boyfriends,' Camilla interrupted them. 'You'll never guess what Andrew did?'

'Don't tell me he proposed?' Viv said. Camilla noticed the sidelong smiles she and the other girls gave each other.

'What are you all smirking at?' she demanded.

'Take no notice, they're just teasing you,' Winnie, always the peacemaker, said. 'What happened?' she asked.

'I'm not telling you now.' Camilla jumped to her feet. 'You'll only make fun of me anyway.'

'Oh, don't be like that,' she heard Winnie say, as she stormed out of the common room.

She paused at the bottom of the stairs, waiting for someone to follow her, but no one did. One of the girls – that spiteful cat Viv, probably – must have made a remark about her, because all the others laughed.

Camilla stomped upstairs, her face burning with anger and humiliation. She tried not to show it, but it hurt that the other girls mocked her relationship with Andrew.

She knew they only did it because they were jealous. Andrew was a catch, and she was determined to hang on to him, whatever happened.

She reached the first-floor landing and noticed that the door to Catrine's room was slightly ajar. When she peeped in, she could see Catrine sitting at her desk. She looked as if she might be studying, but then Camilla noticed she was writing a letter.

Camilla paused, intrigued, her curiosity getting the better of her.

As she watched, she saw Catrine staring at the letter in her hands. And then, as if moved by some impulse, she stuffed it into the envelope and scrawled a name on the front.

Just at that moment, the wretched floorboard under Camilla's feet decided to creak, giving her away.

Catrine turned sharply towards the sound, the letter still in her hands.

'Who is it?' she called out.

Camilla had no choice but to fix a smile on her face and reveal herself.

'Only me,' she called out cheerily. 'Sorry, I was just passing and I noticed your door open.' She stood in the doorway. 'Did you have a nice weekend?'

'Not particularly.'

'Oh, I'm sorry to hear that. What happened?'

'I don't want to talk about it.' Catrine got up from the desk and crossed the room to where her suitcase lay open on her bed. She would be moving to the night staff block.

'I heard you were switching to nights?' Camilla said. Catrine looked at her.

'Who told you that?'

'The Home Sister told one of the girls.' Camilla looked at the suitcase. 'Bit sudden, isn't it?'

Catrine shrugged. 'Matron put me on the roster.'

'How long for?'

'I don't know.'

She sounded evasive. There was definitely something she wasn't telling, Camilla realised.

She watched as Catrine finished packing and closed her suitcase.

'Well, I must say I find it rather strange,' she said.

'Talk to Matron about it, not me.'

Camilla stared at her, offended. 'There's no need to snap,' she said. 'I was only trying to be friendly.'

Catrine paused for a moment, then her slim shoulders slumped. 'I am sorry,' she said, rubbing her temples. 'I am just a little tired, that's all. I had a difficult weekend.'

She looked so exhausted and wretched, for a moment Camilla felt sorry for her.

'Are you sure you don't want to talk about it?' she said, trying to keep the eagerness out of her voice.

'No, thank you.' Immediately the mask was back in place, all trace of vulnerability concealed.

And then she was gone, edging past her out of the door and heading down the stairs.

Camilla spotted the white envelope still sitting on her desk.

'Wait,' she said. 'You forgot your letter—'

But no sooner had the words left her mouth than she heard the sound of the front door closing.

Camilla crossed to the desk and picked it up. It was addressed to Frederick Sutcliffe. Now why on earth would Catrine be writing to the head of the hospital committee?

She examined the letter further, and was intrigued to discover that the envelope had not been stuck down properly. Catrine must have been about to do it when Camilla interrupted her.

She couldn't read it, of course. It was private correspondence, not meant for her eyes. Whatever was in the letter, it was between her and Frederick Sutcliffe.

And yet . . . Camilla stared down at it. Somehow fate had delivered it into her hands. Surely it wouldn't hurt to take the smallest peek?

Her heart was beating fast in her chest as she quickly opened the letter. She was taking a terrible risk. At any moment Catrine might realise she'd left it behind and come back for it. Camilla was poised, ready to run, even as her greedy gaze scanned the carefully written lines.

She felt her eyes widening and her mouth falling further open with every word.

Oh my.

Camilla loved gossip, and this was juicier than she could ever have imagined. She could scarcely wait to tell the others what she had discovered. Wait until they heard what she had to tell them! They wouldn't be ignoring her after this.

But then she had another thought. If she told them, they would want to know how she'd found out and then she would have to admit she had been snooping.

She heard someone coming up the stairs and hurriedly stuffed the letter back into its envelope and slipped it into her pocket.

She would decide what to do with the information later.

Chapter Forty-Seven

At nine o'clock that evening, Catrine reported for her first night duty on Wren ward.

Miss Grace had gone off duty early, so it was left to Staff Nurse Potter to give her report.

'You'll already know most of the cases,' she said. 'Mrs Willis in bed eight had a secondary haemorrhage this morning. Only slight, but you'll need to keep an eye on her. If she starts bleeding again, call the Night Sister immediately. We also have a post-op in room two who'll need watching. Mrs Brookes had a Wertheim's operation earlier today and went into shock. She was all right once she was put on an intravenous drip, but her blood pressure needs to be monitored regularly. The Night Sister will be round to give her some morphia later.'

As she listened to all the cases Potter was reeling off, Catrine was grateful she had a senior student with her. Isabel Blake was a cool, composed third year who instantly took charge once the staff nurse had gone off duty.

'Have you done night duty before?' she asked Catrine. She shook her head. 'Don't worry, it's not as daunting as it seems. It's busy for a while at first, but once all the patients are settled there are only a few we need to worry about. And if it's really serious then the Night Sister can always help out.'

Catrine was aware of the Night Sister, but she had never seen her. She was a shadowy character who was in charge of all the wards during night duty hours. She spent all night flitting from place to place, administering medication and dealing with emergencies wherever they cropped up.

She arrived while Catrine and Isabel were preparing the patients for bed. Miss Campbell was a sturdy, no-nonsense Scotswoman in her fifties, with the permanently hunched shoulders of someone who was used to whispering and tip-toeing everywhere.

While Catrine went round straightening sheets and shaking pillows, Miss Campbell busied herself preparing and administering sedatives to all the patients who needed them, while Isabel Blake wrote them down on each patient's notes.

'How is our post-op patient doing?' she asked Catrine, when they had given out the last dose.

'I checked on her ten minutes ago, and her pulse and blood pressure were still steady.'

'Any pain?'

'She seems quite comfortable, Sister.'

'That's something, at least.' Miss Campbell nodded approvingly. 'But it might be a different story when the morphia wears off. I'll be back in an hour to give her another dose if she needs it.'

The Night Sister left, and they went around turning off all the lights and pinning little green cloths over the lamps near the patients who needed special care. They checked on Mrs Brookes, the post-operative patient, and Catrine made sure Mrs Willis had not started bleeding again.

As Isabel had predicted, night duty wasn't quite as hectic as Catrine had feared. But it was far from restful. Even though the patients were sleeping, there was an endless list of tasks for the night nurses to do. They packed the drum with dressings and swabs ready for the porter to take down for sterilising. They folded and mended laundry, and laid the trolleys for the following morning.

And then, all hell broke loose.

It started with the ring of the telephone shattering the peace of the ward. Catrine was checking on the post-op patient in room two, but she could hear Isabel speaking in hushed, urgent tones.

When she emerged from the patient's room, Isabel was waiting for her. Even in the ghastly green light of the lamp Catrine could see that she looked pale.

'There's been a fire in a pub on the Roman Road,' she said. 'They're bringing the survivors in now.' She nodded towards the telephone. 'That was Sister Casualty. She's asked me to go down and try to help.'

'But what about me?' Catrine whispered, looking around the ward.

'You should be all right. Miss Campbell will be up to give Mrs Brookes her morphia soon. She'll keep an eye on you, I'm sure.' She was already unfastening her apron, ready to go. 'It'll be all right,' she reassured her. 'I'll be back in time to help with the morning routine.'

Catrine glanced at the clock. It had just turned midnight.

'I hope you'll be back before then,' she said.

'Me too,' Isabel said. 'But from what Sister Casualty has just told me, I don't hold out much hope.'

Wren ward was a lonely place with just Catrine there. She sat at the sister's desk, listening to the soft snoring and wheezing of the sleeping women all around her. It felt as if she was the only person awake in the whole world.

She could feel her whole body going heavy, her eyelids gritty with want of sleep. It was her first night duty, and she hadn't got used to the change of hours yet.

Must stay awake, she told herself. *Keep busy.*

She went back to check on Mrs Brookes. She had just finished taking her pulse when Miss Campbell crept in.

'How is she?' she asked, in the flat, toneless voice all the night staff used.

'Her pulse and blood pressure are still steady, but she's getting restless,' Catrine said.

'She probably needs more pain relief.' Miss Campbell produced a bunch of keys and handed them to her. 'Fetch a quarter grain of morphia, if you please.'

'Me, Sister?' It was rare for a junior student to be trusted with the contents of the dangerous medicines cupboard.

'I don't see anyone else here. Unless you want me to wake one of the patients and have them do it?'

Catrine took the key and crept to the medicines cupboard at the far end of the ward, unlocked it and took out the box of morphine ampoules and the drugs book. She found a hypodermic syringe and a small dish, and returned to the private room where the Night Sister was waiting.

Under her supervision, Catrine prepared the syringe and

wrote the patient's name and the dosage given carefully in the book. Then she counted the number of ampoules in the box and checked it against the number written beside the previous injection to make sure it tallied and no ampoules were missing.

When Miss Campbell had finished giving the patient her injection, she handed the syringe back to Catrine for cleaning, and checked the other patients.

'I understand Nurse Blake has been called away?' she said.

'Yes, Sister.'

'I'm afraid many of the other wards are short-staffed, too, thanks to this wretched fire. It's all hands on deck on the Acute ward and in Theatre at the moment.' She checked her watch on the end of its chain. 'I'll try to arrange for a pro to come up later, but I can't promise anything.' She put her watch away and smiled bracingly. 'But you seem like a sensible girl. And you can telephone me at any time if you need help.'

'Yes, Sister. Thank you, Sister.'

And then Miss Campbell was gone, her crepe-soled shoes squeaking softly as she crept down the corridor.

Catrine went to one of the windows and lifted the curtain slightly to look out. On the far side of the building, she could see a string of ambulances lined up outside the Casualty block. Nurses and porters were darting in and out with gurneys and stretchers, ferrying patients inside.

A fire at a pub, Miss Campbell had said. It must have been a bad one, judging by the number of people involved.

It would be a busy night, she thought. She felt for the nurses and doctors who would be working all hours downstairs, dealing with horrific injuries she could not even imagine. At least all she had to do was watch over a couple of dozen peacefully slumbering patients . . .

She turned away from the window and let out a scream at the sight of a ghostly white figure stumbling towards her out of the gloom, hands outstretched, groping blindly in the darkness.

And then it spoke.

'Nurse?' a voice croaked. 'Nurse, are you there?'

'I'm here, Mrs Cashman.' Catrine laughed nervously. 'I'm sorry, I thought you were a—'

She stopped dead, her gaze dropping to the woman's nightgown, and the ominous dark stain that was slowly spreading across it.

'Can you help me?' she whispered, her voice feeble in the darkness. 'I – I think I might be losing the baby . . .'

Chapter Forty-Eight

There was no might be about it. Mrs Cashman's blood-soaked nightdress told its own tragic story.

'Help me, please.' She took a step towards Catrine, but her legs buckled under her and she lurched forward into Catrine's arms.

Catrine felt the panic rising inside her and fought to stay calm.

'Let's get you back into bed, shall we?' she said.

'I'm right, ain't I? I'm losing it.' Brenda sobbed in her arms. 'But it's much worse than last time. The pain . . .' She cried out and doubled over as a wave of pain hit her.

'Come on, we'll get you comfortable.'

Catrine guided her back to her bed and pulled the curtains around her. Even in the darkness she could see the sheets were soaked with blood.

Mrs Cashman's screams had woken up a few of the women on the ward. Catrine could hear them stirring and getting out of bed.

'What's going on?' a voice asked, still half asleep.

Catrine left Mrs Cashman and slipped back through the curtains. There she was confronted with a handful of women in their nightgowns.

'Is it Brenda? Is she losing the baby?'

'Poor girl.'

'Is there anything we can do, Nurse? Can we help?'

'You can help by going back to bed,' she said. 'I've got everything under control.'

Although even as she said it, she could feel her heart hammering desperately against her ribs.

She coaxed the other women back to their beds, and hurried to the telephone to call for the Night Sister. Unfortunately, Miss Campbell had been called to help a pro on another understaffed ward, where a patient had died.

'I'll be there as soon as I can,' she promised. 'I'll try to get hold of a doctor if I can, although I don't hold out much hope since they're all down in Casualty or in Theatre at present. But I'll see what I can do. In the meantime, you know what to do.'

Do I? Catrine thought desperately. Her mind had gone blank with panic.

'Keep her warm and quiet, and let nature take its course. There isn't much more you can do for her, I'm afraid.'

Just at that moment Mrs Cashman let out another scream of agony that ripped through the ward.

So much for keeping her quiet, Catrine thought.

But at least she could keep her warm. She hurried off to make a hot water bottle, and to gather as many blankets as she could from the linen cupboard.

When she returned, she found Henry Tremayne standing by the sister's desk in the middle of the ward.

When he saw Catrine he opened his mouth to speak, but she got in first.

'Thank God. Did Miss Campbell send you?'

'I—'

'Mrs Cashman is losing her baby,' she said, without waiting for an answer. 'The poor woman is in so much pain, she's disturbing the other patients. I want to make up a bed in the private room, but I don't like to leave her alone.'

There was another moan of agony from behind the curtains. Catrine quickly thrust the hot water bottle into Henry's hands.

'Here,' she said. 'Keep an eye on her while I go and make up that bed.'

'But—'

'I'll be five minutes,' she threw back over her shoulder as she hurried away.

When she returned, Henry was sitting on Brenda Cashman's bed. She was clinging to him, her hand gripping his.

'That's it,' he was saying. 'Just keep breathing through the pain. It will be over soon, I promise. You're being so brave . . .'

The pain ebbed away, and Brenda Cashman released him, falling back against the pillows.

Henry glanced over his shoulder at Catrine.

'She's losing an awful lot of blood,' he whispered.

'I know.'

'Shouldn't we call a doctor?'

She stared at him. 'You *are* the doctor, aren't you? I thought you said Miss Campbell sent you?'

'You said that, not me.'

Catrine glanced at Brenda Cashman, then back at him. 'Well, you'll just have to do,' she said briskly.

'But I don't have the training to deal with this.'

'You're still the closest thing we've got to a doctor until someone else gets here. And I can't do this on my own.'

They stared at each other for a moment.

'So what do we do?' Henry asked.

'We need to try to move her to the private room. I've got everything ready for her in there.'

They worked together to try to shift her from the bed, but Brenda Cashman was in too much pain and curled herself into a ball, resisting their efforts to move her.

'Here, let me,' Henry said.

Very gently, he lifted Mrs Cashman in his arms like a child and carried her into the other room. By the time he laid her down on the bed Catrine had made up for her, his white coat was soaked in her blood. But he didn't seem to care.

He watched while Catrine laid her flat and surrounded her with warm blankets. She changed her nightdress for a hospital gown and put a mat in place, but it was hardly enough to stem the blood that flowed out of her.

All the while she clung to Henry's hand like a lifeline. Her nails bit into his flesh, but he did not even flinch. He just kept talking to her in a low, soothing voice, reassuring her that all would be well.

Catrine was grateful for his calm manner, even though she sensed he was as terrified as she was. Brenda Cashman was losing far too much blood. Her pulse was feeble and slow, and she was growing more and more listless.

'I'm so c-cold,' she complained, even when Catrine had banked up the blankets around her and filled an extra hot water bottle.

'Her hands are like ice,' Henry said. He nodded to the sphygmomanometer in the corner. 'Check her temperature and blood pressure.'

Just as they'd both feared, her temperature was low and her blood pressure had dropped.

She had gone into shock.

Henry took charge. 'Help me raise the foot of the bed,' he said. 'She's going to need fluids, too. Do you know how to set up a saline drip?' She shook her head. 'Never mind, I'll do it.'

He showed her how to set up the stand, and how to adjust the flow on the drip. They both stood in silence, watching the slow, steady trickle through the glass connecting pipe.

'It needs to be a little faster,' Henry said. 'Put that pin in the top hole and hopefully gravity will do the rest.'

They sat in silence, their gazes moving in unison between the drip stand and Mrs Cashman, lying still and almost lifeless on the bed.

'She's not improving,' Catrine said.

'No.' Henry chewed his thumbnail worriedly. 'No, she isn't.' He thought for a moment. 'She probably needs a stimulant. An ampoule of Coramine might help.'

'But I don't have the key to the medicines cupboard.'

'Then I'll have to go and beg some from another ward.'

'Don't leave me!' Catrine blurted out as he got to his feet. 'What if something happens to her?'

'I'll be back as soon as I can,' he promised. 'Just keep an eye on that drip and adjust it if it slows down.'

He seemed to be gone for hours. Catrine did as she was

told, checking the drip and adjusting the blankets around Mrs Cashman. She had always prided herself on her ability to cope, but somehow all her cool-headedness seemed to have deserted her as she sat in the lonely, silent ward in the dead of the night.

Finally, Henry returned, bearing the yellow box of Coramine ampoules aloft like a conquering hero.

'I managed to get some from Male Medical,' he said. 'I finally found a staff nurse on duty. I suppose the others must all still be in Casualty. The rest of the hospital's utterly deserted.' His face was grave. 'That pub fire must have been dreadful. I saw the ambulances lined up practically all the way to the gates.'

He administered the medicine, and thankfully it seemed to work. Brenda Cashman's heart rate gradually grew stronger and her blood pressure improved.

They sat on either side of the bed, staring at each other. Catrine wasn't sure whether to laugh with relief or cry.

'You look a mess,' she said to Henry.

'So do you.'

She looked down at her blood-stained apron.

'I do not think I would pass Matron's inspection,' she joked feebly.

'Oh, I don't know. I think she'd make an exception for you, under the circumstances. In fact, I think she'd be rather proud of you.'

She met his gaze. His blue eyes were warm, and there was a hint of a smile on his face.

She looked away sharply. 'Why did you come, if Miss Campbell didn't send you?' she asked.

'I came to apologise.'

Catrine could not hide her surprise. 'Apologise? You?'

'I should never have told you about my father.'

She lowered her gaze. She had washed her hands, but her nails were still rimed with blood.

'I needed to hear the truth,' she said.

'Yes, but not from me. And I did it for all the wrong reasons.'

'What do you mean?'

'I was angry and humiliated after what you said to my father. I wanted to hurt you.'

'I was only trying to help,' she said.

'It didn't feel that way to me. It felt as if you were trying to take over, to push me out.'

'Why should I do that?'

'I don't know. It seems silly now, but that was the way I felt. I suppose I've always felt as if I was different, because I wasn't his real son. And then suddenly along you come, his flesh and blood. Of course I was jealous. You just seemed to fit in while I was struggling to be the son Father wanted me to be.'

Catrine stared at him. 'If anyone was jealous, it should have been me,' she pointed out. 'You were the one who had his name. You were the one he showed off. I wasn't even allowed to look at him when we were in public.'

She hadn't realised how much it had upset her until she felt the bitterness rise up like hot bile in her throat.

'I'm sorry, I didn't think,' Henry said quietly. 'I can't imagine how hurtful that must have been for you.'

'It doesn't matter now, anyway,' she shrugged.

'Are you still thinking of leaving?'

She looked at him in surprise. 'How did you know?'

'Aunt Helen told us.'

'So your father knows?'

'Our father,' he corrected her. 'Yes, he does. And he's heartbroken about it.'

Heartbroken, Catrine thought scathingly. William Tremayne couldn't even begin to understand the meaning of the word.

She thought about the letter she had written that night when she was alone at Lowgill House. All the rage and spite she'd poured out into every line.

She was glad she'd written it. She hoped it would hurt William as much as he had hurt her and her mother.

'Won't you change your mind?' Henry asked. 'I know Father made a mess of everything, but surely you can give him another chance?'

Before she could reply, the door opened and Miss Campbell crept in.

'I'm sorry I couldn't find a doctor to – good heavens!' She stopped short, looking them both up and down. 'Well, you two look as if you've had quite a night of it,' she remarked.

Catrine sat quietly while Henry explained to the Night Sister about Mrs Cashman's symptoms and the treatment they had given her. He sounded calm and measured, and there was none of the nerves she had witnessed before on the wards.

She hoped after this he might realise he was a better doctor than he thought.

'Well, I must say I'm impressed,' Miss Campbell said. 'It sounds as if you two have coped admirably. You make an excellent team.'

Catrine sent Henry a quick sidelong look. He grinned sheepishly back.

Chapter Forty-Nine

Miss Campbell allowed Catrine to go off shift an hour early, after she had coped so well with that night's ordeal.

'Go and get some sleep,' the Night Sister advised. 'You look completely exhausted.'

Catrine was indeed so weary she could barely shuffle back to her room in the Night Nurses' block. But tired as she was, she knew she would not sleep. She had too much on her mind.

She could not stop reliving the events of that night, and everything that had happened with Mrs Cashman. Every time she closed her eyes, all she could see was the poor woman crying out in pain, her nightdress stained with blood.

Thank God for Henry, she thought. She could never have imagined herself saying such a thing, but he had been an absolute rock for her. Miss Campbell was right, they had made a good team.

He had been so calm, too, a million miles from the nervous wreck Catrine was used to seeing on the ward rounds. Being in a crisis had obviously brought out the best in him. She only hoped it would help Henry to realise that he was a far better doctor than he gave himself credit for.

She was surprised at how much she had mellowed towards him in the past few hours. It had come as a revelation to her to talk to him and realise that he was as jealous and insecure of her as she was of him. She had been so wrapped up in her own feelings that it hadn't really occurred to her that her arrival had affected the rest of William's family. Everyone had had to shift to make way for her, and it would not have been easy for them as they had been forced to reconsider their new position. Catrine felt embarrassed that she had been so demanding and ungracious towards them.

Especially her father.

She thought about what Henry had said. A couple of days ago, she might not have been ready to hear what he'd had to say. But now the white heat of her anger had cooled, she was starting to see things as they really were.

She tried to imagine William as a young man, suddenly receiving the news from her mother that she was expecting his baby. Was it any wonder he'd panicked? He would have been every bit as frightened as her mother, she realised.

Of course, that did not excuse him for leaving her mother to bring up a baby alone, but at least it helped her to understand why William had done what he did. And he had certainly done his best to make up for his mistake. Ever since Catrine had come back into his life, he had gone out of his way to make her feel welcome. He had even risked his marriage and his career for her.

She remembered the letter she had written to Frederick Sutcliffe while in the grip of her rage. She had known it was a mistake, even as she was writing it. But at the time she had been hurt and angry, and she had wanted William to feel pain too. So she had lashed out in the only way she could, laying it all out in a letter that she knew would end his career at the hospital he loved.

But now she realised how petty and vindictive it would have been. Hurting someone else did nothing to lessen her own pain.

She went to her suitcase to retrieve the letter. The sooner she tore it up, the better she would feel.

But it wasn't there.

Panic assailed her. She went through her belongings, pulling them out and scattering them, then stared into her empty suitcase. The letter wasn't there.

Catrine sat down on the bed and tried to think. She pictured that Sunday afternoon, how she had just finished writing the letter when she heard Camilla creeping about outside her door. She remembered how the other girl had stood in her doorway, poking and prying and trying to pretend she was Catrine's friend when it was obvious all she wanted was gossip.

Catrine hadn't been able to get away fast enough. She had tossed her clothes into her suitcase and left as quickly as she could . . .

Leaving the letter on the desk in her room.

The other nurses were still getting ready for their shift at the nurses' home when Catrine arrived.

Winnie emerged from her room just as Catrine hurried up the stairs. She was fiddling with the stud that fastened her collar to her striped blue dress.

'Hello, stranger. What are you doing here?' she asked.

Catrine was too preoccupied to reply. Her hand was

shaking as she turned the doorknob to her room and flung it open.

Her room was just as she'd left it, except for one thing.

She swung round to face Winnie, who stood in the doorway. 'There was a letter here. Have you seen it?' she said.

Winnie looked blank. 'I haven't been in your room since you left.'

'Has anyone else been in here?'

'Not as far as I know.'

'Are you looking for your letter?'

There was Camilla, hovering behind them. Catrine stared at her.

'You left it on the desk,' Camilla said. 'I called out to tell you, but you'd already gone. You were in such a hurry—'

'What did you do with it?' Catrine interrupted her.

'I posted it, of course. It looked important, so I thought that's what you'd want.' Camilla looked concerned. 'I hope I did the right thing?'

Chapter Fifty

Helen returned to the Nightingale Hospital that morning to the sad news that Brenda Cashman had lost her baby.

'It happened last night,' Jennifer Grace told her when Helen did her rounds. 'It's such a shame, isn't it? As the days went by, we'd all started to hope that there might be a chance for her.' The ward sister's soft grey eyes were filled with sadness. The plight of poor Mrs Cashman had touched all the nurses on Wren ward.

'What happened?' Helen asked.

'She started haemorrhaging in the middle of the night. Quite badly, according to the report. And of course, it would be the night we had a big accident in Casualty and it was all hands on deck in Theatre. But luckily Villeneuve was on duty. She and young Dr Tremayne did a sterling job between them.'

'Did they?' Helen was interested. 'So they worked together?'

'They might have even saved her life. It was a miracle.'

It was indeed, Helen thought, but not perhaps in the way Miss Grace believed.

'Where is Mrs Cashman now? I'd like to go and see her.'

'I've moved her to a private room. I thought she could do

with some rest.' Miss Grace lowered her voice. 'Her husband's been waiting to see her for a while, but she won't let him come in.'

'Really? That's odd.' Brenda Cashman usually looked forward to her husband's daily visits.

'I know. Perhaps you could have a word with her? The poor man's absolutely beside himself, wondering what's going on.'

Brenda Cashman's face was as pale as the white nightgown she wore, her eyes red-rimmed from crying. But there were no tears now as she sat propped against the pillows. Instead there was a weary, almost resigned expression on her face.

'Hello, Matron.' She managed a wan smile at Helen. 'I suppose you've heard the news?'

'I have.' Helen nodded gravely. 'I'm so sorry, my dear.'

'I suppose it was always going to happen. But as the days went by, I started to hope that this time it might be different – you know?'

'I know,' Helen said sadly.

Brenda Cashman's gaze dropped to her hands, her thin fingers lacing in her lap. 'I suppose that's my lot, ain't it? There won't ever be a baby now.'

Helen was silent for a moment, trying to find the right words, something to give the poor woman hope.

'You're still young—'

Mrs Cashman shook her head. 'I can't put myself through all this again.' She squared her shoulders, smiling bravely. 'I'm just not made to have babies, and that's that. And the sooner I get used to it, the better.'

Do you ever get used to it? Helen wondered. She knew she hadn't. She had found a way to learn to live with it, but the yearning was still there, in her heart.

She looked at Mrs Cashman's knitting, stuffed in a bag beside her bedside locker. She remembered the pride on the woman's face as she'd worked on it. It was like a lifeline to her, giving her something to focus on. Keeping her dream alive.

She probably couldn't bear to look at it now, Helen thought.

'Your husband's outside,' she said, changing the subject. 'Sister tells me he's been waiting a while.'

'I don't want to see him.' Brenda's voice sounded hollow.

'But he's worried about you.'

'How can I face him after this?' She turned her face to Helen. 'I've let him down again.'

Helen felt her skin prickle.

'You haven't let anyone down,' she said.

'I have. His ma was right, he deserves better than me.'

Helen saw the grim determination on Brenda Cashman's face, and she knew exactly what the other woman was thinking.

'You're leaving him,' she said.

Brenda gave her a startled look. 'How did you know?'

Because I did the same thing myself, Helen thought.

Brenda's chin lifted. 'Joe deserves to have a family. He's always wanted to be a dad, and it ain't fair for me to tie him to me when I can't give him what he wants.' Her voice was choked with emotion. 'He should be allowed to go and find someone who can have a baby for him.'

333

'And what about what he wants? Have you asked him?'

'Oh, I know what he'd say,' Brenda Cashman dismissed. 'But I don't want him staying with me out of duty or pity or anything. I couldn't bear that.'

Once again, Helen felt the woman's emotions as if they were her own. She remembered feeling the same way as she had prepared to leave David.

'The man I saw just now didn't look as if he pitied you,' she said to Brenda. 'He looked as if he loved you.'

'And I love him, too. That's why I have to set him free.'

Helen knew there was nothing more to say. She stayed for a few more minutes to straighten the bedclothes and check the flow from the drip stand, and then went outside to where Joe Cashman was waiting.

He jumped to his feet the minute he saw her. 'How is she?' he asked. 'Is she all right?'

'She's doing well, Mr Cashman.'

'Can I see her?'

He looked so hopeful, her heart went out to him.

'She needs to rest now. Perhaps it might be better if you came back later?' Helen suggested.

'I'd rather stay, if that's all right with you, Matron. Just in case Brenda needs me.'

'As you wish.'

Helen walked away quickly, but the image of Joe Cashman's hurt, confused face stayed with her for a long time afterwards.

It was the same look she had seen on David's face the day she told him she was leaving.

Chapter Fifty-One

During his years as a preacher in the Methodist church, Frederick Sutcliffe had stood in the pulpit many times and preached about the power of prayer and God's miracles. And yet he had never witnessed them for himself.

Until now.

He had not been able to sleep since it happened. He had certainly not been able to stop thinking about it.

And now, as he sat at the head of the board room table and faced the extraordinary meeting of the Florence Nightingale Hospital Committee, he could scarcely contain his excitement. It was all he could do to maintain a sober expression as he watched his fellow committee members shuffling in to take their seats.

He could see the bafflement on their faces, and he understood why. He was a man who believed in meticulous order, in sticking to rules and routines and dates in the calendar. Matters were dealt with at the regular monthly meetings, or not at all.

'What's all this about?' Gwen Parry asked. She was the secretary of the committee and clearly most put out at the irregularity of it all.

'Aren't we supposed to be meeting next week, or did I get the date wrong again?' Edward Chalk leaned over to whisper to his neighbour. Mr Chalk was getting on in years, rather deaf and inclined to be confused.

His neighbour, Philip Montrose, the local bank manager, nodded. 'No, it was definitely supposed to be next week. I have it in my diary.'

'I haven't been asked to prepare any minutes for this meeting.' Mrs Parry glared up the length of the table at Frederick Sutcliffe. The main reason she had put herself forward to be Secretary was because she liked being the first to know everything.

But she also liked to be the first to pass on gossip, which was why Frederick had decided not to divulge his secret to her. The last thing he wanted was for her to steal his thunder.

He cleared his throat and rose to address them all. He did not usually stand up, but he felt the occasion demanded it.

'I am aware that our regular meeting is in the diary for next week, but I didn't feel as if this could wait. It concerns the role of Medical Superintendent.'

There was a collective sigh around the table.

'Thank heavens for that,' someone muttered.

'About time,' Philip Montrose agreed.

'You should have told me,' Gwen Parry said in an injured tone. 'I could have put it in the agenda.'

'I'm afraid this is too delicate a matter to be included in any paperwork.'

As if by magic, the table fell silent again.

'What do you mean?' Philip Montrose asked.

Frederick Sutcliffe cleared his throat again. 'As you know, I have delayed making a decision on the matter—'

'You can say that again!' someone muttered at the other end of the table.

'I realise the general consensus was that William Tremayne should be offered the position. However, as many of you are aware, I've had my doubts about his suitability . . .'

He looked around the table.

'And I regret to tell you that those doubts have now been confirmed.'

A tide of muttering swept around the table. Frederick watched them all. He could feel his heart pattering with the sheer excitement of it all.

'What are you talking about?' Edward Chalk asked.

This was the moment he'd been waiting for. Frederick Sutcliffe reached into his inside jacket pocket and pulled out the envelope he'd been keeping close to him.

'Yesterday, a letter concerning Mr Tremayne was delivered to me,' he said.

'And what does it say?' Philip Montrose demanded. 'Spit it out, man, we haven't got all day!'

But Frederick Sutcliffe was not about to be hurried. He took the letter out of the envelope and slowly unfolded it, savouring the moment.

And then, at last, he was ready.

'Allow me to read it to you,' he said.

Chapter Fifty-Two

Joe Cashman was in his usual place outside his wife's door when Helen arrived to do her round the following morning.

'I can't get him to move,' Jennifer Grace said. 'I think he would have slept there all night if Miss Campbell hadn't got a couple of porters to make him go home.' She looked at Helen. 'I'm sorry, Matron.'

'There's no need to apologise,' Helen said. 'I see no reason why he can't stay, as long as he's not in your way?'

'I just feel so sorry for him, that's all,' the ward sister sighed. 'I've done my best to persuade his wife to see him, but she refuses. I've no idea what the poor man's done wrong.'

'How is Mrs Cashman this morning?' Helen asked.

'I'm rather worried about her,' Miss Grace admitted. 'She's very listless, and her temperature's up. I'm worried there might be an infection. I've asked Dr McKay to come and look at her.'

'Dr McKay? I thought Dr Swithin was the physician on this ward?'

'He is,' Miss Grace said. 'But Dr McKay's the best.'

Helen could not disagree with that. Old Dr Swithin was rather set in his ways. If he'd had his way, they'd still be using leeches as standard medical procedure.

'I'll go in and see her now,' she said.

Joe Cashman sat up straight as Helen approached, his shoulders going back, as if priming himself for a fight.

'I ain't going,' he said. 'I don't care what you say, I ain't leaving my Brenda.'

'I wouldn't dream of making you leave, Mr Cashman,' Helen assured him. 'Your place is here, with your wife.'

'That's what I thought.' He looked relieved. 'Only that other woman, the Scottish one, booted me out last night.'

'Yes, well, Miss Grace is in charge now. Now can we get you anything, Mr Cashman? A cup of tea?'

'Thanks, Sister. A cup of tea would be lovely.'

The poor man looked utterly dishevelled, with his rumpled clothes and unshaven chin.

'Anything else? I'm sure I can persuade the ward maid to fetch you a piece of toast. You must be starving.'

'No, ta, miss. I don't think I could eat a thing.' He glanced worriedly towards the door of the private room. 'When do you think I'll be able to see my Brenda?'

'We'll see what the doctor has to say, shall we?'

She gestured to one of the student nurses.

'Fetch Mr Cashman some tea would you, Nurse?' she said. Then she left him and slipped into the private room.

As soon as she saw Brenda Cashman, she understood why Miss Grace had been so worried about her. She looked listless and unwell, a sheen of perspiration on her pale face.

'How are you feeling, my dear?' she asked.

'All right, I suppose.'

Helen checked Mrs Cashman's pulse. It raced under her fingertips, her skin pale and clammy.

339

She was adding the reading to Mrs Cashman's notes when David arrived.

'Good morning,' he said brightly. Brenda Cashman could barely summon more than a weary smile.

Helen stepped back while he carried out his examination.

'Are you in any pain at all?' he asked.

'Not really, Doctor.'

'You're not feeling any breathlessness at all?' David asked, his voice deceptively casual.

'A bit. Just now and then.'

Helen glanced at David. His face gave nothing away but she could see the glimmer of concern in his dark eyes.

'I see from your notes that you didn't eat much breakfast?' Helen said.

'I didn't much fancy it.'

'You need to keep your strength up.'

'Matron's right,' David agreed. 'Good food and rest will do you the world of good.'

'Your husband is waiting outside,' Helen said.

For the first time, Brenda's eyes flashed with emotion.

'I told you, I don't want to see him.'

'But he's been here all night.'

'Then tell him to go home.'

Helen glanced at David. 'Very well,' she said. 'But I don't think he'll go away.'

Brenda Cashman averted her gaze towards the window and said nothing. It was as if all the life had gone out of her.

They left the room, and David explained to Mr Cashman that his wife needed to rest and could not be disturbed for a while.

'Perhaps you should go home for a few hours?' he suggested, but Joe Cashman shook his head.

'I ain't going anywhere,' he said. 'I don't want to leave my Brenda alone.'

They left him sitting there and made their way to the end of the corridor where they could speak without being overheard.

'What did you think?' Helen asked.

'I didn't like the look of her,' he admitted. 'It's not the infection I'm worried about. That's fairly mild, as far as I can see. But it just seems – I don't know, as if—'

'As if she's given up?' Helen said.

He looked at her sharply. 'You noticed it too?' Helen nodded. 'But why, I wonder?'

'I think it's the husband,' she said.

'What about him?'

'From what I can tell, Mrs Cashman believes she's let him down.'

'Let him down? How?'

She paused. Suddenly she did not want to be going down this dark road with David. Especially as she'd already travelled it before.

'She can't give him children,' she said. 'She thinks he'll be happier if she sets him free.'

'But that's ridiculous,' David said. 'You only have to look at the poor man to see he's devoted to her.'

'She's devoted to him, too. Which is why she wants to do what's best for him.'

'And what about what *he* wants?'

Helen looked at him. Suddenly they were no longer

341

talking about Mr and Mrs Cashman. This was personal. They were reliving the moment Helen had told him she was leaving. Only this time, she wasn't the only one doing the talking. David was speaking too, speaking from his heart in a way she'd never heard him do before.

Or perhaps she was so bound up in her own feelings, she had never really listened.

'David—' But before she could say any more, Viv Trent appeared at the other end of the corridor with a cup of tea for Mr Cashman.

She did not look their way, but it was enough to break the spell. Helen stepped back quickly.

'Will you keep an eye on her?' David asked.

'Yes, of course.'

'I have to go back to my rounds, but I'll come back as soon as I can. You'll let me know if there's any change, won't you?'

'Yes,' Helen promised. 'Yes, I will.'

Chapter Fifty-Three

William was already seated at their usual table in L'Escargot when Catrine arrived. Even from across the restaurant, she could see how tired and subdued he looked.

Her heart went out to him. The poor man had seen his whole life fall apart in the space of a day.

And it was all her fault.

But his face still lit up as she approached the table.

'Catrine.' He rose to his feet to greet her, but he did not reach out to hug her as he usually did. He seemed formal, almost awkward, as if he no longer knew how to be around her.

Which was hardly surprising, considering the last time they had seen each other was at Billinghurst, when Catrine had walked out of his life, supposedly forever.

'How are you?' she said, sitting down opposite him.

'Oh, you know,' he shrugged. '*Comme ci, comme ça*, as you French would say.' He paused. 'I suppose you've heard what happened?'

Catrine lowered her gaze. 'Yes,' she murmured. 'I'm sorry.'

'I'm glad you telephoned. After you left Billinghurst I wasn't sure if I'd ever see you again.'

She forced herself to look up into her father's gentle dark gaze. Would he look so kindly on her when he found out the truth? she wondered.

'Helen tells me you're thinking of going back to France?' he said.

She nodded. 'I think it might be for the best,' she murmured.

'I was rather hoping you might have come to tell me you'd changed your mind?'

'How can I, after—'

'After what?'

Catrine dropped her gaze again, just as the waiter appeared with the wine William had ordered. She could hardly wait for him to fill her glass before she snatched it and took a gulp.

William laughed. 'Steady on! If anyone should be drowning their sorrows, surely it should be me?' He regarded her across the table, his expression suddenly serious. 'Unless there's something you want to tell me?' he said. 'Catrine, if there's something wrong—'

'I sent the letter,' she blurted out, unable to cope with his kindness any longer.

William stared at her in silence.

'I mean, I wrote it,' Catrine amended quickly. 'But I did not send it. I was going to tear it up, but then one of the other girls found it and she posted it.' Her words came out in a rush, tumbling over each other. 'There was nothing I could do – I am so sorry.'

'Oh, Catrine.' This time William did reach for her hand, but she pulled away from him.

'No,' she said. 'Do not be nice to me. I do not deserve it. I am the reason you cannot be the new Medical Supervisor.'

'It's worse than that, I'm afraid,' William said ruefully. 'I'm no longer working at the hospital at all.'

'What? Oh, *mon dieu*! That is terrible!' Tears stung her eyes. 'But this is all my fault.'

'No, it isn't.'

'How can you say that? Mr Sutcliffe would not have known anything about it if I had not written that letter.' She balled her hands into fists. If only she could have gone back in time, she would never have put pen to paper.

'The letter made no difference.'

She looked up at him, bewildered. 'What do you mean?'

'Because I resigned anyway.'

Catrine stared at her father across the table. William smiled back at her. 'But I do not understand. Why would you . . . ?'

'I knew nothing about your letter when I went to Frederick Sutcliffe's office,' William said. 'I was actually waiting for him when he returned from the committee meeting. He was rather pleased to see me, I can tell you.' He smiled, remembering. 'He looked like the cat that got the cream. I think he was relishing the idea of giving me my comeuppance, but unfortunately I took the wind out of his sails by telling him I wanted to resign.' He chuckled at the memory. 'Of course, he insisted on brandishing the letter and telling me he knew all about my low moral character, as he called it. But by then there was nothing he could do.'

Catrine stared at him blankly, trying to take in what she was hearing.

'But why did you resign?' she asked.

'Because of you. I needed to prove to you that you mean more to me than anything,' William said. 'I realised how badly I'd treated you, ignoring you all those years and then hiding you away like a shameful secret. You deserved better than that.'

'And so you decided to destroy your career?'

He laughed. 'Hardly! Frederick Sutcliffe might not approve of me, but he can hardly take away my medical degree.'

'But the Nightingale is your life. It means everything to you.'

'*You* mean everything to me. You, and Henry, and Lottie and Tim. You're part of our family now, Catrine. Look, I know I can't change the past, but I'd very much like to be part of your future. If you'll let me?'

He reached out for her hand again.

'Would you be willing to give me a second chance, even though I don't deserve it?' he asked.

Catrine hesitated for a moment, staring down at his hand. Slowly, she inched her hand forward, until their fingers were touching.

Chapter Fifty-Four

By the afternoon, Mrs Cashman was drifting between sleep and wakefulness. There had been a slight improvement in her pulse and respiration, but she was still feverish.

'You don't have to keep checking up on me,' she said when Helen came into the room. 'I'm sure you've got better things to do with your time.'

'Dr McKay would never forgive me if I didn't keep an eye on you.'

She checked her pulse and respiration, then sat down for a while to chat to her. Brenda could scarcely be bothered to make conversation. She looked weary. Her strength might have rallied slightly, but her face still wore the look of defeat that Helen had seen earlier.

At two o'clock the bell rang, announcing visiting time.

'Is Joe still here?' Brenda Cashman asked.

'Yes, he is. Shall I send him in?'

She shook her head listlessly. 'I wish he'd go home,' she murmured. 'He's wasting his time here with me.'

'I'm not sure he sees it that way.'

Helen busied herself arranging the water jug and glass so that it was easily within Brenda Cashman's grasp.

'Are you sure there's nothing I can get for you?' she said.

'How about a book? I know the Lady Almoner keeps a shelf of donated paperbacks outside her office. I could send someone to fetch a couple . . .'

'No, thanks, Matron. I ain't much of a reader.'

'You'll need something to keep you entertained.' She thought for a moment. 'How about a wireless? I could arrange to borrow one '

Before Brenda could reply, a strident voice rang out from the other side of the door.

'Here you are! You could have told me where you were, instead of me having to call round and hear it from your neighbours.'

'Hello, Mum,' Joe Cashman said quietly.

Helen looked at Brenda. She was staring at the door, a frozen expression on her face.

'They've moved her to a private room, I see. Bit much if you ask me,' Enid Cashman sniffed disapprovingly. 'I mean, it ain't the first time she's lost a baby. She should be used to it by now.'

'She's lost a lot of blood, Ma. And she's got an infection.' Joe Cashman's voice was choked with emotion.

'Serious, is it?'

Helen wondered if she'd imagined the note of hope in the older woman's voice.

'The doctor reckons they've got it under control.'

'Oh. Oh well, that's something, I s'pose,' Enid said flatly.

Helen turned and started towards the door, but Brenda put out her hand to stop her.

'No,' she said. 'I want to hear what they've got to say.'

'What are you doing out here if she's in such a bad way?'

Enid Cashman was saying. 'I would have thought you'd be in there with her?'

'She's resting.' He must have mumbled something Helen couldn't hear, because the next thing she heard was his mother saying,

'What do you mean, she don't want to see you? I hope she ain't blaming you for this mess? Because as far as I'm concerned, it's her fault for not being able to carry a baby!'

Brenda was listening intently, her whole body still.

'That's it, I've heard enough.' Helen made another move towards the door, but once again Brenda stopped her.

'Shh, I want to hear,' she insisted.

'I'm just telling you my opinion,' Enid Cashman's voice was low and insinuating. 'You've got to face facts, son. She was never right for you, was she? She couldn't give you what you wanted.'

'What are you talking about?'

'You know very well. I've seen what it's done to you, her losing one baby after another. It's broken your heart.'

'It's broken Brenda's heart, too.'

'Yes, but you don't have to put up with it, do you? You don't have to stay with her.'

Helen looked at Brenda. Her eyes were brimming with tears.

'You think I should leave her because she can't give me a baby? Is that what you're saying?'

'No one would blame you if you did—'

'You don't understand, do you? I love Brenda with all my heart. She's my world.'

'Yes, but you've always wanted to be a father. You deserve it—'

'Do you think I care about kids more than I care about Brenda? If it was a choice between having a family or having her, then I'd choose her every time.'

Helen glanced at Brenda again. This time the tears were spilling down her cheeks.

'I hope you ain't been filling Brenda's head with this nonsense?' Joe said.

'I might have had a talk to her—'

'Jesus, no wonder she's been so upset. I wish she'd told me, I would have done something about it.'

'I was only thinking of you.'

'You should go.'

His mother's voice was reproachful. 'You don't mean that!'

'Yes, I do. I probably should have said it a long time ago. But I'm saying it now. I don't want you anywhere near us if you can't treat my wife with the love and respect she deserves.'

'Respect!' Enid Cashman spat. 'Why should I give her any respect? She can't even give me a grandchild.'

'That's enough, Mum. I think it's best if you stay away from us from now on. And when my Brenda pulls through this, I'm going to make sure she never has to put up with you or your poison ever again.'

'All right, I'm going. But I won't forget the way you've spoken to me.'

'And I won't forget the way you've treated my wife, either!'

In the silence that followed, Helen looked at Brenda. She was staring at the door, as if she could not quite believe what she had heard.

She did not speak, but her face no longer wore that look of exhausted defeat. Instead her eyes shone with hope and determination.

In that moment, Helen knew she would pull through.

'I'll leave you,' she said.

'Thank you.'

'Are you sure I can't fetch you anything?'

'A cup of tea might be nice.'

'Of course.'

She was at the door when Brenda spoke again.

'And Matron?'

'Yes?'

'You could send in my Joe. I quite fancy a bit of company.'

The smile she gave her was so radiant, Helen couldn't help smiling back.

'I'm sure he'd like that too,' she said.

Helen was so elated she almost skipped back to the ward. She couldn't wait to tell David what had happened. He would be so delighted. She smiled at the thought of sharing the good news with him.

She stopped Winnie Riley, who was hurrying past with a dish containing a steaming poultice. 'Have you seen Dr McKay?' she asked.

'I think he's with Miss Grace in her office, Matron,' the girl replied.

'Thank you. Oh, and could you take a cup of tea in to Mr and Mrs Cashman when you've finished what you're doing?

There's no hurry,' she added, glancing back over her shoulder towards the private room. 'I'm sure they'd appreciate some time on their own, anyway.'

Even though they spent most of their time at the desk in the middle of the ward, each sister also had a private office where they could hold meetings or have quiet chats with the nurses. This was also where they kept any confidential files, and the medicinal brandy. Older ward sisters had been known to retire there for an afternoon nap.

Helen was just about to knock when she heard voices inside.

'It's not fair, David,' she heard Jennifer Grace saying. 'She deserves to know. I don't like sneaking about behind her back.'

Helen froze. Cold dread trickled down her spine.

'I know, but now isn't the right time,' she heard David saying.

'You've been saying that for weeks.'

'Yes, but it's complicated.'

'I don't see how. All you have to do is tell her about us. You're getting divorced, it surely shouldn't come as a surprise that you've found someone else. Unless there's a reason you don't want to tell her?'

Helen didn't wait to hear his reply.

Chapter Fifty-Five

'And then what did you do?'

'What could I do? I just walked away.'

Helen could feel the heat rising in her face at the memory. She had been so mortified, all she could think of was putting as much distance between herself and Jennifer Grace's office as possible.

'Oh, Helen.' Dora tilted her head and gave her a sympathetic smile.

It was teatime, and they were sitting in her kitchen. Helen had come to see her friend straight after her duty had ended.

She wasn't sure what had propelled her to her friend's door, except that she badly needed someone to confide in. And Dora was the only one she could trust to understand. She'd been there through all Helen's troubles and traumas over the years, and she knew she could rely on her practical good sense.

'You know, you mustn't read too much into what you heard . . .' Dora began, but Helen shook her head.

'I haven't got it wrong, Dora. I wish I had. But it was clear from what Jennifer Grace was saying that she and David—'

She broke off, lifting her teacup to her lips. She could not bring herself to finish the sentence.

'I'll put the kettle on for another brew.'

Dora rose wearily to her feet. She was still wearing her District Nurse's uniform, and Helen noticed for the first time how tired her friend looked.

'I should go,' she said. 'Your family will be home for their tea soon.'

'Not for a while yet. Danny's playing football with his mates on the rec, so he won't even notice the time. And Nick's working over in Haggerston. He won't be back until late.'

'What about your mum?'

'She's in the other room, putting her feet up. Looks like she's been busy herself today.' Dora nodded towards the window. Outside in the back yard, a line of washing fluttered in the breeze.

'You look as if you could do with a rest yourself,' Helen said sympathetically. 'Busy day?'

'You could say that. I had the antenatal clinic this morning, and then I was on my feet all afternoon on my rounds.'

Helen frowned. Dora never usually complained of feeling tired.

'Here,' she said. 'You sit down. I'll finish making the tea.'

'I won't say no if you're offering.' Dora sank down in her chair gratefully.

Helen watched her out of the corner of her eye as she warmed the pot and spooned in the tea. Dora never usually accepted help, either.

'Are you sure you're all right?' she said.

'I'm fine,' Dora dismissed. 'A bit of backache from lifting

354

patients in and out of bed all day, but that's to be expected. Anyway, it's you we're talking about,' she said.

'There isn't much to say, is there?' Helen poured the boiling water into the teapot.

'I suppose it was bound to happen sooner or later, wasn't it?' Dora said. 'I mean, David's a good-looking man. He wasn't going to stay single forever, was he?'

Helen sent her a sharp look.

'I know, but I didn't think it would be so soon,' she said. 'And not right under my nose, either.'

'But why should it bother you? You were the one who ended it, weren't you?'

Helen frowned. Dora was being rather brutal, considering how upset she was.

'Yes, but—'

'And it's not as if you want him back, is it?'

She caught the taunting glint in her friend's eyes, and suddenly she realised. Dora was testing her.

The next thing she knew, she had broken down, her face buried in her hands.

'I don't know,' she sobbed. 'Oh Dora, what have I done? I thought I was doing the right thing, letting him go. I didn't know it would be so hard . . .' She dashed away the tears that spilled from her eyes. 'I was so determined that David deserved better, that he needed someone who could give him a family. But after listening to Joe Cashman, I realised that perhaps – perhaps all he really wanted was me . . .'

Dora laughed. 'Blimey, girl, has it taken you this long to

work that out? Anyone could see he worships the ground you walk on.'

'Once, maybe,' Helen said sadly. 'But not any more.'

'It's not too late, surely? If you go to him and tell him how you feel?'

Helen shook her head. 'It wouldn't be fair. I let him go, and I broke his heart. Now he's found happiness with someone else, what right have I got to stand in his way?'

'Well, now. Talk about throwing in the towel too soon. I reckon if you really love him you should fight for him.'

Helen smiled in spite of herself. 'Miss Grace and I are not a pair of lovesick probationers fighting over a medical student, Dora. We're not going to start cat-fighting in the sluice!'

'Can you imagine?' Dora grinned. 'That would give 'em something to talk about in the nurses' home, wouldn't it?'

'Yes – for all the wrong reasons!' Helen turned to her. 'And I hope you're not going to breathe a word about this to Winnie? If this got out—'

'As if I would!' Dora glanced towards the window. 'It looks like it's started to rain,' she said. 'Better get that washing in before it gets soaked again.'

'Do you want me to help you?'

'No, you finish making the tea. I won't be a jiffy.' She flung her coat on over her shoulders, opened the back door and stepped out into the rain.

Helen hummed to herself as she rinsed out the cups and poured the tea. It was amazing how much better she felt after talking to Dora. Her problems might not have been solved, but at least she could see the funny side of them.

She was still smiling over the image of her wrestling with

the ward sister when Dora's mother came in, still bleary from her nap.

'Oh, hello, love,' she greeted Helen without surprise. And no wonder; from what Helen could tell, friends and neighbours were always dropping in on Dora for advice or a chat.

Rose Doyle looked up at the clock on the mantelpiece. 'It's never gone five, is it? Have I been asleep all this time? I only meant to shut my eyes for a couple of minutes.'

'You obviously needed the rest, Mrs D.'

'It's my age, love.' Rose rubbed her eyes sleepily. 'Where's Dora?'

'Taking in the washing.'

'She never is?' Rose Doyle suddenly forgot her weariness and rushed to the back door. 'She shouldn't be doing that in her condition!'

'Condition?' Helen said. But she did not get the chance to say any more, because the next thing she knew Rose Doyle had let out a cry of dismay and dashed out into the rain.

Helen ran to the back door in time to see the old woman bent over Dora's crumpled form, lying on the rain-slicked cobbles.

Chapter Fifty-Six

'Pregnant?'

Winnie didn't know who was more embarrassed, her or her mother.

'Don't look so surprised,' her mother said sheepishly. 'It does happen, you know. Even at my age.'

'Yes, but . . .' Winnie was lost for words. Of course she had seen older woman on Wren ward. She and the other nurses even joked about them, wondering how they would cope running after a baby at their age.

But it was a different story when it was her own mum.

'Does Dad know?' she asked.

Her mother shook her head. 'Just your gran. And that was only because she guessed the truth.'

Winnie could hardly take it in. She had been about to go off duty when she and Viv were told to prepare for a new emergency admission. They had grumbled their way through making up a new bed, only to find it was for her own mother.

She could see Viv now, sending her curious looks from the other end of the ward.

'Why didn't you tell anyone?' she asked.

'That's what I want to know.'

Winnie looked round to see her father standing at the

end of the bed. He was still dressed in his work clothes, his boots caked in mud from the building site.

The ward maid would have something to say about that, Winnie thought.

'Your mum told me what happened.' His attention was fixed on Dora, his expression dark. It was the kind of look that had sent Winnie and her brothers running for cover when they were kids, because it meant someone was in trouble.

Her dad was on the warpath, and the best she could do was get out of the way.

'I'll leave you to it,' she said. But neither of them seemed to hear her. They were too busy staring at each other.

Dora had been dreading this confrontation for weeks. But after what she had gone through over the past couple of hours, she felt strangely prepared for it.

'You're angry,' she said flatly.

'Of course I'm angry! How do you expect me to feel?'

'Keep your voice down!' She looked up and down the ward. It was visiting time, and the ward was busy. People were starting to look their way.

'I come home from work, expecting you to be there, and then your mum tells me you've been carted off in an ambulance and that you might lose your baby. A baby I didn't even know existed!' Nick hissed. He glanced down at the blankets covering her, suddenly nervous. 'Is it – are you . . . ?'

'We're both fine.' Dora put her hand protectively over her belly. 'It was only a little fainting fit.'

'A little fainting fit?' Nick ran his hands through his dark hair.

'They reckon I'm just low on iron, that's all. And I've been overdoing it a bit,' she added.

'I'll say you have.' Nick sank down into the chair beside the bed. 'Jesus, Dor, what do you think you're playing at, keeping something like this from me? When were you planning to tell me? Or didn't you think I'd notice?'

'You ain't noticed so far.'

'Why? How far gone are you?'

'Nearly five months.'

'Five months?' He looked horrified. 'You've been keeping this a secret for five months?'

'I wasn't sure for the first couple of months.'

'And you call yourself a midwife?' He wasn't smiling, but there was a twinkle in his blue eyes. 'I'd see the funny side if I wasn't so bloody livid!'

'I'm a district nurse, not a midwife,' she reminded him. 'Anyway, I thought my baby days were over.'

'You and me both,' Nick said grimly. 'So why didn't you tell me when you found out?'

'I wanted to,' Dora said. 'I was going to tell you that night you came home and said you'd lost the council contract. You were so upset, I didn't want to add to your worries.' She looked down at her hands. 'And there was another part of me that didn't want to admit it was happening,' she said quietly.

But since she'd collapsed, it had put a different perspective on things. Believing she was going to lose the baby had made her realise how badly she wanted it.

Without realising it, the pregnancy had crept up on her. She had begun to daydream about the baby, whether it would be a boy or a girl, what they would name it, whether it would have her red hair or Nick's dark curls.

She loved kids, and she realised she was looking forward to it.

'I'm sorry, Nick,' she said. 'I know this ain't what you want. But—'

'Who says it ain't what I want?'

Dora stared at him blankly. 'But you were so angry when you walked in . . .'

'I was angry because I was scared,' Nick said. 'When your mum told me you'd been rushed to hospital, all I could think was that I'd lost you. And I was also furious that you hadn't told me.' He reached for her hand. 'I thought we told each other everything, and there you were, keeping this big secret from me.'

'I thought you'd hate the idea,' Dora said quietly.

'Since when did you start thinking I didn't like kids?'

She lifted her gaze to meet his. 'What about Billy Parsons?'

'What about him?' Nick frowned.

'You said you felt sorry for him, because he had to go to the pub for peace and quiet?'

'From his mother-in-law!' Nick said. 'Have you met Freda Baines? If your mum was like that I'd never come home!' He shook his head. 'Anyway, I ain't Billy Parsons, am I? I love my kids. And I reckon the house has got a bit too quiet lately, what with Winnie and Walter gone.'

Dora stared at him. She still couldn't quite trust herself to believe what she was hearing.

'What about your work, though? Money's going to be tight with an extra mouth to feed . . .'

'We'll manage. We got through the war with baby twins, didn't we? Anyway, something will turn up. It generally does.' He covered her hand with his. His palm was rough and calloused from years working on the building sites, but his touch was gentle and loving. 'Just don't keep anything from me in future, eh? We should share our worries.'

'I'll tell you what I am worried about.' Dora glanced up the ward. 'Our Winnie. She hasn't been able to look me in the eye since I got here!'

'I do wish you'd cheer up,' Viv said. 'Your mum's pregnant, she ain't got a venereal disease!'

'Thanks, that makes me feel a lot better,' Winnie said gloomily. She and Viv were trudging back to the nurses' home together after they'd come off duty.

It had been even more of a relief than usual to escape from the ward. She needed time to think about all that had happened.

'I still can't believe it,' she said. 'My mum, expecting again!'

'I wouldn't be at all surprised if my mum got pregnant again,' Viv shrugged. 'Mind you, I wouldn't know, since I ain't seen her for years!'

Winnie looked sideways at her friend. It could be a lot worse, she thought. Viv's mum had abandoned her and gone off with a GI to America when the war ended. Poor Viv had been brought up by her grandmother, the only family she had.

362

'Anyway, it might be nice to have a baby brother or sister,' Viv said. She leaned over and nudged Winnie. 'It'll be good practice for when you have one of your own!'

'Ugh, no thanks! Winnie pulled a face. 'I don't want to be a mum just yet. I've never even had a boyfriend!'

'You ain't missing anything, believe me,' Viv muttered. 'I've sworn off men myself.'

'So if Henry Tremayne asked you out you wouldn't be interested?'

'There's more chance of Elvis Presley sweeping me off my feet than Henry. He's far too shy,' she said wistfully.

'Perhaps you should ask him?'

'Me, ask a bloke out? That'll be the day!' Viv looked outraged. 'I've got more pride than that, thank you very much!'

As they walked into the nurses' home, the first thing they heard was Camilla Simpson's voice, holding forth from the kitchen. It was her afternoon off so she'd finished on the ward a few hours earlier.

'Someone's excited,' Winnie said under her breath as they slipped off their shoes. 'That can't be good news.'

'Probably someone's died, or broken up with their boyfriend. That's what usually puts a smile on her face,' Viv agreed.

Camilla must have heard their voices because she burst out of the kitchen.

'Have you heard the news?' she said.

Winnie and Viv looked at each other.

'Let me guess,' Viv said. 'Andrew Fule's decided to make an honest woman of you at last?'

Camilla's face flushed, but she ignored Viv's remark.

'They've announced the new Medical Superintendent,' she said.

'Is that all?' Viv stifled a yawn. 'I thought you were going to tell us something interesting.'

'Everyone knows Mr Tremayne's going to get the job,' Winnie chimed in.

'That's just it. He hasn't.' Camilla's eyes gleamed. She was practically hopping up and down on the spot. 'And you'll never guess why . . .'

Chapter Fifty-Seven

'I hear congratulations are in order?'

William stood in the doorway of James Bose's office. His friend sat behind his desk, looking dazed. He had the expression of a man who had just been told he had won the football pools, but could not remember filling in the coupon.

'I don't know what to say, truly I don't.' He sounded almost apologetic. 'I was as surprised as anyone when Sutcliffe offered me the job.'

'Why? With me out of the running you were the obvious choice.'

His friend's face flushed.

'Look, I hope you don't think it was me who told Sutcliffe?' he said. 'I didn't breathe a word, I swear.'

'It never occurred to me that you had, old man.'

'Good. Because believe me, I take no satisfaction from this whatsoever.' He looked grim. 'If I could get my hands on whoever sent that letter to Sutcliffe—'

'What does it matter?' William shrugged. 'As I told you, I'd already decided to resign before the letter arrived on Sutcliffe's desk.'

James Bose frowned. 'Yes, but aren't you in the least bit curious?'

'Why should I be? What's done is done.'

He regarded his friend. James looked rather wretched for a man who had just secured the most senior position in the hospital.

'I'm sorry,' Bose said. 'I just can't understand why you decided to step down. I know how much you wanted the Medical Superintendent's job.'

'I just realised it was for the best,' William said. 'I honestly couldn't see myself working alongside Fred Sutcliffe and his high moral values for more than five minutes. You're far more his type of person, I think.'

James grimaced. 'I'm not sure how to take that!'

'Let's just say the best man won.'

He meant what he said, but it was still a bitter pill to swallow. Even though he'd made the right decision, he still found himself thinking about how much he'd wanted that job.

'I can't believe you won't be here to help me,' James said. 'You're a fine surgeon, and I'll be sorry to lose you.'

'I don't think Mr Sutcliffe sees it that way. The chairman of the hospital committee made it very clear he doesn't want someone of my poor moral character anywhere near the hospital.'

'Then he's a fool. And I don't mind telling him that, either.'

William tried not to smile. James was being very naïve if he imagined he could change Frederick Sutcliffe's mind about anything. Once again, he almost felt relieved that he did not have the burden of working with him.

'Don't waste your breath, old man,' he said. 'Besides, I'm not sure I want to go on working here anyway. I think it might be time for both of us to face a new challenge.'

366

'What will you do?' James asked.

'I'm not sure. I think I'll spend some time down at Billinghurst for a while. Millie's been working herself into the ground running the estate. I'd like to help her, if I can.'

'So you're going to live the life of a country squire?'

'I wouldn't go that far.' He wasn't sure how he would fare running a country estate. And he wasn't sure how long his wife would tolerate him under her feet, either. 'I daresay it won't be long before I'm back in the world of medicine. But I'm looking forward to spending time with my family first.'

'Including your daughter?'

William smiled. 'Especially her.'

James Bose looked at him consideringly. 'You don't think she might have written that letter to Sutcliffe—' he started to say, but William cut him off bluntly.

'Let's not talk about it, eh?' He patted him on the shoulder. 'Some things are best left a mystery, don't you think?'

Chapter Fifty-Eight

By the end of the week, everyone in the hospital knew that Frederick Sutcliffe was in possession of a damning letter that had ended William Tremayne's career.

The contents of this letter varied wildly depending on who was asked. Some said William had been unmasked as an adulterer, or a thief. Others claimed with absolute confidence that he had made a careless mistake during an operation that had resulted in the death of a patient, then bribed the Theatre Sister to cover it up. There were even some who thought he was not a surgeon at all, and that somehow his twenty-year career had all been some kind of elaborate hoax.

The gossip mill was feverish with speculation. Almost everywhere Catrine went, someone seemed to be talking about it. She had listened to all the fantastical stories swirling around, knowing the truth but saying nothing.

Until one day she walked into the classroom of the teaching block for the weekly tutorial and all the other students immediately fell silent.

Catrine's skin prickled, that old warning she had come to know so well as a child. The warning that told her that her secret had once again been discovered.

All eyes followed her as she took her seat in the corner and started to unpack her books. She didn't realise she had chosen the seat directly behind Camilla until the other girl turned round and said loudly, 'We were just talking about you.'

'Oh, yes?'

'Apparently there are rumours that you're William Tremayne's daughter.'

The others were all looking at her. Catrine felt colour flooding into her face.

'Well?' Camilla prompted. 'Is it true?'

Catrine forced herself to look up and meet Camilla's gaze.

'You read the letter I left on my desk, so you know it's true.'

Now it was Camilla's turn to blush.

'You read her letter?' Winnie spoke up. 'You told us it was just a rumour you'd heard.'

'That letter was private,' Viv joined in.

'She shouldn't have left it lying around, should she?' Camilla snapped. 'Anyway, that's not the point.' She glared back at Catrine. 'The point is, she's been lying to us, pretending to be something she isn't.'

Catrine looked around the classroom, at all the dumbstruck faces. She had been here before. At school, or with the other kids in her neighbourhood. No matter where she went or what she did, there was always a point where she was found out, exposed. And then she would run away and hide in shame, build a new life for herself and find new friends until the next time.

But not this time. This time she was not going to run away.

'I have not lied to anyone,' she said, fighting to keep her voice steady.

'You haven't been honest, though, have you?' Camilla challenged her. She was relentless, her eyes gleaming with the light of battle. She reminded Catrine of a hawk, digging its talons into its prey and refusing to let go.

'Do you wonder why, when this is the way you treat me?' she said.

Camilla cleared her throat. 'Well, I don't think my parents will be happy that I'm mixing with someone like you,' she said. She stood up, gathering up her books, then moved ostentatiously to the far side of the classroom, as far away from Catrine as she could get.

Viv sighed. 'For gawd's sake, she ain't got the plague!' she said.

Camilla ignored her, looking at the other girls. 'You should all come and sit with me,' she said.

Catrine lowered her gaze, waiting for them to move. She could feel the hot shame welling up inside her already, knowing what would happen.

But when she looked up again, no one had moved.

'Well?' Camilla looked a little bit shaken. But not half as shaken as Catrine felt.

'I'm all right where I am, ta,' Viv said.

'Me too,' Winnie added, folding her arms defiantly.

There was the sound of a chair scraping back, and then Lou got to her feet. Catrine's heart sank. Not Lou, of all people? She'd thought they were friends. But then, to her surprise, the girl threaded her way between the desks towards her and came to sit beside her. A moment later, the other girls did the same. They surrounded Catrine, leaving Camilla isolated on the other side of the classroom.

Just then, Miss James the Sister Tutor came briskly into the room.

'Settle down, girls,' she said, stepping up to the dais and putting her papers down on the desk. She looked up briefly and caught sight of Camilla, sitting all by herself. She opened her mouth as if to speak, then seemed to think better of it.

'Right,' she said. 'Open up your Materia Medica, if you please.'

As pages rustled around the classroom, Winnie leaned over and whispered,

'It'll be old news soon, you wait and see.'

'And don't you worry about Camilla, anyway,' Viv said. 'We're on your side, mate. You remember that.'

Catrine looked down at her book. But she could hardly see the pages through the tears in her eyes.

'What's all this I've been hearing, then?'

Henry looked up from his notes to see Andrew Fule standing in the doorway.

'I don't know,' he sighed. 'What have you been hearing?'

'I've heard your old man was a bit of a naughty boy. No wonder he got the sack from the hospital.'

'He didn't get the sack. He resigned.'

'That's the official story. But I heard old Sutcliffe gave him his marching orders after he found out he'd fathered a kid out of wedlock.'

Henry froze, his pen still in his hand.

'Where did you hear that?'

'Camilla told me. It's rather useful, having a girl-friend who's so incredibly nosey. Although I must say I'm disappointed you didn't tell me yourself,' he added. 'I thought we were supposed to be friends?'

'I can't think what gave you that idea.'

Henry forced himself to continue writing his notes, but he could feel his room-mate circling him, coming closer.

'And there was me, thinking you were interested in Nurse Frenchie, when all the time she was your sister,' he sneered. 'Must have been a shock for you, finding out your father had been putting it about like that.'

Henry ignored him. Andrew was trying to goad him, but he refused to give him the satisfaction of a reaction.

'Talk about heroes with feet of clay,' his room-mate went on. 'I can understand why the hospital committee didn't make him Medical Superintendent. I'm surprised they didn't fire Frenchie, too.'

'Don't call her that.'

'There are a lot worse things I can call her, believe me,' Andrew smirked.

'Such as?'

'Do you need me to spell it out for you, old man?' He leaned down, his leering face close to Henry's. Tantalisingly close, in fact. 'You know what they call illegitimate kids like her.' His face grew closer, until all Henry could see were his fat freckled cheeks and his wet lips moving. 'She's a bast—'

He didn't finish the word before Henry's fist had connected with his jaw. It wasn't a hard punch, but it caught him unawares and sent him flying backwards across the room. He collided with the wardrobe and slid to the ground.

'You can call her my sister,' Henry said.

Chapter Fifty-Nine

Brenda Cashman was being discharged, and Helen made sure she was there to see her off.

'Well, Matron, I reckon it's the last you'll be seeing of me,' Brenda said as Helen helped her pack her belongings into her bag.

'Oh, I don't know. Never say never, Mrs Cashman.'

Brenda shook her head. 'Joe doesn't want me to try again, not after last time. He said he nearly lost me once, he ain't going to risk it again.'

Helen folded up a nightgown and handed it to Brenda to put into the bag. Joe Cashman had come close to losing her, it was true. Helen shuddered to think what would have happened if Brenda hadn't heard him defending her to his mother.

It might not have been her intention, but Enid Cashman had saved their marriage.

Speaking of whom . . .

'And what about his mother?' Helen asked. 'What does she think about it?'

'I don't know, and I don't care!' Brenda's reply was fierce. 'It's nothing to do with her, so she can mind her own business.' She stuffed a pair of slippers into her bag. 'Besides, we ain't heard a peep out of her since Joe told her where to get off, and that suits me fine.'

'Good for you.'

'And we ain't likely to be seeing much of her in the future, either. Joe's applied for a job out in Essex,' she explained. 'If he gets it we'll be moving out to the country, miles away from his family.'

'That sounds like just what you need,' Helen said approvingly. 'A new start.'

It would be good for Brenda to be away from his mother, not to mention his ever fertile sisters.

'Exactly. A new start.' Brenda closed up her bag and fastened it with a snap. 'And there's something else, too,' she said. 'Joe and me have thought about it, and we reckon once we're settled we might try to adopt a baby.'

'That sounds like a wonderful idea.'

'There's no guarantee we'll be able to do it, of course,' Brenda said shyly. 'But we can give it a try. It's something to aim for, at least.'

'I hope it all works out for you, Mrs Cashman.'

Brenda and Joe Cashman had a lot of love to give. If they couldn't give it to their own child, perhaps there was another one out there who needed it?

Joe Cashman was waiting for his wife outside the private room. He leapt to his feet when he saw her, a look of relief on his face. Helen was suddenly reminded of all the hours he'd sat and waited for her.

'Ready, love?' He reached out and took the bag from her.

Brenda smiled at him. 'I reckon I am.'

'I've got all your paperwork here.'

Jennifer Grace approached them, a bundle of forms in her hand. 'Once you sign these, you'll be free to go.'

'You make it sound like prison!' Brenda Cashman grimaced as she reached for the pen the ward sister was holding out for her.

Helen and Miss Grace stood together and watched them leave the ward. Neither of them spoke.

Helen was painfully aware of the awkwardness between them. Things had not been the same since she'd overheard Jennifer speaking to David.

How she wished she had never heard that conversation! She was fond of Jennifer Grace, but now she found herself looking at her in a different light. Wren had been one of her favourite wards, but recently she had been keeping her distance.

'They're a lovely couple, aren't they?' Jennifer interrupted her thoughts.

'Yes, they are,' Helen agreed.

'I hope they make a go of it. They deserve some happiness,' Jennifer sighed. Then she caught Helen's eye and laughed. 'Take no notice of me, Matron,' she said. 'I'm just a hopeless romantic!'

Helen looked at her. A hopeless romantic. Was that why David had fallen for her? If it was, she didn't blame him. Jennifer Grace was a delightful woman. Not just attractive, but kind and warm-hearted with it. She could imagine the two of them being very happy together.

The only thing standing in their way was her.

She took a deep breath and swallowed down the bitterness that rose in her throat.

'I wonder if I might have a word with you?' she said. 'In your office.'

Jennifer Grace's office was little bigger than a broom cupboard, with barely space for a desk and a couple of chairs.

The ward sister looked concerned as she closed the door behind them.

'What did you want to speak to me about, Matron?' she asked.

'It's a – personal matter.' Helen forced herself to look at her. 'About David.'

'Oh!' Jennifer looked startled. Two bright spots of colour lit up her cheeks.

'I understand the two of you have become close recently?'

'Did he tell you that?' she asked cautiously.

'No, he hasn't said anything. But I overheard you talking in this office a few days ago.'

'Ah.' Jennifer's gaze dropped. 'I'm sorry, Matron. I assure you I'm not in the habit of allowing my personal life to interfere with my duty, it was just—'

Helen held up her hand. 'It's all right, Miss Grace, I'm not here to criticise you.'

'Nevertheless, I'm sorry.' Jennifer Grace lowered her gaze. 'I wish you'd said something sooner. I had the feeling there was some – tension between us.'

So she had noticed, Helen thought. 'I'll admit it came as rather a shock,' she said. 'I needed some time to think about it. But I want you to know you have my blessing.'

Jennifer looked up sharply. 'Your blessing?'

'I think you and David make a very good couple, and I hope you'll be very happy. Obviously, it puts us both in a difficult situation,' she went on, her words tumbling out in a rush. 'But we're sensible women, and I'm sure if we put our minds to it we can—'

'I don't understand.' Jennifer looked perplexed. 'How much of the conversation did you hear, Matron?'

'Well, not all of it,' Helen admitted. 'But enough to know that you quite rightly wanted David to come clean to me about your relationship, and that he was reluctant to do so.'

'So you didn't hear the part where he ditched me?'

That stopped her in her tracks. 'What?'

'Alas, it's true.' Jennifer Grace looked rueful. 'If you'd stayed for a few minutes longer you would have heard David confessing the reason he hadn't told you was because he was still in love with you.'

Helen stared at her, lost for words. 'I – I don't know what to say,' she murmured at last.

'Neither did I,' Jennifer said. 'Although I have to say I did rather suspect it. David's heart was never really in it, you see.' She smiled wistfully. 'I think I was testing him when I asked him to tell you. Trying to force his hand, I suppose.' She looked at Helen. 'And if I'm not mistaken, you feel the same way about him?'

Helen felt herself blushing. 'What makes you say that?'

'I told you, I'm a hopeless romantic. I can tell when two people are made for each other.' Jennifer paused, then said, 'You do know he's leaving the Nightingale, don't you?'

Helen looked at her, startled. 'What? He didn't tell me.'

'He's going back to his GP practice, apparently. Between you and me, I suspect the only reason he came here in the first place was to try to win you back,' Jennifer confided. 'He believes he's failed, but I rather think the opposite, don't you?'

Chapter Sixty

David McKay sat in the station tearoom, his suitcases at his feet, staring at a cooling cup of tea. He was far too early for his train, which wasn't at all like him. But London had lost its attraction for him, and suddenly all he wanted to do was go home, back to Billinghurst.

He should never have come back in the first place. It had seemed like such a good idea at the time – a chance to be close to Helen again, perhaps a chance to make her see that their marriage was worth saving.

He'd realised his mistake very soon after he'd arrived. Helen was not interested in rekindling their relationship. And the longer he spent in her company, the harder it was for him to see a future without her.

And then Jennifer Grace had come along, and he'd decided that if Helen didn't want him then he should make a clean break, move on.

Another stupid mistake.

He felt wretched about Jennifer. He'd really wanted their romance to work, but all it had done was prove to him how hopelessly and utterly in love with Helen he was.

She had his heart, and if it couldn't be her, then it wouldn't be anyone.

'Is this seat taken?'

He looked up sharply. As if he'd conjured her from his thoughts, there was Helen, standing over him. He could scarcely believe what he was seeing.

He shook his head, hardly daring to speak. Helen pulled out the chair and sat down.

'Would you – um – like some tea?' He offered her the pot. Helen took off the lid and peered inside.

'It's stewed,' she said. 'And yours is cold, I see. I'll get us a fresh pot.'

She stood up and headed to the counter. All the while his mind was racing.

What was going on? What was his ex-wife doing there?

Helen returned with a tray containing a pot of tea, two cups and a slice of Victoria sponge. If this was a dream then it was a strange one, David thought.

As she poured out the tea, he said, 'Do you mind me asking what you're doing here?'

'Looking for you,' she said briskly. 'Miss Grace told me you were going back to Billinghurst, but I didn't realise she meant so soon, until I spoke to your secretary.' She handed him a cup, then pushed the cake plate into the middle of the table between them.

'No time like the present,' he said.

'And you were going to leave without saying goodbye?' There was the faintest hint of hurt in her voice.

'It was all very last minute,' he lied. 'Dr Prendergast decided he couldn't wait to come back, and the locum had given notice, so . . .' He picked up one of the cake forks and helped himself. Helen did the same.

They had often shared a piece of cake back in Lowgill

House, but suddenly it seemed like a curiously intimate gesture.

'So this is it, then?' Helen said.

'It seems like it.'

'I thought you were happy at the Nightingale?'

'I'm not sure happy is the right word.'

'Why not?'

He looked up at her. There was a cake crumb stuck to her lower lip and it was all he could do not to reach up and brush it off.

'I think you know why,' he said quietly.

'Because you came back for me?'

He looked down at his teacup. 'I can see now it was a ridiculous idea,' he said. 'And very unfair on you, too.'

'How so?'

'You came to London to get away from me, to make a new start. It was very wrong of me to follow you and try to change your mind. I overstepped the mark. I should have respected you—'

'So you haven't changed your mind? That isn't why you're leaving?'

'How can you even ask me that question?' He shook his head. 'My feelings for you haven't changed, and I don't think they ever will. The only thing that's changed is that I've realised how hopeless it is.'

'I see.' Helen prodded at the cake with her fork. She still ate it in a very orderly fashion, he noticed, starting at the narrowest point and working her way methodically towards the edge. It sometimes drove him mad, just as he drove her to distraction with his random hacking here and there.

And yet neither of them ever suggested they should eat separate slices of cake.

'Perhaps it isn't as hopeless as you think.'

She wasn't looking at him when she said it, and for a moment David wondered if he'd imagined the words.

Then he saw it.

How had he not noticed the small valise at Helen's feet before? He looked from it to her face and back again.

'Are you going somewhere?' he asked.

'I have a few days of leave owing to me, and I thought I might spend it at Billinghurst, if that's all right with you?'

She looked up at him, and he saw the hope and tenderness in her brown eyes.

'I think I'd like that very much,' he said.

Chapter Sixty-One

At two months old, Julie Rose Riley was already a fiery red-head like her mother. And just like Dora, she did not take kindly to being ignored. After hollering her way through her own christening, she was now making her presence felt at the party in the pub afterwards.

'She's got a good pair of lungs on her, I'll say that,' Dora's brother Alfie commented nervously.

'I'll second that!' Her younger sister Bea put her hands over her ears. 'Can't you shut her up?' she pleaded. 'I can hardly hear myself think.'

'In your case, I'd say that was a blessing in disguise. Here,' Dora dumped the baby into her sister's arms. 'You take a turn with her. You can show off those maternal skills of yours.'

'Hang on a minute . . .' Bea started to protest, but Dora was already pushing her way through the crowd of guests.

'Do you think that's a good idea, leaving her with your Bea?' Nick asked. 'You know what your sister's like. She'll probably leave her behind the bar, or put her out in the alley with the empties.'

'I've got my eye on her, don't worry,' Dora smiled.

'Anyway, Julie will stop crying soon. She's just a bit unsettled, that's all. It's been a long day for her and she's overtired.'

'Ain't we all?' Nick sighed.

Dora planted her hands on her hips and faced him.

'Don't you start, Nick Riley. You were the one who wanted a big party for your daughter's christening! I would have been happy with a few sausage rolls in our front room, like we did with all the others.'

'Yeah, but this is different, ain't it?' Nick said. 'We should push the boat out for Julie, since she's our very last one. At least I hope she is?' he eyed Dora quizzically.

'That depends on whether you can keep your hands to yourself, doesn't it?'

Nick grinned. 'Seriously, though, it's nice to have a bit of a do, ain't it? Especially now we've got something to celebrate.'

It was nice to see her husband smiling again, Dora thought. Nick had been so worried about their future, but now they seemed to be getting back on their feet. He'd taken on a couple more contracts, and they had some money coming in at last. Which was just as well, given she couldn't go back to district nursing for at least a few months.

Just recently they'd had some more good news, too. After a year away, their eldest son Walter had written to say he was being allowed home on leave from his National Service. With any luck, he would be back for the new year.

And with the prospect of all her kids being under the same roof again, Dora couldn't have been happier. It really seemed like Julie had been a tiny good luck charm for all of them. Even if she was a greedy little beggar who loved to scream the house down in the middle of the night.

Dora looked around at the friends and family who had gathered to celebrate their daughter's big day. As she'd said to Nick, she wasn't one for big parties. But she was glad she'd pushed the boat out this time, because it meant seeing her friends Millie and Helen again.

Helen looked so happy. She'd surprised everyone when she quit her job as Matron of the Nightingale and returned to Billinghurst with her husband David.

Dora had no doubt she'd done the right thing; Helen looked positively radiant with joy, clinging to her husband's arm as if she did not dare let him go again.

Millie and William were there, too. Dora was willing to bet there weren't many East End pubs that could boast the daughter of an earl among their punters. But that was the beauty of Millie – she was so sweet and totally without snobbery, she was happy to fit in anywhere.

And as for William . . . Dora watched him as he sat down at the piano and began to play a raucous chorus that soon had everyone singing along. Who would believe that they were the hands of a top surgeon?

'Honestly, can't someone shut him up?' Helen pleaded.

Millie smiled fondly. 'Leave him alone, he's enjoying himself.'

'He may be the only one who is,' Helen grimaced. 'Honestly, how do you put up with him?' she asked Millie. 'He can be such an embarrassment at times.'

'Excuse me, that's no way to talk about your brother. Or my partner,' David said.

'It's exactly because he is my brother that I can say what I like about him,' Helen declared primly.

Thankfully William stopped playing and lurched over to where they stood. He was decidedly the worse for wear, Helen thought. But then they were all slightly tipsy, so it didn't matter.

'It feels so strange to be back in the East End again, doesn't it?' William said to her.

'I was just thinking the same thing.'

'Do you miss it?'

Helen shook her head. 'Do you?'

'God, no! Best thing I ever did, leaving the Nightingale. Especially since Bose has been telling me how thoroughly miserable he is. Talk about under the thumb! Turns out Frederick Sutcliffe won't let him open so much as a bottle of aspirin without his say-so.'

'And now we're both under my husband's thumb instead,' Helen smiled.

'Chance would be a fine thing,' David McKay muttered. 'Neither of you ever do as you're told. I thought it would be a good idea taking William on as my partner, but now I find myself doing daily battle with the Terrible Tremayne Twosome instead!'

Helen winked at her brother. 'How can we possibly gang up on you when we never agree on anything?'

'Anyway, let's face it,' William said to David. 'We both take orders from Helen. She's the boss.'

'Now that's something we can agree on,' Helen said.

'So you really don't miss being Matron of the Nightingale?' William said.

Helen thought about it for a moment. 'Sometimes,' she admitted. 'Although I love working with you and David, and living so close to Millie and the children. But I often think about all those years I spent on the wards.'

'Me too,' William said.

'Frankly, I don't know how the place manages without either of you,' David said. 'The Nightingale without the Tremaynes? It's unthinkable.'

Helen and William smiled at each other, each knowing what the other was thinking.

'Don't forget, there's still a Tremayne at the Nightingale,' William reminded him. 'Two, in fact.'

He nodded towards Catrine and Henry, arguing in a corner as usual.

'I wonder what they're bickering about now?' Helen mused.

'If they're anything like you and me, she's probably telling him how to run his life,' William sighed.

'Excuse me?' Helen turned on him. 'I happen to think Catrine's very good for him. I mean, do you honestly think Henry would have summoned up the courage to ask Viv Trent out if it hadn't been for his sister?'

She looked over at the pretty redhead holding Henry's hand. From the shy smiles he kept directing at her, he clearly could not believe his good luck.

'You think that was Catrine's doing?' William said.

'I know it was.' She smiled at the scene. 'They're good for each other, I think.'

'Just like you and me, Sis,' William said, putting his arm around her. 'Just like you and me.'

Acknowledgements

Nurses on Call proved to be a tough project for many reasons, and I'm immensely grateful for everyone who helped me through it.

First of all, to my husband Ken, for his endless support. He usually ends up as a footnote in the acknowledgements, but he really deserves to be at the forefront, because without his patience and encouragement (not to mention the pep talks and cups of tea), there simply wouldn't have been a book. I appreciate you more than I ever let on.

The same goes to the rest of my family and friends, who believed in me and this book when I'd given up. They've all got used to the ups and downs of the writing process, and they know exactly when to make the call and when to leave well alone . . .

Of course, the terrific team at Penguin deserve much credit. They, too, have been endlessly kind and patient. Many thanks to Katie Loughnane for bringing back the Nightingales in the first place, and for being such a wonderful and talented editor. Not surprisingly, being so wonderful and talented has meant she's now gone on to bigger and better things. I'm sorry we won't be working together any more, but hopefully this is only *au revoir*, as my character

Catrine would say. And the biggest thank you to the amazing Katya Browne, who has guided the book smoothly through production, and who manages to stay positive and serene even when I'm sure I must cause her to tear her hair out on a daily basis.

Finally, a big thank you to my agent Caroline Sheldon. She's been with me since the very first Nightingale book, and I'm really not exaggerating when I say I owe it all to her. How she's managed to put up with my hare-brained ideas over the years, I've no idea. Now she's decided to take much-deserved retirement and handed the reins over to Jon Wood. Does he know what he's taken on? Only time will tell, but so far he seems up for a challenge. Looking forward to working with you on the next one, Jon!